The
BUBBLE GUM
THIEF

The
BUBBLE GUM
THIEF

JEFF MILLER

THOMAS & MERCER

Published by Thomas & Mercer
P.O. Box 400818
Las Vegas, NV 89140

ISBN-13: 9781612184838
ISBN-10: 1612184839

Dedicated to Kate, for reasons longer than this book

໖

PART I

THE WHAT

CHAPTER 1

January 1—Bethel, New York

Sometimes big things start small.

Waller's Food Mart felt like the smallest place on earth to Crosby Waller. The gangly teen sat behind the register sipping a Jones Fufu Berry Soda and leafing through a copy of *Sports Illustrated* with Shaquille O'Neal on the cover. A bead of sweat fell from Crosby's forehead and landed on the magazine page, drowning the "Man" in "Manning" and blanching the "Green" from "Green Bay." The radiator was stuck on high, and there was a four-day wait to have it fixed. Crosby tore off his sweater, stripping to an Arcade Fire T-shirt. It was three years old and too small for his frame. It had shrunk, but mostly, he had grown.

Twenty years of his father's cigarettes had left an odor in the store that Lysol couldn't fix, but Crosby was used to it. He wasn't used to the soft flicker of the dying fluorescent bulb above, and it was giving him a headache. Maybe it wasn't the flickering light. Maybe it was just boredom. Business had been slow since the Walmart Supercenter opened in Monticello, and this day had been slower than most.

The door chimed.

A cold blast of air sent a shiver through Crosby. The appearance of the tall, fit man walking through the door sent another. He wore black jeans and a grey sweatshirt, the hood of which was pulled tightly over his head, masking most of his face. The big orange lenses of his aviator sunglasses hid his eyes. Thin white gloves—not winter ones made of leather or wool, but shiny, tight hospital gloves made from rubber or latex—covered his hands. He looked, Crosby thought, like a serial killer.

"What's up?" Crosby asked, surprised by the crack in his voice.

The man nodded in his direction and then wandered down an aisle. Crosby returned to his sullen perusal of the magazine. It was only two fifteen, and Crosby was stuck there for another four hours. When he'd agreed to work weekends and holidays in exchange for a 2002 Alero, it had seemed like a good deal. Selling Manhattan for a handful of beads had probably seemed like a good idea at the time, too.

Stuck. It's how he felt most of the time. Stuck at his parents' store. Stuck in Bethel. Stuck in a world of mediocrity, tedium, and boredom.

When the hooded man reached the soda fountain, he looked over at Crosby and spoke in a deep, deliberate voice. "You're out of the big cups." To make his point clear, the man pointed at the empty cup dispenser below the fountain drinks.

Crosby set his magazine down on the counter. "Give me a second." He glanced at the rifle on the shelf under the register, then walked through the door to the back storeroom and tugged on the chain that hung from a bare bulb. When the light didn't come on, he yanked four more times before the chain broke and fell to the floor. Crosby kicked the nearest box in anger, then squeezed between some shelves toward the lone window. He twisted the rod on the window blind, and bright rays of sunshine permeated the dusty air.

Along the side wall, boxes of various sizes were piled from floor to ceiling. He found one labeled "Biggie-Gulp," pulled it from the stack, and tossed it to the center of the room. When he tore the top flap open, the sharp edge of a one-inch staple cut his index finger. He cursed, shook his finger, and licked away the blood. Reaching into the box, he grabbed a long sleeve of sixty-four-ounce cups.

Boom.

It sounded like a gunshot.

Crosby dropped the cups and dove to the floor. This was his time. Everyone who works at a convenience store is eventually shot, and this was his time. He should have been at Suzi Fenner's New Year's Day party, but instead, he was going to die in his parents' store. At least they'd feel guilty for making him work. The sound of a car door snapped him back to the moment. Standing up, he brushed his hair out of his eyes and peeked through the small square window in the storeroom door. The front door was flapping in the wind, and the man in the hooded sweatshirt was starting the engine of a black Ford Explorer. Crosby watched it kick up gravel as it sped away.

Crosby jogged to the store entrance and tugged the door closed, then ran behind the counter, punched in the security code, and opened the register. He counted the money, and then counted it again. All there. Beer, Crosby thought. He ran back to the refrigerated shelves. Nothing was missing. He must have stolen something, Crosby thought, as he wandered up and down the canned-goods aisle, then around the hot-dog roller. When he turned down the candy aisle, he saw it.

A white business card stood at the front of a box of Chewey's Cinnamon Gum. Crosby had just opened the box the day before. Now one pack was missing. Crosby laughed. The hooded sweatshirt, the glasses, the gloves, even the Biggie-Gulp-cup ploy...all for a pack of gum. He picked up the white card.

THIS IS MY FIRST CRIME.
MY NEXT WILL BE BIGGER.

He turned the card over. A stick of Chewey's gum, still in the foil wrapper, was stuck to the back of the card, held in place by a small piece of Scotch tape. Crosby tore the stick of gum off the card, unwrapped the foil, and folded the gum into his mouth. He balled up the foil and tossed it into the trash. The card, he figured, would make for a good story at school, so he stuffed it into his wallet.

Crosby looked at his watch. It was only two forty. He still had three and a half hours to kill. Suzi's party would be over by then. Cursing his father, he walked around the counter and put on his sweater, then picked up the issue of *Sports Illustrated* and sat down behind the register. Flipping through the magazine, Crosby found the cover story. It began, "On March 6, 1972, Lucille O'Neal gave birth to a seven-pound eleven-ounce baby boy."

Sometimes big things start small, Crosby figured.

CHAPTER 2

....

January 1—Washington, DC

Dagny Gray's 2006 Prius was outfitted with the Option 5 package, which included Bluetooth phone integration, a line in to the stereo for her iPod, and a built-in GPS navigational system that currently showed a street map of Georgetown and a little red triangle that wasn't moving. The little red triangle was Dagny's car, and it wasn't moving because traffic doesn't move in Washington, DC—people just sit in their cars and wait for the earth to turn.

When the earth finally turned, Dagny saw something she'd never seen in Georgetown—an empty parking space on M Street. She flipped on her turn signal and pulled just ahead of the space. A man in a silver BMW ignored the gesture and pulled up behind her. Dagny honked, but the Beamer didn't budge—the man just crossed his arms and smiled smugly, waiting to claim the space. If he'd wanted to block her entry, he should have pulled closer. Dagny sized up her clearance. If she angled it just right, she'd have an inch or two to spare on each side. She threw her Prius into reverse and floored the accelerator, turned the wheel hard to the right, then just as quickly to the left. In one swift, fluid motion, she slid into the space. Even better, she'd come close enough to give the BMW driver a deserved scare.

Dagny's satisfaction faded as she watched the noblesse filtering into Zegman's Gallery. Though she could hold her own among the effete and well heeled, she preferred the warm embrace of a good book and a well-worn couch, or the iPod-assisted solitude of a long run on the Mount Vernon Trail, or the torturous agony of her Arabic study, or a rusty nail embedded in her foot. But she'd promised Julia Bremmer she'd come, and Julia was her last close friend. She'd lost other friendships to geography or dereliction. Julia's friendship was worth saving.

Besides, she had promised herself that this would be the year she'd learn to have fun, even if it was no fun at all.

Dagny was thinking about this promise when her phone rang. She didn't have to check the display to know that Julia was canceling their plans.

"TRO," Julia said. This meant temporary restraining order—and that Julia was stuck working on one. She was an associate at Baxter Wallace, one of the top litigation firms in town. Baxter Wallace was originally Baxter, Wallace, and McCallister, but McCallister got the shaft when some marketing consultants decided that the firm's name was too long. It didn't matter to McCallister, or to Baxter or Wallace, for that matter; all three of them were long dead.

"Blow it off."

"I can't. Not this year." Julia was up for partner—more precisely, non-equity partner, which, like nonalcoholic beer, doesn't taste very good and is no substitute for the real thing. "I'm sorry, Dag."

"It's okay, Jules. I didn't want to go anyway."

Julia's voice rose. "No, no, no. Dag, you should still go in."

"I don't—"

"You *have* to."

Dagny hadn't seen it coming, but this excursion was a setup. "I'm not in dating shape."

"You're never in dating shape. Maybe you need to date to get in shape. Plus, your resolution—"

"I don't think I used the word resolution," Dagny protested.

"Just go," Julia said, before hanging up.

Dagny tucked the phone back in her purse. No matter what it was called—"resolution" or "promise"—Dagny had vowed to change her life, and she couldn't give up on the first day, especially after such a strong start. That morning, she'd picked through the boxes in her basement to find the hair dryer she hadn't used since her last move. After her shower, she'd brushed her long black hair straight instead of tying it in the usual ponytail. Her cheeks were powdered with the slightest blush, while her eyelashes carried the unfamiliar weight of mascara. And under her new red leather swing coat, she wore her favorite black dress. It was padded in all the right places.

Dagny waited for the traffic to wane before climbing out of the car. She walked to the front of the gallery and peered through the windows, eyeing the suits and gowns inside. Some of the women towered over their dates. Dagny's eyes followed their bodies down to their feet and saw that they were uniformly elevated by two- or three-inch heels. She looked down at her own sneakers and shrugged. At five nine, she was plenty tall, and the sneakers were black and almost looked like dress shoes. If she looked out of place, so be it. She never wore heels—not anymore.

Dagny opened the gallery door and stepped into the vestibule. A sign on the interior door announced the name of the show: *A Georgetown Collection*. Dagny picked a program off a nearby table and began flipping through its pages. A couple walked through the entry door, passed Dagny, and continued through the second door into the gallery. They moved effortlessly, gliding through in mere seconds. Dagny wondered how they did it.

Someone had left a copy of the day's *Washington Post* next to the programs. Dagny scanned the front page. The president was urging Congress to enact tougher penalties for white-collar criminals. A young black kid had been shot and killed at a New Year's Eve concert at the 11:30 Club. Trouble in the Middle East. It was the same news every day. Dagny glanced at her watch—5:26 p.m.—took a deep breath, and walked into the gallery.

In the main room, a densely packed mob sipped cocktails and chattered away about their latest successes. Dagny heard snippets of conversation, things like, "I read his piece in *The New Republic*" and, "How old do you think *she* is?" Two long lines snaked through the crowd, leading to cash bars on each side of the room. A woman in a tuxedo vest carried a tray of appetizers—something wrapped in prosciutto—and normally dignified socialites stumbled over each other to grab them before they were gone. Dagny looked for an avenue of escape. Because even the most devoted cognoscenti of art care more about wine and cheese than paint and canvas, the exhibition room to the right was nearly empty, so she went there.

Dagny knew a little about art. She could tell a Monet from a Manet, and a Titian from a Tintoretto. But with a million dollars and the lives of a thousand screaming babies on the line, she couldn't have distinguished most of the dreck on the gallery walls from the thirty-dollar paintings hawked at starving-artist sales in Holiday Inn conference rooms. The first three paintings were impressionistic landscapes, remarkable only for their absolute irrelevance. If there was anything interesting to say about water lilies, Dagny was pretty sure it had been said a hundred years earlier. A black canvas with a red square in the middle had been titled *Red Canvas with a Black Square in the Middle*, presumably to convey the artist's witty and elevated sense of irony. The title didn't make her laugh, but the painting's $1,200 price tag did.

One painting put the others to shame. In it, a man stood at the edge of a cliff, overlooking a city. The city was painted like a dark, violent storm, with thick, swirling strokes, like Van Gogh's *Starry Night*. But the man was rendered in a realistic, even romantic, style. He was strong and athletic, and his features were fine and distinct. He wore a suit and tie, and held his jacket casually over his shoulder, untroubled by the chaos below.

"Isn't it awful?" a voice said from behind. Dagny turned toward the man who said it. First, she noticed that he was tall. Then she noticed his navy-blue Brooks Brothers suit and black wing-tip shoes. These were standard issue for a lawyer or a lobbyist, though the curl of his hair in the back suggested he was neither. Sky-blue eyes and a soft smile. Cleft chin and a square jaw. He was more handsome than beautiful. "Absolutely awful," he continued in a deep, soothing voice. "Glorious man and the savage society. It's sloppy and indulgent. The artist must be a real egoist. Probably insufferable."

"I don't know," Dagny said. "You seem okay to me."

He smiled. "That obvious?"

She figured that he was in his early forties—not *too* old, considering she was rapidly approaching thirty-five. No ring, of course. Julia had made that mistake once before. She wondered if he was divorced. If so, then why did the marriage fail? If not, what was wrong with him? His hands were manicured, but there was still some dirt under his nails. She noticed a small scar above his left eyebrow. His lips were full and chapped. He had a swimmer's build—she liked that. "I'm Dagny Gray." She stuck out her hand and he shook it.

"Cool name. Very Myrna Loy. I'm Michael Brodsky," he replied. "But you can call me Mike."

"I would have anyway."

He smiled at this, which Dagny liked.

"You don't really look like an artist," she continued.

He laughed. "Why not?"

"The suit, for starters."

"You'd expect a horizontal black-and-white striped shirt, beret. Palette in hand?"

"I was thinking more thrift-store chic." As she said it, a man wearing a corduroy jacket, ripped jeans, and black-rimmed glasses walked by. They both laughed.

"Please tell me that you're Julia's friend," Dagny said.

"I am."

"Thank God."

He smiled, then surveyed the room and sighed. "You wanna ditch this? Get a cup a coffee? Maybe sit down and talk? I can't stand these gallery crowds."

"Yes." She was surprised by how quickly she had answered.

He took her arm and led her to the door. As they stepped into the cold, their breath made a cloud in the air. She shivered, and he put his arm around her. If another man had done this, she would have recoiled. But it felt natural, and warm, and right.

They crossed the street, ducked into Dean & DeLuca, and headed for a table in the corner. Mike pulled Dagny's chair out for her and asked, "What can I get you?"

"Decaf. Black."

"No mocha-something-or-other?" he asked, smiling.

"Never." She watched him walk to the counter and wondered if he knew how hard she was trying.

He returned a few moments later with two cups of coffee and a couple of pieces of chocolate. "Try this," he said, setting one of the pieces in front of her. "It's incredible."

The three-quarter-inch cube before her was expertly molded and beautifully accented with a raspberry squiggle across the top and deep, ornate grooves on the sides. It probably cost eight dollars. And it was probably delicious. It was also 90 calories, half of them from fat. Don't blow this, she told herself. She'd just run an extra half mile the next day. She lifted the chocolate to her mouth and took a tiny quarter bite. If this was going to be her treat, she was going to make it last.

"It's delicious," she said, and it was.

"So how do you know Julia?"

"She's my best friend. We went to law school together. What about you?

"She and her husband commissioned a painting."

Julia hadn't mentioned this. "More romantic heroism versus the savage society?"

He laughed. "Something like that. A portrait of her father, actually."

"He's an amazing man, and she adores him. I think you're the right artist for the job."

"Thank you," he said, consuming his chocolate in one bite. Dagny bit off the next quarter from her piece. "I have to ask," he said. "When I came up to you at the gallery, how did you—"

"Your picture was in the program," she said.

"You remember all the faces in the program?"

"Just yours."

He smiled. "What else do you remember?"

"I remember that you teach art history at Georgetown. That you specialize in the Italian Renaissance, but you wrote a book about the Flemish painter Hans Memling. You won the Mare Warrington Award in 2003, though I don't know who she is. Your middle initial is A." Dagny took another bite of the chocolate, leaving only a quarter. It was disappearing too quickly.

He nodded. "You remember all that?"

"I'm amazing," she joked. "But I don't want to talk about me. I want to talk about your work. It's…"

"Yes?"

"…not pretentious." She smiled at him. "Critics must hate you. But you seem to be doing alright."

He laughed. "Critics do hate me, but they don't buy paintings—businessmen and entrepreneurs do. So while you'll never see my work at the National Gallery, you'll find it all over Wall Street and Park Avenue."

"And do you actually believe in what you're painting, or are you just meeting a demand?"

"I believe in every single brushstroke. But what did you think? Did you like the painting?"

"I wouldn't be here if I didn't." And it was true, she thought. "What did Julia tell you about me?"

"Nothing. She just told me to look for the beautiful woman standing all alone, as far away from everyone else as she could possibly be." He smiled, then shook his head. "I don't know anything else about you, Dagny Gray, except that you like my art."

"Then you know a lot." Her phone beeped—a text message. She retrieved it from her purse and read the screen. "I'm sorry, Mike. I have to go." She was happy to see genuine disappointment on his face.

"What is it? A client?"

"Nope."

"Well?"

Dagny flashed open her red leather swing coat. He seemed surprised, but not frightened, by the Glock 23 in her shoulder holster. Now he knew something else about her. Dagny found a pen in her purse, grabbed his paper coffee cup, and wrote her number on the side. She handed him the cup and popped the last bite of chocolate into her mouth. When she got to the door, she turned back and caught his smile. Thank goodness, she thought. He was smitten, too.

CHAPTER 3

January 7—Brooklyn, New York

Everything about Special Agent Tommy Welpers bothered Dagny—from his puffy cheeks and ragged mustache, to the beer belly that poured over his belt, to the single inch-long white hair growing out of his left earlobe. During their six days in the cold abandoned storefront, Welpers had coughed 278 times. In the past hour alone, he had farted four times, twice audibly. Dagny watched Welpers lean back on his chair's hind legs and silently willed him to fall. He had fallen the day before, and it had buoyed her spirits for hours.

When he wasn't farting, Welpers complained endlessly about the conditions of the storefront and their "piece of crap" space heater. He complained about his wife and kids. He complained about the president, about illegal immigrants, and about all the people who were "demanding their rights." She was, it seemed, trapped in a cold abandoned storefront with an AM talk-radio host. No, it was worse than that. She was trapped with an AM talk-radio caller!

And to top it all off, he kept calling her "Dagwood."

They were watching the Alms apartment building on Flatbush Avenue, near Prospect Park. Dagny remembered looking at an apartment a few blocks away when she'd lived in New York. Things had changed in the past eight years. Now nannies pushed strollers down the sidewalks. Sleek and shiny condos made from glass and steel rose from the earth. Greasy dives had given way to sushi bars. Manhattan was moving to Brooklyn. God help it.

Dagny was pretty sure that eighty-eight-year-old Vincent Milano didn't eat sushi. The former head of one of the city's oldest crime families had once lived in a Tudor mansion on twelve acres of Staten Island. Now sick and senile, he lived on the eighth floor of the Alms, in a simple seven-hundred-square-foot apartment. He rarely left the building.

The Bureau wasn't interested in Vincent, though; it was interested in his grandson, Mickey "the Mouse" Milano, who had steered the family business into a field so vile that few gangsters would touch it. The Milanos had become lobbyists.

The *quid* was a $40 million earmark for the construction of a sanitation museum on a nonexistent plot of land in Queens. The *quo* was $300,000 in cash. The mistake was the attempt to deposit the cash into a Wells Fargo checking account. The idiot who made this mistake was South Dakota representative Phil Jenkins.

When Dagny and her fellow DC agents confronted Jenkins, he confessed. When New York agents confronted young Milano, he fled. Now, working together, New York and DC agents were staking out possible hideouts. The local special agent in charge called them "Mousetraps," and there were seventeen of them scattered around the city. Dagny was at one of them, sitting next to Tommy Welpers, who was most of the way through a Domino's pizza. He had eaten seven slices (2,149 calories; 84 grams of fat) to Dagny's none (0 calories; 0 grams of fat).

Dagny looked back and forth between the entrance of the Alms and the screen of her MacBook Pro. She had installed a wireless camera on a tree behind the Alms so she could watch the back entrance of the building from her computer.

"Oooh, check her out," Welpers cooed, pointing at the screen. A young, thin blonde wearing faux fur and high heels was leaving the Alms. "She's a buxom baby."

Despite her best efforts, Dagny laughed. "She looks like an escort."

"I think the Mouse just had a little cheese." Welpers was convinced that the Mouse was staying with his grandfather.

Dagny wasn't quite as convinced. "Lots of men live in the Alms, Tommy."

"Yeah, but they're all ninety, Dagwood."

"Yeah, but Viagra." The buxom baby *was* a good sign, but Dagny didn't want to give Welpers any satisfaction, especially after he had called her Dagwood again.

A few minutes of blessed silence followed, and then a flash of movement on the computer's screen caught Dagny's attention. The Mouse was exiting the back of the Alms, heading north. "Tommy, let's go," she cried, slapping his arm. Agent Welpers had fallen asleep.

The space heater must have been doing some good; it felt bitterly cold outside. Dodging traffic and a fierce wind, they sprinted across the street. A six-foot chain-link fence blocked the rear of the alley. Dagny jumped mid-stride and dug her shoe into one of the links, then catapulted over the top of the fence. Welpers wasn't as agile and fell behind.

The Mouse was running north, cutting toward Lincoln Road and headed toward Prospect Park. Dagny was fast and began to close the gap between them. The Mouse reached inside his coat, turned, raised his gun, and fired a shot. It missed her, but Welpers's scream suggested it had found another target. She turned and ran back to Welpers, who lay on the ground holding his leg.

"Christ, Dagwood. Forget me. Get him!" Welpers cried.

Dagny patted his arm, then sprang from the ground and continued her pursuit of the Mouse. Maybe Welpers wasn't really that bad after all.

Prospect Park was more than five hundred acres of simulated wilderness, tamed lightly by a few streets, a zoo, and a number of nature trails. Dagny had been to the park just once, years ago. She'd watched kids race remote-controlled boats on a man-made lake, wondering if, one day, she'd watch her own kids do the same. When the Mouse entered the park, he sprinted toward the lake then turned onto a footbridge where the lake had tapered to a winding creek. The bridge arched in the middle, and for a second he was elevated and exposed. Dagny raised her gun, tracking him in her sights. He had already fired at her, so she could justify a shot. But if she got closer, she had a better chance of landing a nonfatal one. As always, the goal was to capture the subject alive.

The Mouse felt no similar compunction. As she crossed the bridge, he fired at her and missed. Dagny kept running toward him. The Mouse darted up a hill to Center Drive, followed the road to East Drive, and turned left. Fifty yards down the street, he dove into the woods on the left. If he thought Dagny would just stroll up the street while he hunted her from there, he was wrong. It wasn't 1776, and she wasn't the British army. Dagny darted into the woods forty yards behind the Mouse, hoping to creep up to him from behind.

Using the tree trunks as cover, Dagny advanced on the Mouse, who crouched at the base of a thick oak just a few feet from the edge of the woods. His gun was still pointed toward the street. She crept carefully toward him, leading with her Glock. If she could hit his right shoulder, he'd drop the gun. But to hit her mark, she'd have to get closer. Slowly, she zigzagged from left to right, hopping from tree to tree, closing in on her target—first fifty feet away, then forty-five, then forty. As the wind died, each step seemed louder than the last. When she was thirty-five feet away, her eyes fixed on his shoulder. She stepped a foot closer. And then another. One more step and she'd hit the ground on one knee, resting her elbow on her other knee to steady her aim.

Her cell phone rang.

The Mouse spun quickly and shot toward the sound. The bullet hit Dagny in the chest and she fell backward, dropping her Glock. Even with the Kevlar vest, the shot stung.

The Mouse started toward her. Dagny rolled over onto her knees, groping for her gun. Where was it? She rifled through some fallen leaves, feeling for her weapon. The Mouse fired another shot, and it landed near her hand, kicking a fallen branch from the ground. Another shot hit the tree to her left. He was getting closer—twenty feet away, maybe less.

There were two ways she could go, and neither was great. She was fast, but she couldn't outrun a bullet, so she decided to charge him instead. She barreled into his gut, and he toppled backward, dropping his gun into a blanket of leaves. She dove to the ground, grasping for his weapon. A swift kick to her side tossed her into a tree trunk. The next kick landed on her forehead and drew blood. She grabbed his ankle and twisted until he fell. A flash of moonlight reflected off the barrel of his gun, and she grabbed it. When she spun around, the Mouse was limping through the woods.

With her legs and a gun, it would be too easy. She fired a shot to his left to get his attention. "I don't want to kill you," she shouted.

"You'll have to," came the reply.

She chased him through the trees, ducking under branches, jumping over rocks. With every obstacle, she gained ground. He tumbled over a drooping poultry-wire fence; she hurdled it in one stride. He stepped over fallen tree trunks; she bounced off them.

Dagny spied the park's great grassy meadow through the thicket. Once he left the cover of the forest, she'd have a clear enough shot to bring him down alive.

At the end of the forest, he burst into the meadow with surprising speed. She pounded her feet harder, stretching each stride. Three steps out of the forest, her left foot landed on the paved pathway and she slipped, tumbling forward onto the frozen grass.

All at once, her entire body ached. She tried to move, but couldn't. The blood on her forehead froze and pulled at her skin. Her grip loosened on the gun, and it slipped out of her fingers. The beat of the Mouse's footsteps grew fainter, then disappeared. Dagny lay there, tired and confused—defeated.

She sat in a small white room at the Bureau's Brooklyn-Queens office, waiting for the door to open. An hour passed before it did.

"You had your phone on?" Frank Cooper, the assistant director in charge of Dagny's DC office. Dagny liked Cooper—he was two of her favorite things: smart and quiet. But he wasn't being quiet now.

"I made a dumb mistake."

"I'll say. You're lucky." Cooper put his briefcase down on the table between them and took a seat opposite Dagny. He pulled a Glock from his coat pocket and slid it across to her. "They found it."

Dagny took the gun and holstered it under her arm. "Thanks."

"I'm not going to make a crack about you losing your gun."

"Thanks again." She paused. "I got *his* gun at least."

"Yeah. Even trade." Cooper tilted his head and sighed.

"I'm sorry." She wasn't sure if she was apologizing for losing her gun or losing the Mouse.

"You came close."

"I had him. I had him, and he just—"

"Was faster?"

"No."

"I heard you fell."

"I did."

Cooper pushed his chair back from the table a few inches, then scooted it forward again. "I think we need to talk."

Dagny didn't like the sound of that. "About what?"

"You know I like you. I mean that, Dagny."

"I don't like the start of this."

"Well, you need to know that. You're one of the best agents I've got. Which makes this—"

"Am I in trouble?"

He took a deep breath. "Did you eat anything today?"

So it was this. "I just slipped, Frank. Maybe there was a patch of ice on the pavement."

"Answer the question." He waited, and then repeated, "Did you eat anything today?"

"I can't remember."

"That means no."

"I might have. I can't remember."

"Welpers said you didn't eat anything."

"Okay," she said. "I may have skipped a day."

"Or two. Or three."

"I ate something yesterday."

Cooper laughed. "Do you really think you're going to win this argument?"

Dagny shook her head. "What do I need to do?"

"You need to eat. Isn't that clear?"

"Frank, I run every day. What I eat isn't affecting my work. I didn't fall down because of that."

"This isn't about the Mouse. This is about you. You're starting to look sick. And I'm worried. I think you need to see someone."

"If I do, it goes into my file."

"I knew you'd say that."

"I can get right without it. I've let things slide a bit, but I can fix it. Seriously, I can."

"I knew you'd say that, too."

"A couple years ago, the same thing happened, and I fixed it myself."

"It's not fixed when it happens again." He paused. "I know you don't like talking about this stuff, so I'm just going to lay it out for you. You've got until March fifteenth to get up to one hundred twenty-five pounds. Until then, you're off active duty. I've signed you up for a two-month counterterrorism class at Quantico. Anyone asks me where you are, I'll tell them you're at the class. I've got a friend down there in the medical department. Once a week, I want him to weigh you, just to make sure you're headed in the right direction. You start heading in the wrong direction, and the whole thing is off. If you don't make it to one twenty-five by the fifteenth, I'm putting you on medical leave, and you're going to see a professional. As for what that means for your future in the Bureau—I can't make any promises. You understand?"

"Yes." She wanted to try to talk him down to 120, but held her tongue.

He seemed to read her mind. "At five nine, one twenty-five is still too low. What are you now?"

"I don't know."

"One ten maybe. And headed in the wrong direction. I want you right."

"Okay."

"Dagny, I want to be clear; I'm not punishing you."

"I know," she replied, even though it felt an awful lot like punishment.

Cooper pushed his chair back, stood up, and reached for his briefcase.

"Who's teaching the class?" Dagny asked.

"Timothy McDougal."

"Isn't he crazy?"

Cooper shrugged. "It was the only class I could get you into with such little notice."

Dagny nodded and watched Cooper leave.

She sat there in silence for a while. The phones in the outer offices were still ringing, even at this late hour—Bureau brass inquiring about the Mouse, she feared. An electric typewriter hummed—someone was filling out an evidence card and didn't know how to use the templates on the computer. A group of men were chuckling in the hallway; she wondered if they were laughing at her.

Dagny pulled her cell phone from her pocket and looked to see who had placed the call that had almost gotten her killed. When she saw Mike's name on the screen, she smiled, and suddenly felt a little less alone.

CHAPTER 4

January 15—Warwick, Rhode Island

In retrospect, the best thing that ever happened to Senator R. Brock Harrison Jr. was that hooker falling off his boat.

At the time he'd been a rising star. Upon his elevation from the House to the Senate, Tim Russert had praised his preternatural political skills and visionary eloquence. David Broder had referred to him as "future president Harrison." Maureen Dowd said he was "delicious." Then, amid talk of a presidential bid, reporters began to follow him closely. The attention was flattering, but it cramped his style. The slightest extramarital indulgence required incredible feats of subterfuge and misdirection. Awkward disguises. Switching cars and such. It had been hard enough keeping things secret from his wife, but reporters weren't so easily deceived. Unlike Mrs. R. Brock Harrison Jr., they didn't have a vested interest in maintaining the illusion of a perfect marriage.

So when that hooker fell off his boat, the accolades gave way to denunciations and the man who would be president became just another punch line for the late-night comedians.

But a funny thing happened. The good people of Rhode Island reelected Senator R. Brock Harrison Jr. Although he'd never be president, he realized that virtually no sexual misdeed could ever disqualify him from the Senate. And to the surprise of many, including the senator, Mrs. Harrison stood by her husband after his very public mea culpa and a three-week stint at the Promises Clinic—a medically accredited rehabilitation center/ health spa/thirty-six-hole championship golf resort in the foothills of Tucson, Arizona.

The whole experience was rather liberating, and the past three years had been one long erotic and culinary orgy, conferring upon him thirty-five new pounds and a case of gonorrhea. At forty-six years old, Harrison was in the prime of his life.

As the senator worked the crowd at the Warwick Museum of Art, he kept checking his watch. Across the room, a skinny girl in tight jeans was twisting the cap off a Miller Genuine Draft. She had jet-black hair and when she stretched, her shirt lifted to expose her midriff, showing off her belly ring. Harrison imagined that she owned a secondhand guitar and wrote songs in minor keys about her feelings. Good Lord, she was sexy.

Harrison started toward her, but Margaret Meddlebaum, the museum's matronly director, caught his arm. He concealed his annoyance and turned on the charm. "Margaret, my lovely dear, is it time already?"

"Yes, Senator, if you don't mind."

She walked him to the podium and the crowd grew quiet. While she introduced him, he glanced at his watch. His appointment was at nine thirty, so he had to keep it short. Maybe he'd abandon his ten-minute speech for the five-minute one instead. He surveyed the crowd of social do-gooders, aging hippies, and young free spirits. Every one of them voted for me, he thought, and will again. He flashed his broad smile and pushed his blond hair away from his eyes. Keep it short, he reminded himself.

"It's great to be here, but I have to run."

Harrison had jettisoned the five-minute speech for a five-second one. He offered poor stunned Margaret a quick good-bye, kissed her cheek, and left through the back door. A minute later, he was driving his Lexus down Route 117 into West Warwick, following very explicit directions. Suspiciously explicit, in fact.

If it was a setup, Harrison had his story—he was conducting research for a bill pending before the Senate. This actually seemed like a good cover to Harrison, but then again, he was a little drunk.

The senator parked in a lot at the corner of Saint Mary's Street and Legion Way. It was 9:24 p.m. He fiddled with the radio, then turned it off. When a police car approached on Legion Way, Harrison's throat closed tight and he couldn't breathe. After the policeman drove past, he laughed nervously, then fiddled with the radio again.

At 9:32, a black Ford Explorer turned into the lot and pulled next to Harrison's driver's-side door. The other driver turned off his engine and lowered his window. Harrison did the same.

Shadows hid the man's eyes. "It's five hundred." The man's warm breath drifted into Harrison's car.

"You said it was two hundred." Harrison knew he was being taken, but he wasn't surprised. He had brought $1,000 just in case.

"It's five hundred."

Harrison didn't budge, and the man in the Explorer started his engine. "Okay," Harrison relented. "Five hundred."

The man turned off his car. "It's six now."

Good Lord, if only Harrison were just some street junkie, then the guy would have given it to him for two. "Okay, six." The senator fumbled with his wallet and then placed six hundred-dollar bills in the palm of the man's white latex glove. The man took the cash and then leaned forward into the light, revealing his face.

"Look at me. Do you see me?"

Harrison stared back into the man's eyes. So cold, Harrison thought, as cold as the winter air. Harrison looked away.

"Look at me!" he commanded. "Do you remember me?"

Harrison looked back at the man's face. He did look vaguely familiar.

"Do you?" the man barked.

"No," Harrison said, looking away again.

"You will." The man turned the key to his car, starting the engine.

His voice was so haunting that the senator nearly forgot about the merchandise. "Hey, what about the..."

The man in the Explorer grunted, or maybe laughed. He receded back into the shadows and tossed a bag of cocaine through Harrison's window, onto the senator's lap. A white card was attached. Harrison tore it from the bag. It looked like a business card and had a piece of gum taped to the back. The card read:

THIS IS MY SECOND CRIME.
MY NEXT WILL BE BIGGER.

When Harrison looked up, the Explorer was gone. Yet the image of the man's face and those cold, cold eyes seemed to float outside the car window. Why did his face look familiar?

Harrison ripped open the top corner of the bag and dug his pinkie into the snow-white powder, then brought a pinch up to his nose. Good Lord, he felt alive. He started the car and slammed on the accelerator. If he hurried back to the museum, the skinny girl might be waiting. Maybe he could take her out on his boat.

CHAPTER 5

·······································

January 16—Quantico, Virginia

The FBI Academy is nestled deep in the Quantico woods. Apart from Hogan's Alley and the gun ranges, the Academy's nondescript concrete campus feels like that of almost any small college. Prospective agents live in dorms, eat at a dining hall, and, if they choose, pray in the chapel. In the larger classrooms, agents-in-training sit at long curved tables on elevated tiers. The orange molded-plastic seats at these tables aren't padded, but they do swivel. Sometimes they squeak. When someone from the Behavioral Science Unit flashes bloody crime-scene slides on a large screen and describes the methodical way in which a body was torn to pieces, no one notices the squeaking. But when a Department of Justice lawyer lectures about the technical details of the exclusionary rule, the squeaking seems to grow to an intolerable pitch.

Dagny's chair didn't swivel, and the room she was sitting in didn't look much like a college classroom. It looked like what it was—a large basement supply closet. Pallets of toilet paper were stacked in one corner and an old mimeograph machine sat in another. There was no chalkboard or lectern, just a single easel with a dry-erase board. Overhead, a single bulb hung from a cord that swayed when the air kicked on. The center of the room was packed with old wooden chairs with attached desks—refuse from a middle-school yard sale. A small desk sat at the front of the room, facing the students. Dagny surveyed the other nine agents who had been selected to participate in the Professor's program. It was a motley crew. Two grey-haired men in the back of the room were playing Game Boys. The young woman to her right was sleeping. She wore too much makeup, and her nails were bitten to the quick. The young man behind Dagny looked seventeen; because of his short red hair, the Nintendo agents kept calling him "Opie." Although the class was intended to be a comprehensive overview of counterterrorism techniques, it looked more like a scene from *The Breakfast Club*.

It was five past nine, and the Professor was late. When the door finally swung open, craned necks gave way to disappointment as a handsome black man walked in. Dagny recognized him as Brent Davis, an ambitious agent, two years her junior. Brent had all the markings for success in the FBI—a deep voice, a fighter's body, and a scholar's mind.

Dagny had met Brent just once, three years earlier at the National Institute of Justice's annual conference in DC. He had been working the room pretty hard, smartly building a network of useful connections, and foolishly thinking Dagny could be one of them. They had talked for only a couple of minutes then, so she was surprised that he seemed to recognize her now. When their eyes met, he smiled and gestured for her to step out to the hallway.

"Dagny Gray," he said. "I don't get it. I know it's January sixteenth, but it feels like April first in there."

He'd remembered her name. "You still in California?" She rolled her hair between two fingers, and stopped when she realized she was doing it.

"No. Colorado and Texas since then, but I'm hoping to end up at the home office. Thought this course could help."

"Surprising mistake for a blue-flamer," Dagny said, making a friendly jab at his ambition. "I'm surprised you remember me, by the way."

Brent smiled. "You're not an easy face to forget."

If she'd felt like flirting, she would have replied, "You either." But instead she suggested they go back in.

Brent agreed and followed her into the classroom, claiming the lone empty seat, two away from Dagny.

Another twenty minutes passed without the Professor's arrival. Dagny wondered if he was just a mythical figure, like a unicorn or Sasquatch. After all, McDougal's life did seem to be the stuff of legend. In the late fifties, he disrupted a socialist-terrorist network based in New England, preventing an attack on the New York subway system. A few years later, he stopped a group of pro-Castro dissidents from setting off explosives in a handful of Miami hotels. And then in the late sixties, he infiltrated the Weathermen and helped sabotage a number of planned attacks, including the bombing of a noncommissioned officers' dance at Fort Bragg in North Carolina. McDougal had fought domestic terrorism long before most people were even aware that it existed.

For all his heroics, McDougal had a reputation as a malcontent. When he learned that COINTELPRO—the FBI's Counter Intelligence Program in the sixties—had been gathering evidence against the Weathermen through illegal searches, he refused to work the case. He was rewarded for this principled stand with a stint in the Iowa field office, where he headed the investigation of an interstate cattle-thieving operation. Two years later, the cattle thieves were locked away, and McDougal began to work his way back into the Bureau's good graces. He helped local police catch a serial killer in Des Moines, and then did the same in St. Louis, Detroit, and Indianapolis.

These successes won McDougal an invitation to work at the newly created Behavioral Science Unit at Quantico. At the BSU, he lectured new Academy recruits and his didactic and Socratic style earned him the nickname "the Professor." Despite its derisive origins, McDougal actually liked the nickname and encouraged its use. And since he had no clear title at the Bureau, it was easy for most to simply refer to him as the Professor.

At first, McDougal's work in the BSU was widely appreciated, but as he grew older and crankier, his act started to wear thin. In the early nineties, he started writing predictive and prescriptive articles criticizing Bureau operations and forecasting an onslaught of new domestic terrorism. For a while, they appeared in the FBI's monthly *Law Enforcement Bulletin*, but when McDougal's alarmist tone escalated, publication was refused.

Undaunted, McDougal self-published, faxing *Professor McDougal's Journal* to field offices around the country. Younger agents referred to them as "Letters from Grandpa Simpson." But after the first bombing of the World Trade Center, the Oklahoma City bombing, and the attack on the USS *Cole*, these dispatches seemed more prophetic than crackpot.

Members of Congress quoted from McDougal's missives when questioning Bureau leaders, which only earned McDougal additional enmity within the FBI. He was stripped of his lectures, moved to an isolated office, and given nothing to do.

Things changed when the new president was elected.

The president's father had served as a senator in the 1960s. Some claimed that McDougal had tackled an assassin just as he was raising his gun to shoot the senator. Others said that McDougal dove through the air and intercepted the bullet with his body. Still others insisted that there had never been any gun at all, and that McDougal had discovered that the senator's cook had been poisoning his boss's food. Regardless, the election of the president seemed to change the Professor's fate, because he was subsequently allowed to create his own domestic terrorism course. Bureau leaders were not happy about this, hence the shabby classroom digs.

The years of undeserved indignities were said to have weighed heavily upon McDougal, and the man unfairly maligned as a crackpot had supposedly become one. That's why few had signed up for the class, and why Brent's presence was such a surprise.

Given the Professor's heroic reputation, Dagny had expected him to be big and strong, but it was a short, slight man who finally limped through the door, looking more like an old mad scientist than some kind of James Bond. His small, round head started with a shiny bald spot and ended in a pointy grey beard. Round wire-rimmed glasses sat on his sharp nose. He wore a tweed jacket with patches on the arms, and his frail body shook with a frenetic energy, though he actually moved very slowly. A cane would have helped; Dagny figured he was too proud to use one. She guessed he was in his midseventies, though he could have been as old as eighty, or even ninety. It was hard to tell for sure; he just looked old.

Despite the Professor's appearance, his voice was vibrant and strong.

"Welcome to what I am sure has been described to you as the end to your career in the Bureau." He spoke in a quick, agitated manner. "I am an old coot, a has-been, a crackpot, a lunatic, a madman, right? You've heard all of these things, I assume. There are rumors and stories about me. I won't discuss any of them. That's not why we are here. Suffice it to say, you can look around this room and draw your own conclusions about my stature within the Bureau.

"Some of you—all of you, I hope—are wondering what this program is supposed to be. Six weeks of what, exactly? We already have counterterrorism training, so what is this, besides a vanity project?" He paused a beat and then continued. "I'll tell you what it is: it's another view.

"After September eleventh, the Bureau put four thousand agents on the case. That's what you do with a big case, right? You throw people at it? I'm skeptical. I believe that a handful of people can do a better job than a thousand. We spend too much time looking for information and not enough time analyzing it. We are handicapped by our size. We have too many layers. We are— pay attention to me!" The Professor threw a book at the woman sleeping next to Dagny. It missed, but still woke her. She looked like she was about to cry. The Professor was unmoved. "There may come a time when you are working a case, and you will have to make decisions, and those decisions will have import. If you make the wrong decision, people could die. Perhaps many. Perhaps thousands or even millions. I may or may not be able to tell you something that helps you make the right decision. But God help you if I do and you can't remember it when it matters. This class is important!"

The Professor limped around to the front of the desk and leaned against it. He scanned the room, taking inventory of his disciples. Dagny pegged his look for extreme disappointment.

"Agent Gray?" he called out.

Dagny was startled. "Yes."

"How is practicing law different than practicing law enforcement?"

"In law you can always ask for a continuance."

"Precisely. Now suppose that you know a terrorist is making bombs in Austin, Texas. Where do you suspect he is getting his materials?"

"From a college laboratory."

"Which one?" he asked, with eyes still fixed on her.

"The University of Texas."

"Why not Concordia? Or Austin Community College? Wouldn't these smaller colleges have fewer security measures in place?"

"It's easier to blend in at a big school. At smaller schools, people in the lab know everyone who uses the lab. At UT, there are so many people that no one would think twice about seeing someone they didn't recognize."

"And why else?"

She felt as if she were on the rapid-fire segment of a game show. "The University of Texas is likely to have a larger variety of chemicals, and also a larger supply of each chemical, which means that you might find what you need and be able to take some without a noticeable depletion of the supply."

"Mr. Walton?"

"Yes, sir?" Opie stammered.

"Suppose someone from Concordia University tells you that they are missing small quantities of ammonium nitrate and chlorine gas. Are you worried?"

"I'm actually"—his voice cracked—"a forensic accountant."

"I didn't ask what you are. I asked if you're worried."

"It's not my specialty, so—"

"Are you worried?" the Professor bellowed.

"I am now," Walton said. No one was brave enough to laugh.

"One minute with the Google you kids are always talking about will show you that you need to be worried about the creation of nitrogen trichloride, which will explode violently if heated to above sixty degrees Celsius."

The next three hours were more of the same. The Professor grilled his captives on the explosive properties of various chemical agents, the philosophical treatises underpinning the modern ecoterrorist movement, the historical and biological differences between the tangelo and the clementine, the emergence of three-dimensional imaging in ballistic identification, and the fundamental failings of the legal profession. Each of these digressions was punctuated with periodic outbursts of anger and occasional, but mild, cursing. The Professor threw three more books, confiscated two Game Boys, called one agent fat, and finally drove the sleepy woman to tears.

Most of the students sat in silent, abject horror. Dagny loved every moment of it.

She did not love the trek to the medical center. Since Cooper's ultimatum, she'd eaten less, not more. Maybe it was the stress of the situation. Maybe she thought it would be better to start at a lower weight, so that it would be easier to show progress. She did not try to analyze her behavior; she knew she couldn't justify it.

A man in a doctor's coat met her at the top of the building's steps. His name tag read "Malloy." He looked her up and down, fished some keys from his pocket, and unlocked the door. "Follow me," he said, grimly.

He led her through the waiting area, down a dark corridor, and past a series of examination rooms. With his thumb, he herded her inside the last room and flicked on the light. He opened a drawer under the examination table, withdrew a paper gown, and tossed it at her. "Change into this and then meet me in the hallway."

"I can't just wear my clothes?"

He smirked and shook his head before closing the door behind him. That smirk stayed with her. She'd seen enough smirking doctors to last a lifetime.

She changed as instructed and walked out into the hall. Dr. Malloy was waiting by the scale. He motioned for her to step onto it. Bathroom scales are kinder, Dagny thought. They give instant readings. Physicians' scales require the sliding of weights and the settling of levers, and this only serves to ratchet up the suspense

and maximize the agony. Physicians' scales were suitable for pro-
duce or livestock, not people.

Malloy fiddled with the smaller weight, sliding it back and
forth until the beam finally settled. One hundred eight. It was
actually better than she had expected. She had two months to
gain seventeen pounds.

She changed back into her clothes, and he walked her back
down the hallway to the main doors. There was no humor in
his face. "You would be perfectly healthy at one forty. This one
twenty-five..." He shook his head. "If it had been up to me, your
target wouldn't be one twenty-five," he sighed. "I'll see you next
week."

Dagny nodded and started down the steps. She felt relieved
that the ordeal was over, until she realized that it had just begun.

CHAPTER 6

···

January 17—Alexandria, Virginia

Dagny climbed out of bed and walked blindly through the darkness to the bathroom. She flicked on the light, stripped off her nightgown, and looked at herself in the mirror.

People had told her that she was beautiful, but they were wrong. Sure, there were some things she liked—her high cheekbones, for instance, or her long legs, or her small breasts; the silky-smooth dark hair that hung past her shoulders; the soft olive skin that had slipped down the gene pool from a Korean grandmother she'd never met. But when her gaze shifted from isolated parts to her body as a whole, everything fell apart. She turned away from the mirror and looked over to the bathroom scale, pondered its utility and purpose, and decided once again to leave it alone.

Back in the bedroom, Dagny dressed quickly—nylon running shorts, a sports bra, and the Harvard Law sweatshirt she wore only under the cover of darkness. She pulled on her advanced-performance, friction-free, low-cut socks and the new pair of Nikes that she'd laced the night before. Grabbing her keys, her iPod, and her gun, she raced downstairs.

At five in the morning, all of the homes in the Del Ray neighborhood of Alexandria were dark except for hers: a small Prairie-style two-story—all horizontal lines, overhanging eaves, and intricately cut wood—set back on a heavily wooded quarter-acre lot. It was fifteen degrees outside when Dagny ran out of the house. The cold air felt like a sharp slap against her bare legs, but after a dozen strides, the sting faded.

It was quiet except for the buzz of a dying streetlight, the flicker of which glistened against dangling icicles, remnants of a freezing rain from the night before. No cars filtered through the streets. The morning papers had not yet come. These early hours belonged to Dagny alone.

After five minutes of sidewalks and streets, Dagny reached the Mount Vernon Trail, which snaked along the Potomac from George Washington's plantation toward the District. She turned left on the trail, cranked the alt-piano rock of Ben Folds's *Rockin' the Suburbs*, and sprinted through dark woods and past wet swamps. She followed the trail around Reagan National Airport, under the roar of a United jet taking to the skies. A mile later, she was across Gravelly Point, a large grassy field that jutted out along the Potomac. During the summer, the field was covered in blankets and the air was full of Frisbees. Now, in the cold and dark, Dagny saw only a single homeless man, wrapped in a blanket and leaning against a tree. He followed her with his eyes.

Another mile and she passed the Navy–Merchant Marine Memorial, a sculpture of seven seagulls flying above the crest of a wave. Dagny looked across the Potomac and saw the Washington Monument guarding the city. She'd worked in DC for years, but the monument still moved her. No time for gawking—she ran harder, through the LBJ Memorial Grove, past the Arlington Memorial Bridge, and all the way to the entrance to Theodore Roosevelt Island. She'd run eight miles already. If she kept going and crossed the Key Bridge, she'd end up at Mike's house, many hours too early. She blew out a big white cloud of air and turned around.

There was a time when her feet would have been sore, her legs would have ached; but that time was long past. Some people abandon their warm desks to stand in a freezing rain to smoke a cigarette. Others toss back a shot or two of whiskey after a long day at work. Her father, before he was murdered, always and obsessively tuned the television to Channel 12 before he turned it off. Everyone needed something. Dagny needed to run.

Mike had been away at a conference. Between their busy schedules, they'd managed only three dates—dinner and an art-house flick, a hike through Great Falls Park, and a lecture by Gary Becker at Politics and Prose. In all, Dagny had spent less than twelve hours in his company, but it was enough to make her feel lonely when he was gone.

Mike lived in a three-story Italianate town house on the corner of Thirty-Third and Prospect in Georgetown, just a couple of blocks from Zegman's Gallery and a short walk to the university's campus. Cursive letters had been carved all the way through the cherry front door, and the gaps had been filled with thick, undulating glass. The letters spelled "Brodsky" and rose slightly from left to right, just like the signature on his paintings. Dagny rang the bell. Was it stupid to buy a man flowers? Probably. She tossed the bouquet behind the shrubs just before he answered the door.

He kissed her and invited her in. The entry was a long hallway that extended the full length of the town house. On the right side of the hallway was a red brick wall, accentuated by alternating bay windows and light sconces; on the left, clean white drywall held just three paintings, spaced three feet apart.

She walked over to the first, a Picasso—a cubist rendering of a girl with dark hair. The girl's right eye and nose seemed to float a few inches to the side of her head. Her clothing was a hodgepodge of mismatched patterns. The grooves of brushstrokes announced that this was no print—it was real. She moved to the next painting, a Monet. A girl with an umbrella stood on a hill in a field, white clouds and blue sky behind her. Dagny had seen a similar Monet; but in this one, the girl's hands were outstretched, as if she were dancing in the summer's breeze.

The third painting she recognized right away. It was the portrait of Giovanni Arnolfini and his wife by Jan van Eyck. The original was in the National Gallery in London—she had visited it many times the summer she spent in England before law school.

It was a strange and captivating work. Arnolfini holds the right hand of his apparently pregnant bride while he raises his right hand, as if greeting a guest or perhaps reciting an oath. He wears a large hat that dwarfs his small head. The bride looks down, in shame perhaps, or maybe just in resignation. Her long green dress gathers in a pile at the floor. Both Arnolfini and his bride are pale, their faces smooth, like dolls. They stand between the bedroom window and a bed draped in red velvet. A small dog stands between them; some discarded clogs rest on the floor. The chandelier above is painted in extraordinary detail, as is a small mirror on the back wall. The work is famous in large part because of this small mirror. With proper magnification, the mirror reveals the backs of Arnolfini and his wife, two witnesses, and the artist, Jan van Eyck, who stands in the middle, painting the scene. Dagny squinted at the painting on Mike's wall but couldn't make out the figures in the small mirror.

"I love this painting," Dagny said.

"Me, too," Mike replied. "That's why I painted it."

"You painted this?" Dagny was impressed. It looked so much like the original. "Wait a second." Mike walked back around the corner, and returned with a magnifying glass. He handed it to her. "Look in the mirror."

Dagny held the glass close to the painting. The artist reflected in the small mirror was Mike Brodsky, clutching his palette, cleft chin and all. She laughed. "What about the Picasso? And the Monet?"

"Sadly, those are Brodsky originals, too."

"They're amazing."

"Yeah, well…" he shrugged. Before she could ask him more, he grabbed her hand and led her around the corner.

His home was open and modern, more SoHo loft than Georgetown town house. A thick granite countertop swooped around the kitchen, widening into a rounded breakfast bar, large enough to accommodate six swivel stools, each bolted to the floor. Dagny had tried, and failed, to achieve a similar look on an IKEA budget. His Sub-Zero refrigerator had four deep drawers at the bottom, and the right-hand door was made of glass. The cabinets were beech wood with silver hardware. Calphalon cookware dangled from a hanging rack. Dagny had kitchen envy.

Crushed garlic and chopped onion sat in a saucepan on the stove. Mike doused them with olive oil and then turned on the flame. Dagny leaned against the counter and surveyed the living room. Bright colors, sleek lines. The sofa seemed familiar— she had seen it in a book or magazine. "Is that a Hans Wegner couch?" she asked.

"I'm impressed," he said, adding red pepper flakes to the pan, then stirring the concoction with a spatula. "So tell me about the class."

"He throws books at people."

"I thought you guys only did that figuratively."

She laughed. "I think it's actually going to be a good course. I don't think anyone else in the class is going to like it, though."

He put his hand on her back. "That's how I feel about the classes I teach. I think they're good, but I don't expect anyone else to like them."

She knew that wasn't true. His classes were popular at Georgetown; there was a waiting list every semester. "I'm already tired of the drive to Quantico. Forty-five minutes this morning."

His hand slid down to her waist, and she pulled away. It was instinctual, and more dramatic than she would have liked. They stood in silence for a moment. He furrowed his brow, and seemed to be debating whether to let the moment pass. "I think maybe we should talk about that."

"There's nothing to talk about." She'd said that sentence several hundred times in her life.

He shook his head. "No, see, I like you. I like you a lot. So I want to get this right from the start."

She thought about that, and was going to cry.

He saved her. "About those paintings in my hallway..."

Mike turned down the flame and opened a cabinet door, grabbing a plain glass jar of whole, peeled tomatoes. "I'm going to tell you a story, and it's not a good one." He opened the jar into a large porcelain bowl, then washed his hands. He dug his hands into the bowl and crushed the tomatoes, one by one, into a consistent pulp.

Dagny stared at him expectantly.

"A long, long time ago, I dabbled a little in art forgery." He noticed her surprise and chuckled. "You don't need to read me my rights just yet." He dumped the crushed tomatoes into the saucepan. "I think the statute of limitations has run out. I hope so anyway."

It had started, he explained, as a joke. Trying to prove to his professor that Picasso wasn't that interesting, he'd painted a fake Picasso for his midterm exam. The professor gave him an F—"F for Fake"—and then promptly hung the picture in his home, where he passed it off to visitors as the real thing. One of his professor's friends was a partner at a big law firm in Baltimore. After some heavy questioning from this friend, the professor confessed that it was a fake and sent the lawyer Mike's way. Eager to outfit the firm's walls with a classic on the cheap, the lawyer offered him $1,000 to paint another Picasso.

"Then they wanted a Van Gogh, and then a Monet. And then a Modigliani. Pretty soon, my paintings covered most of their lobby and conference-room walls." He poured two glasses of wine, then added a splash to the sauce.

Mike reached up and grabbed a stainless steel pot from the rack. He filled it with water, set it on the stovetop's lone induction burner, and continued his story. "Some of the lawyers started to send their clients my way—early techies, software developers—people trying to impress the venture capitalists by making them think that they were already successful. The money was good, but it was a pain. I had to study up on every painter, their techniques, their materials, then figure out ways to age the paintings so they would look right. I spent hours tracking down old unused canvas, scraping paint off old junk paintings. I told myself that I wasn't doing anything wrong, because I wasn't lying to anyone, and I didn't have any reason to believe my buyers were going to resell the paintings." He dumped fettuccine noodles into the boiling water.

"But it was wrong," he continued. "These people were using the paintings to lie to people. And I knew that eventually they could end up lost in the marketplace. Look at all the dot-coms that went bust. The longer they held on to the paintings, the more real they would look. Some of the paintings, like the Monet, or especially the Van Gogh, had thick paint that wouldn't dry for years, so they couldn't have fooled an expert when I painted them. But years later when the paint dries?" The pasta started to boil over, so Mike turned down the heat and stirred the pot. He tossed a handful of peeled shrimp into the simmering sauce. "I couldn't sleep at night. I started getting paranoid; every time I saw a man in a suit, I thought he was coming to arrest me. One day I read a story in the paper about a guy named Tony Tetro. Ever hear of him?"

"No."

"Dalis and Rembrandts and Rockwells—he could make anything. A genius. A real genius." Mike shook his head. "They charged him with forty-four counts of felony forgery."

"But I'm sure he was selling them to people who thought they were real," Dagny countered. "You were selling them to people who knew they were fake. That's not a crime."

"Even if mine wasn't technically a crime against the law, it was a crime against art. I was ashamed of myself. I hated myself. So I stopped. It wasn't easy. No one wanted to buy a Brodsky original back then. I worked in a restaurant to pay the rent. Tried to live honestly."

Mike drained the pasta in a colander over the sink, then dumped the noodles into two large bowls, topped them with sauce, and sprinkled fresh parsley on top. "Shrimp Fra Diavolo," he said, placing a bowl in front of her. "So now you know the worst thing about me, Dagny Gray. For a short time, I was a fraud."

"So was I," Dagny said.

He smiled. "How so?"

"I practiced law for four years."

"Yours *is* worse!" he joked. "Tell me about it."

She carried the bowl and wineglass around the counter and sat on a stool. He did the same.

"Always thought I was supposed to be a lawyer, ever since I was a little kid." Ever since Dad died, she thought, but she left that part out. "So I went to law school." She told him about Harvard and the job at the big firm in Manhattan. "On my first day at work, they shipped me down to Houston to review documents in a warehouse for a securities case. *For a year.*"

"Was that Enron?"

"No, it was right after Enron, but it was like Enron. Years and years of records, and we had to go through them all, weed out the privileged stuff, try to contrive legal justifications for not turning stuff over."

"You must have gotten sick of the flying."

"I just stayed in Houston. It was actually cheaper for the client to put me up than to fly me back and forth. Free meals, luxury hotel—it wasn't all bad. They paid me a hundred eighty grand that year to flip through documents, and I didn't have to spend any of it. Finally, the case settled and I moved back to New York and lived in my office." Dagny slurped a long noodle. "This is great, by the way." Great artist, great body, great cook, she thought.

"Thanks," he replied. "You mean you were at the office a lot?"

"No, I mean I literally lived at my office. I never had time to find a place, and I was working late every night—weekends, too. The firm had a dining hall, a fitness club. Sometimes I'd go a week without setting foot outside. I saved a lot of money that year, too."

"The partners must have loved you."

"Nobody noticed," she sighed. "I lived at the firm for a year, and nobody noticed."

"So what got you out?"

"I had a friend who was killed in the London Underground bombing. Not even a friend, really. Someone I knew when I was a kid. Her dad had been killed in the World Trade Center four years earlier. I read about it in the paper—these two tragedies that happened to the same family. Sifting through financial documents in a warehouse suddenly seemed a lot less important. I applied to the Bureau about two weeks later." She realized that they had stopped eating. She twirled some more pasta on her fork. "Did you know anyone—"

"No. Almost, but..."

She sensed that he regretted the *almost*. "What?"

"My ex was supposed to be on one of the planes."

Ex-wife? Ex-girlfriend?

"Fiancée," he said, sensing her question.

Oh. "What happened?" Dagny asked.

"She missed the flight."

"No. I mean with the engagement?"

"She left me."

She wanted to ask why. Instead, she said, "Tell me about her."

"She taught criminal law at Georgetown. Taught English literature, too. Refined, elegant, descended from landed gentry and all that. But she liked me. And she used to be sweet, unpretentious. And then the *Post* asked her to write an opinion piece for one of those show trials in the 1990s."

"O. J.?"

"No. It was right after O. J., but it was like that. It led to an appearance on CNN, and then a recurring segment. Over time, her commentary became less thoughtful and more caustic. When reasoned discourse finally gave way to shouting, they gave her a show. I thought it would end when the trial was over, but there was always a new trial."

Dagny realized her pasta was gone. She didn't even remember finishing it. That never happened to her. "How did it end?"

"One night, over dinner, she said, 'Oh, did I tell you I'm taking that job at Columbia?' And I said, 'What job at Columbia?' She said it would be easier to get on the networks from New York than DC. I just stared at her blankly—trying to understand. She wouldn't look me in the eyes. So I just said, 'We're not getting married, are we?' And she said, in this matter-of-fact voice, 'No, I guess we're not.'"

Mike got up and walked over to the sink. He turned on the water and began washing the dishes. "Afterwards, I walked her home, and she shook my hand, wished me luck. She didn't seem the least bit emotionally affected by the evening. The person I fell in love with…she was gone."

Dagny carried her bowl over to the sink and put her arms around Mike. He turned off the faucet and kissed her. "I really like you, Dagny Gray."

"I really like you, Michael Brodsky."

He took a step back but held on to her hands. "The paintings on that front wall—"

"Yes?"

"The van Eyck—I never sold it—I painted that for me. Sometimes, if I was painting for myself or a good friend, I'd hide myself in the painting as a joke. And so I put that one in the front hallway to remind myself not to take myself, or my art, too seriously. The Picasso and the Monet—I bought those back at auctions. They cost me a fortune—years of sales of my own art. I bought them to prevent others from buying a fraud. If any more come up for auction, I'll be broke. Thought about burning them. Hung them in the front hallway instead, so that I have to confront them every day. So that I can't just forget about it all. So that I have to deal with it."

Dagny looked into Mike's eyes. She understood what he was saying. "Okay." She paused, then exhaled. "I have to gain seventeen pounds by March fifteenth or they're going to put me on medical leave. It's an issue I've struggled with, on and off, for a long time. I was fine for a few years, but I'm slipping. And if you like me, this is something you need to know. Because it's something you'll never understand, and it will probably drive you crazy. If I were you, I'd run from this as fast as possible. This isn't something you can make better. And this probably the most I'll ever talk about it, because even this is hard. I don't hang this painting in *my* front hallway."

He pulled her close and kissed her. "I'm not running. I'm not going try to fix anything. I'm not going to make you talk about this again, unless you want to. You're not going to do this for me. But I'm going to be with you. And you're going to do it just fine." It was everything she had wanted to hear.

They devoted the rest of the evening to lighter subjects and the kissing that new lovers do. Halfway through a second bottle of wine, Dagny noticed it was nearly midnight. "I have to go—"

"No, you don't."

"—get my things from the car."

He walked her to the car and carried her bag inside. They climbed a metal spiral staircase from the living room to the second floor—a large open space that served as Mike's studio. Dagny wanted to linger, but Mike tugged her up another staircase to the third-floor bedroom. He lifted her onto the bed, then lay down beside her, kissing her neck as he unbuttoned her blouse. She reached over and turned off the lamp, wrapped her right hand around his neck, grabbed the hair above his collar, and pulled him to her lips. The blood rushed close to her skin, a familiar feeling that she couldn't place until she realized—yes, this is what it feels like to be alive.

CHAPTER 7

February 1—Chula Vista, California

God, he hated that dog.

Tucker was scratching at the sliding glass door. The kids were screaming about going to bed. Martha was doing the dishes and talking on the phone to her mother.

Fred Lubers rubbed his forehead with his thumb and index finger, trying to stifle the start of a migraine. He slid open the back door and the German shepherd ran out.

"No! No! No!" the kids yelled in unison.

"You have to go to bed right now!" he yelled back.

"Fred, I'm on the phone!" Martha yelled. "The kids won't go to bed. Every night, it's World War Three," she complained to her mother.

Fred lifted six-year-old Gina into his arms and headed upstairs.

"It's not fair. I went up first last night," she complained. Her pigtails twirled in the air as she shook her head.

"You're older, honey. You have to set the example."

Four-year-old Josh stood half-naked at the bottom of the stairs, laughing and pointing at his ascending sister. "You're going to bed first!"

Fred reversed course and carried Gina back down. "Just for that, Josh, you're going to bed first. There's no taunting, okay?"

Josh stomped his foot, but only once before Fred scooped him up and started up the stairs. Gina began singing, "Josh got in trouble. Josh got in trouble!"

Fred shook his head but continued up the steps, carrying Josh into the bathroom and setting him atop a step stool in front of the sink. "Time to brush your teeth."

Josh looked up. "I don't want to."

"It's not an option."

"I don't need to brush them. I drank a lot of water."

Fred didn't follow the logic of this argument but didn't feel like pursuing it further. "Just brush."

"No."

Tucker was barking at something in the backyard. If that dog kept it up, the neighbors were going to complain again. Fred knelt down and looked Josh in the eyes. "Josh, I have a headache. Please just do this for me."

His son smiled. "Okay, Daddy." Josh brushed his teeth, spitting out his toothpaste near, but not into, the sink. Fred cleaned up the mess and carried Josh into his bedroom.

"Jammies, Josh."

"Which ones?"

"You get to pick."

"Football."

"Okay."

Josh put on his pajamas and crawled into bed. "Will you read me a story?"

Fred didn't feel like reading to Josh. He wanted to put Gina to bed and then get some sleep. He had to catch a 6:00 a.m. flight to

Nashville with a layover in Salt Lake City. Steve Hammond from corporate was going to be there for his presentation. He needed to be at his best.

"Which one, Son?"

"The cookie mouse."

Fred grabbed *If You Give a Mouse a Cookie* from the bookshelf. He actually liked this one. "If you give a mouse a cookie," Fred began, then turned the page. "He's going to ask for a glass of milk." Josh fell asleep before Fred could finish the story. He turned off the lights, closed the door partway, and headed down for Gina. She was waiting at the bottom of the stairs.

"Tucker keeps barking, Daddy."

"He probably sees a raccoon or something, honey."

"Tucker sounds mad."

She was right. Tucker was in a frenzy. He lifted Gina up and turned toward the stairs. "I'll go check on Tucker in a minute." Just as his foot hit the first step, something sounded like a gunshot. Tucker stopped barking. Gina screamed and Martha put down the phone. Fred set Gina down and raced into his study, unlocked a desk drawer with one key, and removed another key. He used that key to unlock the gun cabinet, grabbed his rifle, and sprinted to the back door. "Martha—take Gina upstairs." He flipped the switch for the backyard light, opened the sliding glass door, and stepped onto the back patio.

The German shepherd lay motionless in the grass, next to the swing set. Moving closer, Fred saw blood trailing from a gunshot wound just to the side of Tucker's right eye. The dog was dead.

The rustle of footsteps echoed from the woods behind the house. Whoever had shot Tucker was headed toward the 805. Fred chased the sound, dodging trees as the killer moved faster. "Stop right now, you coward!" He tried to hurdle a fallen tree, but tripped and fell forward. The butt of his rifle drove into his chest, bruising a rib. Fred waited on the ground for some audible clue to the killer's whereabouts, but everything was silent. After a moment, he felt ridiculous, and then afraid. Maybe chasing an armed dog-killer through the dark wasn't the best idea.

Fred rose to his feet, grabbing a tree for support. The snap of a branch in the distance caught his attention. A dark silhouette of a man turned toward Fred for just a moment and seemed to wave. It was a quick, halting gesture, and then the figure was gone.

Taking a step back toward the house, Fred realized that he had twisted his ankle in the fall. Limping back to the swing set, he headed for Tucker's lifeless body. A white card was taped to the dog's belly. He tore it away and held it up to the moonlight.

THIS IS MY THIRD CRIME.
MY NEXT WILL BE BIGGER.

A piece of gum was taped to the back. Fred put the card in his shirt pocket and turned toward the back patio. Martha stood at the door with her arms wrapped around their children. He fought back tears and walked over to comfort them.

God, he loved that dog.

CHAPTER 8

February 14—Quantico, Virginia

There was an American flag decal on the long neck of the Detecto 448, and the words "Made in" above it and "USA" below it. A black rod ran from the bottom of the neck to the top, and could extend further when required. Dr. Malloy had used it to measure her height at her last visit: five nine and a quarter. The weights at the top of the Detecto 448 slid across two weigh beams. The bottom beam was marked from zero to 350 in 50-pound increments, although additional notches carried the weight to 450, even though they were not marked. The top beam went pound by pound to 50. The base plate on the machine was solid black, and cold on Dagny's bare feet. On the front of the scale, below the weigh beams, was the name DETECTO and the company's logo—a red outline of a bird alighting on a thin branch. Dagny felt like that bird.

Malloy read the results. Dagny's scale at home had registered an additional pound, but that was okay. She dressed in the examination room, then sent Mike a text: 116, it said. Nine more pounds to go.

In 1818, five-year-old Thomas Alexander Mellon emigrated with his family from Northern Ireland to Pennsylvania. Inspired to seek riches by *The Autobiography of Benjamin Franklin*, Thomas studied hard and became a lawyer, and then a judge. He saved his money, bought vast stretches of downtown Pittsburgh real estate, and opened T. Mellon and Sons Bank, where he placed a life-size statue of his hero, Ben Franklin, above the door.

In 1890, Thomas gave control of the bank to his son Andrew. Andrew transformed the bank into the Mellon National Bank, and as the family fortune swelled, he invested in other industries, too. Some of the investments became Gulf Oil, Alcoa, and Union Steel. Over time, Andrew Mellon served as an officer or director for more than 160 corporations. In 1913, he and his brother established the Mellon Institute of Industrial Research, which later merged with the Carnegie Institute of Technology to become Carnegie Mellon University. During the First World War, he served on the board of the American Red Cross and other organizations supporting America's wartime efforts.

In 1921, President Warren G. Harding appointed Andrew Mellon to secretary of the treasury, and he continued as such under both Calvin Coolidge and Herbert Hoover. As secretary, Mellon was a pioneer of supply-side economics, cutting tax rates in order to spur investment and economic growth, while slashing the national debt by more than 30 percent. Throughout most of his tenure, the nation enjoyed unparalleled prosperity, and his public service and numerous philanthropic endeavors made him a beloved national figure. As *Time* magazine later noted, he was widely considered the "greatest secretary of the treasury since Alexander Hamilton."

And then the stock market crashed in 1929.

Mellon resigned from office in 1931, and Hoover lost reelection two years later. After taking office, Franklin Delano Roosevelt drew up a list of enemies and scapegoats. Mellon topped the list.

FDR demanded that the IRS audit Mellon's tax returns. No irregularities were found. Undaunted, FDR ordered his administration to seek an indictment against Mellon for tax evasion, but the grand jury refused. Finally, FDR's Treasury Department filed a civil lawsuit against Mellon before the US Board of Tax Appeals for underpayment of taxes. Mellon was innocent; FDR knew it, but didn't care. The tax proceedings kept the eighty-year-old Mellon on the witness stand for five days in 1935.

A lesser man might have held a grudge. But in 1936, weak and weary and dying of cancer, Mellon met FDR for tea at the White House and told him that he wanted to create a National Gallery of Art in the nation's capital that would rival the best galleries of Europe. With FDR's approval, Mellon financed construction of the gallery and donated his vast collection of art, then valued at $50 million. He died a few months later, just before the Board of Tax Appeals unanimously cleared him of all charges. The National Gallery of Art was completed in 1941. Thirty years later, a second building was added. It became known as the East Building; the original became known as the West Building.

A statue honoring Mellon now sits in a small park next to the West Building. Dagny and Mike raced past the statue on their way to the East Building. Although they had arrived late, they were greeted by a blinding flash from a *Post* photographer at the door. Mike gave him their names, spelling "Dagny" twice.

Inside, the gallery's atrium was filled with floating red heart-shaped balloons. Below them, the district's high society was at play. Dagny was trying to eavesdrop on George Will's conversation with Senator Mitch McConnell when Mike tugged her toward a heavyset Mexican man wearing a big grin.

"Diego, this is Dagny Gray," he announced.

"She's even more beautiful than you described." Diego hugged Dagny and kissed her cheek.

"It's nice to meet you, Diego. I'm excited to see your exhibit."

"Forget that!" Diego bellowed under the weight of too much wine. "Tonight is about something much more important."

"Raising money for your charity?" Dagny asked.

"No. Dinner!" Diego laughed. "I put you guys with Carville and Matalin. You won't have to say a word all evening." A museum employee called for Diego. "Let's talk after, okay?"

"Of course," Mike replied as Diego jogged away.

"He seems like a very nice man," Dagny said.

"Biggest heart in the world. A good friend. You want to see his work?"

Mike led Dagny up a staircase, then steered her past several paintings to a watercolor of a young Mexican fording the Rio Grande. His jeans were covered in dirt and mud, his shirt was ripped, and he had a scar across his forehead. The man looked tired, but also hopeful. Afraid, but free.

"It reminds me of your work, Mike."

Mike pointed to the young Mexican in the painting. "That's a young Diego Rodriguez. It's a self-portrait. He came over in '81. Took the amnesty in '86. He used to sell his stuff on Sunday mornings at Eastern Market. That's where I met him. He taught me more than any professor ever did."

They walked around the rest of the exhibit. Together, Diego's paintings seemed to tell a single story of Mexican immigrants pursuing the American Dream. Unlike most modern art, Diego's was vibrant and alive and inspiring. It was like Mike's, except that Mike's was better. Mike's work should be here, too, Dagny thought.

CHAPTER 9

February 15—Columbus, Ohio

Melissa Ryder snipped the price tag off her pink lace Victoria's Secret V-string underwear. She tossed the tag into the trash, dropped to her dorm room floor, and sighed. She didn't want to go to the Black Out party at the Sigma Epsilon house, but Janet Hodges was her best friend, and Janet liked skinny white boys in OSU ball caps. That was pretty much everyone in Sigma Epsilon.

It was never much fun to go to parties with Janet, even the cool parties with the introverted boys who liked jazz or read Kerouac. Janet was beautiful. Melissa was "cute enough." Her mom had told her that in high school: "Don't be silly, Melissa, you're cute *enough*." Standing next to Janet made her feel barely cute. Or barely there. When Janet was around, Melissa was the invisible woman, even to the geeks and outcasts.

The Black Out party was an illegal party, a vile and filthy annual affair that had led to a yearlong suspension for the Sigma Epsilon house just three years ago. At Black Out parties, cardboard boxes were ripped apart and taped to the frat house windows, so at midnight, when the frat brothers killed the lights, it was pitch black inside. Under the cover of darkness, things happened that shouldn't, and no one was quite sure with whom they happened. Melissa had heard that the boys would put on night-vision goggles and trade women back and forth without them knowing.

This was not the reason the Sigma Epsilon house had been suspended.

At the Black Out party, all of the men wore blackface. This was the reason the Sigma Epsilon house had been suspended.

"But it's different now," Janet pleaded. It wasn't any different, Melissa thought, as she walked past the two boys manning the door, slathering greasepaint on every guy who entered. Melissa noted that the racist routine had been updated. No longer were the white boys pantomiming slaves and servants; now they were decked out in wifebeaters and grills and bling, and grinding to Snoop, Childish Gambino, and 50 Cent, or "Fitty," as they were wont to call him.

Red lights pulsated to the beat of the music. People were dancing—or moving, anyway—shaking and swaying and stumbling. A girl in a short skirt with a bare midriff was giving a lap dance to a boy sitting on a couch. Two other girls were kissing, to the delight of a group of boys gathered around them. Everyone held plastic cups; none of the cups stayed full very long, and none of them stayed empty either. There was lots of beer but no food.

A black man wearing blackface and a ball cap walked by Melissa. He was smiling and talking with some cute white girls. Wasn't he offended by this? The women at the party were giggling, smiling, laughing, flirting, kissing, and grinding. Didn't they know this was wrong? Didn't they realize that by being here, they were condoning this behavior? Melissa paused for a moment. She was at this party, which meant she was condoning this behavior. When she turned to tell Janet that she wanted to leave, Janet was gone.

Someone put a beer in Melissa's hand; without Janet, she was visible again. Melissa decided to leave after she finished her beer.

Then when she finished her cup, she decided to dance for just one song. But then they played the Jay-Z and Beyoncé hit she liked, and a Fat Joe song after that. While she danced, she thought about how much she hated these people, how mad she was at Janet for ditching her so quickly, and how she had to finish writing a paper for her journalism class. As the evening drew closer to midnight, Melissa noticed that men and women were pairing up and that she was going to be one of the leftovers, again.

A tall man walked over. He seemed a lot older, but it was hard to tell behind the blackface. He wasn't skinny like most of them; he was fit and built. Handing her a seventh beer, he whispered in her ear so she could hear over the noise. "This party sucks, doesn't it?"

He turned his ear to her mouth and she whispered back, "It's awful. It's racist and sexist and awful."

"I'm writing an article about it."

"What?"

"I'm writing an article about it."

"You're a reporter?"

"Yes."

"And they let you in?"

"The guys manning the door aren't exactly at the top of their game."

He was right about that. One of the doormen was crouched on the floor, throwing up. The other was laughing hysterically, and then he fell to the floor as well.

"Are you with the *Dispatch*?" she asked.

"Yeah. Do you read it?"

"Of course, I'm a journalism major."

"That's great. Are you covering this party, too?"

"I should be, but no. I came with a friend."

"Where is he?"

"She."

"What?"

"She!" Melissa yelled over the noise of the crowd.

"Where'd she go?"

Melissa shrugged.

"She just abandoned you?"

"Yep."

"Some friend."

"I know."

"What?"

"I know!"

"You want to go upstairs and find somewhere that we could actually have a conversation?" he suggested.

"Very much."

Grabbing her hand, he led her up the stairs. He opened the first door at the top of the steps, looked in, then closed it quickly. "We don't want to go in there." They continued down the hallway to an empty room at the end. There were no posters on the wall. The shelves were bare. There was just a double bed, neatly made. "Must be a guest room," she said softly. They sat on the bed.

"Would you like some gum?" He handed her a pack of Chewey's. It was already opened, and three pieces were gone.

"Sure." Was her breath bad? She grabbed a piece by its silver wrapper and slid it from the pack, then removed the gum and folded it into her mouth. He was older than she first thought, maybe even forty, but he was very handsome. "How long have you been at the *Dispatch*?"

"I've been there a long time."

"What do you cover?"

"I'm on the crime beat."

"Why are you here tonight? Is this a crime?" She giggled.

"It will be. How are you feeling?"

"What?" It was hard to follow him. "Will be?"

"How are you feeling?"

It was a strange question. "I feel fine. I just feel a little…"

"A little?"

"I just feel a little…" Was it dizzy? Was it tired?

"Maybe you should lie down," the man suggested. Melissa slid down on to the bed, and he lifted her feet up to the mattress. He walked over to the door and locked it. "Because of your father, Melissa."

His words were slurred. Or was it her hearing? "What?"

"Your father." It was the last thing she heard.

Everything after that was hazy. She felt some jostling, some nausea, a heavy weight pushing down on her. After a couple of minutes, everything went black.

When she woke a few hours later, she was certain something awful had happened. She tried to get out of bed but slipped to the floor. Her legs ached. She struggled to stand again, then hobbled to the bedroom door and down the steps. The few people she passed along the way were asleep. Outside, the cold winter air helped wake her as she stumbled across the campus, back to her dorm. She fished through her pocket and found her card key, flashed it at the door, and entered the building. She climbed a staircase and turned right, passed seven doors, and found her own.

She closed the door behind her and finally felt safe. Still, it took a few minutes before she realized that the loud wheezing sound she heard wasn't a neighbor's alarm clock; it was coming from her.

Slumping to the floor, Melissa leaned against the wall and brought her knees to her chest. She tried to count the blocks in the wall, but they were shaking. She tried to count the beats of her heart, but they were too fast. She counted the passing seconds, as they tumbled into minutes and hours. And then a calm came, as the distant hum of a furnace filled her ears like the gentle crash of ocean waves, washing away her thoughts. It could have been a minute or an hour, but she held to it with all her might, even as she felt it slipping away. And when it was gone, the storm returned.

Suddenly, her clothes were disgusting—they had to be removed, maybe destroyed. She jumped to her feet and tore off her shirt, shed her skirt, and ripped away her bra. When she kicked her shoes into the closet, she caught a glance in the mirror. Her underwear—her nice, new pair—was ruined. Stained by her blood. She tore them off and flung them into the garbage. Something was inside her. Reaching between her legs, she removed a blood-soaked piece of paper. She unfolded it and tried to make out the letters.

THIS IS MY FOURTH CRIME.
MY NEXT WILL BE BIGGER.

Her thumb stuck to something on the other side of the card. It was a chewed piece of gum. She tossed the card into the trash, dropped to the floor, and sobbed.

CHAPTER 10

....

February 26—Alexandria, Virginia

In Washington, DC, homes, restaurants, and schools are expensive, but you can sail on the cheap. The Sailing Club of Washington operates out of the Washington Sailing Marina on Daingerfield Island, next to Reagan National Airport, in Alexandria, Virginia. For seventy-five dollars, you can take a SCOW course. If you pass a test, you become a skipper. For an additional hundred dollars a year, a skipper can use any of SCOW's four nineteen-foot Flying Scots.

Dagny and Mike unclipped the blue tarp covering the *Danschweida*, placed it into a dry slip bag, and set it on the grass. They lifted the front of the trailer by the hitch, walked it across the lot toward the dock, and backed its wheels against a concrete parking block next to the water and a twenty-foot crane. Dagny rotated the crane until it was above the boat, then pushed a button to lower a thick steel hook and chain. Mike attached the hook to the boat's hosting bridle, and they lowered the boat into the water. Dagny walked the boat halfway down the wood pier, where she cleated it. Then they returned the empty trailer to its original spot, next to the other boats.

"I didn't realize it'd be such a chore," Mike said.

"A lot more to do."

When they returned, the boat was bobbing in the water, tugging at the rope. Dagny leaped from the pier and landed on the deck, then stepped down into the eight-foot hull. Two molded-plastic benches ran along each side. She sat on the port side. The boom for the mainsail ran across the middle, resting on a crutch and dividing the hull. Dagny smiled over at Mike. He tossed her his backpack and then stared nervously at the boat's deck while the boat thrashed up and down in the waves.

"It's like a three-foot jump, for crying out loud," she teased.

"More like six," he said, "and it's bobbing like crazy."

"Don't be a baby."

That worked. He jumped from pier to deck, then stepped to the starboard side of the hull. Dagny spent the next five minutes explaining how they'd lift the mainsail. Mike interrupted her before she could finish. "Why are my feet getting wet?"

Dagny looked down and saw that water was starting to pool at the bottom of the hull. "We forgot to plug the boat," she laughed.

"*We?*" He shook his head and smiled. "This isn't exactly inspiring confidence."

"I didn't realize you were such a wimp about getting a little wet."

"I didn't realize that I was supposed to bring a bucket." They jumped off the *Danschweida* and walked it back to the crane, then lifted the boat into the air and drained the water from the hull. Dagny plugged the drain, and they lowered the boat back into the water and readied it for sailing once again.

The sails caught wind, and they headed north, around the lighted jetty extending from the airport runway toward the Jefferson Memorial. When the wind died down, Mike reached into his backpack and retrieved a thermos. Hot chocolate. A hundred and thirteen molten calories, Dagny thought. But she needed every one of them, and it would keep her warm. She leaned back against Mike's chest as they floated on the Potomac. He put his arm across her and kissed her cheek. "It's nice, isn't it?" she asked.

"It's wonderful."

Aside from the roar of the occasional airplane, they drifted in a comfortable silence…until Dagny's phone rang.

Dagny looked at the screen. "Oh God."

"Who is it?"

"My mother." She had dodged her mother's last three calls. It didn't feel right to dodge a fourth.

"You should take it."

Before she could decide what to do, Mike grabbed the phone, tapped the screen, and held it to her ear.

"Sorry, Mom. I've been tied up." Dagny pulled away from Mike and slapped his arm with the back of her hand. "How are you doing?"

"I'm worried sick, that's how. You know I worry when you don't answer your phone. Is that why you took that job—so that I could worry all the time?"

"Yes, Mom. That's why I joined the FBI." Mike smirked and she hit him again. "You know I just sit at a desk all day." She had told this lie a thousand times.

"Then why do you carry that gun?"

"Because we all have to, Mom. It's just the rules."

"I don't like it one bit."

Her mother's calls were always like this. "Why are you calling, Mom?"

"Because I miss my daughter, that's why. How's that man you're dating?"

"Just fine, Mom."

"Is he treating you well?"

"Very much so."

"Do you think he could be the one?"

"I don't even know what that means, Mom."

"Of course you do. Why do you have to be so difficult?"

"Look, Mom—"

"Dagny, just tell me if you're falling in love with him."

"I can't talk about that right now."

"Why not? Oh, wait a minute. Is he there right now?"

"Yes, Mom."

"Can I talk to him?"

"Absolutely not."

"I talked to Herb Roseman the other day. They need help in their litigation department."

"I'm done with law, Mom, and I'm not moving back to St. Louis."

"You'd make more money, Dagny. And you wouldn't have to carry that awful gun."

"I'm happy doing what I'm doing, Mom."

"Are you eating?"

"Yes, Mom. I am."

"I want to get one of those camera things so I can see if you're eating."

"You don't even have a computer."

"I want to get one. That's what I'm saying."

"We're not getting webcams."

"Well, we'll talk about that later. But I—"

"Can I call you back later?"

"You promise you will?"

"Yes, Mom."

"Tell Mike I said hi."

"I will."

"No, I mean right now."

"Mom, I have to go."

"Call me later."

"Okay."

"I love you, Dagny."

"I love you, too." Dagny hung up the phone, and then screamed.

Mike wrapped his strong arms around her, pressing her back against his chest, and kissed her neck. "Desk job, huh?"

"She worries enough already."

"I worry, too."

It hadn't occurred to Dagny that Mike would worry about her. "I'm just in class now. There's nothing to worry about."

"And when the course is over?"

"Back to work."

"More gunfights in New York?"

"That's part of the package."

"I know," he said. And then again, more softly, "I know."

Later that night, as Mike slept beside her, Dagny tossed and turned. She hadn't given much thought to how her career might interfere with her future relationships when she joined the FBI. Being an agent meant strange hours, a lot of travel, and too much danger. Signing up for the Bureau had been an admittedly selfish choice she'd made as a single woman with no attachments. It wasn't a great life for a wife, or a mother. Did she even want kids? A couple of months ago, she would have said no. Now, she wasn't so sure.

At one thirty, she got out of bed and descended the spiral staircase to the second floor. Mike had drawn a curtain across his studio space; he had told her he was working on a surprise. Dagny resisted the temptation to take a peek and continued down the next flight of stairs, through the living area and kitchen to Mike's rendition of the van Eyck in the entry hall.

She loved looking at the small details in the painting—the figure of a woman carved into the bedpost, the apple sitting on the windowsill, the leaves of the trees through the cracked window...the wedding ring on the wife's finger, stuck at the middle joint, too small for her. After a few minutes, she walked upstairs and climbed back in bed. It must have been easier to think about the Arnolfinis than her future, because she drifted off quickly.

She woke at four and tiptoed to the bathroom, brushed her teeth, and climbed onto his scale. Three red numerals: 1-1-9. Glancing in the mirror, she saw Mike in the bathroom doorway, wearing his blue boxer shorts and leaning against the doorframe.

"It's early, Dag." He rubbed his eyes.

"I've got to head down to Quantico."

Mike walked to his dresser and picked up his keys. "C'mon, D."

She grabbed the keys from his hand and tossed them onto the bed. "Go back to sleep. I'll run home."

"You're crazy, Dag. That's twelve miles."

"It's barely eight." She kissed his lips and led him back to bed. "Get some more sleep. You've got to teach a class today."

"Let me drive you," he offered, as he slid back under the covers. "Let me drive you," he muttered again, falling back asleep.

They had traded keys a week earlier, and Dagny used hers to lock the door when she left. She took a deep breath of the cold, crisp air. And then she ran.

CHAPTER 11

....

February 27—Quantico, Virginia

The Professor leaned against the front of his desk. "The FBI defines terror as the unlawful use of force or violence against persons or property to intimidate or coerce a government, the civilian population, or any segment thereof, in furtherance of political or social objectives. So was the BTK killer a terrorist? Agent Davis?"

"Arguably, he had a social objective—namely, for society to fear him. It's why he sent letters to the police and to the papers," Brent said.

"If self-aggrandizement is a social objective," Dagny interjected, "then I'm afraid an awful lot of crimes are going to fall within our definition of terrorism. It's not unusual for serial killers to seek recognition. The Zodiac killer sent numerous letters to the media. Jack the Ripper sent a letter to authorities bragging about his crimes. I think that we should expect a criminal to have an objective beyond his own gratification before we call him a terrorist."

The Professor smiled. "So Agent Gray, you're willing to let the definition depend upon the way madmen define their cause?"

"Aren't all crimes judged by the mind-set of the criminal, Professor? Doesn't the commission of a crime itself require a mens rea?"

"Ah, the lawyer has made her appearance." This got a hearty laugh from Brent and a chuckle from Walton. No one else was paying attention.

"You're right, though," the Professor continued. "We do define crimes by the mind-set of the criminal—*at trial*. But when you're in the field, you're not worried about reasonable doubt, are you? Your job is to prevent crimes. Aren't niceties like state of mind better left to juries?"

"Sure, Professor, but aren't we just playing a definitional game? Regardless of whether a criminal meets our definition of a terrorist, we want to catch him. His motive is irrelevant."

"Right, *in part*," the Professor barked. "We want to catch him, regardless of his motive. But obviously, his motive is not irrelevant to us. And why is that, Agent Gray? Why do we care about his motive?"

The Socratic game reminded Dagny of law school. "Motive only matters if it can help us catch him. If we know his motive, we can anticipate his next move."

The Professor grabbed a marker and began writing on the dry-erase board, saying the words as he wrote them. "The WHAT. The WHO. The WHERE. The WHY." He threw the marker to the ground and smacked the word WHAT with his hand. "You show up at a crime scene and do your work, and you've got the WHAT. A dead body. Missing money. Whatever. From that point on, everything is about the WHO and the WHERE," he said, hitting the words with his hand again for emphasis. "If you figure out who did it and where he is, then your case is closed. The WHY only matters if it helps you get the WHO or WHERE. And that's the only reason that motive matters. Agent Davis made a decent case for the BTK killer being a terrorist. But the question is irrelevant. You might not even know if an act is intended to create terror until you're well into the investigation. So why are we even talking about this? Agent Walton?"

"Ummm…"

"No ummms!"

"Because you want us to remember that crime is crime—and that the FBI may be making a mistake by segregating counter-terrorism from other investigative units. Because we need to approach each crime without preconceived notions."

"More or less, Mr. Walton. In any event, I'm hungry, so let's break for lunch."

The Professor gathered his books and hobbled to the door. "Agent Gray, if you would care to join me, I'd like to discuss a matter."

He'd never before extended such an invitation to anyone in the class. "Of course, Professor." Dagny returned the puzzled looks of her classmates with a shrug and followed the Professor down the hallway. He moved slowly, and Dagny found it difficult to match her pace to his.

They took the stairs to an even lower level, wandering under dim, flickering lights, past clanking pipes and boilers, to a thick metal door with a yellow Post-it note affixed to it. It read "McDougal."

"My office," he sneered, pushing the door open.

"This feels like a Terry Gilliam movie," Dagny said.

"I don't know who that is."

Inside, the concrete walls of the ten-by-ten cell were bare. The Professor's metal desk was covered by stacks of books, as was much of the floor. The shelves behind the desk were filled with brown Redwelds, overflowing with file folders and papers. Two framed photographs stood on the top shelf. Dagny guessed that the woman standing against the rail of a ship in the picture on the left was Mrs. McDougal. The picture on the right showed J. Edgar

Hoover presenting a medal to a young, strong, tall agent. Was it the Professor? Dagny didn't believe it was possible. Sure, people shrink, but that much?

"Have a seat," McDougal said.

Dagny removed a stack of books from the chair opposite the desk and sat down. The Professor opened a small refrigerator next to the bookshelf and withdrew two brown paper sacks. He tossed one to Dagny.

"I brought you lunch."

"Oh, thanks, but actually—"

"Don't be rude."

The bag contained a turkey sandwich on rye bread and a bag of baked Lay's potato chips. She took a bite of the sandwich. "Thank you."

The Professor opened a desk drawer and pulled out a bag of Cheetos. "Our program ends in two weeks, and Frank Cooper wants to send you back to New York to work the Milano case— full time, seven days a week, through capture and trial. The detail could last a year or more."

"Oh."

The Professor tore open the Cheetos bag, and most of the contents fell onto his desk. "You don't sound enthusiastic."

"It's a good case. It's just…"

"Yes?"

"The Milanos of the world kill each other. I didn't sign up to save gangsters from one another. I wanted to help—"

"Regular folk? Innocent civilians and the like. That's why you've been teaching yourself Arabic?"

"Yes." Dagny knew there were ten thousand FBI agents, and only fifty of them spoke Arabic. "It's coming, slowly."

"So I assume you'd eventually like to do counterterrorism work, whatever that means," the Professor mumbled, his mouth full of Cheetos.

"I think so."

"Ninety percent of terrorism cases these days are plots the Bureau concocts to entrap Muslim kids."

"But then there's that ten percent," she said.

He nodded. "I understand you're seeing someone. Perhaps you'd like to stay in DC for now?"

How did he know about Mike? She'd never mentioned him to anyone in the Bureau.

"If possible." Not long ago, Dagny wouldn't have cared.

"Well, I have a proposal." The Professor swept the remaining Cheetos into the desk drawer. "I need a research and writing assistant for a few months. If you work for me, you'll have plenty of time to continue your Arabic studies—even enroll in a course if you'd like. Working for me won't help your career, but learning Arabic will. We'd work at my home in Arlington. And when we're done, we can see about getting you reassigned somewhere that lets you protect the regular folk from the ten percent."

It was intriguing. Stay with Mike, learn Arabic, figure out her life.

"You can do this?"

"I talked to Cooper last night."

"And he agreed?"

"He doesn't want to lose you, but I have a little sway," the Professor replied. It's good to know the president, Dagny thought. But then why was he stuck on the boiler-room floor? "I try to pick my battles," he replied, reading her mind. "One more thing. Cooper told me about March fifteenth. You still have to hit the target. That's part of the deal. You understand? I need you healthy, too."

She nodded. That's why he had forced lunch on her.

"So does this interest you?"

It seemed almost too perfect. "Very much."

"Then we have an arrangement." He leaned over the desk and shook her hand, oblivious to the orange dust that coated his fingers. "Now you can go do your run, if that's what you'd like. But take the rest of your lunch with you."

Dagny grabbed the remaining half of her sandwich. At the door, she turned. "Professor, what are we working on?"

"My memoirs," he said. "Until something interesting comes along."

She nodded and started down the hallway past the clattering pipes. As the metal door swung shut behind her, she heard the Professor yell once more, "Eat the rest of the sandwich, Dagny!"

She smiled.

CHAPTER 12

....

March 1—Cincinnati, Ohio

Cynthia Johnson frowned. It was a boring day.

She leaned against the counter and twirled her red locks. Down on the floor, the latest issue of *Us Weekly* peeked out the top of the twenty-eight-year-old's purse, teasing her. The magazine was folded in half, so only "erlake" and "ansson" showed. There was a single security camera in the lobby, and she knew Mr. Waxton studied the footage to make sure they were working. Once, he'd caught a teller flipping through a *Vanity Fair* and docked her pay for each minute she'd spent reading. When the woman had been caught a second time, she'd been fired. So *Us Weekly* stayed in Cynthia's purse.

Because Maxine Campbell's car wouldn't start, there were only two tellers working the morning shift at Waxton Savings and Loan. Even down a teller, it hadn't been busy. Two hours, six customers, and nothing else to do but listen to the clock tick. *Tick. Tick.* Fifty-nine minutes until lunch.

"I'm bored to tears, dearie," Reggie Closter said. Four feet tall and four feet wide, she was an elderly cube. Cynthia hated her throaty, smoke-torn voice, and she really hated being called "dearie."

"I know, Reggie. I'm bored, too."

There were two glass offices in the front of the bank. One was empty; Roy Fielder sat in the other. He had short curly hair and a head that widened from top to bottom, providing ample room for the biggest smile Cynthia had ever seen. Cynthia had gotten to know him a bit, and wanted to know him a bit more, even if he was a little young for her. She wondered why Roy was wasting time working in this rinky-dink savings and loan instead of a prestigious bank like Fifth Third or Citibank. Heck, a piggy bank was more prestigious than Waxton Savings and Loan.

Roy was on the phone. Cynthia couldn't hear what he was saying, but he seemed pretty excited. When he hung up, he grabbed his coat and briefcase and bounded out of his office.

"I'm off to Dayton."

"What's in Dayton?" Cynthia asked.

"Big loan. Maybe very big. If I can get it."

"Great." Cynthia shrugged. "More money for Mr. Waxton."

"Well, it's his bank," Reggie interjected. "Who do you think signs our checks? Santy Claus?"

Cynthia ignored her. "Coming back?" she asked Roy.

"Oh, yeah. Probably by four."

As the door closed behind Roy, Cynthia turned to Reggie and seethed, "You know, Reggie, you don't have to invite yourself into every conversation."

"He wasn't talking to you. He was just talking generally."

"He was *too* talking to me." Cynthia leaned against the counter again. Fifty-five minutes until lunch.

"I'm going outside for a smoke."

"Yeah," Cynthia looked at her watch. "I guess it's been ten minutes."

With Reggie gone, *Us Weekly* was tempting. Maybe she could just sneak a quick peek. She was reaching for the magazine when a large, heavyset woman entered. Most of the bank's customers were elderly folks who had banked with Waxton for most of their lives, so it was unusual to see a fresh face. Fresh face was a generous description for this woman, though. She had a heavy brow, a bar-fight nose, and saggy cheeks caked in rouge. Her green ensemble was more tent than dress. She wore white gloves and carried a large canvas purse.

"Can I help you?" Cynthia asked.

The woman responded with a man's voice. "I have a gun, and I need you to put your hands on top of the counter, and not to say a word." It was a deep, soothing voice, but Cynthia was still hyperventilating when she put her hands on the counter. "If you do exactly as I say, everything will be fine." His saggy cheeks were beginning to tear away from his face—it was a mask of some kind, made of putty and makeup, like they'd wear at the theater. "Do you understand me?"

Yes.

"Answer me!" That wasn't soothing. It was angry. Violent.

"Yes."

"I'm going to come around and watch you open both drawers. At no time should either of your hands go anywhere near the right side of the drawers. You are not to trigger the alarm."

The man walked around the counter, keeping his gun pointed at Cynthia. He nodded toward the drawer and she opened it. The man held his purse open, and she transferred the cash to the bag. "Bottom, too," he said.

Each teller had two drawers, one on top of the other. Cynthia turned a key in the bottom drawer and popped it open, then loaded the money into the man's bag. "Top drawer of that one," he said, motioning to Reggie's drawer. Only the bottom drawer required a key, and he knew it.

Cynthia emptied the bills into the man's bag. "Don't cry," he said. "This isn't about you." She hadn't realized she was crying.

The door chimed. Cynthia looked up and saw Reggie walking back into the bank. "What the—"

The man shot his gun at Reggie, shattering the glass door behind her. Reggie dove through the doorframe and the mostly shattered glass, screaming as she fell on the concrete sidewalk in front of the bank.

The man grabbed Cynthia's wrist, kicked open the door to the back hallway, and dragged her along. At the end of the hallway, he kicked in a door marked CHESLEY WAXTON in black block letters, then yanked Cynthia inside. Mr. Waxton wasn't there. Maybe he had escaped to the back parking lot, Cynthia hoped.

The man fired a shot into the bookshelf behind the desk. "Get up, Waxton!" The bald, spotted tip of Waxton's head rose from behind the desk. Like Cynthia, he was crying. The man motioned for him to stand and then tugged Cynthia by her wrist toward her boss, before placing the barrel of his gun against Waxton's head.

"The sins of the angels remain with them in heaven," the man intoned. "The sins of the angels remain with them in heaven. Say it to me."

"Wha-wha-what?"

"Say it back to me!" He pushed the gun harder into Waxton's temple.

Waxton squeaked, "The sins of the angels remain with them in heaven?"

"Not as a question!"

Waxton was dripping with sweat. "The sins of the angels remain with them in heaven."

"Again."

"The sins of the angels remain with them in heaven."

"This is important, so don't forget it." The man shoved Waxton to the ground, then let go of Cynthia's arm and pointed to the floor.

Cynthia joined Waxton on the floor, and the man walked over to the bookshelves behind the desk. She watched him reach for the autographed baseball resting in a glass sphere, suspended by a stem over a wood base. It was Waxton's prized possession. The man opened the sphere, removed the baseball, and tossed it in his bag with the money. Then he set a small white card inside the sphere so that it stood on its short end. He turned toward Cynthia, and she twisted her face back toward the ground, afraid to make eye contact with him. The man walked over to Waxton and dug his heel into his back. "One more time."

"The sins of the angels remain with them in heaven."

"Exactly." The man sprinted to the door, fired two more shots into the bookcase, and disappeared.

Cynthia began to shiver. A sheen of sweat covered her arms and face, and the air from the vent felt cold. She was lost in the sound of her breath when she heard a car engine fire. He was leaving.

Cynthia sat up, and Mr. Waxton crawled over to her and hugged her tightly. Silently, Cynthia regretted every bad thought she'd ever had about the man. A few minutes later, Reggie appeared in the doorway. Her dress was torn in several places, and her arm was bleeding. She held a lit cigarette in her hand, and in her throaty snarl, she croaked, "That woman was a real bitch, wasn't she?"

As awful as the day had been, this made Cynthia laugh. "It was a man, Reggie."

"Well, she's gone—whatever she is."

Waxton let go of Cynthia and lifted himself up by the edge of his desk. He seemed a little embarrassed by the hug. Cynthia looked at the empty glass sphere, then turned to Mr. Waxton. "He took your ball."

In the past few minutes, she had seen Waxton afraid and nervous and even embarrassed, but for the first time he flashed despair. "My ball?" He started to cry again. "We have a vault here, for Christ's sake. Why the ball?"

While Waxton cried, Cynthia looked inside the glass sphere to the card the man had left behind.

THIS IS MY FIFTH CRIME.
MY NEXT WILL BE BIGGER.

Cynthia Johnson couldn't help but smile. It was not a boring day.

CHAPTER 13

March 3—Alexandria, Virginia

Dagny climbed out of bed and walked blindly through the darkness to the bathroom. She flicked on the light, stripped off her nightgown, and looked at herself in the mirror. Something was different. A puff in her cheeks, maybe. A crease missing from her brow, perhaps. She saw Mike step behind her and she smiled. The smile—now that was different.

She turned away from the mirror and looked over to the bathroom scale, pondered its influence and power, and nudged it to the center of the floor. Mike stood beside her. To let him stand there and watch this was as intimate as she could ever be. She stepped onto the scale and watched the numbers flutter: 1-1-8. She'd lost a pound.

"There's plenty of time," Mike said.

Back in the bedroom, Dagny dressed quickly—nylon running shorts, a sports bra, and a Libertarian Party sweatshirt she wore only under the cover of darkness. She pulled on her advanced-performance, friction-free, low-cut socks and a worn pair of Nikes she'd soon have to replace. "You coming?"

"Yes." He pulled on his shorts and put on his sneakers. "Mount Vernon this time?

"You got it." She grabbed her keys, her iPod, and her gun, and raced him down the stairs.

She knew that a tablespoon of sesame seeds had 52 calories and that 40 of them were from fat. So when she saw the hamburger bun, she tried to guess whether the seeds scattered on top of it amounted to a quarter of a tablespoon, or just a fifth, and even though the difference was only 2.4 calories and entirely inconsequential, she couldn't stop herself from doing the calculation. And then there was the bun itself—which was impossible to estimate. A kaiser roll at the grocery store, similar in size, registered 180 calories, 20 from fat, but this restaurant bun was probably made with more butter and sugar, so it was probably 220 calories, 50 from fat.

The cheese, which she'd ordered only because of the dire circumstance of Cooper's ultimatum, was a Vermont cheddar. A normal slice of cheddar cheese was about 80 calories (60 from fat); this slice was thicker than normal, probably more like 120 calories (90 from fat), she decided.

The burger was tricky, too. She knew that three ounces of extra-lean ground beef had 208 calories (116 from fat); doubling that would be 416 (and 232). But this wasn't extra-lean ground beef, so maybe it was closer to 300 from fat.

As for the toppings, she figured 6 calories for the slice of tomato (none from fat), 10 for the red onion (again, none from fat), maybe 5 for the slice of lettuce (no fat). These things weren't really worth counting, but she counted them anyway.

The tablespoon of ketchup was easy—15 calories, and just 1 from fat. The sweet-potato fries she took from Mike's plate added maybe another 200 calories (80 from fat). All told, this decadent, monstrous meal was about 1,000 calories, and more than 500 from fat.

To do this calculation, Dagny needed neither pen nor calculator. It took no mental gymnastics; she processed it in seconds. She did it while listening intently to Mike's story and laughing at the appropriate moments. He surely had no idea what was happening inside her head. No one did. She was a Rain Man with calories.

They were eating dinner at Ray's Hell Burger Too, a gourmet burger joint in Arlington. Dagny preferred chain restaurants, which posted nutritional information on their websites. Usually, she'd peruse the site and select her meal in advance; for the more popular restaurants, she'd committed the relevant information to memory. The point of this wasn't to avoid the trouble of calculation on the spot; that effort was minimal. The point was to establish certainty, and to avoid the pitfalls of estimation and guesswork. While she believed that there were 1,000 calories on the plate in front of her, she wasn't certain, and this caused her some anxiety.

Another calculation was causing her anxiety. A runner can determine her calorie burn by multiplying her weight in pounds by three-quarters of the number of miles run. She'd run fifteen miles that morning, which translated into a burn of a little over 1,300 calories. The massive meal in front of her didn't even offset the calories she'd burned. And she ran this much every day.

Mike had never, not once, chided her for eating too little or running too much. He was simply there for her. And that was enough to both inspire and shame her. Were she alone this evening, she would not be eating a cheeseburger and fries. Most likely, she would not be eating at all. The task of gaining seven pounds in twelve days would have overwhelmed her. With Mike, she just went along for the ride, trusting that it would work, because it had to.

After dinner, they walked up Wilson Boulevard to Boccato Gelato. The thought of eating more disgusted her, but she did not protest or quibble. She did not suggest Pinkberry or lobby for sorbet. The uphill hike cost her another 50 calories, she guessed, so she more than offset that by taking her treat in a cone. They sat on a bench by the street, eating their gelato, watching pregnant bellies and strollers pass by.

"There are times I feel completely alien," Dagny said. "Where I find myself watching the world with a detached fascination, utterly incapable of relating to it in any meaningful way."

Mike leaned back and put his arm around her, pulling her closer.

"But I don't feel that way now," she said.

CHAPTER 14

March 12—Quantico, Virginia

The Professor slid a piece of paper across his desk. The header indicated that it had been faxed by the Cincinnati Police Department. The paper was blank except for the faint outline of a business card around two lines of rather ominous text.

"Strange font," Dagny replied. "Bookman Antiqua, maybe? I take it that this was left at the scene of some crime?"

"A bank robbery." The Professor handed Dagny a printout from *The Cincinnati Enquirer*'s website. "Man dressed as an old woman takes a couple of drawers and an unusually valuable baseball. The bank was understaffed, as one employee had been called away to a fictitious loan opportunity and another had car problems. An inspection of the car revealed tampering."

"So the thief did some planning."

"Too much for such small stakes," he said. "How'd you know it was Bookman Antiqua?"

"Yearbook and paper."

"What?"

"High-school yearbook editor. Worked for the college paper."

The newspaper article focused on the stolen baseball. It had been caught by César Gerónimo of the Cincinnati Reds to record the final out of the 1975 World Series, and had been signed by numerous players, including Pete Rose, Joe Morgan, Johnny Bench, and Tony Pérez. The bank's owner, Chesley Waxton, had bought the ball for $25,000 at a charity auction thirteen years earlier. He seemed more distressed by its disappearance than by the disruption to the bank's business or the threat to his employees. The article noted the thief's mysterious note in passing, adding that the reporter was unable to find accounts of the implied earlier crimes.

Dagny knew that the Professor's interest had nothing to do with the baseball. "You're curious about crimes one through four?"

"I'm more curious about crimes six and up," he said. "The case is being handled in Cincinnati by Lieutenant Ronald Beamer. He told me that no similar cards have been reported. Maybe the crimes haven't been discovered. Or maybe he's not just committing them in Cincinnati. Or maybe the card is a hoax."

"I assume you want a thorough investigation?"

"Just a little information. Don't make it seem like anything official."

"I'll start right after class."

"Skip class. I'm not talking about anything important this afternoon."

"How is that different from this morning?"

The Professor sighed. "Why aren't you afraid of me, Dagny Gray?"

Dagny smiled, then gathered her things and headed for the door.

"Wait."

When she turned around, a brown paper bag was hurtling toward her. "Lunch!"

This is my fifth crime. My next will be bigger. Dagny searched
Google for earlier permutations, assuming there were earlier
cards. When Google came up empty—the FBI had spent hundreds of millions of dollars building databases, and none of them
were as good as Google—she tried Yahoo!, Bing, Ask.com, and
even HotBot, which she hadn't searched since 1999.

Still nothing.

Dagny logged onto Westlaw and searched through ten years
of newspapers, magazines, and wire services. When nothing
came up, she tried the same in LexisNexis. Nothing.

It was time for a more direct approach. Dagny found a list
of the hundred most populated American cities on Wikipedia.
Then she searched for an e-mail address for each city's police
department, starting with New York, Los Angeles, and Chicago,
and working her way down to Birmingham, Alabama; Gilbert,
Arizona; and Rochester, New York—skipping only Cincinnati.
After dropping the addresses into the bcc line, she drafted an
e-mail describing the Cincinnati bank robbery and requesting
any information about crimes involving a similar calling card.
She asked that each police department forward the e-mail to
smaller neighboring municipalities, and that they in turn pass
it along to villages and townships. If chain e-mails worked for
Viagra spammers and the "Prince of Nigeria," maybe they'd work
for the FBI, too.

After an hour, thirty-nine cities had responded, none with
useful information. A few personal e-mails arrived, too. Julia
Bremmer wrote to say that she and Jack couldn't meet Dagny and
Mike for dinner because Jonathan was sick. The Harvard Law
School Association of DC announced yet another happy hour
that Dagny would skip. A Google news alert told her that Dan
Bern was releasing a new album.

More responses came: Albuquerque, Pittsburgh, Tulsa,
Buffalo, Newark, and Virginia Beach all responded negatively

before Dagny received Officer Eduardo Perez's e-mail from Chula Vista, California. She called him.

"Dad putting the kids to bed hears the dog barking in the backyard, doesn't know what's going on, then hears a gunshot, runs outside, and the dog is dead. Shooter ran off. Guy left a card with the dog—'This is my third crime. My next will be bigger.'"

"When did this happen?" Dagny asked.

She heard the rustling of pages. "February first, around nine p.m."

"Did you guys check the make on the gun?"

"No." Pause. "It was *only a dog*, Agent Gray. But we do have the bullet."

Dagny wanted that bullet, which made her realize that she'd been cooped up in a classroom for too long. The Professor just wanted a little information, not an investigation. She absolutely couldn't ask for the bullet.

"Can you send me the bullet?"

"Sure."

"Shell?"

"Don't have it."

"Anything else you can tell me?"

"Hmmm," Perez hummed. "Well, the card was taped to the dog's head. The dog was a German shepherd. Name was Tucker. And there was a stick of gum on the back of the card."

"What do you mean?"

"He had taped a stick of gum on the back of the card."

"Unchewed?"

"If he had chewed it, he wouldn't have needed the tape, right?" Maybe Perez was still smarting over the unintended implication that he should have checked the make of the gun.

"Was the gum still in a wrapper?"

"It was in the silver foil."

"Do you know what kind of gum it was?"

"Jesus, lady. It was a doggycide, for Christ's sake."

"Officer Perez, I don't mean to suggest that you *should* have checked the make of the gun or the make of the *gum*, for that matter." She wanted to laugh, but restrained herself. "I understand that it is a relatively small crime, and that your resources are better used elsewhere. I'm just pursuing information, not insinuating that you haven't done a thorough and complete job, and I apologize for any implication otherwise."

Perez seemed to realize that he had overreacted. "Yeah, look, I'm sorry if I snapped. It's been crazy lately."

Dagny didn't ask him what this meant, even though it seemed he wanted her to. "Would it be possible for you to scan the file and send it to me by e-mail? When things settle down?"

"Yeah, of course. And you want the bullet? FedEx?"

"That's fine."

"So you think this dog-killer robbed a bank in Cincinnati?"

"Looks like it."

"Have you heard anything about the other three crimes yet?" he asked.

"No. But I'm still waiting to hear from a lot of departments."

"Do you think he stole the gum?"

She misheard him. "The gun?"

"No, the *gum*."

Dagny hadn't thought about it. "You mean as his first crime?"

"If you were going to start small, could you start any smaller?"

"That's a good theory."

Perez seemed pleased with the praise. Dagny thanked him, gave her home address, and said she might call upon him again.

Perez's theory was good, but it worried Dagny. It would be better if the first crime was grand theft or burglary. Stealing a stick of gum was a long way from bank robbery, and such a steep trajectory made Dagny worry about the nature of crime number six.

She surfed the web while a few more unhelpful e-mails came in. At a quarter to five, she packed up her things and headed back to the classroom. Along the way, she stopped at a vending machine and purchased a pack of Wrigley's Extra. She fished one of her business cards from her backpack and held the stick of gum to the back of the card. The gum was shorter than the card by half a centimeter on each side. She folded the gum in her mouth and continued to class.

She was met with cold stares from her classmates as they exited the room. A teacher's pet is never popular. Even Brent's smile was a little forced. Should've been him, right? Even though he wouldn't have wanted it. Dagny peeked inside the classroom, and the Professor waved for her to enter.

"Dead dog in Chula Vista," she began. She filled him in on the details and relayed Perez's theory about the gum. "Was there gum on the back of the card in Cincinnati?"

"You can find out tomorrow when you visit Lieutenant Beamer. You're okay with that, right? Going to Cincinnati?"

"Of course." Little did he know she'd already booked a ticket.

CHAPTER 15

March 13—Cincinnati, Ohio

A balding middle-aged man with a bad cough plopped down in the seat next to her. "Michael Connelly. I love his stuff. I read that one last week." *Cough.* "How do you like it?"

"Uh-huh," she murmured, without looking up from her book.

"I thought about being a cop, always thought I would have been a good detective. But you know how those things go."

Dagny didn't, so she ignored him.

"You from Cincy or DC? Or you connecting somewhere?"

"I'm from DC. I'm going to Cincinnati."

"Business or pleasure?"

"University Hospital. I've got a mild form of leprosy, and they're checking me into a clinical trial."

"Oh." The man left her alone for the rest of the flight. He even ceded the armrest.

When the hills of Northern Kentucky parted, the Cincinnati skyline filled the expanse. Staring out the taxi window, Dagny was surprised by its beauty. Newer cities are all glass and steel, but Cincinnati was a hodgepodge of classical, art deco, and modern architecture. The hills surrounding downtown were dotted with expensive homes and condos feasting on river and city views. Beautiful, colorful bridges spanned the river. But when Dagny's cab crossed one of them into the downtown, she saw boarded-up storefronts and loiterers in front of City Hall. There were hundreds of old houses in distress. Shattered windows and graffiti. Vagrants sleeping on benches. An upturned trash can.

Cincinnati looked better from afar, she decided.

At District One, a short, scrawny bald man waited by the curb. "Ronald Beamer," he said, helping her out of the taxi. The curbside greeting was unexpected, but then again, visitors from Quantico were surely rare.

Beamer led Dagny up the steps and into the station, through a maze of cubicles and desks, to a conference room in the back. One wall of the conference room was made of glass and looked out to the bustling activity of the precinct floor. Dagny sat down in a maroon leather chair with brass nail-head trim. Its rollerball wheels didn't fare well on the plush green carpet. Beamer sat across from Dagny and placed a thin black binder on the wobbly oak conference table. He flashed a nervous smile. "Okay, before we go any further, are you taking the case?"

"No. I'm working with Timothy McDougal at the Academy. He's worked with the BSU for the past thirty years or so, and now he works mostly on independent research projects."

"He's the old guy that I talked to?"

"Yes."

"What's his interest?"

"He was intrigued by the robbery at Waxton Savings and Loan, and wanted me to find out more about it. That's it."

"Why is he intrigued? Because of the baseball or because of the card?" Beamer asked.

"The card."

"So this is just research?"

"Yes."

"We'd like notice and a chance to review before anything is published. Just to protect the investigation, if you know what I mean."

"That's perfectly reasonable."

Beamer opened the notebook and slid it across the table to Dagny. "You can look through it, make copies, whatever you want. I can give you the rundown, too, if you'd like."

"I would."

Beamer spent the next thirty minutes recounting the pertinent details of the investigation. The thief had stolen only a little over $7,000 and the World Series ball. The phone system had logged the call that drew Roy Fielder to Dayton. It was a nonexistent number with a Dayton area code. "There are sites like SpoofCard.com that make it look like you're calling from another number, another area code," he explained. Dagny already knew this, but let him tell her anyway.

Beamer took her through the various witness statements, and noted the thief's strange incantation: "The sins of the devils remain with them in heaven."

"The sins of the devils remain with them in heaven?"

Beamer looked down at his notes. "Yep."

It didn't make sense, she thought. "What about the bullets?"

He reached down toward the floor, lifted a clear plastic bag from a box, and handed it to Dagny. "We found three in the bookshelf in Waxton's office. The other he fired through the front door."

Dagny held the bag up and studied the bullets. Five lands and grooves twisted to the right. "Smith and Wesson," she noted. Beamer handed her two more bags. The first contained the bullet casings. The second held the business card and gum. Dagny lifted the bag containing the card and looked at the other side. "No prints, I assume?"

"Nothing. The guy was wearing gloves. You'll see in the tape when Goldilocks gets here."

The card edges were perforated. Dagny guessed that they had been produced on a home ink-jet printer. She grabbed her camera from her bag and took a picture of it, then flipped the card around and took of picture of the gum, still partially attached to the back in its wrapper. Chewey's was repeated in capital letters a half-dozen times in shiny lettering diagonally over the matte silver surface of the wrapper. "What's the flavor?" Dagny asked.

"I didn't chew it, Agent Gray."

She opened the bag and sniffed. "Cinnamon." She closed the bag. "Who's Goldilocks?"

"Goldilocks is our nice nickname for J. C. Adams. You don't want to hear the bad ones."

"Who is he?"

"J. C. Adams. *The* J. C. Adams." Beamer raised his eyebrows. "You don't know who J. C. Adams is?"

Dagny shook her head.

"He's a local boy that went off to USC to play quarterback. Went all Hollywood while he was there. Dated an Olsen twin for a minute. Would have been a first-round pick, but he got hurt on the first play of the Rose Bowl in his sophomore year."

It sounded vaguely familiar. Maybe she had heard the name before. "Why is he coming here?"

"After the injury, he came home and joined the force. The chief liked having a celebrity around, and soon the kid started to get his ear on all kinds of stuff. Expensive stuff. And most expensively, the video console. He convinced the chief that we would save money long-term by producing training and recruitment videos in-house. So we sold off the old stuff and bought all-new equipment—cameras and lights, too. Turns out, the kid just wanted to use it for some film he's making. Then a few months ago, he won a lawsuit with his insurer over the football injury, so he quit the force. Says he's going to film school in the fall. Now we're stuck with this stuff, and no one knows how to use it. So we're always having to call the kid in for help."

"At least he comes in, right?"

"Sometimes. He'll come in for you, though. I told him you were pretty."

Dagny laughed. "You hadn't even seen me."

"Yeah, but I wanted to make sure he'd come. For the record, he won't be disappointed."

While they waited for J. C. Adams, Beamer excused himself to tend to other matters. Dagny called Officer Perez and confirmed that the gum on the back of the card in Chula Vista was Chewey's Cinnamon. He also confirmed that there were perforations on the edges of the card, and that the bullet (which he had yet to send) had five lands to the right. Probably the same gun, Dagny thought. Maybe the same guy, or maybe multiple unidentified subjects in coordination. No apparent motive. The third crime had occurred on February 1; the fifth, on March 1. Two data points were never enough to draw a conclusion. Still, if forced to place a bet, Dagny would have put her money on January 1 and a pack of Chewey's for the first crime.

Beamer returned with J. C. Adams, who looked more like a surfer than a quarterback. He was tall, but skinnier than she'd expected. His curly blond locks hung around his face, forcing him to constantly shove them away from his eyes. "Yeah, she's hot," Adams said plainly to Beamer, as if Dagny weren't there. Then he turned to her and showed off a white-capped smile. "I'm J. C."

Dagny shook his hand. "Special Agent Dagny Gray, Mr. Adams."

"Nothing sexier than a lady with a gun."

She ignored that. "I'd like to see the security footage from the Waxton robbery."

"Sure." Adams led them along the perimeter of the precinct floor. When they got to the studio, Dagny laughed at the massive array of video and audio equipment. It looked like the control booth for the Academy Awards.

"What's so funny?" Adams asked, defensively.

"You really pulled a con job here," Dagny said.

"This thing could pay for itself if they used it right!" Adams loaded a DVD. The security footage flashed on the screen in front of them.

"No sound?" Dagny asked.

"Nope."

The camera had been positioned above the tellers, and the wide-angle lens showed Cynthia Johnson and most of the lobby, including the front door. The wide angle came at a cost—the image was stretched and distorted. It was hard to see much detail in the robber's face.

"Can I see the other angles?" Dagny asked.

"That's the only one," Beamer answered.

"What do you mean? They only had one camera?"

"Only one working."

"That's crazy."

"I know."

"Nothing outdoors? Drive-through ATM?" Dagny asked.

"Nope," Beamer replied, but he hesitated. Dagny knew he hadn't checked. Hopefully, he would now.

"Can we see where the unsub enters the door again?"

"Huh?" Adams replied.

"The robber," Beamer explained.

Adams rewound the footage to the point where the robber entered the bank. Dagny squinted at the tape measure along the right side of the doorframe. "Six foot exactly?"

"That's what it looked like to us," Beamer said.

At Dagny's request, Adams made a copy of the DVD. She thanked Lieutenant Beamer and Adams, then headed toward the exit. Beamer went back to his office, but Adams followed her. "So you're from DC?"

"And going back," Dagny responded, pushing through the door.

"Right now?"

"That's right."

"I can give you a ride if you'd like."

"I think I'll just hail a cab."

Adams laughed.

"What's funny?"

"You think you're in DC? You can't just hail down a cab here."

"I'm sure I'll catch one." Dagny could see a cab a block away, but it was headed in the wrong direction.

Adams pulled a crumpled piece of paper from his pocket, jotted a number on it, and handed it to her. "After a few minutes, when you haven't seen a cab, call me and I'll swing back and pick you up." Adams pointed his remote key toward a red Porsche parked along the curb and unlocked the doors. "Call me," he mimed as he climbed behind the wheel.

Adams was right—Cincinnati wasn't a cab town. Each minute Dagny waited felt like an eternity. She thought about calling information and getting the number for a taxi company, but it was easier to just call Adams. He was there two minutes later. "I knew you'd call."

"I see you're enjoying the insurance money," Dagny noted as she climbed into the Porsche. "I'd like to make a stop before the airport."

"Sure. My bedroom has a great view of the city."

"I'd like to stop by Waxton Savings and Loan."

"The ATM, right? You think Beamer messed up by not getting the footage. We can go, but you're wasting your time. The ATM's on the wrong side to see the front."

"They should still check the film."

"Beamer will. He was just too embarrassed to admit they hadn't, but he's a good cop."

"How'd you know where the ATM is?"

"I helped them with their security."

Small town, Dagny thought. "How'd that come about?"

"Waxton's a sports nut. He bought one of my high school jerseys and asked me if I'd sign it. I came over to the bank, signed the jersey, and we got to talking. I'd been working with the chief to upgrade the equipment at the station and told Waxton about it. He wanted some advice on security for the bank, so I looked around and gave it to him."

Dagny laughed. "Yeah, well, bang-up job."

"Hey, I just wrote him a proposal! Spent some time on it, too—looked at what other banks were doing. Made a lot of recommendations, but he didn't do any of them."

"How much did you propose he spend?"

"Fifty thousand." He didn't seem to like that she was shaking her head. "Hey, that's not that much. Motion-sensitive cameras, hard-drive recording, remote monitoring. I think the robbery shows I was right and he should have listened to me."

"Counting the baseball, the robber took Waxton for about thirty, maybe thirty-five grand. You were trying to take him for fifty."

Adams pouted but had nothing to say. After a couple of minutes, he said, "If you got to know me, you might like me, you know."

"Shouldn't you be playing with women your own age? What are you, twenty-five?"

"Twenty-four, actually."

"Do you have any idea how old I am?"

"Thirty-eight?"

Dagny ignored this and hoped to ride in silence. Adams wouldn't oblige.

"So what's the deal?" he asked. "You have a boyfriend or something? I don't see any ring."

She resolved to rent a car the next time she came to Cincinnati. "Yes."

"A feeb?"

"No."

"Well, what's he do?"

"He's an artist." She instantly wished that she had said he was a professor.

Adams shook his head and chuckled. "Does he have the earring and everything?"

"You're one to talk, with that surfer hair."

"This is a very normal haircut for people my age," Adams stammered.

"Yeah, I think I've seen it on *The Real World*." She was proud of her dig, though it had no effect on Adams.

Dagny was eager to sit down by the gate and return to her book and the gritty world of detective Hieronymus Bosch, but all the seats were taken. Instead, she leaned against a pole and watched a mother play with her kids. The mom was thirty, maybe younger. Her four-year-old son's jeans were too big, and they bunched under his belt in the back when he rolled a small fire truck on the carpet, chasing his two-year-old sister. The sister toddled like a penguin, crashing to the ground after every few steps, laughing hysterically each time. The mom helped the daughter up after every tumble, holding her by her hands until she could steady herself. Moments later, when the dad returned with ice-cream cones, all play stopped. The two-year-old started clapping wildly, sometimes missing her hands and hitting her arms. The mother shared her cone with the daughter and a smile with her husband. The son devoured everything that made it into his mouth and wore the rest. When they finished, the mom wiped the kids' faces clean while the dad tidied the carpet beneath them.

Dagny started to cry. Usually she was able to keep it together. Sometimes she couldn't. She went to the bathroom and washed her face. When she returned, the plane was boarding. Cheeks still puffy, Dagny took her seat and started to read. A man sat down next to her and looked at her book. "I love Harry Bosch. Haven't read that one yet."

She nodded but continued reading. Mercifully, he pulled out a Jeffery Deaver novel and they took off in peace. A half hour later, the man closed his book with an exaggerated flourish. "Man, that was good. Do you ever read Deaver?" Dagny noticed his shoes—polished brown Oxfords with an impossible shine. "Edward Green," he said.

"You're Edward Green?"

"No, the shoes you're looking at. Edward Greens. From England."

"Oh."

She guessed from his salt-and-pepper hair that he was in his late thirties, maybe forty. He was handsome and fit, with cute dimples and a cleft chin. Deep-blue eyes. His voice was calm and soothing.

"So do you read Deaver?"

"I've read the Lincoln Rhymes."

"I love his twists at the end. You know, how you think the story is over, but then you find out there was more going on, and that someone else did something, too. This one," he brandished the book, "had a triple twist."

"Sometimes he tacks on one twist too many," she said.

"Maybe, but it's always an amazing ride."

She went back to her book. By the time the plane started its initial descent, Dagny was thirty pages from the end.

"So are you from DC?"

"Yes," she said, eyes still focused on her book.

He reached into the pocket of his suit coat and pulled out a silver business-card holder. "I'm going to be in town this week, so if you'd like to get together…" He shook the card holder and a card fluttered down on the page of her book. She slammed it shut and closed her eyes. And then she thought about how lucky she had been to find Mike, and how much she missed him after only a matter of hours.

CHAPTER 16

March 14—Arlington, Virginia

If Snoopy's doghouse could accommodate a pool table and Jacuzzi, maybe it made sense that the Professor's quaint Tudor could hold his absurdly massive, marvelous study. It was at least thirty feet by thirty, maybe larger. Built-in bookcases—made of dark, rich oak—rose from the floor to the fifteen-foot ceiling along each of the walls, breaking only for the doorway, and even then extending on up from the top of the frame. Sliding ladders graced each of the walls to enable book retrieval at the highest levels. The floor was covered in a plush dark-blue carpet. Tall reading tables with flexible brass lights ran down the left and right sides of the room. Two couches faced each other in the middle of the room, perpendicular to the Professor's large oak desk. A glass coffee table sat between the couches; the glass afforded a view of an embroidered FBI seal in the middle of the floor.

The Professor was perched on the couch opposite Dagny, chewing the end of his pipe and stroking his beard. He'd ended the class two days early, ostensibly to ponder the bank robbery but more likely because he'd grown bored with it. Dagny had spent the last hour walking him through the information she had collected in Cincinnati.

"If the third crime was February first and the fifth was March first, it would suggest that the first was January first."

"It's a reasonable supposition," the Professor responded. "If he is as mathematically minded as he seems, the second and fourth crimes would have occurred in the middle of January and February respectively. I wonder…" the Professor said, rubbing his temples.

"What do you wonder?"

"Months are of different lengths, so the middle of January might fall at noon on January sixteenth, while the middle of February is technically the stroke of midnight on the fourteenth. Or is that technically midnight on the morning of February fifteenth? Which way does midnight fall?"

"I think it would fall on the morning of the next day, but—"

"I wonder if he is more concerned with mathematical accuracy or symmetry," the Professor interrupted. "Would he want the even-numbered crimes to fall exactly within the middle of each month, or would he prefer that they fall on the same numerical day each month?"

"I don't think we know enough about him to make an educated guess."

The Professor grabbed a remote from his desktop and pressed a button, causing a large white dry-erase board to descend from the ceiling. He wrote the numbers one through eight across the top of the board. Under the number one, he wrote gum, followed by a question mark. Under three, he wrote dog, and under five, he wrote bank. Then he inscribed a series of dates under each of the crimes. The odd-numbered crimes started with 1/1 and increased to 4/1. The even-numbered crimes began with 1/15 and continued to 4/15. Every date, except for crimes three and five, earned a question mark. When he had finished, the Professor sat back and contemplated the board.

. "Is killing a dog three-fifths of robbing a bank?" he asked. Killing a dog seemed worse than robbing a bank to Dagny. People robbed banks because they wanted money. People killed dogs because they were evil. "I wish we knew about the gum he stole," he said, adding, "if he stole it."

"Chewey's Cinnamon."

"No, I mean the number of sticks in the pack."

"You think he's planning to commit crimes until the pack runs out?"

"Probably."

Dagny took out her laptop.

"I don't have Internet here," the Professor apologized.

So many books, but no Google. "I get the Internet everywhere." Dagny had a Sprint 4G card, which brought high-speed Internet to her MacBook in most metropolitan areas. She searched the web for the Chewey's home page. Scrolling through the list of products, she found Chewey's Cinnamon Gum. "This isn't very helpful," she said. "They sell it in packs of five, ten, twelve, and fifteen. I can't tell if this is an exhaustive list."

"I think we can safely assume it wasn't a pack of five. The card makes it clear that he plans to continue."

"You seem to have a lot of faith that he's sticking to some rules."

"Sometimes they cheat," the Professor said. "But usually not until later."

"What do you think is next?"

"Assuming he started with gum, worked up to dog killing and then bank robbery, I think we're due for a murder." The Professor tugged at his beard. "If he didn't start with gum but started with something bigger, then maybe he hasn't worked his way to murder yet. Maybe the increments are smaller. Maybe a kidnapping."

"You think that it's clearly one person? Even with the geography?"

"Can I see the security footage?" he asked.

Dagny placed her computer in front of the Professor and inserted the DVD. The Professor occasionally nodded, but remained silent until the end of the recording. "Either this person had some help or is very talented with makeup—maybe even a background in theatrical arts." He paused. "Or he just did his research." The Professor scrolled back through the footage and stopped on the culprit's face. The man's cheeks were uneven and seemed to sag. One of the brows extended a little farther forward than the other. "The prosthetics on his face make him appear much heavier than he actually is."

He walked to his desk, picked up the phone, and mumbled something. "Getting a snack," the Professor explained. A short while later, a striking grey-haired woman walked into the room carrying a tray with an assortment of cheeses and grapes. She set the tray down on the coffee table and offered her hand to Dagny.

"I'm Martha McDougal. You must be Dagny?"

"Yes. It's a pleasure to meet you."

"Is he being nice to you?"

Dagny looked over at the Professor, who pretended not to be paying attention. "Very much so."

"Well, that's unusual." She smiled at Dagny and then turned to her husband. "You keep playing nice."

The Professor shrugged off the admonition. "I'll be however I damn well want." It came out meeker than he must have hoped.

"If he acts up, Dagny, let me know," she said, before leaving them to their work.

"Eat something," the Professor ordered.

"I'm not hungry."

"Today of all days, you'll eat it. You're of no use to me on medical leave."

He professed only self-interest, but she sensed some underlying affection. Dagny grabbed a handful of grapes. "Professor, what do we do now? He's probably going to commit another crime sometime in the next couple of days, maybe even today. It may be a murder. That doesn't give us much time to—"

"We wait, Dagny. We have to wait."

"Wait? Until someone dies? Shouldn't we try to do something?"

"I'll send a fax to field offices suggesting that a crime is expected, and asking them to report it to me. You should send a similar e-mail to the local police you contacted the other day. But there's nothing else we can do. It's not our case. And no one is going to take us seriously until someone is dead."

The man was friends with the president; surely he could pull some strings. "Can't you use your sway with—"

"Even if we were given the authority to move forward with an actual investigation, we don't have the time. Sometimes you have to wait."

"But—"

He held up his hand. She nodded, then composed her e-mail and sent it off. "Done."

"Take the afternoon off. We'll reconvene tomorrow morning. I'll call you if something happens before then."

Dagny slipped into the auditorium and scuttled across the back row to an empty seat. The lights were dim so the students could study the Giuseppe Arcimboldo painting projected onto the large screen at the front of the room. It was a portrait of a nobleman—except the man's face was composed of various vegetables, fruits, and flowers. His eyebrows were peapods; his ears were, appropriately enough, ears of corn. Dagny guessed that his nose was a pear, but it was hard to tell.

"He didn't just paint this one painting. He painted hundreds like it," Mike said, flashing a few more examples of Arcimboldo's work on the screen. Upon first glance, the portraits looked like inverted bodies, as if the organs were on the outside. Only when they came into focus were the fruits and vegetables evident. "Born in Milan in 1527. Died in 1593. Spent most of his early years rendering window designs and tapestries. And then in 1562, he moved to the imperial court in Prague and began painting like this," he said, gesturing toward the screen.

"You might think he was mocking the elites of the day," he continued. "Maybe he was, but the privileged lined up for the honor, paying Giuseppe handsomely to depict them like this. His work became so popular that it spawned a number of imitators, and to this day, it's hard to tell whether some paintings were done by Giuseppe or one of his contemporary forgers." Mike turned up the lights and raised the screen.

He lectured with a smooth, lulling cadence, and Dagny forgot about the bank-robbing dog-killer and his calling cards. When they were together, he made her forget everything else. It sounded simple, but it was what she needed, and no one else had done it.

Dagny studied the faces of the girls around her, with their forlorn glances and bobbing heads and longing sighs. Who wouldn't love him? Strong, rugged, smart, talented. Kind, gentle. Tender.

Hers.

After class, Dagny swam against the tide of departing students to Mike. "My other professor let me out early," she explained.

He kissed her, prompting a couple of mock swoons from the few students left in the room. "Let's get out of here," he said. "Your surprise is ready."

"*My* surprise?"

They walked to his house, then upstairs to his studio and the curtain that tempted her each night.

A painting, she guessed. A portrait of me. Even if you don't like it, pretend, she told herself, but she knew she'd like it. "Of everything I've ever done, this is my favorite," he said, slowly tugging the curtain away.

It was a bronze sculpture of a woman—a goddess—who stood, not on a pedestal, but on the floor. "She's beautiful." The woman was Dagny's height. She wore an evening gown. Dagny touched the shoulder straps of the dress, then traced the seams of the fabric. It was her dress—the one she was wearing when she first met Mike. The zipper in the back bent slightly left just like hers. Even the stitching was precise. Dagny dropped to the floor and looked at the shoes—*her shoes*—the sneakers she had worn when they met.

"She's wearing my clothes."

"Of course," Mike laughed. "She's you, Dagny."

But that didn't make sense, because this woman was gorgeous. "Is this how you see me?" Dagny asked.

"This is how you are. It's how you are *right now*." Mike grabbed Dagny's left hand and placed it on the top of the statue's bronze nose, then placed her right hand on her own. He slowly slid both hands down to the ends. "Do you see?"

They were the same.

He moved her hands, and Dagny compared her forehead, her ears, her chin. They were all the same. Her elbows and fingers and knees—the same. Her waist—the same.

"How do you like it?"

"I love it." For the first time in her life, Dagny felt beautiful.

"I love you."

"I love you, too."

Finally, it was said. They embraced for a while. After a minute, he broke the silence. "I made a lasagna."

She laughed. "Thank you."

CHAPTER 17

March 15—Washington, DC

"This is my sixth time," the woman said. She carried three books and a rolled poster in her left hand, and pushed a stroller with her right. There was a bounce in her step when the line moved forward. He tried to ignore her, but she continued. "Seeing her, I mean. And each time it's bigger."

The line to meet Candice Whitman snaked through the bookstore's shelves and twisted between the tables in the café before continuing out the door. He'd waited for nearly an hour, and now stood just twenty feet away. He was trying to concentrate on Whitman's purse—a large black leather bag, slightly open at the top—but the woman behind him kept talking. "The first one I went to, ten people showed up. Now look at it."

He looked up at the round convex mirror above the magazine racks. It took a few seconds to pick himself out from the crowd. The wig, the mustache—if he couldn't recognize himself, Candice didn't stand a chance. Even without the disguise, he'd changed a lot since they'd known each other. She'd changed, too. The Botox and dye job couldn't hide that the softness in her eyes had grown cold. He noticed that her fingers were all bone; her cheeks, too.

Maybe she looked good on camera, but in person, she appeared sickly and frail. Her right hand wrapped around a pen, clutching it as an asthmatic holds his inhaler. He thought about the damage it had done. Just words, but words had consequence. People suffered because of the way she spilled her ink. He'd suffered from it. But she'd hurt him in other ways as well.

Eight people—that's all. Just eight people stood between them. She wore a white blouse with an olive jacket and a little pink flowered handkerchief poking up from the pocket. Gold earrings dangled from her ears; a large diamond pendant hung from her neck. Booty from her crusades. Booty like the apartment on the Upper West Side, and the place out in the country with the pool and the stables and the Venezuelan man who tended the gardens. Booty—that's what she would have called it if she were writing a column about someone else, anyone else.

And yet they loved her.

If you're going to lead a lynch mob and not get lynched, you have to keep it moving. Candice did it better than anyone. From Ken Lay to Duke lacrosse to the runaway bride—guilty, innocent, or just plain confused—it didn't matter, as long as they filled the hour and brought home the viewers. And if she was wrong, as with the Duke lacrosse team, then she just moved on to the next villain-of-the-day. No one held her accountable. But he would.

And then there were three between him and Candice. He closed his eyes and slowed his breathing, relaxed his grip on her book, and told himself that this was just.

And then there was just one, a frazzled young woman who spoke with a nervous quiver. "Your work has really meant a lot to me, Ms. Whitman. My nephew was Andrew Higgins." Whitman didn't seem to know who that was. "You know, the little boy who was kidnapped in McLean? Kidnapped, and then—"

"Oh, yes," Candice responded, mustering indignation. "An absolute monster."

"I just want you to know that your work helped get us through that, and I don't think they would have given him the sentence they did if you didn't keep everyone's attention on it."

Whitman smiled and signed the woman's book. "The cases I cover are so heartbreaking that I sometimes think I can't keep going, but then I meet people like you and it reminds me why I do." Whitman clasped the woman's hands in hers and nodded.

It was his turn. He slid his book across the table. "I'm a big fan of yours," he lied, making no effort to disguise his voice.

"Thank you." She smiled, though had she recognized him, she wouldn't have.

"Can you make it out to Brutus?"

She paused for a moment. "Brutus?"

He shrugged. "It's a little joke for an old friend."

When she opened the book, he leaned down to tie his shoe. As she scribbled away, he thrust his arm quickly into her purse and dropped the card. In less than a second, it was over. He rose. She handed him the book. He thanked her. No one noticed anything. He paid for his book at the third register, the one where the camera captured only the back of the customer's head, and walked out the door.

There was a taxi parked at the curb. The driver leaned against the passenger door with the *Post* and a cigarette. He wore a plaid ivy cap and a red-checked scarf. "Need a ride?" he asked the man.

He thought about saying yes and ending it all right there. Instead, he ignored the cabbie and walked around the building, taking his place in the bushes across from the store's loading dock. Whitman's Mercedes SL Roadster convertible was parked by the back exit. When the signing was over, she'd descend the back steps. Would his old friend be with her? He hoped so, though he hadn't seen him in the bookstore. Still, there was plenty of time for him to come, and it didn't really matter that much anyway. There just had to be two to keep the math right, and someone would be with Candice. She had her signs and banners, and she'd never carry them herself. Someone would carry them for her.

The next hour moved slowly. He crouched in his hiding spot and rolled the handle of an eight-inch dagger in his palm, growing comfortable with its weight and shape, until it felt like a natural extension of his arm. The first time the back door opened, it was just a stocky teenage boy carrying out the trash; the second, a middle-aged woman who stood at the top of the steps, leaning against the rail for a smoke. He watched that cigarette burn down to the stub and then watched the embers die after she'd tossed it to the ground.

An hour is a long time when you're waiting to kill.

It had taken all of the past year to plan the crimes—to develop the sequence, to visit the scenes, to choose the victims. But it had taken every one of the ten years before it to muster the strength to commit the crimes, to understand that he could be violent and vulgar, even cruel and savage, and still not be evil. Indeed, he was fighting evil—exposing it. Judging it, as it should be judged.

And then she was there, pushing through the door, carrying only her purse, as a crisp breeze blew through her hair. From the distance, she looked like her younger self, before the Botox and the collagen. She leaned against the rail, arching her back, smiling. Their old friend was there, too, following behind, carrying two boxes as if they were nothing. He looked the same—just as young, just as fit.

The friend leaned the stacked boxes against the rail and chuckled at something Candice said, and the laugh carried across the lot to the bushes as if it had carried across twenty years. His grip on the dagger grew a little soft when he heard the laughter. He almost dropped it altogether—the dagger, of course, but also the murder and his contempt for her and all the others. It was funny that something as simple as a laugh could change the course of everything. It could have, but it didn't.

He hid the knife under his jacket and walked toward them. They didn't even notice his approach—indifferent to him even at the end. She started down the steps toward the parking lot. When her left foot hit the second step, he raced toward her, withdrew the knife, and stabbed her quickly in the chest, right through her pink handkerchief. The first jab hit bone, but the second slid between her ribs and into her heart.

She fell to the ground.

Her friend dropped the boxes and lunged at him, but he shoved the bloody knife into the man's chest and tore it toward his heart. And though he should have run right then, he lingered to watch the life drain from his old friend's eyes. Before it did, there was one last look of recognition. *You?*

The man nodded. "This is my sixth crime. My next will be bigger."

CHAPTER 18

March 15—Quantico, Virginia

At 9:30 a.m., Dagny stood for the final time on the Detecto 448. Dr. Malloy slid the weights back and forth, then managed to flash a rare, quick smile. "One twenty-six." She'd made it, with a pound to spare. It was probably the lasagna.

She called Mike from the car on the drive back. When he didn't pick up, she left a message in which she rambled more than she would have liked. "One twenty-six. I made it, and it's thanks to you, Mike. I couldn't have done it without you. I mean that. I love you so much. I do. I really do. Let's celebrate tonight, if I don't get caught up with work. Love you." She hoped there would be no crime this day—it would give them two reasons to celebrate.

After Dagny arrived at the Professor's house, they worked on his memoirs; she took dictation while the Professor paced around the room and recounted tedious and inconsequential details from his childhood. While they worked, a muted CNN played in the background on a sixty-inch plasma TV that descended from the ceiling at the push of a button. Every few minutes Dagny looked up at the screen, waiting for news of the sixth crime. There was nothing. And so the Professor dictated and Dagny typed.

The sixth crime had already occurred when Mrs. McDougal brought them lunch—a spinach-and-ham quiche with a strawberry-and-walnut salad. If she had known about the crime, Dagny wouldn't have touched her lunch. But Dagny didn't know and it tasted good, so she finished every bite.

If she had known what had happened, she wouldn't have joked with the Professor, trying to get him to confirm the rumors about his undercover work with the CIA. He brushed aside her inquiries, insisting that they proceed chronologically. "We must finish with the third grade," he insisted, which made her laugh. They had already spent an hour on the third grade. Not one single noteworthy thing had happened to the Professor in the third grade.

If she had known what had happened, she wouldn't have been fixating on the letter C. The third and fifth crimes had occurred in Chula Vista and Cincinnati, and she wondered if Charlotte, Columbia, or Cambridge could be next. She also wondered about the number ten. Chula Vista and Cincinnati each had ten letters, just like Kansas City, Alexandria, and Chevy Chase, and she could have added Washington and Georgetown, but she didn't know. When she told the Professor all of these thoughts, he dismissed them. "You can tell very little from two data points and an awful lot from three."

The bodies weren't discovered for twenty minutes, and even then, it took another ten for the cops to arrive. Forty more minutes passed before one of the detectives found the card in the woman's purse. A half hour later, someone called the FBI, just in case the card meant something to the Bureau. The agent who took the call fired off an e-mail that sat in someone's in-box for another forty minutes. When the e-mail was finally read, three phone calls were placed, the third of which rang the phone in the Professor's study. A few seconds into the call, the Professor grabbed the remote and flipped to Channel 9. An aerial shot showed police barricading the crime scene, and the yellow type at the bottom of the screen read "Murder of Two in Georgetown," before giving way to a slow crawl: "Candice Whitman and a companion were stabbed to death behind a Georgetown bookstore this morning. Whitman had just finished signing copies of her latest book, *The Ides of March*. The acerbic legal commentator was forty-five." It scrolled past seven times before "UPDATE" flashed in bold, bright letters at the bottom of the screen, and then a new crawl began: "Police have identified the second victim as Michael Brodsky. He was professor of art history at Georgetown and a respected artist. He was forty-three."

PART II

THE WHO

CHAPTER 19

March 15—Arlington, Virginia

Dagny must have screamed, because Mrs. McDougal ran into the room. Everything else was a blur. The Professor seemed to know who Mike was, though she had never mentioned him by name. Mrs. McDougal handed her a glass of water, but she dropped it, unable to grip anything, just trembling, shaking. She felt dizzy and nauseated. Her stomach cramped. A chill settled upon the room, and she shivered. They covered her with a blanket and turned up the heat. It was still too cold.

Her thoughts began to run together and pile upon each other. She thought mostly of Mike's arms squeezing her—of how safe she felt with him, and how she'd never feel safe again. She thought about the way he kissed her neck. A silly joke he told her at the zoo. The smile he flashed to the children they'd passed on the street. Reading the paper in bed. Ice-skating on the Mall. The way he drove so cautiously. Two months of memories that would have to last a lifetime. Fifty years that would never happen. Children who would never be born.

The things they'd never had hurt more than the things they'd never have again. They'd never known summer or fall together, nor spring either, really. She had never seen him in swim trunks. They had never walked on the beach, gone to a Nationals game, or watched the fireworks on the Fourth of July. They'd never shared a Christmas, not even a birthday—his was March 23, hers was April 12. She'd never met Mike's mother, an industrious woman who ran a bed-and-breakfast on Cape Cod. They had planned to visit in June. Mike had never met her mother either. They had planned to visit for Passover. Dagny had been dreading the trip and was ashamed of herself for that now.

She was also ashamed by the one thought that kept crowding out the rest: Why was Mike with his ex-fiancée?

"Dagny?"

She opened her eyes. The Professor was standing over her.

"Dagny, some men have come. Are you able to speak to them?"

She glanced at the clock on the Professor's desk. It was four thirty. An hour had slipped away. When she opened her mouth, her throat was dry. "Yes," she managed.

The Professor walked out of the room and came back with two men. The older one was a Caucasian with a buzz cut and a thin mustache. His tie was fastened in a big, loose knot, and he introduced himself as a detective from DC Homicide. The younger one was an African-American in his late twenties. He wore cuff links and a broad, nervous smile. Although he was with the FBI's DC field office, Dagny couldn't remember his name. Under different circumstances, she'd have known it instantly.

Before they asked a single question, a thought flashed through her mind. "J. C. Adams," she muttered. She jumped from the couch and ran to her computer on the Professor's desk. Dagny typed her own name into Google and clicked the fourth link. There, in *The Washington Post* Style section, among a hodgepodge of pictures of Washington's elite, was a photograph of her and Mike at the National Gallery. That's how he knew, Dagny thought.

"Agent Gray?" The detective walked over to Dagny. "What about J. C. Adams? You mean the football player?"

"I told him I was dating an artist. He must have googled me. That's how he knew about Mike. And the bank robbery—he had an inside track on that, too." She spoke her thoughts as quickly as they came. "He did a security proposal for the bank, so he must have known how everything worked. The camera, and the baseball, and the double drawers. And the makeup the bank robber wore—Adams makes films. He'd know how to do that. Plus, he hasn't worked all year. He just came into all that money."

The detective put his hand on Dagny's shoulder and gave a gentle squeeze. "Agent Gray, there's a lot of stuff you just said, and it could be pretty important, so I'm going to ask you to slow it down just a bit, if you don't mind."

Dagny took a deep breath and started from the beginning. She told them about her relationship with Mike, and his relationship with Candice. She described her investigation of the bank robbery in Cincinnati, and her discussions with Officer Perez in Chula Vista. And she described her interactions with J. C. Adams and gave them Adams's cell phone number. She recounted all of this in a clear, measured tone, anticipating their questions, elaborating where required, and suspending her emotions, as she'd long been trained to do.

When she finished her narrative, she peppered them with questions. *Was there video of the killing?* Just some grainy footage from a nearby bank. *What about the card?* In Whitman's purse, probably placed during the book signing. They hadn't watched the video from inside the bookstore yet. *Any chase by foot?* The murder wasn't discovered for a while; they were still canvasing, but he probably got away. *Eyewitnesses?* So far, none. One guy thought he saw someone running down by the canal, but people ran there all the time.

"Did he suffer?"

The young agent folded his hands and stared down at the floor. "At this point, it's really hard to—"

"No, Agent Gray," the detective interrupted. "He died very quickly."

"Oh." The detective was probably just telling her what she wanted to hear, but she was willing to believe it.

The two men thanked her for the information, expressed their condolences, and left. Dagny collapsed on the couch. Agent Maxwell, Dagny remembered. The young guy's name was Terrance Maxwell. She pulled her knees tightly toward her chest. The room felt as if it were spinning. Mrs. McDougal came in and handed her another glass of water. This time, Dagny clutched it for dear life—she would not drop it. It took every ounce of concentration she could muster, but it did not drop.

The Professor sat across from her and turned his pipe over in his fingers. "It wasn't because of you, Dagny."

She just shook her head. Of course it was.

"No," he said. "Mike was just a bystander. *She* was the target." The Professor unfolded a piece of paper he had in his pocket. "The detective gave it to me. It's a flyer from the bookstore." He handed it to Dagny. It announced that Candice Whitman would be signing copies at a release party for her new book—a collection of fake editorials about famous murders in literature. Apparently, she had applied her modern-day invective to the likes of Raskolnikov, John Jasper, and the unruly orangutan in "The Murders in the Rue Morgue." Her book's ominous title was *The Ides of March: Bringing Justice to the Murderers in Great Literature.*

"Today is March fifteenth. She was stabbed on steps, just like Caesar. The card was in *her* purse. These things suggest that Whitman was the target," the Professor explained.

Dagny handed the flyer back to the Professor. "That could just be a coincidence."

"Either the crime's connection to you *or* Whitman's release of this book is a coincidence. The murderer would have known of the book release long ago. He could have put this crime in play before the year began. If, on the other hand, you were the connection to this crime, then our murderer's making it up as he goes and, given what we know already about the other crimes, that seems unlikely. I don't think it's J. C. Adams, and I don't think it has anything to do with you."

It was no comfort.

The Professor and his wife had begged her to stay, but she wanted to curl up on her own couch, in her own house. Climbing the steps to her porch, she knew it was a mistake. The house had become cluttered with memories of Mike, and being home just made her feel more alone. When she opened the screen door, a small package fell off the threshold. The return address read "Chula Vista." It was the bullet that killed the dog. She opened the front door and tossed the package onto the kitchen counter, then walked upstairs, undressed, and climbed into the shower, where she fell to the floor and cried.

CHAPTER 20

March 16—Alexandria, Virginia

Her cell phone vibrated across the top of the dresser. One more call would push it off the edge. The calls had come steadily through the evening, slowed some during the night, then picked up again in the morning. She hadn't bothered to answer the phone, or for that matter, get out of bed. She hadn't slept much, either—maybe a minute here, another there. Mostly, she mourned.

The next call sent her phone to the floor. She slid her right leg out from under the covers and planted it on the carpet. It took all the strength she could muster to pivot to the right, sit up, and plant her left foot on the floor. When she stood, she was surprised that her legs held firm. It didn't feel any better to stand, but it didn't feel any worse either.

Dagny picked up the phone. The last incoming call began with a 513 area code. J. C. Adams, she thought. When she'd called him for a ride to the airport, her number had been saved to his phone. She scrolled through the list of missed calls. The fact that the thirty-four calls had come from only four people was a measure of her pathetic life. Julia, her mother, and the Professor had called numerous times. J. C. Adams had called twice.

Dagny dialed her voice mail. Despite the many calls, Julia left just one message. She offered her condolences, promised to do anything she could to help, and invited Dagny to stay with her. Her mother left seven messages, each more panicked than the last. The Professor's message was awkward and sweet. He told her to take whatever time she needed to "resolve" her emotions, and asked if there was anything he could do to help her during this "awful, awful period."

Adams's message wasn't sweet. "What the hell, Gray? I was just flirting with you. Jesus Christ! What's your problem?"

Dagny hung up the phone and set it back on the dresser, then changed into her running clothes and grabbed her iPod. It took her four attempts to tie her left shoe, another three for the right. She walked down the steps and opened the front door. Stepping outside, Dagny was blinded by afternoon sun. Mothers were pushing strollers along the sidewalks of Del Ray. An elderly man was fixing the shingles on his roof. Two kids were skateboarding down the street, doing spins and jumps off the curb. By running, she turned their world into a blur. The iPod drowned the thoughts in her head, and when that stopped working, she counted each thud of her feet as they hit the pavement. Three-ninety-four. Three-ninety-five. It almost cleared her mind.

Her legs carried her along the Potomac into the District, and over the M Street Bridge into Georgetown. When she got to Mike's house, it was cordoned off by crime-scene tape. She had been to hundreds of crime scenes. There was a key in her pocket that opened the door to this one, but she couldn't use it.

Two agents emerged from the house and walked over to a dark-blue sedan. Carl Milton and Dave Bourner—she'd worked with them before. Carl was pushing his thick fingers through his dark-brown hair and laughing, while Dave was nodding his head and taking drags off a cigarette butt. A robin landed on the top of the sedan, and the men turned toward it. The bird toddled around the car top in circles, like a drunken man stumbling out of a saloon. Carl stopped laughing, and Dave flicked the last bit of his cigarette to the ground and tilted his head, mesmerized by the robin. The bird danced on the roof of the sedan for three full minutes, and the agents watched in silence. Finally, the bird flew off, and Dave pulled out another cigarette.

Dagny turned and ran. She didn't count her footsteps or blare her iPod. Instead, she let herself hear the hum of traffic, the murmur of overlapping conversation, the deafening blasts of the planes leaving Reagan National, the rattle of the Metro cars rolling above on elevated rails. Everything before had seemed jumbled, but now all was clear. The rest of her life would be for grieving. Right now, there was work to do.

CHAPTER 21

March 17—Arlington, Virginia

"Media attention. A celebrity death. Political interest. Six crimes, spread across the country, it seems. I think it's safe to say that this will be heavily manned."

"A wise man once said that we'd be better off with just a small handful of people on cases like this."

"You already convinced me, Dagny." Traffic had come to an abrupt stop, and the Professor slammed on his brakes to avoid hitting the black Cadillac in front of them. He undid his seat belt, reached to the backseat for a stack of folders, and handed them to Dagny. "You might as well look at these now."

They were her classmates' files. "Why?"

"Because you need a partner, and I can't run around like I used to."

"That's why we'll use the webcams."

"Not good enough. You have to partner with someone if I'm going to sell this thing."

"We could try to sell it with just me first…"

The Professor sighed. "Dagny, *I* need you to have a partner. *I* want someone with you. It's not negotiable."

Dagny thumbed through the files. Brent Davis was the logical choice. He was smart and confident, polished and professional. But Dagny didn't want an equal—she wanted a body. If the Professor insisted that she have a partner, she was determined to pick the least intrusive partner she could. And that, she determined, was Opie.

Special Agent Victor Walton Jr. was barely twenty-five years old. After three years at Deloitte & Touche, he'd signed up with the Bureau. Although he'd scored exceptionally well on each of the nine academic exams administered during the seventeen-week New Agent's Training Unit course, he'd fared less admirably on the physical tests. He also failed to score above 40 percent on any of the three shotgun tests, even though new agents were required to exceed 80 percent on two of them. In the past, the Bureau had strictly enforced its training standards, but in recent years, it had relaxed its policies for specialized candidates. In the wake of Enron and WorldCom, the Bureau had a particular need for forensic accounting expertise, and Walton's future assignments would likely involve calculators, not guns.

Brent Davis would have been a partner; Walton would be a potted plant. She closed the files.

"You've chosen?" The Professor changed lanes in front of the Holocaust Museum; the abrupt movement sent the files from Dagny's lap to the floor.

"Yes," she replied, gathering the loose pages and returning them to their folders.

The Professor issued a disapproving "hmmm."

After a few more reckless maneuvers, he turned down a ramp and headed under the concrete blight known as the J. Edgar Hoover Building. The DC field office, where Dagny worked, was only blocks away, but she'd been to headquarters only a few times, and had met the director just once, as part of a group accepting his congratulations after her class completed its training.

The Professor took his reserved space underneath the building, as well as a good part of the space next to it. "Now listen to me, Dagny," he said. "I was easy to play because I wanted to be played. The Director is not going to be easy. I'll do the talking, but he will probably ask you questions. You have to hold it together. You can't go in there like this."

"What do you mean?"

He reached up to her cheek and brushed away a tear. She hadn't realized that she was crying. "Ready?"

"Okay."

They flashed electronic badges at the security desk, then walked down several long stretches of hallway until they came to the Director's waiting room. A receptionist offered them a seat. Twelve chairs lined opposite walls. The only one that was occupied was taken by a lanky man in a navy suit. His long, thin face was red and peeling with sunburn, and his dusty-brown hair was peppered with grey specks, cropped trim and neat. The man rose from his chair, grabbed the Professor's hand, and whispered in his ear loud enough for Dagny to hear, "Fuck you." The man pulled back from the Professor and flashed a smile, while still shaking the Professor's hand. Then he broke free from the hold and grabbed Dagny's hand with his right hand while clasping her arm with his left. "I'm Justin Fabee, Dagny. It's nice to meet you. I wish it had been under other circumstances. I've very sorry about your loss." He spoke in a soft Texas drawl.

"Thank you."

"You both did a nice job at the start of the case. I'd like to commend you on that." When he wasn't cursing in the Professor's ear, Fabee had a real dignity and charm. No wonder he had risen so quickly.

The FBI had eighteen assistant directors. Three headed the field offices in New York City, Los Angeles, and Washington, DC. The rest headed divisions at FBI headquarters. Fabee was the head of the Criminal Investigative Division, which was one of the better assistant director positions, since other divisions included the IT Services Division, the Laboratory Division, and the Human Resources Division. Fabee was in his early forties, young for an Assistant Director in Charge. Only the director and four executive assistant directors were higher on the Bureau's organizational chart.

The Professor and Fabee took seats at opposite sides of the waiting room and simultaneously lowered their heads, silently rehearsing what they'd say to the Director. Dagny just tried to keep from falling apart. Clasping her hands, she stared down at the carpet, looking past its surface until it was a blur. She slowed her breathing, inhaling deeply, then exhaling slowly, and counting to four before reversing the flow. After a few minutes, she felt calm.

She held that calm when the Director came. He was a short, stocky man with wire-rimmed glasses and a growing bald spot on the top of his head. A cartoonist would have drawn his face with nothing but circles. His forehead gleamed with perspiration. Although the Director was not the prototypical Hoover man, he was regarded as uncommonly fair-minded, and only moderately prone to political capitulation. That was about the best the Bureau could do.

The Director grabbed a handkerchief from his pocket and blew his nose, then put the handkerchief away and extended his hand to the Professor. "Timothy, it's good to see you." It didn't sound as if he meant it.

"You're looking well," the Professor replied, and Dagny *knew* he didn't mean it.

The Director nodded at Fabee, then turned to Dagny. "It is nice to meet you, Special Agent Gray."

She shook his hand. "My pleasure, sir."

The Director led them into the big, dreary room that was his office. The carpet was a bland cream color, as were the draperies that covered the windows on the left side. Three chairs faced the Director's desk. The wall behind was covered by dark wood cabinets with glass doors. Under the cabinets, a long Formica countertop had been modified to hold a computer. A maroon leather couch rested against the wall by the entrance to the room. The right wall was lined with more shelves, an American flag, and a tall reading table. Aside from a few framed government plaques, the walls were bare.

The Director took his seat behind the desk; the others sat down in the chairs arranged before it. "Now, Timothy, I assume you're here to give your ideas about the Whitman murder?"

It bothered Dagny that he was calling it the *Whitman* murder.

The Professor began in a cool, deliberate tone. "As you know, Dagny and I started looking at this case prior to the murder. We located the third crime—the dog killing—and Dagny flew to Cincinnati and talked to the police about the bank robbery. We'd like to continue looking at the case, with the Bureau's permission, of course. We wouldn't do anything to interfere with Justin's investigation, and in fact, would provide him any information we uncovered."

Fabee forced a smile. "Now, Timothy, I'm very appreciative of the work that you and Dagny have done. But if you're proposing a parallel investigation of some kind, I'm afraid I'll have to register my objection. I don't think it would be possible for you to continue to look at this without interfering on some level. I mean, what do you envision—two teams at each crime scene, two sets of witness interviews?"

Blowing his nose again, the Director shook his head. "I'm inclined to agree with Justin. Parallel investigations? Is that what you want?"

"Two agents, that's all. Dagny and another. Going to crime scenes, talking to witnesses. But not interfering. We won't run the tests. We'll take second dibs on the witnesses. We'll be off to the side. Just another set of eyes on the situation, that's all. We wouldn't compete with Justin's investigation. We'd supplement it."

The director leaned back in his chair and removed his glasses, then polished the lenses with the same handkerchief he'd used for his nose. Fabee leaned forward and spoke softly. "I don't mean to bring up something unpleasant, but there is the matter of SA Gray's conflict of interest. I mean, she is a potential witness," he whispered, as if Dagny couldn't hear him. "Ancillary, at that," he added.

The Professor edged toward the front of his seat and spoke as softly as Fabee. "Since it appears that Ms. Whitman was the primary target, it's likely that Dagny's connection to this case is coincidental." Dagny wondered if he really believed it.

"Nevertheless," Fabee barked, before continuing more calmly, "I think her personal stake in the resolution of the case could influence her judgment."

The director tapped his fingers on his desktop. "Timothy, regardless of the conflict, you haven't really given me a compelling reason to allow your request."

The Professor shrugged. "Maybe we should call the president and see what he thinks." He glanced at the Director's phone. "The number is four-five-six, one-four—"

"I know the damn number!" The Director pushed the phone a few inches away. "Really, Tim? You want to spend your capital on *this*?"

The Professor leaned back in his chair. For a second, Dagny thought he was going to put his feet on the Director's desk. "Yes."

Fabee clenched his teeth so tightly Dagny thought they might shatter. The Professor and the Director locked eyes, and neither seemed willing to look away.

"Alright, then," the Director said, breaking the standoff. He took out his handkerchief again and blew his nose. "Allergies. I blame the cherry blossoms. I really do. Send them back to Japan,

I say. It'd solve some of the traffic problems, too. People with their cameras on the side of the Parkway, for Christ's sake."

He grabbed a pen from his desk drawer and began to scribble notes on a lined yellow pad. "First," he said to the Professor, "you defer to Assistant Director Fabee at every turn. He will not interfere with your work, but he can impose some timing and logistical restraints. You are to let him know your movements. Second, you are not to pester the actual investigation. Information *may* be shared with you, but we are not under any obligation to do so. Third, you are to report any substantial findings from your investigation to Assistant Director Fabee, or his designee, each day. Fourth, should Assistant Director Fabee request your assistance on any matter, unlikely as that may be, you are to render the requested assistance. Should a dispute arise, I shall arbitrate, but you know that I don't want to have to do that. And if a dispute were to arise, I'm sure the president wouldn't be happy about that, regardless of any past histories. And fifth, stay off the Whitman murder. You can look at anything before or after, but not Whitman. The last thing I want is some vigorous cross-examination about a personal conflict of interest messing up a trial. Is this understood?"

"Absolutely," the Professor responded. It was the best they could hope for.

"Yes, sir," Fabee added, without much enthusiasm.

The Director shifted his gaze to Dagny. "Special Agent Gray, I know that you are going through a difficult time. I do not believe that you should be working this case, but I will defer to Timothy's judgment for the time being. If, at any time, you feel you cannot work on this case, for whatever reason, I encourage you to exercise proper judgment and recuse yourself. Under the circumstances, we'd be more than happy to grant you an extended paid leave."

"Thank you, sir. But I will be fine." Her words didn't sound convincing, even to Dagny.

On the way out of the office, Fabee grabbed Dagny's forearm and pulled her aside. He wasn't happy and his voice showed it. "I got copies of your notes and the security footage. You got anything else?"

"Just the bullet that killed the dog."

"That goes in the file. Drop the bullet off at my house tonight." He scribbled his address on the back of his business card, grabbed her hand, placed the card in her palm, and closed her fingers over it. "Don't lose that." He must have meant for the gesture to seem tough or strong or authoritative. He must have meant for it to remind her that he was in charge of the case. But whatever he meant, it just seemed creepy.

Fabee lived forty-five minutes out of the city, in a redbrick farm house on five acres of land, surrounded on all sides by thick woods. Its genuine seclusion easily beat Dagny's faux seclusion on her quarter-acre lot in Del Ray, and she felt a tinge of envy as she turned into Fabee's private gravel drive. Not that the property was well kept. The grass was overgrown and the paint on the shutters was peeling. A chain on the front porch swing was broken, so the seat hung to the ground. One of the gutters had slipped from the roof.

Dagny grabbed the FedEx box from the passenger seat and climbed out of her Prius. Walking to the front door, she passed two windows. Peering through one of them into the living room, she saw four folding chairs, a card table, and little else. She walked past the front door, toward the two windows on the other side of the porch. One of them looked a little different from the other—crisper, cleaner. Fabee had recently replaced the window and hadn't taken the care to match the new one to the others. He hadn't even removed the sticker from the windowpane. Dagny figured that Fabee lived here alone, because no woman would have stood for mismatched windows, peeling paint, and folding chairs. But then again, she'd also noticed a wedding ring on his hand.

Dagny walked back to the front door and rang the bell. Fabee answered with his sleeves rolled up and a chopping knife in his left hand. "Makin' chili," he said, motioning for her to follow him over a scuffed tile floor to the kitchen. Dishes were piled high in the sink. The wallpaper was peeling above the stove. Fabee wielded his knife at a chopping board, slicing through a jalapeño and picking out the seeds. "That my bullet?" he asked, nodding toward the box in Dagny's hand.

"Yes."

"Set it on the table."

The kitchen table was covered with stacks of paper, two and three feet high. Dagny set the box on top of one of the piles.

"Is this all related to the case?" she asked.

"It is."

"What is it all?"

"Witness statements. Measurements. Photographs. Calendars and e-mails from the victims' computers."

"All from the sixth crime?"

"Mostly."

Dagny saw an e-mail from Mike's account on the top of one of the stacks. She wanted to thumb through the stack to see if any had been exchanged between Mike and Candice. She wanted to do a lot of things she wasn't allowed to do. "Anything promising in there?"

Fabee ignored the question. "I know the place is a mess. Wife and the girls are in Texas. Things are a little rough. Trying to make everything work. Me being here, and then always on the road. Sometimes..." He didn't finish the thought. "Everything is hard except when I'm working, Dagny. But when I'm working, it's all fine. I guess you're that way, too."

"Yes."

"Misery can wait," he said. "Misery can wait." Fabee tossed the sliced jalapeño into a pot, then leaned against the counter.

"When our man stabbed Michael, it wasn't just one quick jab and done. He stuck the knife in his gut"—Fabee mimed the action with his own knife—"and yanked it slowly up to his heart, then wiggled the blade around in a circle a few times. Man, he wiggled that thing around for at least ten seconds and then held Michael's body up by the blade and watched the life flow out of him. Maybe took another twenty seconds. And when he was done, he didn't just pull the knife out—he shoved Michael's body until it fell away from the knife, and his face hit against the rail on the way down. Knocked a couple of teeth loose."

Dagny could feel Fabee's eyes move over her, waiting for her to break. She'd figured out that she could avoid this by biting down on the sides of her tongue just hard enough to hurt a little. After a moment, she said calmly, "I'm aware that murder is ugly."

"If someone hurt my wife, or my kids...you bet I'd want in on the case. I'd want blood. But they wouldn't let me, and thank God for that. I couldn't take working a personal case like that, and I'm a coldhearted prick, not a nice girl like you. The Professor may be buddies with the president, but he's done you no favor. I'm going to do you the best favor anyone could. I'm going to do my best to give you nothing on this case. Nothing. You have my word on that, Dagny Gray."

Driving away from Fabee's home, she no longer envied its deep seclusion. It seemed like a lonely way to live.

CHAPTER 22

March 18—Arlington, Virginia

When Dagny pulled into the Professor's driveway at a quarter past six, Victor Walton was pacing on the porch, hands stuffed in the pockets of his oversize suit pants.

"Hey," she yelled, running around to the Prius's hatchback. "Help me bring this stuff inside."

Victor shuffled toward the car, then tripped over his own feet and fell to the pavement. "Look, I'm not sure about this," he said.

"Not sure about what?" She grabbed his hand and helped him up, then handed him a large bag from the Apple Store.

"I'm not sure if you really want me to work with you on this." His voice cracked as he said it.

"Of course I do." Dagny lifted two more bags from the back of her car and closed the door.

"I'm just an accountant. I don't know what to do."

"When in doubt, just follow my lead." Dagny jogged up to the front door and rang the bell. Victor scurried behind. "Did you bring your gun?" Dagny asked.

"What? No." He rolled his eyes, then sighed. "Are you serious?"

"I brought an extra."

"Do I really need a gun?"

"An agent always carries his gun."

Mrs. McDougal answered the door and greeted Dagny with a warm, motherly hug. "Good to see you, dear." The gesture was meant to be comforting, but it only reminded Dagny that she was operating within a personal tragedy. When they broke their embrace, Victor walked over to Mrs. McDougal and gave her a hug, too. "Mrs. McDougal, I'm Victor Walton Jr. It's nice to meet you."

Mrs. McDougal seemed to be taken aback by the unexpected embrace. "Nice to meet *you*." She laughed nervously.

After breaking the hug, Victor followed Dagny on a serpentine path through the house to the Professor's study. "Cool room," Victor observed when they entered. He ran his fingers across the spines of the Professor's book collection. "The rest of the place is a bit of a dump, but this room is stunning."

A stern, severe voice boomed from the back of the room. "I'd like to think the rest of our home is nice as well." The Professor walked over to Dagny and gave her a hug. It felt like the first hug the Professor had ever given—not a trinket handed out casually, but something held in reserve for special people in extraordinary circumstances. In the short time she had spent with the Professor, Dagny sensed that certain emotions—rage, anger, and envy, for example—came easily to him, but affection and compassion did not.

"How are you doing, Dagny?" he whispered in her ear.

"Hanging in there," she replied, which was about right.

When Dagny withdrew from the embrace, Victor was waiting. He threw his arms around the Professor, squeezing him tight, and patting his back. "I just want to say that I'm honored that you picked me."

The Professor stood still, with his hands at his side, building into a slow simmer. His face grew red and his body began to shake. The Professor threw his arms up to break Victor's embrace. "Special Agent Walton, for some reason you won Dagny's lottery. I can tell you that you wouldn't have been my first choice."

"I know, sir. In fact, if Agent Gray would like a do-over—"

"Sorry, Walton, but you're stuck." The Professor eyed Dagny's gift bags. "What goodies did you bring?"

They spent the next hour setting up and testing the Professor's new computer system. It violated protocol, but Dagny liked to use her Mac, since the Bureau's computer system was hopelessly out-of-date and unreliable. Bringing the Professor off the Bureau grid with her would give their investigation a little privacy, just in case Fabee had prying eyes.

Dagny helped the Professor create a Gmail account, then filled in the POP settings in the mail application so messages would automatically download to his hard drive. They practiced initiating videoconference calls. She showed him how to save images to iPhoto, the computer's photograph-management software. He begged her to teach him how to use the iTunes music store, but she demurred. They had a flight to catch.

Dagny had reserved a compact car, but that didn't prevent the rental-car agent from trying to push an upgrade. It took three clear refusals to end the sales pitch, and only then did the clerk admit that they were out of compact cars and that Dagny would get the upgrade for free. She refused the insurance, too, until Victor's hectoring insistence wore her down. "Always get the insurance," he argued. "Especially if you can get it reimbursed."

On the drive into downtown Cincinnati, Dagny relayed most of the important details of the case to Victor. She left out *the* most important detail—her relationship with Michael Brodsky— because she couldn't discuss it while maintaining composure.

At District One headquarters, they hopped out of the car and bounded toward the steps. Dagny handed Victor his Glock and an underarm holster. "You need to look like an agent, Walton." She noticed that his sleeves were flapping in the wind. "Why are your suits so big? They make you look small. Hand-me-downs from your dad?"

"My dad? No, these are my suits."

"Were they on sale or something?"

"They used to fit. I lost about thirty-five pounds in training."

"Seriously?"

"Yeah. I was a little pudgy."

The familiar face of Lieutenant Ronald Beamer met them at the door. He wore a warm, sad expression and gave Dagny a big hug. The top of his bare scalp came up to her chin. "Dagny, I'm so sorry," Lieutenant Beamer said. "My condolences." It was her third hug of the day, and it wasn't motherly or fatherly like the first two. It was the hug of a brother. Law enforcement stuck together in times of tragedy, regardless of rank or affiliation.

When Beamer let go of Dagny, Victor threw his arms around the lieutenant for a big bear hug. "I'm Victor Walton." Victor's body towered over and seemed to engulf Beamer's.

Squirming, Beamer stuck his head out from under Victor's arm and looked at Dagny. "This your partner?"

"Apprentice," she replied.

They retired to the conference room, where Dagny explained that she'd been given permission to work the case, but that Fabee had frozen her out. Beamer told her that the case had gone "completely federal," and that five or six agents had arrived with Chuck Wells, the local Special Agent in Charge, to lift the Cincinnati Police Department's file the day before. Wells was keeping Beamer in the loop since he knew he'd have to work with him in the future. The other agents weren't local—Fabee preferred to use "his men."

Beamer told her that they'd searched Adams's home, but hadn't found anything incriminating. Adams wasn't there when the search began; when he returned home around noon the next day, the Feds were still picking apart the house. Adams cursed Dagny's name and ran off—presumably, that's when he'd left the angry message on her phone. He returned with his lawyer and two receipts—one from a gas station, another from a liquor store—that indicated purchases in Columbus on the afternoon of the fifteenth, around the time of the murder in Georgetown. Adams also produced a credit card bill that suggested he was in Cincinnati on February 1, and not in Chula Vista, killing a dog. "I don't think Adams is a serious suspect right now," Beamer explained. "Besides, he's too lazy to pull off so mething like this."

Victor scribbled notes on a legal pad. Luckily, the lieutenant didn't seem to mind. When they finished, Beamer wished them luck and walked them to the door.

Once outside, Dagny collared Victor. "Listen, you've got to stop hugging people. It's really, really awkward."

"Hey, I thought it was strange too, but you said to follow your lead!" Victor protested. "I don't want to hug these people. And why is everyone hugging you? And why did Officer Beamer offer you condolences?"

Dagny ignored his questions. "Another thing, don't take notes when we talk to people like Beamer. Notes are for suspects and witnesses. The last thing Beamer wants is a record of him helping us." She grabbed the loose arm of his suit jacket and pulled him toward the rented Impala.

Dagny wanted to head straight to see Chesley Waxton, but Victor insisted that they eat lunch. They stopped at Camp Washington Chili, a diner on the west side of town. Victor ordered a "four way"—chili over spaghetti with onions and two inches of shredded cheddar. It had to be nearly 800 calories and 44 grams of fat. Dagny asked for a cup of vegetable soup. "I can't believe you're not having the chili," Walton said. "You can't come to Cincinnati and not eat the chili."

"It looks disgusting."

"Yeah," Walton replied with a mouthful of molten cheese. "But it tastes *so* good." He tossed some oyster crackers into his chili and shoveled the mix into his mouth. "So why did the officer offer you condolences?"

"He's a lieutenant."

"Okay. Why'd the lieutenant offer you condolences?"

She'd evaded the question as long as she could. "Because Michael Brodsky was my boyfriend."

Walton dropped his fork, and it bounced off the plate and into his lap. He dabbed his napkin in his water to wipe away the stain. "Seriously? Oh, my God, I'm sorry, Dagny."

She slid her hand across her cheeks to make sure they were still dry. "That's why I wanted this case so badly."

"And they let you?"

"Yes."

"Because the Professor is buddies with the president? Did he call the president and get him to intervene?"

"He threatened to. The Director seemed to know how that would play out."

"Yeah, the Director's already in hot water with the president."

"How do you know that?"

"Don't you watch *Meet the Press*?"

"It's been awhile."

"Well, the Director's kinda on thin ice. So are the weird things about the Professor true?" It was a sudden turn. "Like that he was a CIA mole spying on Hoover?"

"I don't know."

"Aren't you working on his memoirs?"

"We're mired in grade school."

"I heard that he once killed another agent."

"That's ridiculous."

"I don't know. He's pretty intense."

"The man's a pussycat."

Walton leaned back and laughed. "Were you sitting in the same classroom I was?"

"He's harmless."

"I don't think so."

"Hey, would you do something for me?" she asked. "And I don't want you to take this badly or—"

"Sure. Whatever. What do you need?"

"Would you mind talking less?"

"Huh?"

"Silence is golden, right?"

Victor slumped in his chair. "Okay."

Dagny didn't feel like finishing her soup, so she just watched Victor scoop up the remaining remnants of his chili with little of the exuberance he had shown at the beginning of the meal. She thought it was strange that he hadn't asked a lot of questions about Mike. She couldn't tell if this was a sign of emotional intelligence or ignorance. Either way, she appreciated it. She was tired of hugging people.

Silence turned out to be just as bad as noise. "So why'd you join the Bureau?" she asked.

He smiled, happy to be engaged again. "My dad was an agent, so everyone assumes I'm just trying to follow in his footsteps. But mostly, I was bored. I couldn't see myself at Deloitte forever, and didn't want to stick around and make partner, because that would just make it harder to leave. You worked at a law firm, right? So you know what I mean?"

"Yeah." She knew.

He finished the last bite of chili, then crushed some more oyster crackers onto the plate to sop up the last of the sauce. "You're not finishing your soup?"

"I'm not very hungry," Dagny replied.

"I am." Victor pulled her soup bowl across the table and finished it off.

Chesley Waxton unlocked the door to his bank and let them into the lobby. Within a single sentence, Waxton's voice fluctuated from a whisper to a shout and then back again. "I already talked to some of your guys." He was an old and ugly man. His back arched forward, cheating him of at least three inches of height. A few remaining strands of hair were combed across the great bald expanse of his head. He wore his cuffed pants high enough to show some skin above his socks, and his white dress shirt was so thin that Dagny could see his nipples.

"We'd like to get a little more information."

"So you don't have my ball?" Waxton's lip quivered with disappointment.

"No, Mr. Waxton."

"Phooey." He led them to his office, and sat behind his desk. Dagny and Victor took their seats across from him.

"Mr. Waxton, tell me about the ball." She took out a pad of paper and began taking notes.

Waxton reached down beneath his seat and pumped his chair a bit higher. "I bought that ball twelve years ago. My pride and joy. Most important ball in Reds history if you ask me."

"More important than '76?" Victor asked.

"That wasn't as good a series!" Waxton yelled, perhaps unaware of his volume.

"How much did you pay for the ball?" Dagny asked.

"Twenty-four thousand three hundred and eleven dollars." Waxton turned back to look at the empty spot on his shelf where the ball once rested. "And it's worth a lot more."

"It seems like the robber knew where the ball was. He went right to it."

"Oh, he knew. But anyone who watched the news would have seen it. It was right there behind me," he said, pointing over his shoulder, "when I was on Channel Nine."

"You were on the Channel Nine news? When was that?"

"Twelve years ago. When I bought it."

"To your knowledge, has there been anything else written, anything else in the media since then that would suggest where you kept this ball? Subsequent interviews, photographs?"

"I don't think so. The whole thing was a story for about a day."

"Who had access to this office? Who would have seen the ball?"

"My employees, of course. And we have a cleaning service. I've had business meetings here. But I gave my calendars to you guys already, so you should have all that."

"So lots of people?"

"Yes. A lot of people over the years."

"Tell me about J. C. Adams."

"I thought that was already cleared up. J. C. grew up around here. I knew his mom and dad. Good kid. Great athlete. After that injury at USC, he was down on his luck a bit. Joined the police. I asked him to sign some jerseys—gave him some money for that."

Victor perked up. "Wait a minute. J. C. Adams is *the* J. C. Adams? The football star?"

Waxton leaned forward, as if noticing Victor for the first time. "Is this kid really a federal agent?" he asked Dagny.

"It's Take a Child to Work Day," Dagny responded. "Adams said he did some security work for you?"

Waxton laughed. "It was more like unsolicited advice. He came to my office and signed the jerseys, and I gave him fifty bucks. As we're walking out, he starts looking at the cameras. Tells me I need a security upgrade. Asks me to give him a tour, so I point out the cameras, tell him a little about what they do. A couple of the cameras are dummy cameras. He tells me that I'm fifty years behind the times, and that he could design a new system for me. I try to be polite, tell him that I'll think about it, and next thing I know, he sends me a written proposal for a system that would cost close to fifty thousand. He claimed that the bank could make commercials, that the whole thing would pay for itself. Said he'd direct the commercials if I let him use the equipment on some film he wanted to make. Ridiculous. So that was the end of that."

Victor raised his hand. "Why'd you have dummy cameras?"

"Most bank robbers only take a few thousand dollars. It doesn't make sense to spend much more than that on security," Waxton explained.

"Why do they take so little?" Victor asked. "You've got a lot more in the vault, right?"

Dagny answered before Waxton could. "It takes too long to get into the vault. A robber figures he has two minutes after the silent alarm is pushed. So he usually takes what's in the drawers and runs." She turned to Waxton. "Tell me about what he said to you. Something about sins."

Waxton seemed to fall into a trance, as if he were reliving the robbery. Finally, he shivered. "It was the strangest thing. He kept making me repeat, 'The sins of the devils remain with them in hell.' He made me say it over and over."

Dagny had read the CPD report, but it didn't jive with Waxton's new account. "In the report, they had 'The sins of the devils remain with them in *heaven*.' Now you're saying 'hell.' Do you remember which it was?"

"Devils wouldn't be in heaven. I'm pretty sure it's 'hell.'"

Dagny wrote "Angels?" on her notepad and underlined it twice.

After concluding their interview with Waxton, Dagny and Victor wandered out to the bank's lobby, where Dagny snapped pictures and Victor leaned against the front doorframe and pretended to write notes on a pad of paper. "How tall are you?" she asked. "Five eight?"

"Six foot, exactly." He seemed to take umbrage at the question. "Do you think I look five eight?"

"The tape measure on the doorframe says you're about five eight."

"Well, it's lying."

"Switch with me." Dagny took Victor's place. "How tall?"

"Five five and a little."

"I'm five nine and a little. Every foot on this thing has an extra two-thirds of an inch." She grabbed a pair of gloves from her backpack and tugged along the top of the tape measure. It lifted easily from the frame. Magnetic. Another magnet held the bottom of the measure at the floor. The tape hung loose between them. Dagny rolled the measure and dropped it into a Ziploc bag.

She returned to Waxton's office and asked about the door marker. "Didn't even realize we had it," he replied. "Maybe it was something Adams did."

"It came from Adams?"

"I don't know. Maybe it was in his proposal."

"Can I get a copy of that proposal?"

Waxton opened the bottom drawer of his desk. Dagny looked down at the unruly stack of mangled papers that filled it. Waxton shuffled through them, then shuffled through them again. He stuffed the papers back into the drawer and walked out to a large lateral cabinet, five shelves high, in the hallway outside his office. Waxton opened the top-shelf lid. Several stacks of papers were crammed into the space. Half a pile fell to the floor. Dagny looked through the papers that fell while Waxton thumbed through what was left in the drawer.

"Maybe you can keep looking and fax a copy to me?" Dagny handed Waxton her business card. "It's important, Mr. Waxton, so we need for you to keep looking."

"I will," he promised.

Victor drove while Dagny worked on her laptop. She found J. C. Adams's address on the Hamilton County auditor's website, traced the route to his home on Google Maps, and fed Victor the directions. "So our guy isn't six foot, he's six four?"

"He's called an unsub; and yes, he's six four."

"You know, J. C. Adams is six four."

"How do you know that?"

"He was on my fantasy team. What's unsub short for?"

"Unidentified subject, which you should know." Whether or not the unsub in question was J. C. Adams, it was easier to find someone who was six four than someone who was six foot even. Fourteen percent of men are six foot or taller; fewer than one percent are six four or more.

Jumping on Google, she searched for "The sins of the devils remain with them in heaven." She found nothing. Then she tried "The sins of the devils remain with them in hell." Still nothing. She tried both with "stay" instead of "remain," but found nothing. She tried "The sins of the angels remain with them in heaven" and several other permutations to no avail. Dagny went to the LexisNexis website and tried the same searches in the news database, hoping an old article might contain the phrase. It took several attempts, but she finally found it in the fourth paragraph of a newspaper article from Memphis in 1996: "The tellers at Hammerty Bank report that the man wore a blue-and-orange ski mask, and muttered 'The sins of the angels remain with them in heaven' repeatedly during the holdup." The article indicated that the identity of the bank robber was unknown and that he was still at large.

Dagny ran another search: "rob! W/10 Hammerty." The first few stories concerned another heist in 2001, but the eighth story reported that someone named Reginald Berry had been convicted for the 1996 robbery. Dagny e-mailed both stories about Reginald Berry to the Professor and then told Victor what she had found.

"I saw you write it on your notepad when you were talking to Waxton," he said. "You wrote 'angels.' If you thought Waxton had the quote wrong, why didn't you ask him if it could have been about the sins of *angels* in heaven? Was it because you didn't want it to get back to Fabee if they interviewed him again?"

The kid was smarter than he looked.

J. C. Adams lived, appropriately enough, in Mount Adams, a wealthy hilltop community that overlooks downtown Cincinnati. Row houses lined the narrow, steep streets. His house was a three-story contemporary stucco marvel, hanging over the hillside on cantilevered beams. Dagny and Victor pulled into the short drive-way, walked to the front door, and rang the bell.

The golden-haired quarterback answered wearing a USC T-shirt and boxer shorts. It was dark inside, and he shielded his eyes when he spoke. "Jesus, do you know what time it is?"

Dagny looked at her watch. "It's four thirty in the afternoon."

"Really?" He smelled of alcohol. "Well, I guess you're here to apologize?"

"I have nothing to apologize for."

"Oh, yeah, well, why don't you come in and see the mess they made."

The home was indeed a mess. Papers were strewn across the floor. DVDs and compact discs lay in piles at the bases of shelves. There was a hole in the wall next to a La-Z-Boy, and another one in the kitchen. The carpet was stained and stiff in spots. A glass trophy case was cracked.

"They did all this?" Dagny asked.

"Huh?" Adams replied, confused. "No, they did this," he said, pulling a black leather couch away from the wall and pointing to a scuff mark.

Dagny laughed. "You're not exactly ready for *Cribs*."

"I just bought a place in LA, and it's completely pimped. In a week, I'm out of this hellhole. *Cribs* was canceled, by the way. Who's your friend?" Adams asked.

Victor smiled and extended his hand. "Victor Walton Jr."

"*Special Agent* Victor Walton Jr.," Dagny corrected.

"I was such a big fan of yours. I thought you were great, man."

Adams's frown flipped to a smile. "Thanks, man." He turned his attention back to Dagny and brought the frown out of retirement. "So why'd you send your goons here? Because I guessed you were thirty-eight?"

"I didn't send anyone here, Mr. Adams. I told them what happened, and someone else made that call." Dagny paused, then added, "But for the record, when a woman asks you to guess her age, always subtract five years from your approximation."

"I did!"

She ignored that. "I need a copy of the proposal you made for Mr. Waxton."

"You still think I did this? I was in Columbus—"

"I know. I just want to see what you recommended. Waxton's security measures were pretty lax, and I'm just curious about what he turned down."

"Fine." Adams ran off to his bedroom. After a moment, they could hear a printer churning out pages. Adams returned with the proposal and handed it to Dagny.

Dagny flipped through the proposal. "Did you give Waxton the tape measure that runs up the side of the doorway?"

"No."

"Was it there when you wrote your proposal?"

Adams shrugged. "Beats me."

Victor grabbed the proposal from Dagny's hands. "Can you autograph this for us, J. C.?" Victor handed the proposal and a pen to Adams, who obliged, signing his name in big, round letters.

"How's that, buddy?" he asked.

Victor grinned like a schoolboy. "Thanks, J. C."

"Are you really that happy about an autograph?" Dagny asked, settling in behind the wheel. "Because it's going straight into the evidence file, you know."

Victor held the pen in front of Dagny, then dropped it into a plastic bag. "We've got his fingerprints." Victor pulled another bag containing another pen from his briefcase. "I swiped one of

Waxton's pens, too, in case we need to distinguish his prints." The kid was certainly trying.

Dagny didn't have the heart to tell him that they already had Adams's fingerprints on the proposal he'd just given them. Waxton's prints were a good catch though.

"Can we get some dinner?" Victor asked.

"No." She backed into the street and threw the car into drive. Finding her way was difficult. Mount Adams was a confusing maze of steep one-way streets, and parked cars on each side made for narrow clearances and tight turns. It was hard to navigate the Impala through the neighborhood, so it must have been nearly impossible for the black Chevy Suburban that pulled up behind them. Four wrong turns made Dagny wish they'd sprung for GPS. When the Suburban followed her on each wrong turn, coincidence seemed unlikely. Darkly tinted windows hid the driver from view, and there was no front license plate. Halfway through an intersection, and without signaling, Dagny spun the wheel left, tossing Victor into the passenger-side door.

"Jesus, Dagny," Victor cried.

The Suburban was still on their tail. Dagny took another sharp turn down the long slope of Martin Drive, which led downtown. The Suburban only drew closer, filling the Impala's rear window, then grazing its rear bumper. Dagny floored the accelerator.

"Why are you driving like a maniac?"

"Because we're being followed, Victor."

When the light at Fourth and Broadway turned red, Dagny punched the Impala and shot through the intersection, forcing oncoming traffic to screech to a halt. The Suburban followed behind, shooting across traffic. She knew she could lose the tail if she wanted, but catching it would be trickier. Dagny grabbed her phone and called Lieutenant Beamer, running two more lights while they concocted a plan to trap the Suburban. She circled the federal courthouse to give a patrol car time to get into position, then swung back onto Fourth Street and headed west to Vine.

Lining up the patrol car was easy. Getting Victor involved in the plan would be hard. "When we trap him, jump out," she explained. "Aim at his tires and shoot if he won't stop." Victor's face turned white, but he nodded. She turned left onto Vine, and then turned right into a small alley called West Ogden. It wasn't as desolate as Dagny had hoped—a drunk had just stumbled out of a bar called O'Malley's. The Suburban followed.

When they reached the end of the alley, she slammed on the brakes. Dagny and Victor hopped out of the car with raised guns. The Suburban stopped, then shifted into reverse, and the drunk ran back into the bar. A CPD car slid across the back of the alley, blocking the Suburban's exit. The Suburban crept slowly to the middle of the alley and stopped, a hundred feet behind the Impala. Steadying her gun with both hands, Dagny started toward the Suburban, waving for Victor to follow.

"Hands out of the window!" Dagny yelled. "Hands out!" Eighty feet away, no hands. Sixty-five, and still nothing.

The Suburban lunged toward them when they were fifty feet away. Dagny sent four shots through the windshield. Victor aimed for the tires and squeezed the trigger, but no bullets came out. The Suburban didn't slow, forcing Dagny and Victor to dive to opposite sides of the alley. It raced past them, plowed through the Impala, and was gone.

Dagny hopped to her feet. "Why didn't you fire?" she screamed.

Victor stood up slowly, holding his back. "I did. Nothing came out. Maybe the safety's on."

"There's no safety on a Glock." Dagny grabbed the gun from Victor's hand and squeezed the trigger, sending a bullet into the brick wall. "The only safety mechanism is a lever that makes it so you have to pull the trigger from the center in order to get it to shoot. You'd have to be an idiot to squeeze the trigger any other way." She tried to pull from the bottom of the trigger, but even this sent another bullet into the wall. "I have no idea how you *couldn't* shoot this thing."

Victor lowered his head and put his hands in his pockets. "I didn't want to carry it anyway."

She'd been rough with him, but he deserved it. "If you want to be an agent, you've got to act like one."

"I'm not an idiot, Dagny. KL9-EZJ. State of Kentucky." He'd caught the rear plate on the Suburban as it had passed them.

The Impala had been thrown across the street into a light post. The driver's side was crushed, and when Dagny tried to open the door, it wouldn't budge. She walked around to the other side of the car and climbed through the passenger door. Victor slid in behind her. She turned the key, but the car only wheezed.

Victor turned to her and smiled.

"What?" Dagny asked.

"Aren't you glad I talked you into the insurance?"

They spent the next few hours at District One, waiting for news about the black Suburban. A few witnesses saw the Suburban race through red lights on its way to the I-75 North ramp. Later, a gravedigger reported an explosion at Spring Grove Cemetery. The fireball left little of the Suburban behind. The license plate was a dead end—it had been reported stolen that morning from a car across the river in Covington, Kentucky.

Dagny and Victor spent another hour filling out paperwork for the rental car company. When they finished, she called the Professor and caught him up on the day's events. He told her that Reginald Berry—the "sins of the angels" bank robber—was an inmate at Coleman prison in Florida.

"We'll head down now."

"You can't. Fabee's sending you elsewhere."

"Where?"

"Bethel, New York."

CHAPTER 23

....

March 19—Bethel, New York

Dagny was curled up in the passenger seat of another rented Impala, sucking on a fat-free sourdough pretzel nugget to keep awake and shielding her eyes from the reflection of the sunrise in the side mirror. Her head throbbed. The air inside the car was stale and smelled like ten years of cigarette smoke. Victor drove with his left hand and shoveled an Egg McMuffin into his mouth with his right.

After they'd caught the red-eye to LaGuardia, they'd spent two hours at a Red Roof Inn—just enough time to nap and shower. The Garmin GPS they'd rented from Avis called out street directions, sparing Dagny the task. Steve Miller's "Abracadabra" was playing on the radio. It kept Victor awake and alert, so she lived with it.

"So why is Fabee sending us here, Dag?"

"Don't call me Dag." She rubbed her fingertips against her forehead in a circular motion, trying to push the pain away. "Because it pulls us off the rest of the case. He knows there's nothing to find here."

A stolen pack of gum, two and a half months ago. It was a dead end, but they'd be stuck questioning people in Bethel for days. What could they even ask? *Do you remember anyone coming here on New Year's Day flashing a lot of gum around?* It was hopeless.

Victor chuckled. "It's funny, though."

"What's funny?"

"If we find the chewing gum thief, we've caught a murderer. Solve the smallest crime in the world and we solve the biggest. That'd be some way to catch him."

Yeah, she thought. It would be. But Fabee had already had his men take a statement the night before. The boy didn't remember anything useful. Red Ford Explorer. Maybe the guy was tall. Didn't see his face. Left behind a card. No video from the security camera. That was it. Dagny hoped to determine how many sticks of gum were in the stolen pack. She didn't expect much else.

Bethel was two hours and a million miles from New York City. It was a strange town, full of burnouts and soccer moms, hybrids and Hummers, vegans and hunters. They passed twelve American flags, four rainbow flags, and one Confederate flag, painted on the roof of a barn, before they finally found Waller's Food Mart at a quarter past seven. Victor pulled into the gravel lot and parked. Dagny opened the car door, and the wind caught it, ripping it from her hand. Another burst of wind nearly toppled her as she climbed out of the car. Victor walked around the front of the car, pushed her door closed, and placed his hand on her back, steadying her as they walked toward the entrance.

A chubby, middle-aged man with a round face and sideburns looked up from behind the register when the door chimed. "You the feds?" he asked, making his way around the counter to greet them. A pack of Camels peeked out of the pocket of his flannel shirt.

"Special Agent Dagny Gray," Dagny said, flashing her creds.

"I'm Jeff Waller." He shook her hand. "I hope this helps. I mean, I just wish he knew more."

"I'm Victor Walton."

"*Special Agent* Victor Walton," Dagny corrected him.

"I'm new," Victor explained, shaking Waller's hand.

"Let me get my boy." Waller walked to a door behind the counter and called, "Hey, Crosby! Get out here!"

"Crosby?" Victor asked. "Like Crosby, Stills, and Nash?"

"And Young," Waller admonished.

Crosby came through the door wearing a baggy Yankees jersey and loose-fitting jeans. He brushed the hair out from his eyes and smiled at Dagny. Cute kid, she thought.

"Are you guys special agents?"

"We are," Dagny replied. "I know you talked to a couple of agents last night, but I was hoping we could go through what happened again. Is that cool?"

"It's cool." Crosby stuck his thumbs in his jeans pockets and kicked back his head. He took them through his New Year's Day, from the moment he woke up, to his dubious claim of having chased the thief out of the store, to his subsequent discovery of the theft.

"Show me where the card was," Dagny asked.

The kid led them to the candy rack and tapped the front of a Chewey's Spearmint Gum box on the far left side of the second shelf. "The card was standing up in the front of this box."

"Spearmint?" Victor asked. "Are you sure it was spearmint?"

"Nah. It could have been any flavor. These things get shifted."

"Was there a stick of gum attached to the back of the card?" Dagny asked.

"Yeah."

"What happened to it?"

"I chewed it." Crosby's dad shot him an angry look, but Crosby shrugged. "What? Were we going to sell a single stick of gum?"

"Do you remember the flavor?"

"No. Does it matter?"

"It might. If I said it was cinnamon, would that sound right?"

"Could be."

Dagny studied the cartons of gum on the shelves. All of the packs of Chewey's held fifteen pieces. "Mr. Waller, have you always sold Chewey's in packs of fifteen?"

"No, it can vary. Sometimes it's twelve. Sometimes it's ten. Depends on the deal we get from the wholesaler."

"Is there a way to figure out how many sticks were in the packs you were selling on January first?"

Waller led them through a cluttered storage room to a small office in the back of the building. "Whenever we take an empty box off the shelves, we order another box, so we always have one on hand," he explained. He opened a file drawer and pulled out several thick manila folders. "The orders are in these."

"So the last order you placed before January first is when the pack in question would have been put out on display?"

"Yeah, that's right. So the pack you're looking for would have come from the order before that one." He thumbed through the first file, then started through it again. "Sorry if I'm going slow. I'm a little nervous. I don't want to miss anything."

"I understand. Do you mind if I look through one of the other folders?" Dagny asked.

"Me, too?" Victor added.

Waller handed them each a folder. Though Waller seemed to have a comprehensive set of order forms, they were not in any particular order. "Let's just pull everything that says Chewey's," Dagny suggested. Within a few minutes, they had stacked about twenty forms. Victor put them in chronological order, and they thumbed back through them, looking for an order for Chewey's Cinnamon Gum.

"December thirty-first," Victor said. "On New Year's Eve, you guys ordered another box of Chewey's Cinnamon."

"So we need to go one more back," Waller remarked.

They sifted through the orders and found that another had been placed on September 20. "That's it?" Dagny asked.

"Should be," Waller said. "But it don't say how many were in each pack. I guess that's not on the form?"

"Can you tell by the price? Five dollars and eighty cents?"

"Nah, it fluctuates. Could be the ten, twelve, or fifteen."

"Do you have a specific person you deal with at the wholesaler?"

"Just whoever answers the phone. They've got a big call center. Lots of people there."

Dagny glanced at her watch. It was eight thirty. Maybe the call center would be open. She found the phone number on the order form and called from her cell. A bright and cheery female voice answered.

"This is Sandi at HLP Wholesale, can I help you?"

"This is Special Agent Dagny Gray of the FBI. I need to find out some information about an order placed by Waller's Food Mart on September twentieth, last year. Is it possible for you to look it up on your computer system?"

"I'm going to have to transfer you to the legal department."

"No, I just think…" It was too late. She heard a few seconds of overwrought instrumental music before an answering machine informed her that the legal department did not open until nine. She hung up her phone.

Victor laughed and grabbed her phone. "Did your rep have a name?" he asked.

"Sandi."

Victor hit redial and then held up his hand for silence. "Hi, this is Crosby Waller," he said in an inexplicable Southern drawl. "Hey, Barbara, I'm so glad you are there. My daddy owns Waller's Food Mart here in Bethel, and I work here. I think I did something wrong, so I was wondering if you could help me out?…Yeah, you see, when I order stuff, I'm supposed to write down exactly what was ordered, and my daddy's going through the papers and checking, and I realized I didn't write down some information on one of them, and I know it's stupid, but if that information isn't there, I'm going to get a whuppin' like you wouldn't believe… September twentieth of last year…Yeah, I know, it's completely stupid. My dad's insane—likes to rip that belt off mighty fast." Mr. Waller frowned, but Victor shrugged. "I know I ordered Chewey's Cinnamon, but I don't know if it was a ten- or twelve- or fifteen-pack, or what…Order number two-one-two-three-three-eight… Yeah, thanks…Okay, I got it. You have no idea what you've saved me from." Victor ended the call and handed the phone back to Dagny. "It was a ten-pack. But if you want," he said, "you can send a subpoena to their legal department to confirm it." Dagny was impressed; her potted plant had some skills, after all.

Ten sticks, ten crimes? Maybe.

Dagny turned to Waller and his son. "Thank you for your help today, gentlemen. I would like to ask one more favor—that you don't talk to the press about this."

"Of course we won't," Waller said. "That's what we told the man last night."

It was strange that Fabee had sent only one agent the night before. "You remember his name?"

"Brian, I think. Black guy." Waller reached to his back pocket and pulled out an overstuffed wallet. A few loose papers fluttered to the ground when he opened it. He leaned down to pick them up and found the card he was looking for. "Not Brian. Brent." He handed the card to Dagny. "Keep it. He gave Crosby one, too."

She smiled. Brent Davis was working for Fabee.

They spent the rest of the day canvasing Bethel homes, inquiring about a man in a grey hooded sweatshirt who stole some gum on New Year's Day. In the evening, they checked into the Econo

Lodge in nearby Monticello. Victor dropped his suitcase in his room, then joined Dagny in hers.

"Time to learn something," she said, withdrawing a fingerprint kit from her bag. She put on a pair of nitrile gloves and removed the doorway tape measure they'd bagged at Waxton's Savings and Loan. The magnetic strips at each end were about six inches long and an inch wide. She brushed the magnets with a white powder, coating the entire surface.

"What kind of powder is that?"

"Lanconide," Dagny replied.

"Why not carbon black?"

"You can't use black on black. You use carbon black on white or clear surfaces." Dagny lifted the top magnet by its edges and tapped the side gently against the table. "To create an even distribution," she explained. She blew softly over the top of the strip, but the powder didn't adhere.

"No prints?" Victor asked.

"None." The top magnet was of no help. She tapped the bottom magnet against the table, revealing a couple of prints—a thumb and an index finger. Dagny photographed the prints with her digital camera, then lifted them with a long piece of transparent tape, which she stuck to a piece of black card stock.

"The photographs actually work better," she explained, "but you always keep a copy." Dagny placed the tape measure back in its bag and retrieved the pen with Waxton's fingerprint. It was a Bic—white plastic with recessed black lettering. "Round surfaces are always tricky."

She grabbed another brush and dusted the pen with carbon black. "Partial thumb, partial index. That should be enough." She photographed the pen, then lifted the prints with tape and stuck them to a white piece of paper.

"Since the prints are rounded, they might not show well in the photographs, so the paper is actually the more important record in this case." She compared the features of the fingerprints on the black paper with those on the white. It wasn't even close.

"Those prints aren't Waxton's." She repeated the process with the pen Adams had used to sign an autograph for Victor, but the prints were too smudged to be of use.

"Drat," Victor said.

"Drat?" Dagny removed Adams's security proposal from her bag, tore off the front and back pages, and set them down on top of a newspaper. She coated the pages lightly with ninhydrin. "You use ninhydrin with porous objects—paper, cardboard, fabrics. You can't use too much pressure, though, or you'll destroy the print."

"Aren't they supposed to turn purple?" Victor asked, peering down at the pages.

"Sometimes it takes a little while to develop."

"Cool." He sat down on the bed and folded his hands in his lap, then began to whistle the theme song from *Growing Pains* until Dagny shook her head. "Can we get some dinner? I can't keep skipping meals like this."

She'd been living off pretzel nuggets and adrenaline. It was hard to understand why anyone would need more than this.

At Loretta's the tables were lined with chrome, the booths were covered in vinyl, and a tiny jukebox sat at the end of each table. Dagny flipped through the selections—a lot of Neil Diamond and Billy Joel. Victor ordered the diner's world-famous chicken potpie. Dagny ordered a salad and picked around the feta cheese.

"So we didn't need the pen, I guess? The one with J. C.'s fingerprints. I forgot that his prints would be on the proposal," Victor said.

"It's always nice to have a backup. You still did well."

"Can I ask you a question? And if you don't want to talk about it, I'll drop it completely."

"Go ahead," Dagny said.

"How are you doing this? How are you keeping it together?"

"I'm not keeping it together, Victor. I'm just tossing it all in the closet to deal with later. Believe me. It's eating me up inside."

"Why work the case, then? Why throw yourself into the vortex? The case doesn't need you. It doesn't need us. Fabee wants to catch this guy, too, even if it's only to stake his career."

He was right, of course. Fabee was perfectly competent and adequately motivated to work the case. "I wish I could give you a good reason, but I only have bad ones."

"Revenge? Retribution?"

Those things and more. "I'll drop you off this boat before it sinks. You'll come out okay," she promised.

"I don't care about that."

"Well, you should. You've already got a mark against you for signing up for the Professor's class." It must have bothered him to hear this, because he set his fork down and stopped eating. "Don't worry. You've got potential. You could actually be something. Someday. If they give you a chance to learn."

"I'm learning a lot right now."

"This isn't the way to learn, Victor. We're not working the case like someone should. We're just picking up scraps."

"What are you talking about? We know there are ten sticks of gum, right? So maybe our guy's planning ten crimes. And we know he's a tall guy—around six four or so. And that he quoted a bank robber doing time in Coleman—so maybe he knows this robber, maybe he used to be in jail with him. And now we have some prints that might match something. Do you think Fabee's fabulous team has that much?"

It was a good question. "Let's find out what Fabee's Fabulous has." She pulled out Brent Davis's card and dialed his number.

"Hello?" he answered.

"Have a little time for an April fool?"

"Dagny Gray! How's Bethel?"

"So you know about my banishment here?"

"Wasn't my idea."

"Where are you?"

"Sitting at the counter, staring at you."

Dagny looked across the room. Brent waved, and she called him over. Victor slid over in the booth to make some room, and the handsome black man in a fitted suit sat down next to the pale boy in a floppy one. The contrast between the two of them made Dagny happy.

"Nice to see you both," Brent said.

"You stalking us?" Dagny asked.

"I was actually here first. Get the cheesecake, by the way. It's delicious."

"Why are you still in Bethel?"

"Antiquing."

"So you're not going to give me anything."

"We're under strict orders not to."

"Well, you just divulged your strict orders, so—"

"Open the floodgates?" Brent laughed.

"What flavor?" Victor asked.

"Marble. Get the marble."

"What if we got something you missed?" Dagny asked.

"Sounds unlikely."

"But maybe you'd trade? Give us a glimpse into the magic of Fabee's Fabulous."

Brent chuckled. "Is that what you're calling us?"

"Victor came up with it. So a trade?"

He paused. "You didn't get anything."

"We did."

Brent looked at Victor. "Did you get anything?"

"We did," Victor said.

"Offer it up. If it's good, I'll give you something in return."

"Only a fool would take that deal."

"But you're an April fool, remember."

Dagny figured she had nothing to lose. "Twelve sticks. Twelve sticks means twelve crimes."

"I already knew that, Dagny."

"It's not twelve, Brent."

He offered a sheepish smile. "Okay, I don't know. How many then?"

"What can you give me for it?"

The waitress approached, and Victor ordered the marble cheesecake. Brent drummed his fingertips on the tabletop. "I had a sketch artist meet with Crosby this afternoon. So we've got a good idea of what he looks like. I can get you a copy of the sketch."

"When?"

"I'll e-mail it when I get back to the motel. You can't reveal where you got it."

It was something. "Okay."

"So how many sticks?"

Dagny paused. "Ten sticks." She explained the methodology behind this deduction.

"Okay then." He nodded. "I'll send you the sketch."

Back in her motel room, Dagny checked Adams's proposal. Several prints had turned purple. She held them next to the prints from the magnetic strip. And though she was no expert, it looked as if Adams's prints matched those on the faulty tape measure.

Adams had an alibi for Mike's murder, so he was either an accomplice or he was being framed. The latter seemed more likely to Dagny; no one, not even a murderer, was likely to put up with Adams's company for long. She photographed the fingerprints and sent the images to the Professor. While she did this, an e-mail arrived from Brent. She opened the attachment and looked at the sketch. The man in the drawing was hidden behind big sunglasses and a hooded sweatshirt. He looked exactly like the Unabomber. She called Brent.

"Not helpful," she said. And when he laughed, she followed with, "Not funny."

"Okay, I may have oversold its utility. But it has some value. The guy does a Brutus thing in DC, and he does the Unabomber in Bethel. He likes a good homage. That's something."

"You still owe me."

"I know. And I'll deliver. I promise. But for now, I'm just a cog in the machine. I don't know anything you don't know. If I get something, I'll get it to you."

"I'm sure."

"You have my word." He paused and then added, "You're not someone I want mad at me."

After hanging up, Dagny took a shower and changed into a long Georgetown T-shirt—a gift from Mike. It had only been four days since his death. She felt tired and weak. It hurt to breathe. She thought about ants, and how they carried fifty times their body weight. She wondered if it hurt them as much as it was hurting her. The bed called, and she climbed beneath the covers.

At 4:00 a.m., she woke and dressed for her morning run. Outside the motel, a man was loading the newspaper boxes. The day's *New York Post* featured a picture of Crosby Waller on the cover. The front headline blared, "The Boy and the Bubble Gum Thief."

CHAPTER 24

March 23—Washington, DC

The crowd for Michael Brodsky's funeral overflowed from the All Souls Church onto Harvard Street, where a long line of mourners waited to pay their respects. Inside, Marjorie Brodsky, a thin and stylish woman, sat by the closed casket, her right leg crossed firmly over her left, her clasped hands resting on them. She wore no veil to hide her tears—they flowed freely and quietly while a succession of friends and colleagues paid tribute to her son. There were no prayers or homilies—just stories and anecdotes. Fellow professors talked, with only slight exaggeration, about his love for teaching and his prodigious intellect. Lydia Brodsky, Michael's younger sister, placed a sheet of paper on an overhead projector; an untitled watercolor by the artist at age four filled the screen in front of the congregation. Diego Rodriguez talked about Michael's final days, noting that he was happy, and that he was in love. He didn't mention Dagny by name. Few in the church would have known who she was. Those who did probably didn't think much of her, because she wasn't there.

CHAPTER 25

....

March 23—Coleman, Florida

Dagny's phone had finally stopped vibrating. The service must have started. She kept her eyes focused on Highway 301. Her cell had been ringing with regularity since Mike's murder, and Dagny had ignored all calls except those related to the case. Julia's name had flashed up so often that it threatened to burn into the screen. Maybe Julia wouldn't understand, but Dagny couldn't talk to her right now. She couldn't talk to anyone.

Except Victor, it seemed.

Victor held an Egg McMuffin in one hand and a road map in the other. "Should be up on the right," he said, dripping egg juice on his tie. "Dammit. Third one."

"What?"

"Third tie I've ruined this way."

"With an Egg McMuffin?"

"Yep."

Coleman Federal Correctional Complex looked a little like an industrial park—bland, expansive block buildings, all gated and fenced. A clear glass sign hung from the brick entrance, with white block letters and directional arrows. Minimum security to the left. High-security USP 2 to the right. Straight ahead for low security, medium security, high-security USP 1, and central administration.

"Actually, one was a Bacon, Egg, and Cheese."

Dagny flashed her creds to the guard in the booth at the front of the medium-security lot. They parked their rented Buick in the small parking area and walked through the red stone arched doorway into the prison. An old, thin man sat at the front counter and opened the glass window to greet them. The nameplate on the counter read "Maurice Jones."

"Can I help you?"

"We're from Quantico." Dagny flashed her creds, and Maurice nodded and looked over at Victor, who was fumbling through his pockets.

"I swear I have them," Victor said.

Maurice shook his head and looked back at Dagny. "He your partner?"

"The community college has an externship. He gets two credits."

"And what do you get?" Maurice asked.

"Mostly annoyed."

The old man laughed. "How can I help you?"

"We're here to see a prisoner. Reginald Berry."

"Reginald Berry," he mumbled, starting to type the name into his computer. Then he stopped typing and laughed. "Oh, *Reginald Berry*. I'm sorry ma'am, but you're at the wrong facility. You need to go down the road a bit."

"What do you mean?"

"As of a couple of years ago, Reginald Berry is Regina Berry. She's at the women's satellite camp."

"You mean he—"

"She."

"Really?"

"Yes, ma'am."

"I didn't know that a sex change would get you transferred to the women's prison."

"I don't believe there's an actual policy on this kind of thing. Most prisoners can't afford the surgery, and the government won't pay for it. So it hardly comes up."

"How'd he get the transfer if there's no policy on it?"

"How does anyone get anything in prison? He filed a lawsuit."

"Pro se?"

"No, he had a lawyer."

"How'd he get a lawyer?"

Maurice shrugged. "Berry's got to have a little money—he paid for his surgery."

"The lawyer must have been pretty good to get the transfer."

"Maybe, but then again, he drew one of them liberal judges."

"Hey, do you think our guy dressed as a woman during the bank robbery as some kind of nod to Berry and the sex change?" Victor asked, groping around the backseat of the car.

"Maybe." She'd actually been thinking the same thing herself.

"Found them," Victor exclaimed triumphantly, creds in hand.

As they pulled into the parking lot and the women's prison came into view, Berry's surgery started to make sense. The men's prison was a medium-security facility, but the women's was a minimum-security camp. Thus the women's warden didn't lead them to a sterile concrete room with a table and chairs, but rather to an outdoor picnic table in a grassy clearing next to a large oak tree. A gentle breeze rustled through its new leaves. "Ah, spring," Victor said.

A guard escorted a small and slight African-American woman to their table. She looked a little like a woman, anyway. In a dark bar, perhaps even an attractive one. But her hands, her throat, her brow—all retained a masculine quality.

"You the feds?" Regina asked in a husky rasp.

"I'm Special Agent Dagny Gray, and this is my associate, Special Agent Victor Walton," Dagny replied. "We'd like to talk to you about a bank robbery."

"I ain't done nothin'—I've been in prison."

"I mean the one that got you here," Dagny explained.

"What's to tell, really? And why should I?"

"You'll be coming up for parole sometime."

"Shit, there ain't hardly any parole anymore. Maybe you drop a year or two from twenty-five, but that's all."

Victor jumped in. "That year or two will seem important when it comes."

"Alrighty," Regina relented, throwing her hands up and pretending that Victor had convinced her. "I'll tell y'all about the bank robbery, but I don't know what it's gonna do for you. It's ancient history."

"Please tell us about it," Dagny said.

"I was working construction, doing houses and stuff. It was hard work, and we was working with illegals, long days in the hot sun. Plus lots of overtime, and they was stiffin' us. So one day I'm complaining out there to a guy I worked with a lot—Ed Cooper was his name, or so he say. Big white guy. And he's telling me how he has a plan so he don't have to keep doing shit jobs like this. Gets me all interested—real mysterious like—telling me just that he got a plan. This shit goes on for days, maybe weeks, just telling me he got a plan, but not telling me what it was. Finally, I tell 'im I think the whole plan thing is bullshit and he ain't got no plan, and so he tells me he's got one, really, but he ain't gonna tell me unless he can trust me. 'Can I trust you?' 'Sure you can.' So he tells me he wants to rob a bank—he's got the whole thing planned, 'cause he has a cousin who runs security at the bank, and the cousin can be the inside man. His cuz would let him know when the staff was down. You follow?"

"Yes. Please go on," Dagny replied.

"He tells me that on Thursdays they have their biggest load. That they normally got only about twenty grand on hand, but on Thursdays they got five hundred, 'cause that's the change-out day. Says he wants me for the car, but only if he can trust me. I tell him he can trust me, but I don't know about robbin' no bank; I ain't never done nothin' like that. But times was tough, and he says he my angel, come to save me.

"The day we do it, I pick him up in my new Chrysler—it was a year old and the only nice thing I ever bought me, took a lot of house work to get it. I'd stolen a plate and swapped it out, in case there was gonna be a chase. Then Ed Cooper comes up to the car with a cast on his leg, tells me he broke it falling off a roof. Tells me the whole gig's off, unless we switch roles, 'cause he can't run but he can still drive. 'Shit, I ain't gonna do that.' And he says he figured so, but he's gonna have the cast for two months and he can't wait that long since he can't even do construction with the cast. Says he'll find someone else to do the stickup work. I say, 'Wait, man, we had an agreement.' He says, 'If we a team, then you do the job.' I say no way. He says he'll go fifty-fifty with me, and he and his cuz will split his half. That was persuasive.

"I give him my keys and he drives me to the bank. I sit there, just thinking, how am I gonna do this, and maybe it's wrong, 'cause I know it's wrong. But he explained that the bank was insured, and no one would lose anything, and they be happy to give it to me, 'cause it wouldn't trouble them none. Then he hands me a bag, and I open it and see a gun, and he says, 'You're not even gonna have to fire it. You just need it for show.' So I take the gun from the bag and hide it under my jacket, and I just tell myself that two hundred and fifty and I'm set, man. I can buy a new TV and move to a new place. He give me one of them hats you pull down over your head with the eyes cut out and says, 'Don't put this on until you're at the counter and the gun's out.' So I take the mask and put it in my pocket, and I get out of the car and start up toward the bank. Real slow like. And I'm shaking, and wanted to say fuck it, but it was too late, 'cause then I was in the bank and there was like, no one there. No customers and only couple of tellers. So I walk up to the counter and I tell the lady I need the money, but I mumble it like, 'cause I can't even believe I'm saying it. And she's like, 'What?' And so I pull out the gun, you know, for clarification. And I put on the mask. And I tell her to put the money in a bag and give it to me. I didn't even have the bag—man, this shit was not thought through—but she had a bag, so she starts putting money in. It don't look like half a mil, so I tell her I know there's more. But she says, no, that's all, and that there's more in the vault but she don't have access to it. So I grab the bag and run out the door, but my car ain't there. And then it's clear— my friend, my angel—he never had an inside man, no cousin. He ain't even wanted to rob the bank. He just wanted my car. So I run back into the bank and tell the lady, 'I need your car,' and I wave my gun at her, and she digs in her purse and tries to find her keys. But she can't find them, and she's crying, and I hear sirens, and I say, 'Shit, woman, did you call the police?' And she just nods. I fall to the floor, man, 'cause I know there's nothin' I can do. Lady finally finds her damn keys and tosses 'em to me, but by then the police are through the door, guns raised. And it's over."

"Did they catch Cooper?" Dagny asked.

"They didn't even believe he existed. I said, 'Then how the hell I get to the bank?' but they wouldn't listen."

"I read that you kept muttering, 'The sins of the angels remain with them in heaven.'"

"Y'all make me sound like a crazy mofo, but yeah, I said what I said, and I still hope it's true."

"When did you say it?"

"When I dropped to the floor, realizin' just how I'd been played."

"What did you mean by it?"

"I meant just what I said. Damn angels may ride up to heaven, but they gonna have to live with what they did." Regina looked over to Victor. "Fool, don't you say nothin'? You let this lady run you?"

"You're a lady, too," Victor replied.

"Damn straight I am. Beats the hell out of where I was."

"So you had the sex change just for the transfer?" Victor asked. "Was it really that bad?"

"You ain't got no idea what it's like. Five forty in the morning, and I'm awake 'cause some jackass is screaming on the block above. I'm laying on the top bunk, and I know it gonna be six soon, so why bother falling back asleep. Teddy Jack is on the bunk below, and he's jackin' it like he does every morning. At six the lights come on and the gates go unlocked. I jump down from the bed and take a dump, after Teddy. Get dressed. Check to see who's going to the showers. If it looks clear, I might go in. If I get a bad look, figure I can wait 'til later, or even a couple of days if need be. But have to be back at the cell door for the eight o'clock count. Wait for that count to clear. Sometimes it takes fifteen minutes, but sometimes it takes an hour, just standing there. Skip the cafeteria, 'cause bad stuff goes down there in the morning, and just eat the stuff in the box I got at the commissary. Then down to the factory, working the presses, squeeze 'em down seven hundred times until it's close to noon, so I run back to my cell for the noon count. Maybe decide to get a hot lunch in cafeteria after count, so I check it out, see who's there, and if it looks okay, then I get in line for the mac and cheese, and grab me some Kool-Aid. Nobody too happy to have me sit down with 'em, so I eat standing up, real fast, just shovel it in, 'cause the line's long and I need to get back to the factory anyway, keep them presses going. Got one bite of cookie still in my hand, as I'm walking out the door, when guard busts me, calls me a thief, threatens to put me in the hole. Can't take food out the room. They want to sell that stuff in the commissary. Takes my last bite of cookie and tosses it away. Man the presses until the four o'clock count. After count, go outside, get some sun before it goes down. Ain't part of no gang, so I'm just chillin' with Rex and Reed. They've got nothin' going on, just like me. Then Birdy and the Loo come up to Rex and say he forgot the yeast. Rex works the cafeteria, so Birdy and Loo need his help to make wine. Rex just got out of the hole for stealing yeast, and he ain't happy to do it again. Birdy flashes a knife and says there are worse things than the hole. Rex promises he'll get the yeast at dinner tonight. Me, I'm just glad I work the presses. Seventy cents an hour and low stress. Skip the cafeteria and chow down a can of tuna and some crackers for dinner. Eat that most nights. Maybe check out the TV lounge, but sports is on, and that ain't good. Always gonna be a fight, 'specially if it be something like New York or Philly, but even if not, people got too much money on the game. Thousands of dollars. Too much temper in one room, so I head back to my cell and write another letter to Momma. Tell her I'm sorry again. Maybe this time she'll read it and cry, maybe even decide to come visit her son. Ain't had no visitors, not once. 'Cept you and Red, and the lawyer. But maybe Momma will come. Watch a guy polish the floors each night before bed. The whole prison stinks of men, but that floor shines like a beaut. Just keeps shining away, even when it ain't scuffed, when it's clean as day. See, in prison, it don't matter what something needs—every floor gets cleaned whether dirty or not—ain't nobody care, 'cause a floor's a floor and they're all the same to the man cleaning 'em. And the machine he uses, it hums, but real soft. Sounds nice. Gets me ready to sleep. Ten o'clock, lights out. Day is done."

"Coleman's really that bad?" Victor asked.

"That wasn't even at Coleman, but it's all the same. And bad? That was a *good* day. That was the best day I ever had. Not just one time, either. That day, I had hundreds of times. But that's still not a normal day. Most days don't go smooth like that. If every day were like that one, though, don't think I'd be where I am right now. Have I told you enough? Birdy and Loo killed Rex the next morning. And Reed? He was spread down by Skinhead Fred later that night, treated like a woman."

Since she wasn't there to learn about Skinhead Fred, Dagny tried to get the interview back on track. "Did you talk to anyone in prison about your bank robbery?"

"Hell, I don't tell nobody nothin'. In here, everyone's innocent and they don't say otherwise."

"Surely you told someone."

"Wouldn't tell you if I had."

"Why not?"

"Talk in here's confidential. I ain't saying nothin'."

"You tell anyone about what you said about the angels? How 'the sins of the angels remain with them in heaven'?"

"Maybe. Someone else use it?"

"You tell me," Dagny pressed. Regina's face was hard to read, but Dagny was certain she knew something.

"I don't know nothin'. We don't get no papers here."

"Of course you do," Victor said, pointing to an inmate at another table who was reading a newspaper.

"I'm saying I don't read them, is all."

"Regina, if you know something, telling us could help you out," Dagny reminded her.

"It can't do shit for me. Can you bust me out for helping you? Can you tell me that right now?"

"It might get you an earlier release. I can't promise you anything. But we can see if we can move up the parole hearing a bit. Maybe make things easier for you while you're here."

"You're about two years too late on that one. No one was making it easier on me, so I had to do it myself. Now you can't promise shit. I ain't unhappy here. This side is real nice. Martha Stewart put this place on her list of five. That told me right there that it wasn't a bad place to be."

"How'd you pay for your surgery, Regina?" Dagny asked.

"Ain't none of your business."

"I'm investigating a crime, Regina. It's my business."

"Oooh, scare me then. What you gonna do? Lock me up for not tellin' you nothin'?"

"How'd you pay for your surgery, Regina? I know the state doesn't pay."

"Then you're real smart, I guess."

"Where'd the money come from?"

"Ain't no money, fool. Act of charity. And I don't know nothin' more, so don't even try. Don't even know the doctor's name. White guy, though. Or maybe there ain't no doctor at all, 'cause I'm done talking."

"That's not actually lunch," Victor said, motioning to Dagny's glass of water. They had stopped at a truck stop for lunch. Victor had ordered a bacon double cheeseburger. Dagny had asked for water.

"I'm not actually hungry."

"I've never seen you hungry."

"I don't want to talk about this, Victor."

"Fine." Victor leaned back and crossed his arms. "I know what this is, though. I've got a sister."

"You want to go for a run, see who's in better physical shape? You want to talk about eating? 'Cause it looks like you're trying to fill out those suits again." Dagny immediately regretted her outburst. "I'm sorry."

"It's okay," Victor said. "It's okay. It's just—"

Dagny's phone rang. She looked at the screen. Brent Davis.

"What is it?" she asked.

"No hello?"

"What is it?" she repeated.

"They found a stolen Matisse under J. C. Adams's bed."

"What does that even mean?"

"Beats me," Brent said.

"Where is it now?"

"Cincinnati."

"Do they think it's the second crime? The fourth?"

"Neither. It was stolen two days ago from a home in Buffalo. CPD found it today."

"Under J. C. Adams's bed?" she asked.

"Yep."

"Why were the Cincinnati cops there in the first place?"

"As far as I can tell, that's your fault. McDougal forwarded Beamer the results from the prints you took and CPD got a warrant. Don't ask me what they thought they would find. I think they were just harassing him—they seem to have some kind of vendetta against the guy."

"Where's the painting now?"

"Cincinnati field office."

"How long is it staying there?"

"I've told you everything I know."

"Where's Adams?"

"I've told you everything I know."

"Okay."

"I repay my debts, Dagny."

"Debt paid."

"You did not hear this from me. You heard this from CPD. You heard this from Santa Claus. But you did not hear this from me."

"Agreed."

After hanging up, she caught Victor up on the news and then called the Professor.

"I've narrowed it down," he said. He'd been working on a profile.

"To what?"

"To nine hundred sixty-two suspects."

Well, it's a start, Dagny thought. "Why did you send Adams's prints to CPD?"

"I wanted to see if something would happen," the Professor said.

"Something did," Dagny replied.

CHAPTER 26

March 24—Covington, Kentucky

Dagny pulled on a pair of shorts and a T-shirt, tied her sneakers tightly, then took the elevator down to the lobby of the Embassy Suites and ran out into dark. It was four thirty, and the streets were empty. She ran east a couple of blocks, then headed north on the John A. Roebling Suspension Bridge, leaving Kentucky and heading over the Ohio River into Cincinnati. Once across, she circled the National Underground Railroad Freedom Center, a large undulating block of travertine stone and copper panels. She headed west toward Paul Brown Stadium, where the Bengals usually lost.

Her left leg gave way, and she tumbled to the ground, spilling to the concrete and scraping her knee. Dagny looked back to see if something had tripped her, but nothing had. Blood dripped down her leg and onto her sock. She leaned against a light post, gathering the strength to stand. A dirty middle-aged man sidled up to her. Dark stains spotted his flannel shirt and torn jeans, and he smelled as if he hadn't bathed in days. His hair hung over part of his face, and Dagny couldn't see his eyes. He stepped in front of the streetlight and became just a silhouette.

"Excuse me, lady, but my car broke down and I need just a few dollars to get gas. Someone stole my wallet and my cell phone battery died." He held up a cell phone to make the point. "I have to get to my daughter, who was left behind at a party by her friends, and I don't really want to leave her there. Bunch of wild boys—and I don't trust them. Is there any way you could lend me five dollars, just so I can get the gas and get her home? I'll take your address and send you back six."

"I don't have anything on me," she said, and it was true. "I wish you luck with your daughter." The homeless man started to scuffle away. "Hey," Dagny called out to him. "What's your daughter's name?"

He stopped, turned around, and regarded Dagny for a few seconds. Then he shrugged and walked away. She thought about how shrinking cities like Cincinnati were scarier than big cities like New York and DC. In big cities, people were everywhere and there is safety in numbers. But something awful could happen in the middle of downtown Cincinnati and no one would ever know.

The FBI's Cincinnati field office was located in the John Weld Peck Federal Building, across from the Potter Stewart United States Courthouse and within a single block of three Starbucks shops. Dagny sipped a Venti cup of plain black coffee from one of them on the world's slowest elevator ride to the ninth floor. When the doors finally opened, the local SAC, Chuck Wells, greeted her.

"Fabee's here," he warned.

"Why? Is it time for a press conference?" When Wells laughed, she knew he was on her side.

He led her past a sea of half-manned desks. Everything was a muted shade of grey—the carpet, the walls, the chairs, even the food. The drab furnishings of the DC field office seemed inviting compared to this. They found Fabee standing in a conference room, staring at the recovered Matisse, which was on the floor, leaned against the wall.

"Dagny," Fabee said, with his Texas twang emphasizing the last syllable of her name. "I want to thank you for the work you did in Bethel." It sounded sincere, but lots of things *sound* sincere.

"I didn't get much, Assistant Director Fabee."

"Sometimes it's the stuff that you *don't* get that matters." It was the type of thing that sounded true, and then didn't, and then did again.

"This looks like it matters," Dagny said, nodding at the Matisse.

"Yeah, it might. How'd you hear about it anyway?"

"I'm in good with the CPD."

"I'm sure. Where's Victor?"

"Sick." This was a lie. Victor had stayed in Coleman to find out who paid for Regina's surgery.

Dagny studied the painting. It felt familiar, but Dagny couldn't remember where she had seen it before. Maybe in book or at a museum? A topless woman sat in a wood chair, strumming a guitar. The lines were rough and had a sketched feel. The woman's eyes were black dots, her eyebrows black lines. The fingers of her left hand blurred together, gripping the neck of the guitar like a claw. Her mouth was slightly open. Maybe she was singing. She wore a long white skirt that hung down to her ankles. Black shoes, or perhaps socks, covered her feet. Behind her, a mass of cloudy dots was arranged in curved lines that suggested an audience. Dagny dug her camera out of her backpack. She stood five feet from the painting, adjusted her angle to reduce the glare, and took several snapshots of the Matisse. Had she seen it before? No. But the unsub had given it to them for a reason, so she was going to find out everything she could about it.

The flight to Buffalo was miserable. The Williamsons were worse.

Ted Williamson was a slight, effete man in his early fifties. Dagny could see his bare scalp through the sparse black hair combed across it. Williamson wore a blue blazer with six gold buttons on each sleeve, and a red ascot. He tore his glasses from his jacket pocket, studied Dagny's credentials carefully, and handed them back to her.

"A man of my position has to be very careful," he said. "Please come in."

The front foyer was larger than any room in Dagny's house. A curved staircase descended into the room, each step at least eight feet wide; the middle six were covered with plush red carpet, held tightly to the staircase by gold rods. She suspected that the Oriental rug beneath her feet cost more than her Prius. Williamson saw her looking at the rug and then looked down to her feet.

"Shoes by the door!" Williamson barked, clapping his hands three times. "Shoes by the door!"

Dagny looked over at Williamson's feet, clad in brown suede loafers, and wrinkled her nose.

"These are house shoes," he explained. "I don't wear them outside."

"Bureau protocol requires that I wear footwear while working."

Williamson's wife, Barbara, was waiting for them in the living room. She wore a red kimono that would have looked absurd on the tall, bony Caucasian woman if it hadn't been so beautiful. Her hair was tied up in a bun, with two chopsticks pinned through it. "My wife is in a Japanese phase," Williamson whispered.

"I understand," Dagny said, though she really didn't.

For the next hour, they recounted the events of the night of the theft. Dagny was more interested in the painting itself.

"When we bought it, we couldn't find it in any books on Matisse," Mrs. Williamson said. "But I call it *The Guitarriana*, which is Spanish for a female guitarist."

Dagny had taken four years of Spanish in high school and was pretty sure that "guitarriana" was not actually a word. "How did you know it was an actual Matisse if you couldn't find a record of it?"

Mr. Williamson answered. "The seller had commissioned an expert to authenticate the painting; but you can't trust that, of course, so we had three other experts study the painting, too, including Raúl Manuel, who wrote the book on Matisse."

"What do you mean when you say he wrote the book on Matisse?"

Mr. Williamson jumped from his chair and raced out of the room, then returned a few seconds later, out of breath. He handed Dagny a hardcover book. "He wrote the book on Matisse," Williamson explained.

Dagny leafed through the biography, which seemed to deal equally with Matisse's life and his artwork. "So Mr. Manuel—"

"*Señor* Manuel," Mrs. Williamson corrected.

"So *Señor* Manuel concluded that the painting was authentic?"

"As did the other experts," Mr. Williamson said. "Technique, materials, subject matter—there was no question in their minds."

"We were careful," Mrs. Williamson interjected, "since it was a private auction and the previous owner was undisclosed."

That seemed strange. "Why was he undisclosed?"

"Sometimes that's how it works," Mr. Williamson explained. "We bought it from Cecil Rowanhouse. You've heard of him, I assume?"

"I'm afraid I haven't."

"Well, he's well known in *our* circles," Mrs. Williamson said. "He handles transactions for those who desire anonymity. An *interesting* man," she added, with disapproval evident in her voice.

"Why would people desire anonymity?" Dagny asked.

"Lots of reasons," Mr. Williamson said. "And most of them perfectly legal," he added, seeming to remember that he was talking to an FBI agent.

"Such as?"

"Suppose your father gave you a Picasso, but never told your brother about it. If times were hard, you might want to sell the painting without your brother knowing. No need for him to resent both you and your father. So you sell through Cecil."

"A lot of what goes through Cecil is just being laundered," Mrs. Williamson added. Her husband seemed to recoil as if she had said something profane.

"Barbara, dear, Cecil is a *gentleman*. I wouldn't dare suggest that he was engaged in improprieties."

"Well, I would," Mrs. Williamson said. "Because there aren't that many people trying to keep their brothers from knowing about paintings." She turned to Dagny. "Sometimes, in anticipation of divorce, husbands liquidate assets that their wives don't know about and set up accounts to hide the proceeds of the sale. Often they liquidate art."

"Why art?"

"Because most of these rich old men marry young, pretty, stupid little girls; and while these girls are keenly aware of the value of cars, yachts, and homes, they don't know a thing about art. So when it's time for the divorce, the husbands sell off a few paintings, artifacts, historical pieces, and that money goes into an account. After the divorce, the men withdraw the cash."

"Preposterous." Mr. Williamson shook his head and pursed his lips.

"No, dear, I know it happens. I'm not a stupid young thing."

"Well, maybe it does, but I think you overstate it."

"Mr. Rowanhouse sounds like an *interesting* man," Dagny said. "Could I get his address and number?"

Mr. Williamson darted out of the room again and returned a moment later with Rowanhouse's business card.

"Bermuda?" Dagny asked, looking at the address on the card.

"I told you he's not legitimate," Mrs. Williamson replied.

Dagny spent two more hours with the Williamsons before heading to the airport. She called Victor on the way. "Let's meet at the Professor's tomorrow morning. Then the next day, we'll head to Bermuda."

"Bermuda?" Victor said. "How do *you* know about Cecil Rowanhouse?"

CHAPTER 27

March 25—Arlington, Virginia

Victor pulled a picture of an Indian man from a stack of papers and passed it around. "Dr. Santosh Vyas, originally from Calcutta. Has a wife, two kids, and a healthy fear of law enforcement. He gave me this." Victor pulled a manila folder from his briefcase and tossed it onto the Professor's desk.

"So much for physician-patient confidentiality," Dagny noted.

"The file indicates that Berry's operation was paid for by RLD Inc., a business that didn't exist until two weeks before the surgery, and as far as I can tell, hasn't done anything other than pay for his surgery. According to filings with the Florida Department of State, RLD was incorporated and is owned by a guy named Franco Chavez. In fact, Mr. Chavez is the sole owner of a lot of corporations in Florida that don't seem to do very much. So I looked up Mr. Chavez. Turns out that he's an eighty-year-old Cuban immigrant with Alzheimer's. Lives in a Miami retirement home. Can't remember his own name. Thought I was his son. Barely functions. I convinced the nursing home to let me see who is paying his bill, figure maybe there's a connection there."

"And they gave you his file without a warrant?" Dagny asked.

"It was just like with the Indian doctor. If you come back with a broad warrant, you're going to find something wrong, so they'd rather just give you the file you ask for than risk something worse. Plus, they figure this guy isn't going to complain, since he doesn't even know where he is." Victor sat down in the Professor's chair and put his feet up on the Professor's desk. "And he kept telling people I was his son, so they figured I had a right to see the file."

The Professor glared at Victor, who removed his feet from the desk.

"So what did you get from the file?" Dagny asked.

"Not much," Victor began. "Chavez's bills are paid by money order, so I couldn't trace them back to a bank account. I figured that we could trace the timing of the money orders, go to the issuing bank, try to look at their records or video, and figure it out that way, but that would take forever. So instead I went back and looked at the name of the statutory agent for the corporations, and it was the same for all of them—Peter Flust, a Miami lawyer—solo practitioner. Specializes in international law according to his bio on Martindale-Hubbell. I searched court cases for Flust and the names of all the dummy corporations for which he was named a statutory agent. Figured maybe one of them had been sued. It was a long shot, since none of them seem to do any real business. But one had been sued—purely by accident.

"Someone meant to sue LNR *Products* over some mislabeled medicine, but they screwed up and sued LNR *Productions*, one of Flust's front companies, instead. Flust filed a motion to dismiss, claiming mistaken identity. Judge denied it—said the plaintiff was entitled to discovery to see if it really was the wrong company. In the process of discovery, the plaintiff subpoenaed documents from third parties, including local banks, just trying to figure out if LNR Productions had any relation to LNR Products. No surprise, there was no relationship, but one of the documents showed that LNR Productions was sending a guy named Cecil Rowanhouse a steady stream of checks. I figured this Rowanhouse guy might have a connection to the other companies as well, including the one that fronted the money for Berry's surgery.

"I waited by the elevator bank at Flust's office, hoping he'd step out for a meeting or something in the afternoon, and after an hour or so, he did. Then I went up to his office and told the receptionist that I was supposed to meet Mr. Flust and Mr. Rowanhouse, but that I might have gotten the date wrong. She told me that Rowanhouse doesn't usually fly in to meet with Flust until later in the month, and she checked her schedule and said he wasn't due for a week. I took a chance and asked her if she'd ever seen Rowanhouse's place, and that it was beautiful, and she said she hadn't, but who cares what it looks like, it's in 'freaking Bermuda,' and that she'd live in a tent if it meant waking up by the ocean."

"Impressive," Dagny said.

"I called up the prison and asked if they had a record of Rowanhouse ever visiting Reginald Berry. Nope, nothing. But then I asked about Flust, and it turns out that Flust was the lawyer who got him moved to the women's prison. Since Rowanhouse seems to do regular business with Mr. Flust, maybe Rowanhouse paid for Reginald Berry's surgery."

"The kid's got game," Dagny said to the Professor. "Perhaps Rowanhouse is our man."

"Rowanhouse launders transactions for a living," the Professor said. "If he were our man, he'd have the sense to hide behind someone else. And living in Bermuda—it would be easy enough to see when he's been in and out of the country. No, I think our man is probably a client of Rowanhouse. And that would mean that he has money, and that Rowanhouse is handling it for him."

"Here's what I don't get," Victor remarked. "The unsub gave us both the stolen Matisse and Regina Berry. Both lead to Cecil Rowanhouse. Why give us two roads to him?"He must really want us to meet with Rowanhouse," Dagny said.

"And he didn't think we'd be smart enough to pick up on just one of the leads," the Professor added. He pressed a button, and the white dry-erase board descended from the ceiling.

Dagny and the Professor had drawn a mostly empty chart a week earlier, listing each of the crimes across the top. They spent the rest of the day filling out the chart with everything they now knew. And at the Professor's insistence, Dagny ate every bite of the oversize 700-calorie turkey club his wife had made for her.

At the end of the day, she headed home with some trepidation. Hotel life had been simpler. At home, she saw herself in everything around her. The walls *she'd* painted; the pictures *she'd* hung. In a hotel room, she could look around without thinking about herself at all.

Dagny parked in front of her house, walked up the steps, and turned the key. Once inside, she turned on the television to make some noise, and then walked to the kitchen to pour herself a glass of water. A three-inch stack of mail sat in the middle of the counter. Had she left it there? She thought it had been on the kitchen table. She scanned the rest of the kitchen and then the living room. Everything seemed fine. But the remote…had she left it on the arm of the sofa? Yes, of course she had. She was just being paranoid.

Maybe it was time to look at the box again.

She went upstairs and opened her closet, pushed back her clothes, and found the safe. She turned the combination, withdrew the box, and carried it to her bed.

The box was an octagon, twelve inches deep, made of mahogany. Each of the eight sides and the top framed a red-and-gold padded fabric panel. Each panel depicted a scene in a story about a bird breaking free from an egg and learning to fly. Dagny inserted a small key into the box and unlocked it.

Some of the letters he'd sent from his business trips. Some he'd slipped under her pillow. He'd written them from the day she was born to the day he died, but none of them were written to a child. They recounted stories from his youth, and described his fears and aspirations. They gave advice about the future—as if he had known that this would be all she would have of him. And they all told her that he loved her.

After she finished with her father's letters, Dagny washed her clothes, packed her bags, and crawled into bed. At two in the morning, she woke up feeling sick, ran to the bathroom, and vomited every bit of Mrs. McDougal's turkey sandwich into the toilet.

CHAPTER 28

March 26—Saint George's, Bermuda

According to the brochure, Saint George's was the oldest continuously inhabited English settlement in the Western Hemisphere. Most of the buildings in the town looked to be two or three hundred years old and were painted in bright pastel colors—pink and yellow and baby blue. The streets were narrow and made of cobblestone. Kids on mopeds raced in and out of traffic, weaving dangerously close to the cars they passed. Along the side of the road, a soaking-wet tourist stuck his face and hands through public stocks while his equally drenched wife took his picture. The man waved to them as they drove past. Farther ahead, a sign on a wall read TOWN CENTRE, with arrows pointing both left and right. Around the corner, an antique high-wheel bicycle leaned against an orange three-story building with white stone trim. The lettering on the building read ST. GEORGE'S CYCLE LIVERY.

"Quaint," Victor said.

It was hard to hear him over the clatter of rain pounding against the roof of the cab.

"Huh?"

"Quaint!" Victor yelled.

The taxi driver looked back over his shoulder and nodded his head. He was Portuguese, but spoke with an Indian accent. "Is this your honeymoon?"

Dagny laughed. "No, it's not." Thinking about it some more, she laughed again.

"It's not that funny," Victor mumbled.

The driver turned onto a narrow road that curved up the side of a hill. "His house is on the other side." He eased the car to a crawl, building suspense. "Wait for it..."

The home was made of smooth, rounded white concrete, glass, and steel. Its curved, parabolic walls arched back from the front door, spreading toward the ocean, appearing to rest upon the bright, gorgeous blue water and white bubbling foam. The back of the roof was much higher than the front, making the house seem a bit like a half-open, postmodern oyster that had washed onto the shore. The rain washed off the roof, shunted into waterfalls on each side of the front door, and drained into small streams that ran around the sides of the house, back to the ocean. The driveway circled around a large abstract bronze sculpture— undulating wavelets that zigzagged higher and higher, reaching at least fifty feet from the ground. "Some say they are waves," the driver explained. "Others say that it's a graph of Mr. Rowanhouse's bank account."

Dagny paid the cabbie, and they ran through the rain to the shelter of a small overhang above the front door. She rang the bell and tried to peek through the thick, opaque windows that lined the doorway. A figure walked slowly through the entry hall toward the door. Dagny took a deep breath, prepared to confront the man with the answers, but the door opened to reveal a young, thin blonde woman instead.

"This is totally cool!" she screamed. "He said you were coming, but I didn't believe him." Her skin was tan and smooth, her teeth were straight and white, and her eyebrows were plucked into Roman arches. The bottom of her sheer yellow dress showed off her underwear when she jumped, while the top of the dress hung round her neck and split between her breasts, plunging low enough to reveal the silver stud piercing her belly button. She was maybe twenty-two and looked like the cover of a magazine.

And she was exceptionally thin, Dagny thought. Perfectly thin.

"Follow me, kids!" she yelled, motioning for Victor and Dagny to follow, and then skipping down the entry hall.

"His daughter?" Victor whispered to Dagny.

The girl overheard. "No, silly!" She giggled.

Rowanhouse's home was furnished in a modern, minimalist manner. Though a few abstract pieces hung from the walls, there was little ornamentation. The furniture was sleek and utilitarian. Simple monochromatic rugs covered the shiny bamboo floors. Everything was well lit and clean. Although the furnishings were simple, Dagny could see that they were not cheap.

The young woman spun around and extended her hand. "Silly me! I forgot to introduce myself. I'm Jana."

Dagny shook her hand. "Nice to meet you, Jana."

"You're Special Agent Gray, right? Dagny Gray?"

"That's right." Dagny wondered how she knew, but didn't ask. Maybe the airport had tipped them off. Maybe the driver.

"And you're Special Agent Victor Walton? Junior, right? Victor Walton Jr.?"

Victor shook her hand. "That's right, ma'am," he said, inexplicably trotting out the fake Southern accent he'd used at Waller's Food Mart. "Nice to meet you, Jana."

"You're a cute young thing to be working for the FBI," Jana said, flipping her hair out of her eyes with one hand while gently brushing Victor's arm with the other. Then she turned abruptly and continued down another hallway. "He's back here."

She led them to a large glass room that was suspended over the ocean by cantilever and cables. Twenty or thirty lounge chairs circled a long pool, where a man was swimming laps. "I'll leave you with him!" Jana yelled, so as to be heard over the rain that thundered against the glass roof. Lightning flashed in the sky, and huge waves crashed against the beach below; the crests of some smashed against the bottom of the glass wall near Dagny's feet. On a nice day, it was probably the most beautiful place in the world. In a storm, it was a little scary.

The man swam to the side of the pool. The storm seemed to calm as he climbed out of the water. He pulled off his goggles and swim cap, grabbed a towel from a nearby lounge chair, and dried his hands. "I'm Cecil Rowanhouse," he said, firmly shaking Dagny's hand, and then Victor's. He spoke with deliberate and careful enunciation. "I've been expecting you."

Rowanhouse had the body of a twenty-year-old swimmer, but the hair on his head was grey and thinning, and his face was wrinkled from too much time in the sun. He was sixty, at least—but the healthiest sixty-year-old Dagny had ever seen.

"Did Jana offer you two anything to drink?" he asked.

"No," Dagny said.

Rowanhouse mumbled something, then wandered over to a poolside bar, grabbed some ice cubes from a bucket, and dropped them into a glass. "Scotch? Whiskey? Can I recommend a Gosling's and Coke?"

"Nothing for me," Dagny said.

"You have ginger ale?" Victor asked, abandoning his Southern accent.

"Of course." Rowanhouse grabbed a bottle, twisted the cap, and poured Victor a glass. "Now, if you don't mind, I must change. We'll have dinner in a few minutes. I hope you're hungry."

"With all due respect, Mr. Rowanhouse, we didn't come for dinner."

"Then you shall delight in the surprise of getting more than you bargained for, Agent Gray. And seeing as you were not explicitly invited to my home, I'm sure you will appreciate the hospitality." Rowanhouse scurried off before Dagny could reply.

Victor downed his drink, walked over to the bar, and poured himself another. "Do you think Jana's his lover?" Victor asked.

"I don't know," Dagny said, nodding toward the entry to the room. "Why don't you ask her?"

Jana had returned. She'd changed into a pink-and-blue sundress and carried a towel over her shoulder.

"Hey, Jana. You're from the States, right?" Victor asked.

"That's true!" Jana gushed. "I'm from Atlanta, Georgia, though I'm working on losing the accent."

"Why is that, Jana?" Dagny asked. "Do you want to be an actress?"

"I *am* an actress, Ms. Gray," she responded, with some indignation. "I've been in several films. *Frightmaker Seven, Annie's Girl, The Devil's Daughter.* I also had a small part on *The Hills* for a while."

"Is that how you met Mr. Rowanhouse? Through the movies?" Victor asked. "Was he a producer or something?"

Jana laughed. "Mr. Rowanhouse? Movies? He doesn't know the first thing about movies. Hasn't even seen any of mine, as far as I know." She tossed her towel on a lounge chair, then grabbed the bottom of her sundress and lifted it over her head, revealing a very little white bikini and a lot of skin. She giggled and dove into the pool.

Victor watched Jana swim back and forth as though she were a hypnotist's timepiece. "She's like a perfect inversion of my fiancée," he muttered.

"Fiancée?" Dagny asked.

Before Victor could explain, Cecil Rowanhouse walked back into the room. He wore a pristine white suit, with matching white shoes, white belt, and white shirt. His laces, cuff links, socks, belt buckle, and buttons were all black, as was the flower pinned to his lapel. "Dinner is ready. Please follow."

"Hey, Jana! Dinner!" Victor yelled.

Jana bobbed her head up from the pool. "I don't eat dinner," she said, then ducked back beneath the water.

Rowanhouse led them back through the house to an oval dining room with rounded walls, like an egg with a flat bottom. Though the oblong granite table was big enough for twelve, it was set for three. "Please, have a seat."

Dagny sat next to Victor and across from Rowanhouse. Two Latina women wearing aprons and hairnets carried salads to the table, laying them down carefully at each of the place settings.

"Mr. Rowanhouse, I would like to ask you some questions—"

"Of course, but I must insist that you eat, too. I can't eat if my guests don't, and I'm awfully hungry."

Victor hadn't waited for the invitation—he'd already shoveled most of his salad into his mouth. Dagny speared a piece of arugula with her fork and ate it, then set her fork down on the table. "Now, Mr. Rowanhouse, I'd like to know where you got the Williamsons' painting."

"Agent Gray, it's my job to provide anonymity to those who request it. Surely you have other questions."

"Why does your client require anonymity?"

Rowanhouse set his fork on his plate and placed his hands on the table, palms down. "I will speak only generally of my clients, Agent Gray. And forgive me if my tone becomes one of a lecturer. We live in a world that is sometimes fair, but often not. There are those who are dealt with less fairly than others. Occasionally, there is a way to even things out, and if this requires anonymity, I am more than happy to oblige. I'm sure you look at my house— my life—and suspect that I have made my way through illegitimate means. I am not a thief or a scoundrel. I provide services to people who need them, and I provide them only to those who deserve them. The person who brought me the painting was someone who deserved my services."

Dagny nibbled at her salad, concentrating on the greens and the carrots, while ignoring the goat cheese and walnuts. "Mr. Rowanhouse, you are aware that the painting in question might be linked to the crimes of a murderer."

"So I have surmised."

"Doesn't that upend your notion of the justice of anonymity?"

"Agent Gray, based upon what I know and what you don't know, my conscience is clear. I have made commitments and have pledged to keep them, knowing full well what would come. And I have done so, in part, because the government you represent is not the arbiter of right and wrong. Your agency has carried out much injustice, and while I don't question your motives, I do question the seal on your credentials. Credentials which mean little here in Bermuda."

"There are extradition treaties, Mr. Rowanhouse. If you were found to be conspiring with a felon—"

"I don't think you'd find extradition as easy as you think. I have many friends in Bermuda."

The servants replaced their salad plates with seared tuna and steamed vegetables. Victor grabbed his knife and began cutting into the tuna steak. Dagny started to speak, but Victor kicked her under the table. She decided to let Victor have his run at Rowanhouse. For all his flaws, the kid had a certain talent for getting people to talk.

"So do you think Regina Berry really felt like a woman trapped in a man's body, or do you think she just really wanted out of that men's prison?" Victor asked their host.

Rowanhouse leaned forward and studied Victor carefully. "Regina Berry, you ask?"

"Yes," Victor replied, with his mouth full of tuna. "Are you surprised we know of her?"

"Agent Walton, if I didn't want you to know about Regina Berry, then I would have made sure you didn't know."

"So what do you think? About Regina Berry?"

"Have you ever talked to anyone who has spent any significant time in a federal prison, Agent Walton? How about you, Agent Gray?" he asked. "Do you know what it's like to be locked up by a nation of *laws* and placed in an environment without them?" Rowanhouse raised his voice. "Prisons are black holes—no light can escape them. Beatings. Rapes. And nobody cares. 'They deserve it'—that's the popular sentiment, right? Even if that were true, what about the innocent men sent there? We don't care—because once they're in the great big empty of a silent black, we don't see it. So I guess I'm inclined to think that Regina Berry just wanted out, no matter what it required. And I don't blame her one bit."

"But Regina Berry was guilty," Victor said.

"In the eyes of man, yes. In the eyes of a jury, yes. But in the eyes of God? You can't judge with God's eyes, Agent Walton. I'm not against prison. The dangerous should be segregated from society. But as for retribution? Only God should have the power to send people to hell."

"But what is your client doing, if it isn't retribution?" Victor leaned forward and stared at Mr. Rowanhouse, waiting for his answer.

"Perhaps, Agent Walton, he's making a statement."

"By committing horrible crimes?"

"If you want the FBI's attention, you commit crimes, Agent Walton."

"And what is his statement?"

"That is for you to discover," Rowanhouse replied, pushing his plate away. "Maria," he called. "We are finished with our dinner." He looked over to Dagny's plate. She had taken only a few bites.

"I'm just not very hungry," Dagny said. Rowanhouse had just admitted that his client, the man who sold the painting to the Williamsons, was in fact the man committing the crimes. Why would he admit this?

Rowanhouse stood. "I have arranged for you to leave tomorrow morning. A car—"

"We'll leave tonight, Mr. Rowanhouse."

"You've missed the last flight for the day, Agent Gray. Even if there were another flight, I doubt you'd want to take it in this weather. I have guest quarters that should prove quite satisfactory. Maria will show you to your rooms. A car will pick you up tomorrow at ten. Use the kitchen as if it were your own. I have a small theater where you can watch movies if it interests you. Jana usually watches something in there, but I'm sure she'd be glad for the company."

"Cool," Jana said, bopping into the room.

"We could watch one of your movies," Victor suggested.

"Sure. Or we could watch something good," Jana replied.

The last thing Dagny wanted to do was spend the night in the home of a man who had befriended Mike's killer, but she felt more tired than angry and didn't have the energy to leave. Maria led Dagny and Victor to their rooms. Dagny's opened onto a balcony that overlooked the ocean. It was dark outside, but the skies had cleared and a full moon illuminated the night. She opened the sliding glass door and stepped outside. The ocean smelled fresh and clean and pure.

Nothing else did.

Her head ached, and she felt dizzy. When she rolled off the side of the bed, it was only dumb luck that landed her on her feet. Too much travel, she thought, grabbing her running shorts from her bag.

The house was still and quiet as Dagny tiptoed through the hallway to the back door. It wasn't yet six in the morning, but outside, it was already warm. The sky was still dark but for a brilliant red-orange hue along the horizon. She climbed down the steps to the beach, then jogged along the ocean. It was hard to run in the loose sand, so she moved closer to the water, where the waves had beaten a hard surface and the foam tickled her feet. She turned on her iPod and followed the jagged shore. A mile later, she passed a young couple on the beach. The girl was leaning against her man, watching the sun rise. He had his arms wrapped tightly around her; every few seconds, they kissed. Dagny turned away from the couple and looked out at the bright-blue glow of the ocean. As blue as Mike's eyes. She began to run faster.

After completing one loop around the island, she was too weak to try a second. She collapsed to the beach behind the Rowanhouse estate, and sat there, staring out at the endless ocean, trying to make sense of the little they knew. Adams's fingerprints, the baseball, the stolen Matisse, Reginald Berry, the gum in Bethel, the dog in Chula Vista, the murders of Mike and Candice, and Rowanhouse. Pieces that seemed to belong to different puzzles. It was enough to make her head hurt.

"Water?"

His voice startled her. "Thank you," she said, taking the glass of ice water from Rowanhouse.

He was wearing long white flannel pants, cuffed to his knees, and a striped, unbuttoned shirt. He pushed his sunglasses on top of his head and sat down in the sand next to Dagny.

"Twenty years ago, my wife was shopping in Manhattan, carrying her bags, going from one store to the next." He spoke slowly and softly as he looked out toward the horizon. "A drunk driver—*in the middle of the day*—drove up onto the sidewalk and killed her. Not instantly. She suffered. Spent a week in the hospital. I never felt more helpless in my life, sleeping on the chair in that room as she slowly died, knowing there was nothing I could do about it." He sighed. "I moved here because New York felt like an ugly place, and I needed something beautiful."

"What happened to the driver?"

"I don't know," he replied. "It didn't matter to me, Agent Gray. Whatever happened to him wasn't going to bring Susan back." He said it innocently—without hidden meaning or duplicity, without subtle reference to Dagny's own situation, and without bias for his client. She knew, from this, that he didn't know about her relationship with Mike.

"You know who Michael Brodsky is, right?"

"I read that he was killed as part of this crime you are investigating. I was very sorry to read that. He was a very talented artist. I've sold some of his work."

"You know that he and I were lovers, don't you?" Lovers? "Dating" sounded trivial, but "lovers" sounded scandalous. There wasn't a good word for what they were.

He seemed genuinely surprised. "I did not know that, Agent Gray. I am very sorry for your loss." Rowanhouse grabbed a fistful of sand and let it fall between his fingers. "I did not know that," he muttered again.

"Then maybe you don't know your client as well as you think you do." She stood up, brushed the sand from her legs, and walked back to the house to collect her things.

"What movie did you watch?"

Victor set down the *SkyMall* magazine he'd been perusing and looked up, surprised by her interest. "*Deathplane.*"

"That a Jana film?"

"Third billing," he smiled.

"Who's this fiancée you mentioned? And why haven't I heard of her before?"

"Her name is Jennifer, and she's a nurse out in Herndon. You haven't heard of her because, well, I guess we haven't really talked about anything other than the case."

He was right. Dagny didn't know anything about Victor's personal life. "When did you meet her?"

"Two years ago. I went in for an appendectomy."

"And it started up just like that?"

"Yep." He picked up the *SkyMall.*

He wasn't getting off that easy. "How'd you woo her? Use that silly fake Southern accent?"

"Nope," he replied.

"What then?"

"Just old-fashioned charm."

"So you have a date for the wedding?"

"August fifteenth. If she doesn't leave me."

"Why would she leave you?"

"She liked it better when I was just an accountant."

"I imagine she's pretty upset that you're gone, working this case?"

"Yeah."

It hadn't occurred to her that she'd disrupt Victor's life by bringing him into the investigation. "I'm sorry I pulled you into this. I should have asked if it was something you could afford to do."

"No, Dag, it's great," he said, and he sounded sincere. "I mean, I didn't ever think I'd be doing something like this, but I'm enjoying it. Is that wrong? To enjoy it?"

"You have to enjoy it, or you won't last long." Dagny wondered whether she enjoyed the work. She couldn't remember how she felt before Mike was killed.

"It doesn't make Jennifer feel any better when I tell her I'm having fun doing this. It actually seems to make things worse."

"Well, if things fall apart with Jennifer, you've always got Jana."

CHAPTER 29

....

March 29—Washington, DC

When the director said that Dagny could work the case, he'd forbidden her to investigate the Whitman murder.

He hadn't said anything about the *Brodsky* murder, though.

Still, as Dagny walked the sidewalks of Foggy Bottom, she knew full well that she wasn't supposed to be doing what she was going to do, and it wasn't just because of the Director. After Bermuda, the Professor had ordered Dagny and Victor to rest for the next couple of days. "Neither of you looks well," he explained. "I would swear that your cumulative weight has stayed the same, it's just shifted." He was resigned to the fact that they needed another murder if they were going to get anywhere. The earlier crimes were too stale. A fresh murder would bring new evidence.

Although the Professor had called a break, none of them had actually stopped working. The Professor was still gathering information on released inmates from Coleman who had served time with Regina Berry. Victor was ferreting out more details about Rowanhouse and Flust, and their financial dealings. And Dagny had spent the previous day reading Candice Whitman's essays, trying to understand why someone would want to kill her, and why Mike had loved her. It wasn't hard to see both.

In her early work, Candice was thoughtful and eloquent, ruminating lyrically on esoteric topics like the romance of the common law. Over time, her tone shifted from sublime to sarcastic, from soft to hard. Early essays advocated tougher sentences for white-collar criminals; later diatribes embraced the rough justice of prison rape. Though Candice had begun as an advocate for the judicial system, she had slowly morphed into an advocate only for the victims of crime, and then finally, an advocate only for herself.

Gloria Benton's office was on the first floor of a burgundy brick row house. Dagny rang the bell and waited. When there was no reply, she rang it again. She'd turned to leave when the door finally opened.

"I'm with a client," Benton said, narrowing her brow. Her kinky blonde hair was disheveled and her bright-red glasses were askew.

"Are you almost finished?" Dagny asked, flashing her credentials to replace the question mark with a period.

"Whitman?" she asked. Her expression changed from anger to sadness.

Dagny nodded.

"Hold on a second." Benton disappeared. She returned a couple minutes later with her client, a large man dressed in a muumuu. She dispatched him with a half hug and an air-kiss.

"Okay," she said to Dagny. "Come on in."

Dagny followed her to a small, dark office and took a seat next to a standing ashtray, where a cigarette butt burned its final ember. Benton sat behind a cluttered desk. There were no books on the shelves behind Benton, just framed pictures of the publicist with various men and women—presumably her clients. Aside from a picture of Benton with Candice Whitman, Dagny didn't recognize anyone.

"Winston doesn't like the sun," Benton explained, rising from her chair to open the blinds. When she sat back down, the sunlight was shining directly into her eyes. Benton squinted but made no move to adjust the blinds again. "I've already talked to you guys for what seemed like days. What else can I tell you?"

"We don't always do a very good job at the Bureau of sharing information. Forgive me if you've answered some of these questions already."

Benton sighed. "It's okay. I don't have another appointment for a couple of hours."

"How long had you been Ms. Whitman's publicist?"

"Fourteen years, I think. Thereabouts."

"How did she come to you?"

"You know, I don't even remember. Maybe through someone at the *Post*. I couldn't really say."

"What was she like? Was she always…"

Benton lowered her head and peered over her glasses at Dagny, "Are you asking if she'd really become a bitch, or if she just played one?"

"Yes."

"Everyone changes when they become famous. And very few become nicer. But I always liked her. If she were a man, they'd have called her 'confident' and 'strong.'"

"Her latest book—"

"*The Ides of March*."

Dagny nodded. "Did you plan her book tour?"

"I did."

"Including the launch in Georgetown?"

"Yes."

"When was it announced?"

"Last fall, I think." Benton opened a drawer and sifted through some papers, retrieving a black appointment book. "People think it's a mess in here, but I know where everything is." She flipped through the pages. "No, when we announced in September, it was going to be at Long Beach. And then"—she flipped through a couple more pages—"Okay, yes. We moved it to DC in December."

"Long Beach?"

"She was going to launch it at a writer's conference in Long Beach, California, but they canceled the conference, so we moved it back here to DC. I guess you want to know when the Bubble Gum Thief might have planned the murder."

The newspaper's awful moniker seemed to be sticking. "Something like that."

When Benton closed her calendar, the paper cut her index finger. "Dammit!" She dug through her purse and found a Band-Aid. "I cut myself all the time," she said, wrapping it around her finger.

"Did Ms. Whitman have enemies?" Dagny continued.

Benton laughed in a loud, halting manner. "Have you ever read her work? Of course she had enemies."

"Had she received death threats?"

"Hundreds of them. Thousands, probably. You should have them already."

"Do you know why Michael Brodsky was with her when she was killed?" Nothing Dagny had asked before this had mattered much to her. This question was the reason she'd come to see Benton.

Benton tilted her head and flashed an anguished frown. "You loved him, I guess?"

"Why would you say that?" There was no way she could have known.

"Because you're crying." Benton handed her a box of tissues. Dagny took a few and wiped her eyes. When she looked down at the tissues, they were soaked with teardrops.

No use pretending. "I loved him very much."

"Then you must be in awful pain right now."

"You have no idea."

"I think I do." Benton opened another drawer and pulled out a photograph and handed it to Dagny. It showed a young Candice Whitman holding hands with a young Michael Brodsky. They stood to the side of a stage in a television studio. "Candice loved him, too."

Dagny stared at the photograph. His hair was longer then. Stubble on the face. Eyes the same. "When—"

"It was her first time on television. She was nervous as could be. Could hardly speak a sentence. But he calmed her. He was *always* a rock, for her. Helped her gain confidence. She had been timid, fragile. But he gave her..." She didn't complete the thought. "When they drifted apart, I told her it was a big mistake. That she was letting something wonderful slip away. She would nod in agreement, but she didn't really hear me. Didn't hear anybody. Everybody was telling her that it was a mistake. And yet I helped her do it." Benton grabbed a tissue and dabbed her eyes. "I helped her climb further and further away. Got her jobs in New York, sent her all over the world, always traveling, always chasing something bigger. But that's what she wanted. And it was my job to make it happen."

"Why was he at the book signing with her?"

"We had dinner, the night before. Candice and I. I could tell she wasn't happy, and I pressed her on it. She was almost always up, up, up, so it was strange to see her so down. I asked her what was wrong, and she looked at me and her face started to crinkle real tight, which isn't easy to do with all that Botox, and I realized that she was holding in tears, forcing herself not to cry. And she said, 'What have I been doing?' It was the first time I heard her doubt herself. The first time ever. She shook her head, and just kept shaking it. I thought she was trying to shake herself out of it, shake off the pain. I don't really know what she was trying to do. And then she said, 'I miss him so much.'" Benton grabbed another tissue.

"And then?" Dagny whispered.

"The next morning, I called Michael. Asked him to meet her, talk to her, just to check up on her. He was as close as anyone had ever been to her. Wanted to see if I should really be worried for her, or if it was just a fleeting sadness. So it was my fault he was there. It was my fault he was killed. It was my fault she was killed, too, because I put her there as well." Benton started to sob.

Dagny waited for Benton to regain her composure, and then grabbed a couple of tissues in case she lost hers. "What did Michael tell you when you talked to him? Did he say he was single? That he was still interested in Candice?"

"Oh, no, no, no. Honey, no. That wasn't why he went. When I asked him to come, he said that he had fallen in love, that he'd found 'the one,' and that Candice was someone from his past. That he and Candice were over, but he still cared about her and that he would show up and check on her. But that was as far as it could go because...well, I guess, because of you."

Dagny finally had an answer to the question that had troubled her most, and even though it was the answer she wanted, it left her feeling hollow, empty, and mostly, ashamed. Ashamed that she had doubted Mike, and ashamed that she had used the investigation to mollify her insecurities.

The key turned. No one had changed the locks.

Dagny pushed open the door and stepped inside. She moved slowly along Mike's Wall of Shame, lingering at the van Eyck. Rounding the corner, she entered the kitchen and fetched a glass of water.

She remembered visiting Thomas Edison's Florida home when she was little. Even though it had been preserved to look exactly as it did when Edison was alive, it didn't feel like a home. It felt like a museum. That's what Mike's house felt like now—a museum. Straight ahead, you'll find the couch where Mr. Brodsky liked to read the newspaper. And here is the kitchen. Mr. Brodsky liked to cook. He wasn't much for measuring things. A pinch here, a handful there...

She shook off a couple of tears, set her glass on the kitchen counter, and wandered upstairs to his studio and her beautiful bronze doppelgänger. This room, she thought, should feel like a museum, but instead, it felt like home. She ran her fingers along the arm of her twin, then closed her eyes and touched its face and hers. She compared cheek to cheek, nose to nose, mouth to mouth. It was her—Mike had gotten her completely.

"He was in love with you," a woman's voice rang out, startling Dagny. "More in love than he had ever been before." Dagny opened her eyes. The woman before her wore a navy blazer and matching skirt. Her grey hair curled inward at her shoulders.

"Mrs. Brodsky?" Dagny asked.

The woman nodded, then approached the sculpture. She looked it up and down, and then did the same to Dagny. "You weren't at the funeral."

"I was—"

"You should have been at the funeral. I don't care what you were doing." Mrs. Brodsky circled around the sculpture, tracing a line around its waist. "You've lost weight since he made this."

"Maybe," Dagny muttered. She should have been at the funeral.

"It was a lovely service. No bland sermonizing or forgetful pastor. Just a lot of friends and family members sharing stories about Michael." She spoke with a confidence and authority that made Dagny feel like a little girl.

"I'm sorry, Mrs. Brodsky."

"You could have shared some things about him, too, Ms. Gray. If you had come."

"I'm sorry."

Mrs. Brodsky touched the forehead of the sculpture, then touched Dagny's forehead to compare. "You feel warm. I think you have a fever."

"I'm okay."

"I'm sure you're not." She started to walk toward the stairs, then looked back at Dagny. "Please come."

Dagny followed her down to the first floor and took a seat on the couch in the living room while Mrs. Brodsky mixed herself a drink at the bar. "I'm not an alcoholic. I'm just in mourning. Would you like something?"

"No, thanks."

Mike's mother went to the kitchen and poured a glass of orange juice. "You need *something*," she implored, handing the glass to Dagny before sitting in the chair across from her. "Now tell me why you weren't at the funeral. Were you working on his case?"

"Yes." Dagny sipped the orange juice. Aside from water, it was the first thing she'd put in her body in two days. "How did you know?"

Mrs. Brodsky pointed at Dagny's glass. "Don't just sip it. Drink the whole thing." Mrs. Brodsky finished her drink and walked to the bar to pour herself another. "Do you have any leads?"

"We've started down the right path, I think, but we're still a long way from identifying a suspect." One hundred thirty calories—a big glass of sugar. At least it was fat free. Dagny drank every drop, hoping to avoid another reprimand.

"Will you catch him?"

"I don't know. Probably not."

"But yet you chase him?"

"It's the only thing I know how to do."

"Mr. Fabee told me that you weren't supposed to be working on Michael's case, and that I should tell him if you approach me about it."

"I'm not working Michael's case, per se. I'm working on the predecessor crimes."

"If you're not working his case, *per se*, then why are you here?"

"Because I miss him. I miss him so much."

Mrs. Brodsky sipped her drink more slowly this time. She leaned back in her chair and sighed. "My name is Marjorie. It's nice to meet you. My son loved you very much."

"I loved him very much, too." She started the sentence calmly, but was in tears before she finished. Marjorie walked over and embraced her. "I loved him so much, Mrs. Brodsky."

"Please, dear. Call me Marjorie."

CHAPTER 30

······································

April 1—Salt Lake City, Utah

Rachel Silvers was thinking about Rolland Feller when she raised her hand and said, "*Necesito ir al cuarto de baño.*"

"*Tome el pase y apresúrese.*"

She didn't really have to use the bathroom—she just wanted a five-minute reprieve from the pluperfect tense. She could stretch it to fifteen if she walked slowly. A hustle to the classroom door and then a leisurely stroll down the halls, counting floor tiles and reading the flyers on the bulletin board. Drummer wanted. Yearbook sales. Tickets to Prom.

Prom.

In some ways, Mount Tyler wasn't much different from any other high school in America. The administration complained about the budget, and parents complained about the curriculum. Some of the teachers were good and some were bad. There were smart kids and dumb kids and kids in between, and most of them eventually found their place in standard-issue high school cliques, like the Jocks and the AP Geeks and the Vegans and the Boys Who Grew Beards at a Freakishly Young Age. But there was one clique at Mount Tyler that subsumed all the others. And because Rachel didn't belong to this clique, she felt forever out of place at Mount Tyler High School, forever out of place in Salt Lake City, indeed, forever out of place in all of Utah. Because her parents didn't believe that Joseph Smith discovered God's message on golden plates buried in the ground of Hill Cumorah in Manchester, New York, she was a social outcast.

Something looked different in the bathroom mirror, and then she realized it was a smile. And not just a slight smile, but a big, dumb, goofy grin. A very cute boy had asked her out during lunch, and not just any very cute boy, but Rolland Feller. He was a junior—the starting tight end for the football team, a benchwarmer for the basketball team, and he could have played baseball, too, if he'd wanted, which he didn't. It was just dinner and a movie—a simple little date, but maybe an audition for Prom. And since Rolland hung with the popular crowd, an invitation to Prom could be an entrée into a better life.

As long as she didn't blow it with Rolland.

Back in Señora Bertlesman's class, her eyes drifted out the window, watching her brother climb into his beat-up Camry. Early dismissal was the big perk for seniors at Mount Tyler, but Rachel was just a sophomore. She couldn't leave early. She couldn't even drive. Not yet, anyway. But next year Jack would be away at Stanford, and the Camry would be hers.

If the bell rang, Rachel didn't hear it, but she noticed that students were gathering their books and leaving the classroom, so she did the same. She stopped at her locker to pick up some books. A picture of Grace Kelly hung on the inside of the locker door. She tore it down. It made her weird, and she had decided not to be weird anymore.

She felt silly riding the school bus. It made her feel young—like a kid—and she didn't feel like a kid anymore. She couldn't wait to drive—for Jack to leave, and for the stinking Camry to be hers. Maybe they could trade in the Camry for something nicer. It didn't have to be expensive or fancy. Maybe a cute little Kia, even a Honda Civic.

"Heard about Rolland," Penelope Morton sang in her ear from the seat behind. Penelope was on the cheerleader squad—not one of the most popular three members, but still a lot more important than Rachel. "That's pretty cool."

What's pretty cool, Rachel thought, is that you're talking to me. "Yeah. We should have a good time." Was that stupid?

"He's a good guy. Better than most boys."

It suddenly occurred to Rachel that she hadn't the slightest clue how to propel a conversation forward. Something—she had to say something. "Are you still dating Bobby?"

"Yeah."

"How long have you guys been going out?"

"Two months and twelve days."

"You guys going to Prom, I guess?"

"We are. I just picked out the dress."

Somehow it worked. They were talking. "What's it like?"

"It's lavender, and it's silky, and it has layers that sweep across like this." Penelope made a diagonal line with her hand, cutting left to right across her chest. "But it's not at all tacky. It looks nice."

"It sounds nice. Where did you get it?"

"Nordstrom. But it was on sale. It's not like it cost that much or anything. You should look there. The sale ends next week."

"I haven't been asked to Prom."

"I'm sure you will be. Just don't blow it."

Yikes!—what did that mean? "Yeah, I know," Rachel said. But she didn't know.

"Just remember that if you need to do something, you can always just use your hands."

Was Penelope kidding? Rachel hoped she was kidding. The bus stopped in front of Rachel's house. "Gotta go."

As she walked up the driveway, she noticed that the house looked strange. It took a second to realize that the blinds were down and the house was dark. Maybe no one was home, she thought. But Jack's car was in the drive. Weird. She heard a loud whir overhead. Just the KSL traffic copter, flying low. She watched it pass. The Crane boys were shooting baskets in their driveway, and the smaller one waved to her. She waved back and fished through her backpack for her keys. They must have fallen to the bottom, buried beneath the books. She knocked on the door, but there was no answer. She fished some more, found her keys, pushed the house key into the lock, and turned the knob.

"I'm home!" she yelled, tossing her backpack next to the door. She walked through the foyer to the living room. The bodies—her mother, father, and brother—were tossed in a pile on the floor, blood still flowing from their wounds. She took one step toward them, and then a hand reached around from behind and covered her mouth. Another reached around from the other side and held a card in front of her eyes.

THIS IS MY SEVENTH CRIME.
MY NEXT WILL BE BIGGER.

The assailant tossed the card to the ground and brought a gun to her head. She wanted to die with a happy thought, so she was thinking about Rolland Feller when the bullet tore through her skull.

CHAPTER 31

April 2—Salt Lake City, Utah

The Silverses' house was in a treelined subdivision, nestled in the woods at the base of the mountains, set back on a yard now cordoned off by yellow tape. Neighbors gathered in their driveways, wearing their robes and pajamas, sipping coffee and sharing gossip. About twenty cars, most rentals, lined the streets. At least thirty agents stood outside the house, waiting for something to do. Only a handful had been allowed inside. Each additional person represented another contaminant.

Dagny grabbed her backpack as she and Victor hopped out of the car. An old woman in a bathrobe and slippers approached from the side and tugged at her elbow. "Are they okay?" she asked, but Dagny just ignored her and kept walking toward the house.

She and Victor held open their credentials as they pushed through Fabee's Fabulous toward the front door. A tall man with a severe buzz cut blocked their entry. "Sorry, but we're full."

"Is Fabee here?" Dagny asked.

"*Assistant Director* Fabee is here," he said sternly.

"Tell him Dagny Gray would like to come in."

Buzz Cut leaned over to another agent and whispered something in his ear. A minute later, Fabee appeared at the door. "Sorry, Dag, but we're a little full right now." His Texas twang was in full force. "If you let us finish up, we'll get the scene in presentable order for you."

"With all due respect, Justin, I need to see the scene before it's picked apart. I'll leave Agent Walton outside." Dagny worried that this might hurt Victor's feelings, but he actually looked relieved.

"We've got eight in here right now, and that's a heavy load."

"I'm small," Dagny said. She needed a fresh scene, so it was time to press the issue. "I don't want to have to tell the Professor we weren't allowed in."

Fabee laughed. "Like he's going to call his buddy over this."

Dagny just held his gaze.

"Yeah, well, fuck you, too," he said, handing her plastic bags to wear over her shoes.

"Over here is where he stacked them," Fabee said, pointing to the living room. A pool of mostly dried blood had stained the carpet a deep red, but there were no bodies to be seen. Two trails of blood led to the large pool in the center of the carpet; one from the left rear opening of the room to the kitchen, the other from the right rear entrance to a hallway. A technician was gathering blood samples. Another was lifting fibers from the living-room carpet.

"We figure that one of the kids—the boy, probably—was in the living room when he was shot, causing mom to run in from the kitchen and dad to run in from the study."

"How do you know? You have bullets?" Dagny asked.

"Two in the kitchen wall, one in the hall. We figure the unsub got in from upstairs and came down the steps. He was firing from the foyer when he shot the first kid, then stepped into the living room while he waited for mom and dad."

If the bullets were in the hall and kitchen walls, it meant mom and dad didn't get very far into the living room when they were shot. The unsub was quick on the draw. Dagny stepped back into the foyer and looked up the staircase. Turning around, she saw that a cluster of family pictures hung on wall at the bottom of the steps. A bullet had shattered one of the photographs that hung at eye level. "This went through the second kid?"

"We think so. Boy gets home from school before the girl. Maybe our guy kills the son and the parents, then waits for the girl to come in. Piles the bodies on top of each other for the girl to discover, and while she stands there in shock, he shoots her, too."

"Was she shot in the front or back?"

"From the side, right against the temple. So we don't think she was running. Maybe didn't know it was coming."

"Where are the bodies?"

"Follow me." Fabee led her up the stairs, walking as close to the wall as possible. Dagny followed in like manner. If you were going to destroy part of a scene by walking through it, you made sure that you kept destroying the same narrow path.

There were four bedrooms on the second floor. Fabee led Dagny down the hallway to the girl's room. Two agents were collecting evidence from the girl's corpse. She was lying in bed, facing the wall. Her covers had been peeled away, but they were covered in blood. "She was under the covers when we found her," Fabee explained. Her hands and ankles were tied behind her with a thin rope. Reading Dagny's thoughts, Fabee said, "Fifteen."

Fifteen was so young. Dagny was glad she couldn't see her face. "Why would he tie her up if she was already dead?"

"Beats me."

Dagny inched closer to the body, until one of the other agents held up his hand, asking her to stop. She saw that it wasn't rope around the girl's wrists, but something thinner. A cord, like the kind used to adjust venetian blinds. Dagny walked to the window.

The cord to adjust the blinds had been cut. Fabee followed Dagny over to the window. "Okay," he said. "So he used this cord. But why?"

"I don't know," Dagny said. One of the agents was scraping under the girl's fingernails. Another was lifting hairs from her clothing. She started to feel better about their chances of catching the killer; there was a lot of physical evidence at the site. Dagny lifted her camera from her bag and snapped a few pictures of the scene. When she finished, she asked Fabee to show her the other bodies.

Across the hall Jessica Silvers's body had been propped up on her son's bed. Her hands were tied in the front and tethered to her ankles. A handkerchief dangled from her left hand. Her head tilted forward, as if in prayer. Dagny walked closer and saw that the cord from her ankles was tied to the footboard of the bed. One of the agents tilted Mrs. Silvers's head backward. Duct tape covered her mouth. Her eyes were wide open. Red thumbprints stained her forehead. "He opened her eyes," Dagny said.

"Yep. Those prints are from his latex gloves."

"No clean prints?"

"Not yet, but we're not done."

Dagny snapped some more pictures before following Fabee to the other two bodies. She knew they'd be in the basement. She wondered if Fabee had also figured out the staging.

The basement was cluttered, filled with boxes from the last move—Christmas decorations, an unassembled workbench, baby furniture never passed along. Jack's body lay in the corner of the basement on a table. Dagny knew that the body was supposed to be on a couch, but the table must have been the best the murderer could do. The boy had been gagged, and his mouth had been taped. His arms and legs were tied like his mother's. Dagny stepped closer to get a better angle for the photo and Fabee stopped her. "Don't get too close, Dagny. We haven't started to process these two yet."

Dagny saw a door at the other end of the basement. "That leads to the furnace?"

"Yep."

"And the dad is in there?"

Fabee opened the door and pulled a chain attached to a bare bulb on the ceiling. Dagny peeked inside. Max Silvers's body lay atop a large cardboard box. Tape covered his mouth and circled the back of his head. His ankles had been tied with cord, but his hands were free. Fabee pointed to the ceiling. A piece of cord hung from a pipe down toward Mr. Silvers's body. "It's as if he had been hanging by his hands and his body collapsed," Fabee explained. "Except there is no cord around his wrists. None of this makes any sense. They were all dead before he moved them in place, so why tie them up?"

Dagny knew why they had been tied up. It was a performance—a reference or homage to an infamous murder. "How were the bodies discovered?"

"A boy was supposed to go on a date with the teenage girl. He came by to pick her up at seven, and no one answered. Figured he'd been stood up. Stewed a bit, then called her house at eight and then nine. A little after ten, he decided to stop by again, started to think something was wrong. Banged on the door for a while, then peeked through the living-room window from the back of the house. Police got here a little before eleven. Around midnight, they called in the card." Fabee pointed to Mr. Silvers's left hand, which clenched a white business card.

"No one's moved it?"

"Locals lifted a finger just enough to read it. Knew it wasn't their case anymore and called us."

"What do we know about Mr. Silvers?"

"CFO of an Internet company. Takes restaurant reservations online, or some such thing."

"Any enemies?"

"Never made one. Loved by everyone."

"Where's he from?"

"Born and raised here. Never left."

"Mormon?"

"Everyone here is."

They went back upstairs. Dagny looked out the window. "Why are the men just standing around outside? Why aren't they canvasing?"

"I've got forty agents canvasing. These guys are the next shift. You and Walton will be joining them."

She hadn't realized that so many resources had been devoted to Fabee's investigation. Over the past few days, she'd started to believe that she and Victor were actually ahead of the game, but with so many agents at his disposal, Fabee was undoubtedly in the lead. He probably knew everything she did and much, much more. And now she and Victor would be stuck canvasing, probably for days. "You don't need us," she implored.

"Until we catch this guy, we need everyone we can get."

She sighed. "Can I take pictures of the other rooms first?"

He nodded. "Just stay out of the crime scenes." In other words, stay away from the bodies. The whole house was a crime scene.

Dagny wandered into the kitchen. A large pot sat on top of the stove. Mrs. Silvers must have been cooking dinner. She wondered if an agent, or the killer, had turned off the burner. Dagny touched the side of the pot. It was cold. Maybe the killer didn't want to burn down the scene he had worked so hard to stage. A calendar was affixed to front of the refrigerator by a half-dozen magnets advertising realtors and pizza delivery. On the second of April, Mrs. Silvers was supposed to play bridge. On the fifteenth, just two weeks away, someone had written "taxes" in capital letters. The fifteenth was also the day the killer would kill again, if they didn't catch him first. Dagny thought of the Ben Franklin quote: "Nothing is certain but death and taxes."

She went back through the living room to the short hallway, passing a small powder room and entering the study. Mr. Silvers's desk was in the middle of the room, facing the hallway door. His computer was still on, but the screen was dark. Dagny tapped the mouse with a pen, bringing it to life. Three windows were open on the desktop. One was a spreadsheet—it looked as if Silvers had been drafting some kind of financial report. The second was an e-mail with a link to a web page, sent by one of his friends. The third was a web browser, opened to a page with a picture of Paris Hilton. Her dress had fallen off her shoulder, exposing her breast. Good old Mr. Silvers, Dagny thought. He was so worried for his family that he didn't stop to close the embarrassing web page. Dagny moved the mouse with her pen, placed the arrow over the corner of the browser, and closed the page. He deserved that much, she figured.

Next to the desk was a wall of bookshelves, meticulously arranged so that the bindings of all the books were perfectly flush with one another. One book had been pulled forward. She walked over to the shelves with a pretty good idea of what book it would be. Sure enough, the spine read *In Cold Blood* by Truman Capote.

Had he found the book on the shelf and used it for reference as he tied and bound the bodies? Maybe he'd brought the book with him for reference. Or maybe he'd brought it with him because he wanted the FBI to find it. Dagny took a photo of the book as it stuck out from the shelf. They'd have to test it for prints. It would probably come back to J. C. Adams somehow.

Dagny knew what she was supposed to do. She was supposed to tell Fabee that the bodies had been staged to look like the killings from *In Cold Blood* and let his team test the book for prints.

But then she'd never get the results. They had different goals—she and Fabee. He wanted to make a case for trial. She didn't want there to be a trial.

Snapping on a pair of latex gloves, Dagny carefully slid the book out from the shelf, turned it so it faced forward, then leaned it against the other books. She removed a canister of ninhydrin from her backpack and sprayed the cover lightly. After a few minutes, a series of prints began to appear in purple. Dagny photographed the cover of the book a dozen times, from different angles and distances, to minimize the glare, hoping that at least one of them would be usable.

"Fabee!" Dagny finally yelled, after tucking the canister back in her bag. "I've got something for you."

Fabee appeared a few seconds later, looked over at the book, and saw the prints. "You fuckin' bitch," he said.

"It's *In Cold Blood*. It's the scene he mimicked."

"No shit, Dagny!"

"This book was sticking out from the others. It's got solid prints on the cover. You guys should check every page."

"I'll decide what the fuck to do in my investigation. Right now, I want you out of this house."

Dagny grabbed her bag and headed toward the front door. Fabee followed close behind, stopping at the doorway. Dagny turned around as she walked down the front steps. "I'm sorry," she said.

He took a deep breath. Or maybe it was a sigh. "We don't use ninhydrin. Not on a case this big," he said calmly. "We use the laser light first, so we don't damage the evidence. We try to be the least destructive we can be."

"I understand. I'm sorry."

"It's okay," Fabee said. "Sorry I yelled. It was a good find."

"So you knew it was *In Cold Blood* the whole time?"

"Of course."

"Why didn't you say anything?"

"For the same reason you didn't," he said, closing the door behind him.

Dagny walked through the crowd of agents toward her car. All of them were men. Though Dagny was used to being in the minority, she would have expected at least a few women on Fabee's team.

Victor was down the street, shooting hoops with a couple of middle school kids in a driveway. Dagny tossed her backpack in the backseat of the car and walked over to them, motioning for the ball. The taller of the two kids passed the ball to Dagny, and she took a shot from outside a chalk-drawn three-point line. The ball hit the backboard and dropped in the basket. The shorter kid shook his head. "You weren't trying to get it off the backboard."

"Nope," Dagny said, "but sometimes you take what you can get."

Dagny and Victor spent the rest of the day going house to house, interviewing parents and children who hadn't seen anything suspicious or relevant the previous day. When it grew dark, they retired to a nearby Best Western. Victor went off to get an "actual meal," while Dagny showered and then flicked on the television. It had been a few weeks since she'd paid attention to the outside world. She hadn't missed much. On CNN, Jack Cafferty was ranting about immigration. On Fox, Sean Hannity was kowtowing to some Republican senator. On MSNBC, Ed Schultz was calling people racist. Dagny was about to give up on the television when she flipped to CNN Headline News and caught Nancy Grace on a tirade about the Bubble Gum Thief.

The unsub had now killed six people, and everyone was still referring to this monster as the Bubble Gum Thief. It made Dagny sick. She fired up her computer and searched Google News for "Bubble Gum Thief." It returned some eleven hundred hits. Some were even using the acronym BGT, maybe because it sounded a bit like the BTK killer. BGT was idiotic. He hadn't even stolen bubble gum, Dagny thought. He'd stolen chewing gum.

Dagny downloaded the photos she had taken in the Silverses' home to her MacBook and imported them into the iPhoto library, then created a photocast folder in the left pane of the program, which automatically uploaded the photographs to a server and generated a hyperlink that she sent to the Professor. When he clicked on the link, the photos would download to the iPhoto library on his laptop, and he'd be able to view the pictures in full resolution. If she had simply e-mailed the photos, Dagny would have had to reduce their size, and these pictures, gruesome as they were, had to be seen at full resolution. The photographs of the fingerprints on the book were particularly important—she wanted the best quality possible for IAFIS matching.

After the photos had uploaded to the server, Dagny initiated an iChat videoconference with the Professor. She reviewed the events of the day, described how she found the fingerprints on the copy of *In Cold Blood*, and complained that Fabee was tying them up with pointless witness interviews. "Sometimes we have to play nice so we can do what we want later," he explained.

"We don't have much time. In less than two weeks, he's going to kill six or eight people, and—"

"Six or eight? That's if we're lucky."

"You think he's going for—"

"I'd bet on sixteen. I pray it's only eight."

"You think he's increasing exponentially?"

"I pray to God he's not. If he goes to eight, then he finishes with sixteen and thirty-two. But if he's going to sixteen—"

"Then he goes to with two fifty-six and..." She tried to do a rough calculation in her head, but the Professor was faster.

"And finishes with sixty-five thousand five hundred thirty-six."

"My God, that's an office building *and*—"

"A stadium. It's like Oklahoma City *and*—"

"Hiroshima."

CHAPTER 32

....

April 6—Columbus, Ohio

Melissa sat at the edge of her bed, her feet planted flat on the ground, and her head turned down. Dagny sat across from the girl, on her roommate's unmade bed. Dagny had ditched her navy-blue suit for jeans and a baggy sweatshirt from the T.J. Maxx down the street, and kicked off her shoes so she could sit cross-legged. Normally she'd be taking notes, but this time she left the notepad in her backpack. Victor waited in the car.

After four pointless days of canvasing in Salt Lake City, Fabee was giving her a real witness. Melissa Ryder had called the Bureau's BGT Hotline (even the FBI was using the name) the night before. Fabee had interviewed her by phone, but he was letting Dagny have the first crack at her in person.

She let Melissa tell the story at her own pace, only gently pressing for details when necessary. Melissa sheepishly described the Black Out party and her reluctance to go. She told Dagny about the older man who had handed her a drink and whispered in her ear. About going upstairs to talk. And she told her about waking up, certain that something had gone wrong.

"And then I ran back here. *Here*," she sighed. A cluttered mess of cheap furniture and dirty clothes. It wasn't much of a refuge. Dagny noticed that the walls on the roommate's half of the room were decorated with music and art posters, but Melissa's walls were bare, save for a few stray pieces of tape. Dagny had known a girl in college who'd torn down her posters, too, after she'd been raped.

"You didn't see him again, when you left, when you were running? Since?"

Melissa shook her head, lifting her knees to her chest and hugging them tight. "I can't even see him now."

"Did you tell anyone you were going to the party? Maybe post something about it or tweet it?"

"It was on my Facebook page. Do you think he picked me out specifically?"

"I don't know, Melissa. I don't know." Probably, Dagny thought. "What about the card?"

"When I got back here, I felt it. It was...it was inside of me." The girl wiped away another tear, determined to finish the story. "It was wet and bloody, and it had gum stuck to the back of it. But I could still read it. 'This is my fourth crime,' it said. 'My next will be bigger.'"

"The gum. What did the gum look like?"

"Just regular chewed gum."

"It was chewed?"

"Yes."

"Do you know who chewed the gum?"

"No." Of course not, she seemed to say.

If he'd been the one to chew the gum, then there were would be DNA evidence on it. But it was gone, so they'd never know. "And you threw the card away?"

Melissa nodded. "I tossed it in the garbage can and sat on this bed, hating it. Hating him. Staring at the wastebasket, just staring at it, until I couldn't take it anymore, and then I dumped the whole thing in the Dumpster behind the dorm."

Dagny walked to the window and pushed up the shade. "That one?" Dagny asked, pointing to a big garbage bin in the alley. Melissa nodded. It was suddenly clear why Fabee had sent her to interview Melissa. "Was it in a trash bag when you tossed it?"

"No," Melissa said. "It was just at the bottom of a plastic trash can. I threw the whole thing away. Can and all. Replaced it with another just like it," she said, glancing at the trash can by her desk.

It was frustrating. Melissa had seen him, heard him, touched him, smelled him. But another hour of questions yielded nothing. Dagny offered Melissa a hug and invited her to call at any time, even if she just wanted to talk to someone.

As Dagny reached for the door handle, Melissa stopped her. "Hey, I want to apologize."

"For what?"

"I should have called sooner. I guess I thought maybe you'd catch him, but then he killed that family."

"You have nothing to apologize for," Dagny said. "There's only one person at fault in all this, and I'm going to kill him."

Melissa jumped back, startled by Dagny's promise.

"Catch him, I mean. I'm going to catch him," Dagny said.

Melissa smiled, most likely her first smile in a long time. "Killing him would be fine, too."

Victor was leaning against the car, dressed in one of his increasingly right-sized Brooks Brothers suits. He lowered the business section of *The Columbus Dispatch* as Dagny approached. "Well?"

Dagny had bottled up her rage when she was talking to Melissa, but it was time to vent. "What kind of maniac thinks a rape is smaller than a bank robbery?"

"A homicidal maniac," Victor offered.

She led Victor around to the alley behind the dorm. "You're not going to like this," she said, eyeing the Dumpster.

It only took him a moment to guess what was coming next. "You can't be serious."

"I am."

"Aren't there people to do that sort of thing?"

"What people?" Dagny said, looking around. "It's just us. Sorry, we can't outsource the investigation."

"And what are we looking for?"

"A tiny, crumpled, bloody card."

"From two months ago?"

Dagny nodded. Somewhere, she was sure, Fabee was laughing.

She dialed the Ohio State Facilities Operations and Development department and arranged for a clean bin to be placed next to the one they would search. They borrowed jumpsuits and gloves from the city's hazardous materials unit and bought masks from Home Depot. Once outfitted, Dagny climbed up on the side of the Dumpster and surveyed the contents.

Victor winced as he joined her. "I will never forgive you for this, Dagny."

Almost any Dumpster would have been better than one behind a college dorm. Little of the garbage was bagged—most of it was loose: pizza boxes, soiled clothes, used condoms, chicken bones, and the like. Dagny stepped carefully onto a rail along the inside of the Dumpster and began to pick up pieces of the garbage, inspect them, and then toss them into the clean bin. By dusk, they had sifted through only half of the contents. They sealed the Dumpster and retired for the night.

After they checked into a motel, Dagny showered until the hot water was gone. She was getting ready for a run when Victor rapped at her door.

"Let's get some dinner."

"I'm good."

"Actually, I don't think you're good. C'mon. Let's go eat."

"I'm not hungry, Victor." She started to close the door, but he stuck his foot in the doorway.

"At this point, it doesn't matter if you're hungry. I think you need to be eating."

She was used to conversations like this. Everyone was always trying to get her to eat when she didn't want to. There were more important things than her diet right now. "I don't want to talk about this."

"This isn't over, Dagny."

Dagny sighed. "It never is." She closed the door. Too tired and worn to run, she climbed into bed instead.

If anything, the smell was worse in the morning, having festered in a sealed space overnight. There were literally hundreds of pieces of gum stuck to the bottom of the Dumpster, but none stuck to the back of a card. If the crime gum was still there, at least part of the card would still be stuck to it. Still, they collected every piece of gum and placed them in separate bags, marking the time and place found with a Sharpie.

If Dagny had learned anything at the Bureau, it was this: sometimes unlikely leads pay off, but usually you're just sifting through garbage.

They finished as evening settled, changed out of their jumpsuits, and headed back to the motel. As Victor drove, Dagny checked her phone for messages. She skipped several from Julia and her mother. The Professor had left one: "Still waiting for the fingerprint results from the book—Fabee's holding it up, I'm sure. Also, your mother tracked me down. She wants you to return her calls." Her last voice mail was from Chesley Waxton. Dagny dialed his number.

"I found it. I just wanted to let you know that I had one of the girls scan it and e-mail it to you."

"You found what, Mr. Waxton?"

"The security proposal you wanted."

"From J. C. Adams?" She already had the copy from Adams.

"Yeah, that one, too, but I forgot about another guy who came through and gave us advice. Name was Roberto Altamont."

CHAPTER 33

April 8—Cincinnati, Ohio

"Maybe he was tall."

"Can you give me something besides his height?" She'd asked him this twelve times. They had spent nearly an hour enduring digressions, bizarre non sequiturs, and occasional, inexplicable racist asides. The room was spinning, and Dagny just wanted to lie down.

Victor leaned forward and spoke softly. "Mr. Waxton, this man—Mr. Altamont—may have killed six people, and if so, he's going to kill even more in less than a week, so you can see why it's so important that we figure out who he is."

"He either had a mustache or didn't. I can't remember. It was one way or the other."

"Was he Hispanic? Latino?" Victor asked, since the unsub had used the name Roberto.

Waxton folded his hands together and closed his eyes. "He may have had a dark complexion, but I don't think he was a wetback, if that's what you're getting at."

"Did he speak with any accent?"

"No. He sounded normal."

"How did Altamont contact you?" Victor asked.

"He called me on the phone. I had one of our girls show me the website, and it looked good."

Slowly, the pieces started to come together. Using the name Roberto Altamont, the unsub, it seemed, had created an elaborate and impressive website for his fake security company. (The site was now gone, but Dagny and Victor found a cache of it at archive.org.) When Altamont offered a free security consultation, Waxton jumped at the offer. "Never turn down anything that's free," Waxton counseled, though Altamont's consultation turned out to be rather costly in the end.

Altamont had apparently met briefly with Waxton, who must have told him about J. C. Adams's previous proposal. This would have given Altamont the idea to frame Adams. Dagny guessed that Altamont had planted a magnetic strip somewhere that Adams was likely to touch—on the handrail leading to his front door, perhaps—and then attached it to the misleading tape measure. On a follow-up visit to inspect the premises, Altamont had placed the tape measure with the magnetic strip containing Adams's fingerprints along the doorway.

"Next day, he sends me the report. Everything he recommended was overkill, even more stuff than J. C. recommended, so I ignored it."

"Is there anything else you remember about him? What was his hair like? How did he dress?"

"He had a full head of hair, cut real short, like that actor from around here—you know, his daddy anchored the news." Waxton rapped his fingers on his desk. "Clooney! That's it. Dressed very well. Nicely tailored suit. Slick. Hey, you guys don't think that Clooney kid is the guy, do you?"

"No, Mr. Waxton. We don't think that George Clooney is the murderer," Dagny said.

"Nevertheless, could you search Clooney's house? See if you can find my baseball," he implored.

"Yes, Mr. Waxton. Of course we will," Dagny replied, starting to stand. They thanked him for his time and wandered out to the lobby. Dagny called Lieutenant Beamer and requested that a sketch artist meet with Mr. Waxton. Dagny didn't have high hopes for the sketch, but sometimes people remember a face more clearly when they see it take shape.

As they left the bank, Victor asked, "We're not really going to search George Clooney's house, are we? Because that would be—"

Dagny fell to the ground. Her right knee hit the concrete first, then the left. She braced her fall with her hands, scraping her palms but protecting her head. Dagny sat up and looked back to see what had tripped her. There was nothing. She felt tired and weak, and a little dizzy. Her hands weren't bleeding, but they were sore, and small chips of asphalt were embedded in her skin. Victor extended his hand and helped her up.

"Give me the key," he said. "I'm driving."

"I'm fine." She dug through her bag and found the car keys. Victor grabbed them from her hand.

"*I'm driving*," he repeated.

Dagny climbed into the passenger seat. She could barely keep her eyes open. Maybe she was sick. Dagny felt her forehead, but she wasn't warm. Just tired. She hadn't been running in the past few days. Maybe the lack of exercise had left her feeling depleted. There wasn't time to feel sorry for herself. "Let's head back to Washington and talk to the Professor. Figure out where we are, where we need to go. Maybe he's got a return on the prints."

"Okay," Victor whispered, but it felt like he wasn't listening.

They approached the highway, but Victor passed the on-ramp. "You should have turned," Dagny said, but Victor ignored her. She closed her eyes again and felt the car gliding across the road, riding the hills, taking turns. When Victor stopped the car, they were in front of a Target.

"C'mon," he said, opening his door.

"I'll wait in here." She was too tired to move.

Victor walked around the car, opened the passenger door, and gently took her hand, helping her up from the seat. "C'mon," he said and put her arm around his shoulder to steady her.

"You want a candy bar or something?" she said. She didn't feel like walking.

"Just follow me." He led her into the store, past the clothing section and home furnishings, all the way to the bathroom section, and then ducked into one of the aisles and scanned the shelves. Dagny leaned against a pole, watching as Victor grabbed a box from the shelf, opened it, and set a bathroom scale on the floor in front of Dagny. "Step on this."

"No," Dagny said. "Not this. Not here."

"Step on this, Dagny."

"I'm not getting on that, Victor."

"Why not?"

"Weight is a very private thing."

"You're my partner, Dagny." He said it with affection, as if he were talking to a member of his family. "Please."

"Not partner. Not yet, kiddo." She hadn't stepped on a scale since Mike was killed. What would it read? Maybe 115. Maybe less. Okay, almost certainly less. But was it a pound or two? Or something more? She had no idea what it would read, and that scared her. "Victor, I don't want to," she mumbled. It was the first time she'd been weak in front of him. She hoped that he understood how hard that was.

"Dag, you have to. You need to see it." He walked behind her and put his hands under her arms, then whispered in her ear, "I'm with you on this, okay. No matter what, I'm with you." He lifted her in the air and set her down gently on the scale. As he released her, the dial spun upward, flittering back and forth, before finally settling on a number.

Ninety-eight.

Ninety-eight pounds. She had dropped twenty-eight pounds in three and a half weeks. That wasn't possible. "The scale is wrong," Dagny protested.

"It's not wrong, Dagny." Victor grabbed another box from the shelf—a round tempered-glass scale with a digital display. He opened the box and placed the scale on the floor. "Try it." Dagny stepped onto the scale. She waited for the red numerals to settle the way a defendant waits on a jury.

Ninety-nine pounds. Just one pound more than the other.

"It's not right, Victor." But this time she knew it was.

He grabbed another scale from the shelves and placed it on the ground. Dagny stepped on it. The dial flittered upward and settled quickly. It registered 100 pounds. One more pound than the last one. "See," she laughed through her tears, "just twenty-six more scales and I'll be back at my old weight." She was joking, but Victor still took a fourth scale from a box and placed it before Dagny. She stepped onto it. Ninety-nine pounds.

Victor lifted Dagny off the scale, turned her around, and embraced her. "Let's get you back on track so we can catch this guy, Dag. Okay? We can only catch him if we get you back on track. But you're going to have to let me help you."

Dagny had been through interventions before. They'd only worked when she'd let them. And it was hard to let them.

Victor put his hand on her shoulder and squeezed gently. "I've been reading up on this, and I've got it all figured out. We'll buy one of these scales and take it around with us. Heck, I need it, too," he said, patting his belly. "We'll use the scale every day, just to make sure we're on track. You and me both. What do you say?"

She nodded. "Okay." She'd do this for Mike. Not for herself. "About the scale—"

"Yeah?"

"Let's get the one that said one hundred pounds."

Confrontation number one. In twelve years of schooling, Dagny had never been called to the principal's office. She couldn't imagine why she was being summoned now, with three days left in her senior year. She worried that her mother must have been killed in some horrible accident, but her mother was sitting across from Principal Weathers, tending to her fingernails with an emery board.

"Please sit down," Weathers said. Her familiar smile seemed forced.

Dagny sat in the chair next to her mother. "Is something wrong?"

The principal leaned forward, resting her elbows on her desk. "You were told that you would be valedictorian the other day?"

"Yes." Oh, God, they were taking it away.

"Traditionally, the valedictorian makes a speech at graduation. This year, we've decided…" The principal's gaze moved to the ceiling. "We have decided not to have a valedictory speech at graduation this year."

"Why?" Dagny demanded, nearly jumping from her chair. "I don't understand." She had already written a first draft.

"I could lie to you and say that we want to shorten the ceremony, or that we want more time for the guest speaker." Weathers sighed, then returned her gaze to Dagny. "In light of your health, we don't feel it would send a positive message if we let you speak."

"What are you talking about?" Dagny asked, her voice settling between reasoned discourse and a scream.

"I am referring to your anorexia, Dagny."

The word felt like a slap. Where had this come from? Rumors, whispers, the unkind gossip of jealous classmates? Dagny's mother continued to file her nails and spoke without lifting her eyes. "My daughter is not an anorexic, Mrs. Weathers. I would know. I am her *mother*."

"How much do you weigh, Dagny?"

How dare this woman ask such a personal question. "One hundred and five." It was a lie, but maybe the sweatshirt would fool her.

"I think it's probably less than that. Someone your height should weigh at least one twenty, don't you think?"

"Everyone is different," her mother said, working on her cuticles. "There is no ideal weight across the board. It depends on the particulars of the body. Dagny has small bones. Of course she's going to weigh less. She's lucky."

She wasn't lucky, of course.

Two. "I'm calling your mother," Lindsay announced, standing over Dagny. Her head blocked the overhead light, giving her face an angelic glow. Dagny pulled the covers over her eyes and didn't respond. Lindsay had threatened to call her mother a number of times throughout the semester. This was the first time that Dagny didn't object.

Her first year at Rice had gone well. She'd bulked up to 110 pounds and had held that weight through most of the year. But this year she'd slipped into old habits, and a few new ones—an apple for breakfast, a slather of peanut butter on a piece of low-fat bread for lunch, some lettuce and a tomato for dinner. For the last two months, she'd subsisted on little more than carrots, Diet Coke, and sugar-free mints. It had taken a toll on her body. She hadn't had her period since November. She fell a lot—her knees would buckle on steps and hills. Her skin grew paler, whiter—like a ghost.

And she'd started to grow fur.

April in Houston is like July in St. Louis, but it felt like the Arctic to Dagny. When her body wasn't able to generate enough heat from the few calories she ingested, she began to grow lanugo—a soft, downy fur—on her chest and arms. Lanugo grows on fetuses and the malnourished. The fetuses shed the lanugo before birth.

During all of this, Dagny maintained near-perfect grades. She was president of the debate team. She edited the opinion page of the *Thresher*, served on the school's honor council, and won the state's collegiate mock trial tournament. She pursued all of the varied interests of her life with the same passion that fueled her anorexia, and she was just as successful in these endeavors as she was at starving herself. To be anorexic requires discipline and determination. It was a point of pride for Dagny—though not one she dared voice aloud—that she had never binged and purged. Bulimia was for the weak. Anorexia was for the strong.

Dagny expected the usual indifference and denial that accompanied her mother's visits, but this time was different. "My God," her mother exclaimed, mouth agape. It was enough to scare Dagny. If her mother thought something was wrong, then it was way past wrong.

After exams, Dagny checked into the Sunny Hill Treatment Center in St. Louis. She spent the first month there envying thinner anorexics, looking down on the bulimics, trading techniques, and finding ways to hide food so that it would look like she was eating. When she dropped from 83 pounds to 72, the medical staff moved her to another wing, where monitors watched her eat and the bathroom doors wouldn't lock. Though it helped change her behavior, it didn't change her mind. It took the death of Becky Ettinger to do that.

Becky was a mirror image of Dagny—a brainy white girl from the suburbs, just one year older, an inch shorter, and five pounds lighter. Dagny didn't know her well—they'd spent one evening bonding over music and another playing checkers. One morning, Becky was gone—her bed cleared, her belongings gathered. A rumor spread that Becky had escaped—that she had slipped out in the middle of the night and caught a bus, heading somewhere west. Maybe California. But then another rumor spread that Becky had died from cardiac arrest. Becky's roommate confirmed it. Twenty-one and dead.

Dagny spent the next two months trying to change.

She left treatment healthier and far more self-aware than when she had entered. Armed with tools to carry her forward, she was determined not to backslide. She had learned that a healthy diet and lifestyle could require just as much discipline as starvation, and that reaching the concrete goal of 120 pounds could be satisfying in a way that "thinner" never was. For a while it worked.

Three. "You haven't eaten in a week." Julia dragged a chair over from a neighboring study carrel. "You're scaring me, Dagny."

"That's not true." Dagny had eaten some nuts that morning and a bowl of cereal the day before.

"I mean a meal."

"Do we have to do this here?" The Harvard Law School Library hardly seemed like the place for an intervention.

"No. Let's go to student health."

"Not interested. I have to study."

"How much do you weigh?"

"What?"

"How much do you weigh?" Julia asked.

"How much do *you* weigh?" Dagny retorted.

"One eighteen."

Really? That seemed so high, Dagny thought. She didn't look that big.

"How much do you weigh, Dagny?"

"Ninety-nine," she said, adding ten pounds to the real number.

"If you're going to lie and make up a weight, you should pick one that's reasonable. Even if you were ninety-nine, that would be way too low."

No, it would have been too much.

"Come with me."

"I don't want to, Julia."

"You know you're not healthy, don't you?"

"No." Maybe.

"Come with me."

Four. "You're getting too bony."

"What?" They were under the sheets. His hand was on her hip bone.

"You're all bone, Dag. You need to gain some weight."

"So you want me to get fat, Nick? That's what you want?"

"Calm down, for crying out loud. I'm just saying that you're too skinny. You need to put on a little, that's all."

"How much should I weigh, Nick? What do you want me to be?"

"I don't know. How much are you supposed to weigh? Aren't there guidelines for that sort of thing?"

She pulled his hand off her hip. "So you don't find me attractive?"

"No, of course I do." He kissed her cheek, then her neck. "But you're too skinny, that's all. I don't want you to feel like you can't eat for my sake."

It wasn't for his sake. It was just who she was. She liked it when her hip bones stuck out from her body. She liked it when she could look in the mirror and count her ribs. She liked it when bracelets fell off her wrists, or when a shirt from the juniors' department fit comfortably.

She liked being anorexic.

She knew it was a problem, and she vowed to change. But she didn't change fast enough for Nick.

Five. "I think we need to talk."

Dagny didn't like the sound of that. "About what?"

"You know I like you. I mean that, Dagny."

"I don't like the start of this."

"Well, you need to know that. You're one of the best agents I've got. Which makes this—"

"Am I in trouble?"

He took a deep breath. "Did you eat anything today?"

So it was this.

Six. They sat in a window seat at the Waterfront, a posh steak house on a barge parked along the Kentucky side of the Ohio River. She ate most of her salad and some of her salmon, and it was more than she had eaten all week. They didn't talk about her weight or Roberto Altamont. They talked about movies and college and music and travel. Still, she wondered how long Victor had been planning his intervention, and how he could have known that forcing her onto a scale would be so effective. Numbers meant something to her that words didn't. They were facts, not characterizations; they were statistics, not generalizations. Words were words, but numbers were real. She realized that maybe she was ignoring Julia's calls, and her mother's, not because she was so busy with the case but because she knew she was in trouble again. Was she running from them? Running from help?

After dinner, they checked into the Marriott. Dagny showered, then tossed on a robe and climbed into the bed with her computer. Lieutenant Beamer had sent her an e-mail with the scan from the sketch artist attached. It looked like George Clooney.

An invitation to video chat flashed on her screen, and Dagny accepted. She caught the Professor up on their interview with Waxton and his identification of a man who looked like George Clooney.

"Gerry Cooney?"

"No, George Clooney."

"I don't know who that is. My source in the lab was finally able to get me results from the prints."

"From the copy of *In Cold Blood*?"

"Yes. They're a match."

"Who?"

"The prints belong to an agent."

"You mean one of Fabee's idiots touched the book before I got to it?"

"No. A retired agent. Jim Murgentroy," he replied. "Pack your bags. You're going to Nashville."

CHAPTER 34

April 9—Nashville, Tennessee

From a distance, Jim Murgentroy's home in the Nashville hills appeared to be crumbling, less a dwelling than a small barn or shack sheltering a moonshine still. Largely obscured behind overgrown trees and shrubbery, its weathered plank walls were irregular and crooked. The whole thing looked as if it would topple in a light breeze.

Two large dark sedans belonging to the Bureau—Bucars—were parked in the gravel drive in front of the house. Dagny parked next to them and Victor knocked on the door.

Fabee answered. "I figured."

She was surprised when he let them in.

Despite the ramshackle exterior, the inside of the house was rich and refined, open and airy. Shined blond hardwood floors, red interlocking molding around the ceilings and doorways, Japanese fusuma sliding doors made of bamboo and rice paper. And books. Thousands of books, filling the built-in shelves that lined nearly every wall of the house, even in the bathroom and kitchen. Murgentroy was in the living room, slumped on a plush purple couch. Three male agents stood over him. Fabee motioned for Dagny and Victor to join them.

Jim Murgentroy was drinking a glass of wine, and from the way he was spilling it, she guessed it wasn't his first. He looked about fifty. The wrinkles on his face cut deep. Murgentroy's eyebrows were thick and bushy. He hadn't shaved in a few days, and his hair hung down to his collar in the back. Despite his disheveled appearance, he was a tall, strapping man, and Dagny could see the former agent in him.

Two of the agents with Fabee looked familiar to Dagny. One was tall and thin, the other was tall and fat. Maybe she'd seen them among the Fabulous in Salt Lake, huddled in front of the Silverses' house. The third agent was bald, short, and stocky. He had a thin mustache, wore a tan overcoat, and waved a lit cigar in his hand. He spoke with a high, squeaky voice. "Jimmie, we're just asking for you to help us out. No one thinks you did it." The agent raised his cigar to his mouth and puffed smoke toward Murgentroy, then reached into his inside pocket and found another cigar. He rolled it between his fingers—a neat trick—and then extended it in Murgentroy's direction.

Murgentroy shook his head. "I don't smoke them anymore, Jack."

"There ain't much left in life if you can't enjoy a nice cigar every now and then." Jack held it in front of Murgentroy for a few seconds, but Murgentroy didn't bite. Jack put the cigar back inside his coat pocket.

"The smoke messes up the wood," Murgentroy said, slurring his words.

"Nah," Jack said, walking toward the bookshelves along the back wall. He ran his index finger along the spines of the books. "Nice collection, by the way," Jack said, punctuating it with a ring of smoke.

Murgentroy laughed, then grabbed his glass, splashing more wine onto the table. "I told you the book was mine, jackass."

"But that's not what we're asking."

"If the Bureau didn't want me, why should I want to help it?"

Jack blew a big puff of smoke. "Because you don't want to go to jail."

Murgentroy jumped up from the couch and hurled his glass over Jack's shoulder; it exploded against the bookshelves. Dagny jumped to avoid the flying shards. One landed on Victor's arm and he brushed it off. No one said anything. Jack kept puffing on his cigar. Murgentroy sat back down on the edge of the couch and buried his face in his hands. Fabee and the other two agents stood perfectly still.

Finally, Jack walked around the coffee table and sat on the couch next to Murgentroy. He reached into his pocket, retrieved the cigar, and offered it again. Hand trembling, Murgentroy grabbed the cigar and placed it in his mouth. Jack pulled a lighter from his pocket and lit the cigar for him. After a few puffs, Murgentroy seemed to calm.

"Now look, Jimmie. Someone wants us to think you killed a family in Salt Lake City. We have a plane ticket in your name from Nashville to Salt Lake before the crime, and one after the crime coming back. Plus, we've got you on a flight from Cincinnati to DC right after the bank robbery and before the murder in Georgetown. Now me? I don't think you did it. But the appearance of the whole thing...Plus, you live like a hermit. Nobody's seen you in months. Now, I know it's not you. But I need to know how someone got *that* book with *your* prints from *your* shelf. If I get that, then maybe I can find how he flew under your name. But I need to know about the book."

Murgentroy rolled the cigar from one side of his mouth to the other—another neat trick, Dagny thought—then reached toward the table for his wineglass and laughed when it wasn't there. "In the last year, I've read probably five hundred books. I'm reading two a day. Three sometimes, if I'm not sleeping.

I had seven copies of *In Cold Blood*, each a different edition, including a pristine first printing. I don't know who took the seventh copy, but I'm damn glad he left me the first. As for who could have taken it, I can't help you there, but I wouldn't be inclined to even if I knew." Murgentroy looked up at Dagny and Victor, tilted his head and squinted a little. "I don't know you two, but I'm Jim Murgentroy. You can call me Jimmie. I used to be one of you."

Dagny nodded at the former agent. He smiled back. She wondered what awful thing had led him to retreat to a world of expensive books and cheap wine.

Fabee tapped Jack on his shoulder, then took his place on the couch. "I'm on your side, Jimmie. But how can I clear you if you won't help me?"

"Do what agents do, Justin. Watch me."

The six of them gathered on Murgentroy's gravel driveway. The tall, skinny agent stood on Fabee's right; the tall, fat one on his left. Jack paced back and forth, puffing on his cigar. Victor and Dagny leaned against Fabee's car, which seemed to bother him, so Dagny leaned back more.

Fabee folded his arms and stared back at Murgentroy's house, shaking his head. "Bones and Chunky will take midnight to eight. Dagny and Victor have eight to four."

"On what?" Dagny asked.

"Surveillance," Fabee said.

"We're going to watch him twenty-four seven?"

"Through the fifteenth. See what happens."

Fabee was effectively pulling them from the case again. "You've got a hundred men on this case! You don't need to stick us here."

"It's my case, Dagny. You should be glad I'm putting you at the center of it."

"He's not the guy. You know that."

Fabee walked up to Dagny and leaned in close. "Jack and I are taking four to midnight until I get a couple more goons down here. If I'm not too good for this, you sure as fuck aren't. Christ, I gave you the day shift, you ungrateful bitch!"

"You shouldn't be out here either!"

Fabee stepped back. The red drained from his face, and he smiled. He flashed between crazed and congenial a little too quickly for Dagny's taste. "He's a real suspect. He doesn't have an alibi, and his prints were at the scene. And we've got him flying to Salt Lake City and DC."

"No, you don't," she said. "You've just got tickets in his name. Our man isn't dumb enough to leave a book with his prints at a murder scene, sticking out from the shelves, begging us to find it. And the wrinkles on his face? Melissa Ryder would have noticed something like that." Plus, nobody could mistake that man for George Clooney, Dagny thought. Not even a senile old coot like Waxton.

"Your shift is on," Fabee said, forestalling negotiation. He ducked into his sedan and emerged with a walkie-talkie. He tossed it to Victor. "Bones has another one," he said.

Dagny walked over to the tall, skinny agent, but he shook his head. "I'm Chunky, he's Bones," he said, pointing to the tall, fat agent.

"You're Chunky and he's Bones?"

"That's right."

"I get it," Dagny said. "What do you call Fabee? Handsome? Einstein?"

Bones handed Dagny a walkie-talkie. "We call him Boss, which is what you should call him, too." Bones and Chucky climbed into their sedan and drove off. Fabee started to head to the other sedan, then stopped and turned back to Dagny.

"Bones used to be skinny and Chunky used to be fat. Then the one went on a diet and the other guy's wife died and they kind of traded places. But we'd been calling them by their nicknames for so long...who's gonna change it. As for me, I scored fifteen sixty on my SATs. And since you only managed a fourteen ninety, I don't think you're in a position to denigrate my intelligence." Fabee and Jack walked over to their Bucar, climbed in, and drove away.

Standing next to Dagny, Victor pressed the transmit button on his walkie-talkie and his voice came from Dagny's. "You *were* kind of a bitch," his voice boomed, peppered with static. "I'll camp in the woods behind the house."

Dagny nodded, agreeing to both statements, and Victor ran to the back of the house. Dagny hopped onto the hood of the Impala and leaned against the windshield, staring up at the front porch. The drapes parted and Murgentroy waved, sipping another glass of wine. She knew that a lot of agents retired to lives of family and travel, but she worried that her path would end, like Murgentroy's, with loneliness and solitude.

"Hey," Victor called over the walkie-talkie. "I bought a sandwich for you at the airport. It's in my bag in the car."

"Thanks." She'd had a bowl of Cheerios that morning, along with a banana and a glass of orange juice. It would be a few hours before she was hungry again.

"Are you going to get it?"

"Yes." Maybe later.

The worst part of practicing law had been sitting on a folding chair in a windowless warehouse, sifting through thousands of documents, looking for something that didn't exist. The worst part of the Bureau was sitting on the hood of a car, watching a house, waiting for something that wasn't going to happen. Her eyes rolled left across the front of the house—window, window, door, window, window, carport—and then back again—carport, window, window, door, window, window. Back and forth. Like a typewriter...*tap, tap, tap*, return. She listened to the breeze blowing through the leaves. A squirrel running across a branch. The hum of a car on the road down the hill. A plane flying overhead. Her own breath, in and out, in and out. All the while, her eyes moving...*tap, tap, tap*, return.

The fifteenth of April was only six days away.

Static, then Victor's voice. "This is boring."

Transmit. "The good news is that you can retire in twenty years with a pension."

Another plane buzzed above. A dog barked in the distance, at first loud and ferocious, then just a sad whimper. She saw a flicker of light through one of Murgentroy's windows—the flashing images of a television screen. A glance at her watch. Three more hours until the end of their shift. Three hours until she could—

Victor screamed.

Not an alert or a call for help. He screamed like someone who'd been hurt.

Dagny drew her gun from its holster and jumped from the hood of the car. She sprinted to the side of the house and ducked down behind the bushes. She started a slow, careful crawl toward the back corner, but the sound of two gunshots sent her into a dash. When she rounded the corner, she saw Victor lying on the ground fifty feet away, at the edge of the back woods. Murgentroy stood on the patio with his rifle raised in Victor's direction. He didn't see Dagny.

"Drop it!" Dagny yelled, aiming her gun at Murgentroy.

Murgentroy glanced over at Dagny but kept his rifle focused on the woods.

"Drop it!" Her finger curled against the trigger, ready to fire. Murgentroy wasn't paying attention to her; he was just staring into the woods. "Drop it!" If there was any chance of saving

Victor, this negotiation had to come to a fast end. One more chance. "Drop it, or I'll shoot!"

Without looking at Dagny, Murgentroy dropped the rifle—his arms fell to his sides, and he stumbled back. Then he reached up with his right hand and rubbed his left shoulder. His head dropped forward, as if he'd fallen asleep, and then his whole body collapsed to the ground.

Dagny ran over to Murgentroy and grabbed his rifle, then ran back to Victor. Twenty feet away, she didn't see any blood. Ten, and he still looked fine, almost as if he were sleeping. She was five feet away when she felt a sharp sting pierce her chest, just below her right shoulder. For a second or two, she thought she would be able to carry on, but then she fell to the ground and everything went dark.

CHAPTER 35

April 10

The rough concrete floor felt cold against her cheek. Waking, Dagny took a deep breath. It smelled like old magazines, chlorine, and mold. Other than the faint hum of a fan in the distance, it was quiet. A basement, Dagny surmised. She pushed herself up to a sitting position. It was too dark to see. There were no windows. No light seeped under doors or around corners. She heard something scamper across the floor, just a few feet away. A mouse, maybe. Or a rat.

She reached under her blouse and felt the wound on her chest. It had scabbed over—too small to be a bullet wound, more likely a tranquilizer dart. Had it been hours? Days? She didn't know.

Dagny didn't have the strength to stand, so she started to crawl. It only took her a few strides to reach a wall. She placed her fingertips against the rough brick and moved slowly along it until she reached the corner of the room. Further along the perimeter, she found a small cot. The mattress was only a couple of inches thick and was covered by a rough wool blanket. On top of the cot was an empty metal bucket. Continuing her crawl, she reached another corner, then started to edge along the next wall. Ten feet later she reached out her hand and felt the slick, polished shine of his right shoe.

"Hello, Dagny." His voice was deep, and it glided over the sound of the fan. "Did you sleep okay?" Soothing, yet eerie. Highly enunciated. Practiced, perhaps. Rehearsed.

She grabbed hold of his calf and tried to pull him down. "You're in no condition to do that," he said, stepping out of her grasp. She swung for his leg but missed. She was too tired to chase his voice.

"Who are you?"

"What, no pleasantries first?"

"Who are you?" she repeated.

"Now, now, Dagny, I'm not about to do your job." He was pacing now. The wood soles of his shoes were clicking against the concrete floor with the regular beat of a metronome. "I didn't bring you here to answer questions."

"Then why did you bring me here?"

"I like you, Dagny. I like you very much. But I'm concerned for you."

"I doubt that very much, Altamont." She used the name he'd used with Waxton.

The man stopped pacing. Maybe he was surprised that Dagny knew his pseudonym.

"What happened to my partner?"

"Victor? If I had any faith in him, Dagny, you wouldn't be here right now. Sure, the kid meant well, with that scene in the store, with the bathroom scales and all. But he's no match for you. Don't worry about Victor. Victor is fine."

He'd been watching them in Cincinnati. "Why am I here?" Dagny asked.

"You're here because you're sick. You're here so I can help you get better."

"I don't need the help of a murderer."

"When you need help as much as you do, Dagny, you take it from wherever it comes." He started pacing again.

"So first you try to run me down, now you want to save me?"

"I never tried to run you down."

"In Cincinnati."

"I never tried to run you down."

She was losing patience with this. "Why did you kill Michael Brodsky?"

"Now *that* is a very good question. But I'm not here to answer questions, and you're not here to ask them. You're here to eat." Dagny felt something hit her hand. A tray. On top of the tray, a plate. A sandwich and some pretzels. A chilled plastic bottle, turned on its side, covered in condensation. "I expect you to eat everything I feed you." The taps of his shoes receded.

"And if I don't?"

A couple more taps and the swish of a pivot. "You're of no use to me unless you're well." More clicks against concrete, and then the ping of shoes climbing a metal staircase. A pause. "The door is steel and bolted. I have cameras and microphones planted around you, so I'll be watching. I'll turn the light off whenever I come down here—I have infrared goggles, so I can see you. There's no bathroom—that's what the bucket is for. If there's something I can do to make your stay more comfortable, just ask. You've done nothing to earn my enmity. I know I've done much to earn yours."

She heard the turn of a handle, and saw a sliver of light at the top of the steps. And then there was a blinding light. She closed her eyes and covered them with her arm. It felt like a giant spotlight, the kind they use on car lots to announce clearance sales, or at prisons, to catch escapees at night. Slowly she opened her eyes, squinting. It was just a single bare bulb, hanging from the ceiling.

When her eyes adjusted, Dagny looked around. Four brick walls made a twenty-foot square. No windows. A metal staircase rose at the far corner, a steel door sat at the top. The ceiling was eight feet high and made of concrete. In the center of the ceiling was a small, round grate; the fan suspended above it kicked on, whirring again. Cameras were mounted in the four ceiling corners. Apart from the cot, the bucket, and the hanging bulb, the room was empty.

"Eat!" His voice bellowed from a speaker lodged above the grate but beneath the fan above her. She pushed herself off the ground, grabbed the tray of food, and walked back to the bed. Turkey on rye. Not just the processed turkey from the local deli, but chunks of actual turkey. The kind of sandwich she used to eat the day after Thanksgiving, back at her parents' house. The bread was fresh and thick. Warm. Homemade.

"Eat!"

She raised the sandwich to her mouth and took a bite, then another. Soon, the sandwich was gone, then the pretzels and water, too. When she finished, he commanded her to leave the tray at the bottom of the stairs. She carried it over and set it down, then walked to the top of the steps and tried the door. It wouldn't budge. She climbed down the steps and stared into one of the suspended cameras. "How do I know Victor's okay?" she yelled.

His voice came through the speaker. "I would never lie to you, Dagny."

Lying was beneath him, but murder was fine.

She lay on the cot, her eyes fixed on the metal grate above her head, watching the oscillating fan and thinking about Victor. When she'd seen him on the ground and Murgentroy with the rifle, she'd assumed that Murgentroy had been the shooter. But maybe Altamont—or whoever he really was—had shot Victor with a tranquilizer dart, and Murgentroy had drawn his rifle in self-defense. That made sense. Victor had screamed before she'd heard any gunshots. Maybe he'd screamed when Altamont hit him with a tranquilizer dart, and then Murgentroy came out with his rifle and fired twice at Altamont before Murgentroy himself was felled by another dart.

Or maybe Altamont had shot Murgentroy with a gun. Maybe he and Murgentroy had each fired a shot, and only Altamont had hit his target. Or maybe Murgentroy had fired off two shots but missed with both, and Altamont had used a silencer on his gunshots. In which case, both Victor and Altamont could be dead.

Or maybe Murgentroy was Altamont. But that couldn't be. Murgentroy hadn't shot her—he'd fallen to the ground before she was hit.

It was all a blurry haze. Altamont had said that Victor was fine. For some reason, she believed him.

An hour or two or ten later, she was still staring at the fan, and wondering why he needed her to be healthy. Maybe it was all a game to him and he needed an adversary on the other side. But there were plenty of worthy adversaries. Fabee was a good enough foil. Or Jack. Even the Professor was a worthy enough opponent. Why did Altamont care about her? Maybe it was personal. Perhaps someone from her past? No one she knew matched the profile—it had to be someone intelligent and educated who was knowledgeable about art, reasonably wealthy. She didn't know anyone like that. (Well, Mike had been all of those things.)

So why her? Was he attracted to her? Some criminals were known to develop a romantic attachment to the female investigators who worked their cases. Dagny remembered reading about a murderer in Manhattan who was caught leaving flowers at the front door of the lead homicide investigator. But Dagny's captor seemed genuinely bothered by the necessity of healing her. She doubted there was romantic interest.

Dagny looked up at one of the cameras, wondering if he was watching and listening. "Can I get something to read?" she asked, testing his willingness to accommodate. A few minutes later, the light turned off and the door opened. There was a thump on the ground. When the lights came on, Dagny found a few magazines and a couple of novels at the foot of the stairs. She brought them back to her bed.

The novels were about serial killers—one by Patricia Cornwell, the other by Jeffery Deaver. The magazines were recent issues of *Cooking Light, Sports Illustrated, Rolling Stone,* and *Newsweek.* The *Newsweek* cover pictured a colorful pack of bubble gum and the words "The Bubble Gum Thief: The Latest in Serial Murder." Had the story become this big?

The article was a paean to the glory of Justin Fabee. It began:

FBI Assistant Director Justin Fabee oversees the investigation. The 39-year-old Texan is a tall, thin man, with a piercing stare and a sharp mind. Instead of running the investigation from the FBI's headquarters in Washington, DC, Fabee has taken a hands-on approach, inspecting each of the crime scenes and personally interviewing witnesses. "If you're afraid to get your hands dirty, then you shouldn't be in this line of work," he explains in an accent straight from the West Texas plains. "I'm an assistant director now, but a special agent always." This kind of dedication has earned the admiration and respect of many Beltway insiders. Catching BGT before he strikes again could catapult Fabee to the top of a short list to become the next FBI director. "I don't think about that, not one bit," Fabee says. "I just think about how we are going to catch this guy."

Dagny surreptitiously tore the page from the magazine, folded it into a small rectangle, and stuffed it in her sock. Maybe his fingerprints were on it, and maybe it would matter, if she ever escaped.

She spent the next few hours studying the walls, the ceiling, the stairs—trying to find some way out, some flaw in the design—but there was none. Occasionally she'd look down at her wrist, only to be reminded that he'd taken her watch. Without it, she couldn't tell if time was passing quickly or slowly.

When he turned off the light and delivered dinner, she figured it was evening. The bulb flashed on to reveal sausage lasagna and a mixed-greens salad covered with goat cheese, walnuts, dried cranberries, and a balsamic vinaigrette dressing. Nine hundred seventy-six calories. Plastic silverware. No beverage. "Something to drink would be nice!" she yelled.

A few seconds later, the light went off, and when if flashed back on, there was a bottle of Dasani on the floor. She twisted off the cap and drank. It was cold and refreshing. She picked up the plastic fork and tore into the lasagna. It was good—very good. Made with fresh mozzarella. She tried the salad. The greens were fresh, crisp. When he turned off the light again and came for the dishes, she tried to engage him. "Dinner was good. Did you make it yourself?" He didn't answer.

A few hours later, he killed the light again. Over the speaker, he said simply, "Good night, Dagny." Maybe he had drugged her, because it wasn't hard to fall asleep, even on the cold, hard cot.

When she woke, the light was already on and breakfast was waiting—a ham and spinach omelet, with bacon and melon on the side. She ate the melon and then set the tray on the floor.

"Finish it." The voice reverberated through the speaker.

She needed to engage him. "How did you learn to cook?"

"Just eat, Dagny."

"I'll eat if you tell me how you learned to cook."

Nothing for a few seconds. And then: "Do you know how long it takes to become accustomed to bad food?"

"No."

"You never become accustomed to it. Now eat." And she did.

On the third day, she felt a little stronger. In between her meals, she passed the time doing sit-ups, push-ups, and jumping jacks.

When she'd worked in New York, her office had been on the seventy-third floor. The elevator ride took nearly a minute—more if there were stops along the way. When that elevator door would finally open on her floor, she'd burst out like a SWAT team did on a raid. Now she was living in an elevator that didn't make any stops. Much more of this and she'd go crazy.

After dinner, the lights went dark for a minute, and then a lone cupcake on a tray appeared on the floor. A small lit candle dotted its center. It was April 12, her birthday. Thirty-five years old. She made a wish, blew out the candle, and ate all 300 calories and 14 grams of fat.

Dagny grabbed the Patricia Cornwell novel and climbed onto the bed. She pretended to read, even turning the page every couple of minutes, while she plotted an escape.

After another day of eating, exercising, and plotting, she woke feeling vibrant and energetic. Breakfast was waiting, and she ate all the French toast he left, even though it had been dusted with powdered sugar. (She didn't, however, use any of the maple syrup that had been provided in a small cup on the side.) Lunch was chicken potpie, and though she knew it was full of fat, she didn't complain.

After lunch, Dagny pulled the cot to the middle of the cell and stepped onto it. She stretched her arms up to the grate in the ceiling. Standing on her toes, she was able to feel the grooves on the plate that covered the duct. Tugging on the edge of a groove, she tested the grating. It was solid. Strong. Dagny removed the belt from her pants and looped it through the grating, then back through the buckle. She tugged it tight so that the belt buckle was flush with the grating. Then she tied the other end of her belt around her neck.

Dagny looked into the camera and said, "Good-bye." She kicked off the bed and swung from the ceiling. The belt pressed against her windpipe, cutting off all air. Instinctively, her hands went to the belt, trying to create some space between it and her neck. It wasn't much help—as light as she was, she still was too heavy a force on the noose.

And then, as she'd hoped, the man burst through the door and ran down the steps, flying through the light. She tried to watch him, but it was impossible to focus; she was suffocating. He jumped onto the bed and raised a serrated knife to the belt, chopping through it in three strokes. Dagny fell to the ground and tore off the noose, wheezed for a second, and then ran toward the man.

Diving at him, she knocked him onto the floor and then kicked him in the back. She hurtled over him and toward the stairs, but he grabbed her leg and pulled her to the ground. The knife fell from his hands and just a few feet from Dagny. She stretched, trying to reach it, but he pulled her further away. The full weight of his body fell on top of hers. His hands held her arms. Quick, heavy breaths warmed her ear.

"You know, Dagny, if things had gone differently, you and I would have been great friends."

She twisted her right wrist and slipped it out of his hold, reached forward, and grabbed the knife. Swinging her arm, she drove the knife into his thigh. He screamed, and she rolled out from under him, then threw herself at the steps. His heavy hand slapped down on her shoulder, then shoved her into the wall. Dagny felt the corner of a brick slice into her shoulder. Blood was dripping from her forehead—somehow she'd scraped that, too. Leading with his shoulder, he barreled into her, knocking her head against the wall. She dropped the knife and fell to the ground. Everything blurred for a second. When her eyes found focus, he was standing on the bottom step, holding the knife. She watched as his brown leather shoes tapped their way up the metal steps. In the scuffle, she never managed to see his face.

Dagny pushed herself off of the ground. When she coughed, blood shot from her mouth. Her shoulder ached. She was dizzy and tired and weak, and mostly mad at herself. This had been her one chance, and she had failed. Now people were going to die.

She crawled toward the bed and leaned against it. It slid out from under her, and she fell back to the floor. The blood from her forehead was dripping down into her eye again. She removed her shirt and tore off the right sleeve and wrapped it around her forehead to stop the bleeding, then tore off her left sleeve and wrapped it around her shoulder.

It took all of her energy to stand and push the cot back against the wall, before falling onto the bed into sleep.

When she awoke, she shouted questions at him. Finally, one provoked a response. "How is a bank robbery bigger than a rape?"

A pause, and then, "Sit on the bed."

She complied. The lights went dark, and the clink of his heels fell down to the bottom step. "I didn't rape her," he said calmly.

"Your card was in her vagina."

"I just used my hand." This was less calm, defensive.

"That's still rape." No response. She tried again. "How is a bank robbery bigger than a rape?"

"You tell me, Dagny. You tell me."

"I can't."

He sighed. "The average rapist spends sixty-five months in prison. Under the federal guidelines, a bank robber who discharges a weapon must be sentenced to between eighty-seven and a hundred and eight months! I'm not the one who says it's bigger. You are."

"I don't make the law."

"You *are* the law." A minute passed. Maybe more. "Can't you see that I like you? Can't you see that I'm helping you?"

She stared at the darkness that was his voice. "No."

"What do you want, Dagny?"

Only one thing, really. "I want to kill you."

"That's fair." The clink of his heel meant he'd gone up a step. And then he said, "Mr. Waxton spent quite a bit for that baseball, and nothing on security for his bank." Another clink. "Why do you think that ball was more important to him than his bank, Dagny?"

"I don't know."

"Sometimes there's no explanation for the things we love, I suppose." *Clink, clink.* "But he loves that baseball. So here's a little advice." Three more clinks. "At the end of the day, you won't be able to bring back the Silverses, or Michael Brodsky, or the children I'm going to kill tomorrow. Or even that dog in California. But you can still get Mr. Waxton's baseball back to him. I really hope that you do."

The pain of hearing him say "Michael Brodsky" was quickly eclipsed by the word "children." Dagny tried to speak, but her voice failed her. She spent the night awake, staring into black, thinking about the children, and wondering if he would kill six or eight, or if the Professor was right, and he would kill sixteen.

CHAPTER 36

April 15

The Temptations jarred Dagny from her sleep. She was sitting, blindfolded, and her head was pulled to her right. Whatever held her head in place tugged at the skin of her forehead. She guessed it was electrical or duct tape. There was something stuck in her mouth—maybe a rag—held in place by more tape, which tore at her skin when she tried to move the muscles in her cheeks. She took deep, slow breaths through her nose, trying to squelch her gag reflex. Her arms were tied behind the seat by twine or rope that scraped at her skin. Her feet were bound together. When she tried to kick them forward, she heard a metal clang. She guessed that she had been handcuffed to the base of the seat.

And then the seat jumped.

A bump in the road. She was in a car. More likely the bucket seat of a van. A cool, steady breeze tickled the left side of her face. Air conditioning. She was in the front passenger seat. He was sitting to her left. She knew this because he was singing along with David Ruffin, acknowledging that she wanted to leave him, but refusing to let her go.

Every minute or two the van would stop. Traffic lights meant traffic. She wondered whether anyone could see her. No, surely the windows were tinted. She felt a lingering, piercing pain in her right shoulder, and figured that he had shot her that morning with another tranquilizer dart.

He lowered the volume of the radio. "Dagny? Shake your arms if you're awake." She ignored his request. "Fine, be that way. I know you're awake. I saw you squirming around. We don't have to talk. I just thought you might like coming with me. A field trip, so to speak. Remember field trips?" He paused for a moment. "When I was seven, we went to a farm. We were given pieces of chalk and asked to draw on the cows, labeling the different cuts of meat. Rump. Round. Loin. It was bizarre, really. Meeting these really cool cows, and then drawing on them precisely how they were to be slaughtered. I hope they don't have kids do that anymore. That wasn't a fun field trip. Of course, this one isn't really much fun either." He raised the volume of the radio. First Herman's Hermits. Then Tommy James and the Shondells, followed by Paul Revere and the Raiders, and then the Lovin' Spoonful. She kept a count of the songs to keep track of the time, and distance. Finally, she felt the car shift into reverse. He was parking, and then turning off the engine. The music stopped.

"Well, we're here," he announced.

She heard him open the door and jump down to the ground, and then she heard the rear side door slide open. He grabbed something, then opened the front door and climbed back up to the driver's seat. Dagny felt him lean toward her. His breath was warm on her neck as he spoke. "I guess I'll let you peek for just a second." She felt his fingers graze her forehead, and then he peeled down the top of the blindfold. Even though the window was tinted, the light hurt Dagny's eyes. Then he lowered her window. At first she saw only a blinding flash of sunlight. As her eyes adjusted, a building appeared as a blur, then slowly came in focus. Dagny struggled to make out the white recessed letters on the wood sign just a few feet away: HAYSWORTH ELEMENTARY SCHOOL.

"So I'm sorry about this, but…" Dagny felt a sharp prick in her arm. "We haven't been together very long, Dagny. I'd like to think you've gained a few pounds, and that you're sufficiently motivated to stay on the right course. I'm putting my trust in you, and I hope it isn't misplaced. I expect to see you again, and next time, you'll have the upper hand. I can't wait to see what you do with it." He paused, and then added, "Oh, in case you were wondering…it will be sixteen."

CHAPTER 37

April 15—Nashville, Tennessee

She sat on the swing, gripping the chain links with her hands, struggling to tap the dirt below with her feet. Most of the boys were playing tag; the girls were standing around on the black-top, talking, laughing. Maybe laughing at her. Cassie was alone, always alone.

A man came around the corner of the school and started walking to the back of the lot, toward Cassie. He was wearing grey overalls and work gloves; a duffel bag hung off his shoulder. A janitor, she guessed, though she'd never seen this one before. When he got closer, he smiled. Cassie smiled back. He seemed nice.

"Mind if I join you?"

She shook her head and he sat on the swing next to her.

"All by yourself over here, I guess?"

She nodded.

"What about the teacher? Doesn't a teacher usually monitor recess?" Cassie pointed over toward the far corner of the play-ground, where Ms. Jenkins was sitting on the curb, reading a book and smoking a cigarette. He nodded. "She really shouldn't be smoking." The man kicked his legs just a little and started a slow swing. "Nice day."

She watched his eyes survey the playground, scanning back and forth.

"Where's Danny Deardrop today?

She shrugged.

"Is he here today?"

She shrugged again. Danny wasn't in her class. She'd seen him before, but not today.

"Well, that's a real kick in the pants, isn't it?" he laughed.

She laughed, too. It was a pretty funny expression.

"What are you? I'd guess you're about eight years old, right?"

She nodded.

He pointed over to the girls on the blacktop. "I guess those girls think they're too cool for you? I know what that's like. I've been shut out before, too." He shook his head back and forth a bunch of times, then looked down at his watch. "I guess I'm procrastinating. You know how sometimes you have to do something, but you don't really want to, so you just wait a little while longer, hoping it will go away."

She did know this feeling—like when her mom wanted her to clean her room.

"Well, I guess I can't wait any longer." He hopped off the swing and opened his duffel bag, then reached in and pulled out a small white card. "Honey, I need you to do me a favor. I need you to take this card and run back to the woods on the side of the school. And I need you to stay there for a long time…maybe count all the way to five hundred. Can you do that?"

She nodded. Five hundred was easy.

"And when you come out, I want you to give this card to an adult. A teacher or the principal or a policeman…just any adult. This is really important. Will you do that for me?"

She nodded. Finally, someone wanted to play with her.

He handed her the card. "Now go," he said, patting her bottom as she ran toward the woods.

When she got to the end of the playground, she turned around and he waved for her to keep going. She continued into the woods. *One, two, three, four...*five hundred was going to take a long time, but she could do it. *Eleven, twelve, thirteen...*he didn't say she couldn't look at the card. *Nineteen, twenty, twenty-one...*

THIS IS MY EIGHTH CRIME.
MY NEXT WILL BE BIGGER.

Cassie heard the shots and the screams, but she stayed in the woods, counting to five hundred, standing alone. Always alone.

CHAPTER 38

April 16—Alexandria, Virginia

Dagny opened her eyes and saw a quarter moon peeking through the clouds. The rain had soaked her clothes, and she was cold. She curled her fingers around slick blades of grass and pushed herself to a sitting position. A clump of wet hair smacked her face, and she pushed it back. She felt awful. There were grooves on her wrists and arms from the rope. Her shoulder still hurt. She stood slowly, bracing herself with her arm, then straightening her legs.

Where was she? Dagny noticed the pitcher's mound and then the tennis courts. The sign prohibiting dogs. The basketball court with the eight-foot rims. She was at the YMCA, just four blocks from her house. It was almost considerate. Even monsters have a good side. This one was a good cook, kept his shoes shined, and returned his kidnappees a few blocks from their homes. He even had a certain charm. Of course, so did Ted Bundy...

He kept his shoes shined. The brown Edward Greens. The Deaver book. Flying from Cincinnati to DC. The man sitting next to her, hitting on her. Was it him?

Dagny splashed through the puddles, weaving between parked cars and streetlights. When she reached her house, she plowed through three inches of wet flower bed, grabbed her spare key, and unlocked her front door. Bedroom, maybe? She ran upstairs. When it wasn't on her nightstand, Dagny raced back downstairs and scanned her bookshelves. Adams, Ambler, Baldacci, Block, Bowen, Burke, Cannell, Chandler, Child, Christie, Clark...Connelly. Connelly!

She grabbed the Connelly book and carried it to the kitchen counter. The card fell on the counter when she turned the book upside down. "Roberto Altamont, Consultant." Dagny didn't touch the card, but leaned closer to study its edges. They were perforated. She stared at the phone number under Altamont's name. If she waited, maybe they could trace it. She couldn't wait—she had to know. Dagny grabbed the phone and dialed the number.

At first she heard ringing only in the earpiece. Then she heard it, faintly, from her backyard, too. Dagny grabbed a chopping knife from the block on her kitchen counter and headed to the back sliding door. *Ring.* She slid the door open, and it was louder. *Ring.* There was a small, wet cardboard box on her patio. He'd probably tossed it from a neighbor's yard. *Ring.* She reached down, picked up the box, and opened it. The cell phone inside it rang one more time before going to voice mail. "Hello, Dagny. I'm not available right now, but I'll see you soon, I hope. And remember, always ask, Why?"

Dagny hung up her phone and dialed another number. "Professor, I'm home. I'm home. I'm..." She dropped the phone and fell to the ground.

An hour later, Dagny was in a private room at George Washington University Hospital, being scraped, poked, and prodded, first by a female agent collecting evidence, then by physicians assessing the state of her health. When they had finished, Justin Fabee walked in and closed the door. He took off his raincoat and hung it on a hook, then grabbed a chair and carried it to the side of Dagny's bed.

"Is Victor okay?" she asked.

Fabee sat down. "He's fine. How are you?"

"Is Victor here? Where's the Professor?"

"Victor's in Tennessee. The Professor is on his way."

"What about the children?"

He just shook his head. Her heart sank. Sixteen kids were dead because they'd failed to do their job. With the Silverses, Mike, and Candice, that was twenty-two lives lost.

"I know you're going to have a ton more questions," he said, "but first I need to talk to you about what happened to you, and then there will be some visitors, if you're up for it. A lot of people are happy you're okay. I'm one of them, by the way." It seemed sincere. Even a blue-flamer can have a heart, Dagny figured.

She spent the next two hours telling him most of what had occurred, omitting a few details, like her anorexia and the fact that Altamont, or whatever his real name was, had kidnapped her in order to nurse her back to health.

"Why do you think he took you?" Fabee asked.

"I think he wants to be caught," she replied. "And I think he wants to be sure that we investigate why he did what he did, even after we catch him."

Fabee furrowed his brow. "So he's got some kind of message or political cause?"

"I don't know," Dagny said, though she had some thoughts on the matter.

"You really think he wants to get caught? Did he give you any clues about what we should be looking for?"

"No. He refused to answer any questions. Did Victor ID him?"

"Victor never saw the guy."

"What about Murgentroy?"

"Murgentroy is dead."

"Dead?" Dagny was surprised. She'd assumed that Murgentroy and Victor had both been hit with tranquilizer darts, and that the two shots she heard had been fired by Murgentroy at Altamont. That seemed to make sense, since Murgentroy fell slowly, several seconds after she had heard the gunshots. Most people fall pretty quickly after they've been hit by a bullet. "I thought he was hit by a tranquilizer. He wasn't?"

"Bullet, in the heart. Matches the gun used at the other crimes."

"Are you sure?"

"I lifted the bullet myself."

Dagny was always suspicious of eyewitness recollections. In stressful situations, people pay attention to their immediate needs—an escape path, for instance, or the safety of their children. They don't pay much attention to the cause of the stress. Later, they're likely to merge assumptions with actual recollections. Maybe she'd done this with Murgentroy's fall. But why would Altamont kill Murgentroy? Had Murgentroy seen his face?

"Kidnapping looks pretty good on you, aside from the scrapes and bruises," Fabee said. He rose from his chair and picked up Dagny's medical chart from the foot of the bed. "One-oh-seven. Hmmm. Maybe we can get some ice cream in here." He set the chart down. "So you never saw his face?"

"Not from the kidnapping, but I remember it from the plane. He—"

The door flew open, crashing into the wall behind it. Dagny expected a hulking mass to be standing in the doorway, but it was a slight, balding man with a pointy grey beard and a briefcase. "Thank God!" The Professor hobbled to her bed and grabbed Dagny's hand. "I'm so glad to see you. You have no idea." His face seemed worn by worry, but his smile betrayed his relief.

"Not as glad as I am to see—"

"Enough with the mushies. Did you see his face?"

"Not this time, but last month, on the flight from Cincinnati."

This should have provoked a wide range of questions, but the Professor seemed unfazed. He opened his briefcase and pulled out a manila folder. He handed the folder to Dagny. "Is this him?"

Dagny opened the folder to find a single photograph—the mug shot of a chubby dark-haired man. Chubby? She studied his face more closely—his cheekbones. Dimples. The cleft chin. Could it have been him a decade earlier? Now he was fit, and his hair was greying. Prison could have done that to him. The deep-blue eyes. Yes, she was certain. "That's him. He's thin now. Strong." She looked up at the Professor. "How did you—"

"Profiling. What, did you think I was just twiddling my thumbs this whole time?"

She laughed. "I had no idea."

"I figured it was a Caucasian white-collar type who'd known Berry. Every white-collar Caucasian inmate released from Coleman within the past five years was accounted for. But Berry also spent a short amount of time at other institutions, either awaiting trial or testifying in other cases. Ashland, Elkton, and Memphis. I was able to account for one hundred and forty-eight potential white-collar criminals who had spent time in those prisons. There was one that I couldn't account for. He was six four and named Noel Draker."

Noel Draker. Now they had a real name. A prior case file. Coworkers, family members, friends. If only they had prints to confirm it. Dagny remembered the *Newsweek* article in her sock. She reached down for it, but it was gone. Draker must have found it. Still, it had to be him.

"Why was he in prison?"

"Securities fraud," the Professor said.

"When was he released?"

"Last May. Almost a year ago. Served ten years at Ashland."

"Long sentence." She handed the photograph to Fabee. "You ever heard of this guy?"

Fabee studied it. "Securities fraud, you say?"

"Yes," the Professor answered.

"Never heard of him." Fabee handed the photograph back to Dagny. "Should I have? Is he famous?"

"No, not really," the Professor said. "The case had some notice when it broke. Regional story, mostly."

Dagny handed the photograph to the Professor and tossed her right leg to the floor.

"Just where do you think you're going?" Fabee said.

"To work," Dagny replied. She tried to spear her right shoe with her foot and tumbled to the ground. Fabee helped her up. "Just a little dizzy," she explained. The Professor frowned.

"What?" Dagny reached down and grabbed her shoe, but Fabee tore it from her hand.

"Sorry, Dagny, but you're stuck here 'til the doctors say so."

"Forget that. I feel great." Actually, she didn't feel great, but she felt good enough.

"It's not your call, Dagny. Plus, right now, you're evidence. I don't want you out there," Fabee said.

Dagny turned to the Professor, but he offered no relief. "Sorry, Dagny, but he's right."

"Like you could keep me here," Dagny muttered, apparently not quietly enough. Fabee whistled, and two agents poked their heads through the door. "You've got guards to keep me here?"

"For Christ's sake, Dagny, you were kidnapped. This guy obviously has a thing for you."

"Are they to keep him out or me in?"

"A little of both," Fabee answered, gathering his coat. "Gotta run."

Fabee left, but the Professor remained behind. He sat at the edge of her bed. "You look good, Dagny." And then softly, "We were really scared. You don't know this, I'm sure, but your disappearance was quite a big deal. A lot of people were out there looking for you. It was a big story—in all the papers."

"By name? *My* name?" Dagny hated the thought of being in the press.

"Your mom is in the hallway. Don't know how she tracked me down. Maybe she has an investigative spirit, too. She cares about you a lot."

"I know."

"I'll send her in," the Professor said as he stepped out of the room.

When Meryl Gray walked through the door, her hair seemed whiter than Dagny remembered. She walked slower, and there were more lines on her face. For the first time, Meryl Gray looked like an old woman to her daughter.

Dagny braced for a lecture. Her mother walked over to the bed and leaned forward, then kissed Dagny on her forehead. "I'm so glad you're okay."

"Mom, I'm sorry that—"

"It's okay," she said. "The only thing that matters is that you're fine." It wasn't the hysterical performance Dagny had been expecting.

"I know I haven't called you, but I've—"

"Been dealing with a lot. I know. I understand."

"Who are you, and where is my real mother?"

Meryl Gray smiled. "I don't want to fight anymore, Dagny. I know you need to be you. If that means you're not going to sit at a desk, then I guess you're not going to sit at a desk."

"I'm sorry I told you—"

"I think I always knew. When you were a little kid, I knew. And law school, well, I knew then, too. It was too good to be true. But I don't want to fight. You and I have both lost people that we loved. Let's not lose each other." They talked for a while, about Mike, mostly. After some prodding by hospital staff, Dagny's mother agreed to let Dagny rest. As she was leaving the room, Meryl turned around and started to say something.

"Please, Mom. Don't ruin the moment."

"I'm not going to ruin anything. But if you can't see that this job is crazy after all of this, I don't know what. Herb Roseman would hire you in a minute, and you'd make good money, too."

Dagny grimaced.

"That's all I'm saying." She pantomimed the zipping of her lips and left.

Dagny fell into a long nap. After she woke, Julia and Jack Bremmer came to see her, followed by less familiar faces, drawn by morning news reports that Dagny had been found. Friends and professors from college she hadn't seen in years. Former coworkers from the firm in New York. Marjorie Brodsky and Diego Rodriguez.

Those with past grievances forgave her for the unreturned calls and unanswered e-mails. Eventually the crowd dwindled, and the nurses turned away a few last stragglers, explaining again that Dagny needed her rest. She was surprised at how much she'd enjoyed seeing old friends and colleagues, and at how much she missed the one person who hadn't yet come.

"Hey, Lindbergh baby!" Victor was carrying a vase full of red and yellow tulips. "I know, I'm late; I'm completely late. You wouldn't believe what I had to do to get past the nurses." He set the flowers by the windowsill and walked over to Dagny, reaching out to shake her hand.

"You idiot," she laughed. "This time a hug is actually appropriate." She squeezed Victor tightly.

Victor chuckled. "Are you okay?"

"Apart from the fact that we let this madman kill sixteen kids, I'm doing okay. What happened at Murgentroy's?"

"I was hit by a dart."

"Yeah, I know. I heard you scream like a girl. What do you remember after that?"

"Waking up in an ambulance. And I didn't scream like a girl. That's just how a scream sounds."

"What about Murgentroy? Did you see him come out with his gun before you were shot?"

"No. I guess I was down before that."

"How long did they keep you in the hospital?"

"Overnight. Checked out the next morning and went looking for you."

"That's cute."

Victor seemed hurt, and Dagny regretted it immediately. "It's not cute, Dagny. I almost found you. Was a heck of a lot closer than Fabee's million-man army, too. This morning, in Nashville, I found his place."

"You found it?"

"Just north of Nashville, in Goodlettsville."

"And you know it's the place?"

"I was standing in the basement when I got the call that you were okay."

"Seriously?"

"Yes."

"Wow. How did you find it?"

"I kept tracing Rowanhouse's dummy corporations, looking for property holdings. When he killed those kids in Nashville yesterday"—God, was that only yesterday, Dagny thought—"I figured he might have a place nearby. There were forty properties around Nashville that these companies had purchased at one time or another, thirty-nine of which seemed to be in the hands of legit people. One didn't—and we hit it this morning."

"Who's *we*? Fabee and his crew?"

"You kidding? They weren't paying any attention to me. I had seven of Goodlettsville's finest with me."

"You got a search warrant from a federal judge for that?" Ownership by a dummy corporation hardly seemed to be enough to justify a warrant, and even if it were, it would have taken days to explain the convoluted circumstances to a judge, including Reginald Berry's sex-change operation and the theft of the Matisse.

"Heck, no. We got one from a Davidson County judge."

"On what grounds?"

"On the grounds that the local property tax for the house was eight months delinquent."

"You're better at this than I ever imagined." Dagny playfully punched him in the shoulder. "What did you find there?"

"Not much. Your hair, his. A couple of prints. He kept it pretty clean. Nice kitchen—really well stocked. Not much else in the house."

"ID on the prints?"

"It's Noel Draker. It's him, Dag."

That's all they needed. Between Dagny, the Professor, and Victor, they had a physical ID, profile, and now prints. "Fabee's got a hundred men on the case," Dagny said, "and yet the three of us identified him first. How is that possible?" But it didn't matter—all that mattered was that the man she was going to kill finally had a name.

"I still don't get it. What was it all about?" Victor asked.

"What?"

"Kidnapping you. Why'd he do it?"

"He said he was worried about my health." She paused. "About my eating. He fed me. Gourmet meals, even. Said he could never become accustomed to bad food. I guess he was talking about prison food."

"It doesn't make any sense. He tries to run us down in Cincinnati, but now he wants to save your life?"

"He says he didn't try and run us down in Cincinnati."

"You believe him?"

"I think so."

"Then who tried to run us over?"

She shrugged. "You got me. Just how upset is your fiancée about you working this case?"

He laughed. "Almost that upset."

"What about my stuff?"

"Computer, gun, bag? It's in my car."

"Then let's get out of here." Dagny jumped out of the bed and slipped on her shoes.

"You're supposed to stay."

"Draker killed sixteen elementary school kids yesterday. I'm not going to hang out in a hospital bed. Help me distract the guards."

Victor's stern grimace slowly melted away. "Okay." He headed toward the door, then turned to Dagny. "So have I reached partner status yet?"

"You're up to master apprentice."

PART III

THE WHERE

CHAPTER 39

April 17—Cincinnati, Ohio

Chuck Wells reached down, grabbed the handle of the rolling steel door, and pushed it up. Dagny stepped forward and surveyed the warehouse holdings. "It's like the last scene of *Raiders of the Lost Ark*."

"Raiders of the what?" the Professor asked. Victor was back in Virginia, tracing through Rowanhouse's and Draker's finances, so the Professor had decided to hit the field with Dagny. She was glad he hadn't said anything about her escape from the hospital, and was worried that he would slow her down.

"Like the last scene of *Citizen Kane*."

"Oh, yes."

She surveyed the first row of boxes. All of the boxes had been taped shut, and all of the tape had been slashed. "Fabee's team has already been through these?"

"Fabee himself was here last night," Wells said.

"Alone?"

"No, he had an entourage. A fat guy, a skinny guy, and a guy with a high voice."

"I've met them," Dagny said.

"I'm sorry," Wells replied. She really did like Wells. He wished them luck, then left them to the files.

There were 451 boxes, stacked five tall and three deep, against the left wall of the room. Two folding tables and a couple of chairs were crammed between these boxes and the first of twenty-eight rows of metal shelves, each filled with more boxes. Fluorescent bulbs flickered overhead. There were no windows. The room smelled like sawdust. Dagny had spent weeks in similar warehouses when she was a lawyer. Back then, she was billing a client over $300 an hour, staying in posh hotels, and indifferent to her work. Now she was staying in a Radisson at the government rate and trying to save lives.

With less than two weeks until Draker's next atrocity, it might have seemed absurd to spend several days looking through boxes of old documents. But the government had spent a year investigating Draker's securities fraud case, and if Dagny and the Professor could spend a few days learning a year's worth of knowledge, it seemed like a good investment of time.

They started with the investigators' documents, poring through case summaries, 302s, grand jury transcripts, warrants, pleadings, and motions. The files were a mess. Pleadings were mislabeled. Folders were out of order. Some of the interview memoranda and photographs listed on the file index were missing.

When they finished with the Bureau's case file, they moved to boxes of seized documents and artifacts: photo albums, checkbooks, e-mails and calendars, contracts, pay stubs, tax returns, deeds, tens of thousands of pages of incomprehensible spreadsheets, an equal volume of lines of code. Luckily, most of the financial documents had been scanned or saved in electronic format. Dagny sent copies of the discs by overnight courier to Victor, who stood a better chance of understanding them than they did.

They sifted through Draker's personal items—clothes and trinkets and credit-card receipts. While the Professor thought it was useful to know that Draker had once purchased a 1787 bottle of Château d'Yquem, it meant little to Dagny. She was looking for signs of personal animus and finding little. At times, the whole endeavor felt like a waste. Some of her time felt more wasteful than others, like the hour she spent thumbing through Draker's college yearbooks, wondering how the smiling kid in the pictures had turned into a monster.

They ate junk, mostly. Pizza and burgers and fried chicken. Deli trays. Egg McMuffins. The Professor tried his first burrito and liked it. Dagny forced herself to eat. Time was slipping, and the stakes were high. She needed her energy and health.

After seven days, they'd looked through every box, if not every page. None of the documents individually set forth a complete narrative, but altogether they told the story of the rise and fall of Noel Draker.

The rise: Noel Draker was born in Bethel, New York, on August 16, 1969. When he was seven, his parents moved to Cincinnati, where his father managed a record store, and his mother sold crafts at Findlay Market. Neither parent seemed to know what to make of their extraordinarily gifted son, a chubby and awkward boy who skipped the first, third, fifth, and seventh grades.

When he was ten, Dewitt Country Day, an exclusive private high school, offered the young prodigy its first academic scholarship, perhaps anticipating that Draker might one day be a valuable alum. On his first day of class, a teacher stayed late to teach Draker how to program in BASIC. Two weeks later, Draker taught the teacher how to program in COBOL, Pascal, and Fortran.

The computer lab was a refuge for a poor prepubescent kid surrounded by the rich and spoiled scions of Cincinnati's elite. When Draker was twelve, the school asked him to develop software for recording attendance and grades. Draker's final product did both, and kept track of the school's budget, analyzed teacher performance, and generated automated tuition invoices. Draker tinkered with these programs obsessively—slashing unnecessary lines of code and adding new features. During his senior year, the thirteen-year-old sold copies of the bundled software to a few local schools, and then, as word spread, to schools across the country. He used profits from these sales to pay off his parents' mortgage and buy a plane ticket to Boston, where he enrolled at MIT.

For Draker, the MIT computer lab was a geek fraternity, full of jokes and pranks, kinship and camaraderie. Fellow students accepted the fourteen-year-old whiz kid as one of their own. It was a welcome antidote to the high school years spent as an outcast. Draker gained contacts and knowledge, and most importantly, confidence. After graduation, he moved to Washington, DC, where he spent two years developing troop- and supply-tracking software for the Department of Defense. Convinced the same tools would be valuable for corporations, he moved back to Cincinnati and started Drakersoft, Inc. Within three years, his company had grown to three hundred employees and was coding complex database software for some of the nation's biggest companies—billing software for Procter & Gamble, reservations software for Delta, and asset-management software for banks and investment companies. Although his company grew considerably, Draker did not simply recede into corporate management. He was reputed to have reviewed every line of code that left his company.

With wealth came women—an endless parade he marched into ballrooms and galas. Cincinnati was a family town, so the old-money establishment disapproved. He bought some acclaim with a series of extravagant fund-raisers, philanthropic donations, and a whole fleet of "ships"—sponsorships, fellowships, and scholarships. In 1990, Drakersoft's long-awaited IPO pushed its CEO's net worth to more than a hundred million dollars. He moved to a mansion in Indian Hill, the suburb of choice for the city's wealthy elite. Locals called Draker's impressive estate "the Playboy Mansion."

The fall: At the time of Draker's IPO, there was lots of money in the company. Revenue had grown exponentially, and investors expected this to continue. Draker knew that it could not. A competitor's package of database-and-accounting software started to gain market share, and while its database design was inferior to Draker's, its accounting system was much better. But the best accounting software on the market had been developed by Seymour Dutton, a twenty-two-year-old college dropout who had founded a start-up in Atlanta called Systematic Software.

Draker and Dutton negotiated a deal; Draker would package Systematic's billing software with Drakersoft's database software and pay Systematic 25 percent of the net profit.

The deal with Systematic helped Drakersoft maintain its market share, but Draker was hardly assuaged. Convinced that the software industry was headed for a downturn, Draker instructed his financial officers to invest the company's savings in a diverse array of non-technological holdings. The corporation established separate, affiliated entities to manage these investments. A shopping mall in Columbus. A resort on the coast of South Carolina. An automotive parts factory in Oregon. Dozens and dozens of other varied interests. Draker's managers served as officers for these corporations, overseeing their operations while continuing to spend most of their time fulfilling their duties to Drakersoft.

The funds Draker invested in these holdings were recorded as loans to be paid back at a stipulated rate of interest. Draker hoped that these payments would provide a steady stream of income to the company, but many of the businesses struggled to make the promised payments. Under SEC regulations, Drakersoft was obligated to disclose the poor performance of these investments in its quarterly and yearly financial reports, and write off the bad debt on its balance sheets. And if it had, the company's share price might have dropped a bit, and shareholders could have raised issues with the company's management, perhaps even scrutinized executive pay. Still, it was something the company could have weathered. But instead, the company committed fraud.

In order to mask the investment losses, Drakersoft recorded some of the sales of the Drakersoft-Systematic suite as stand-alone sales of Drakersoft's database software, pocketing Systematic's 25 percent, while recording this money as though it had come from its affiliated entities as payment of interest on their debts. Eventually, an account manager, Frank Ryder, noticed what was happening and notified some of the company's large institutional investors. Two days later, lawyers filed a class-action lawsuit on behalf of Drakersoft's investors. Chesley Waxton was one of the named plaintiffs. News of the lawsuit prompted the SEC and DOJ to investigate Drakersoft's books.

During the two years before the fraud was exposed, Noel Draker threw lavish parties. He established foundations and endowed libraries and schools, splashing the Draker name on every invitation, sign, and plaque along the way. He was revered around town for his civic philanthropy and envied for his private wealth. But after he was accused of fraud, Draker was reviled and despised. His personal holdings no longer inspired people, they just made them angry. His charitable work, once admired, now engendered disgust. The Draker name, plastered on so many things throughout the city, became a badge of shame.

After the civil suit was filed, Draker held a press conference and promised that there had been no fraud. Three months later, he held another press conference and admitted fraud had occurred, but claimed he didn't know about it. He said nothing more on the subject for nine more months, and then he said only one word. The word was "Guilty"—it was his plea in Judge Nagel's courtroom.

The nine months between his proclamations of innocence and guilt must have been difficult for Draker. His employees caved, copping pleas and pushing the fraud higher and higher up the corporate ladder. Twice he was assaulted while walking to his car. The first time was at night, with no witnesses around. The second time was in the afternoon. A crowd watched Draker's assailant beat him until he bled. His first attacker was never caught; the second was sentenced to thirty days in jail. When reporters asked him why he beat Draker, the man said only, "He had it coming." Around the water coolers in Cincinnati, people agreed.

Though the fraud had been designed to obscure small financial problems, its discovery created big ones. Customers canceled orders, unsure whether Drakersoft would be able to provide customer support. Banks withdrew letters of credit. Creditors foreclosed on secured property.

Throughout the investigation, one group stood behind Noel Draker—his loyal cadre of gifted programmers. They wrote letters to the paper and spoke to television reporters, defending the honor and integrity of their boss. But even their support flagged when an FBI agent, Jim Murgentroy, found a smoking-gun memorandum to Noel Draker from his CFO outlining the plan to hide investment losses. Draker denied knowledge of the memorandum, but several distinct fingerprints on the paper suggested otherwise. The government offered the CFO, Max Silvers, a deal; and Silvers corroborated the memorandum.

"Murgentroy and Silvers are dead. Ryder's daughter was raped. Waxton's bank was robbed and his prize baseball stolen," Dagny said.

"He's settling scores," the Professor said. And there would be no bigger score to settle than one with the man who sent him away for ten years. They decided to visit Judge Edward Nagel.

CHAPTER 40

....

April 25—Cincinnati, Ohio

Judge Edward Nagel was eighty-eight years old but didn't look a day under a hundred. Aside from a few random patches of white hair and the whiskers sticking out from his ears, he was entirely bald. His forehead was covered in dark spots and sloped down to a long, thin nose that supported round wire-rimmed glasses. He wore a maroon, pin-striped vest that clung tightly to his chest; a gold chain dangled from his vest pocket. He smelled like old cologne.

"Please, please, have a seat," Nagel insisted, gesturing to the chairs in front of his desk. His amiable, gracious nature surprised Dagny. In her experience, federal judges were rude, insufferable egomaniacs, though still preferable to state judges, who were rude, insufferable buffoons.

First appointed to the bench by President Johnson (Lyndon, Dagny assumed, but it could have been Andrew), Nagel was the longest-serving judge in the Southern District of Ohio, and as such, had the largest courtroom and nicest chambers. The dark mahogany shelves behind Nagel's desk held ancient law treatises, long obsolete. His walls were covered with awards and commendations issued by lawyers hoping to curry favor. Nagel's portrait hung high on his wall and stared eerily down upon them.

"I'm sorry, but who are you two?" Nagel asked with a big smile and a befuddled air.

Was he senile? They'd just introduced themselves less than a minute before. "I'm Special Agent Dagny Gray, and this is Timothy McDougal, also with the Bureau." Because the Professor had no formal title, she'd been introducing him by name only. It made introductions a bit awkward. "We'd like to talk to you about Noel Draker."

Nagel leaned back in his monstrous chair. "I've read in the papers that Noel Draker is suspected of being this Bubble Gum Thief," Nagel said. "Is this true?"

"It is, Your Honor," the Professor replied. "If you wouldn't mind, we'd like to ask you some questions."

"I am but a public servant, so of course I will oblige. But I should warn you that elements of professional responsibility may require me to defer comment on a case."

"I understand completely," the Professor said, though Dagny knew of no professional limitations on the judge's candor. "You met Noel Draker during the case, I presume. He appeared in your courtroom?"

"Yes, and here in chambers several times as well. I saw the devil in that man, you know. That's why he went away for ten years. Would have been more if I could have managed it, but my hands were tied. Sentencing guidelines. Gave him the most I could. Good Lord, I wish it could have been more. Wouldn't be doing all this nonsense if he were still in jail."

"What do you mean when you say you 'saw the devil in that man,' Your Honor?" the Professor asked.

"I've been on the bench for a long time." Nagel looked over to Dagny. "Longer than you've been alive, sweetheart." The befuddled old man seemed to disappear as Nagel's tone became serious and angry. "And I've seen many guilty men. Some thieves, some murderers, and some monsters. When you see enough of them, you learn. Now me, I don't begrudge a man his wealth, if it's *earned*. But it has to be *earned*. The rich are not devils, per se, but you'll find devils amongst them. And Noel Draker was the devil. I said it in chambers to his face once. I told him he was the devil. And now he's proved me right."

"You called him the devil?" Dagny asked. "Had he said something to upset you, Your Honor?"

"The opposite. The man didn't talk. Just stood there. The prosecutor would say the most awful things about him, but Draker just stood there. I would say awful things about him, and Draker just stood there. When they found that smoking gun—his own fingerprints on that document, for Christ's sake—they brought it to chambers. Draker was right there," he said, pointing to Dagny, "right where the young lady is sitting, and he just smiled. Smug little bastard just smiled. His fancy-pants lawyer starts yelling and screaming about an ambush, finding this memo so late in the game, but Draker just smiled. Smug little bastard. The devil, you see."

Edward Nagel wasn't senile at all, Dagny thought. He remembered small details from the case—the memorandum, the defense attorney, even Draker's smile. "So Mr. Draker never said anything to you?" Dagny asked.

"No. But the smug bastard smiled. I'd have given him twenty if I could've, just for that smile."

As the crime beat reporter for *The Cincinnati Enquirer*, Bill Lusenhop had spent the better part of two years tracing the trials and tribulations of the Draker case. Dagny guessed that Lusenhop was in his mid-thirties now, which would have made him just a kid when he covered the Draker case the first time. The reporter rolled a couple of extra office chairs into his cubicle for his guests.

Lusenhop was so excited by their visit that he was rocking in his chair. "Editor wants the whole front page, now that they're saying he's the Bubble Gum Thief. I get a leg up since I wrote about him before. Can you confirm that he's the primary suspect? You're the one he kidnapped, right? I mean—"

"I'm afraid we need to ask our questions first," the Professor interrupted.

"Fair enough. Ask away." Lusenhop kicked his feet up on his desk and leaned back, resting his hands behind his head.

"Did you ever talk to Draker?" the Professor asked.

"Not on the record. But he called once in the middle of the frenzy, all hot under the collar about something I wrote. Wanting a correction."

"About what?"

"Chickenshit. We ran a picture of him at a party, dressed to the nines, living it up even though his company was under investigation. Ran it with the headline 'The Party Goes On.' He called me, indignant, insisting that the photograph was three years old, that he wasn't partying. Said we were defaming him."

"Were you?" Dagny asked.

"Defaming him?" Lusenhop laughed. "The man was a thief. How can you defame a thief? But he was right about the picture. Who knew? People send you things, you take their word. It was chickenshit. On the big stuff, though, we were right all along. When he pled guilty, it was vindication."

"How did you get assigned to the case?" the Professor asked.

"First the business page had it, and then the legal beat, but within a couple of weeks they realized it was going criminal, so they gave it to me. I'd just started and didn't have a lot on my plate. It was all I did for two years."

"How do you sustain a story like that for two years?"

"You cover every angle. Tell the stories of the investors. Track down his failed investments and show what went wrong. One day, you give voice to the employees who lost their jobs. The next day, you get one of his teachers to talk about what he was like in high school, and it turns out that his shop teacher knew all along that the kid was no good. They even sent me up to MIT, and I talked to people there. Spent a few weeks working the angle that he might have defrauded the DOD. There were a couple of congressional hearings—one led by former representative Alden Brownman, another by Senator Henry Watkins. They didn't go anywhere, but looked promising at the time. Found a girl who claimed to have slept with him, talked about the secret life of Noel Draker. She failed a lie detector, so who knows. And then there was the stuff from the investigation. A little more would leak out each day. One of your guys used to call me all the time. I'd give him stuff and he'd give back. So I always had something."

"Who was feeding you information?" Dagny asked.

"I don't give up sources." Lusenhop plopped his feet back onto the floor and picked up a pad of paper and a pen. "Not for free anyway. If you've got some good information for me, then maybe—"

"Just one more question from us, and then we can get to yours," the Professor said.

"Shoot." Lusenhop was drawing a circle over and over again at the top of his pad, trying unsuccessfully to contain his glee.

"Was there anyone he loved?"

"Loved? I don't think so. If you want to know about his sex life, you'll have to ask Knippinger—he wallows down in that gossipy stuff. I report on real news."

"Who is Knippinger?" Dagny asked.

"He's our society man. Now it's my turn to ask the questions."

"It will have to wait for another time," the Professor said. "We've got to go."

Charles Knippinger was waiting at the bar in the Hilton Netherland Plaza hotel, an elegant art deco shrine clad in marble, velvet, and rosewood. It was a massive space—the ceilings were at least thirty feet high, adorned with giant murals framed in gold. It was the kind of place where you expected to see Cary Grant or the Thin Man.

Knippinger was a slight man, however, with a round face and thick eyebrows, probably in his late fifties, Dagny guessed. He wore a light-blue suit with a white handkerchief peeking up from the monogrammed pocket and a mischievous smile. Spotting Dagny and the Professor, he set aside his martini and tapped the seats of the nearest barstools.

"Nothing could delight me more than talking about the curious case of Noel Draker," he said.

They took the offered seats, and the Professor began the interview. "I assume you've read that Noel Draker is suspected of being—"

"The deliciously named Bubble Gum Thief? How tacky is that? You'd think they'd drop it now that he's killing children, but no, they keep using it. Once a name grabs hold, I guess it won't let go."

"What was your impression of the man?" the Professor continued. "You wrote about him often."

"Well, this isn't Tinseltown. You write about what you have. And in Cincinnati, that's always been Pete Rose, Marge Schott, Jerry Springer, and the occasional Noel Draker. Oh, and Draker was a particularly wonderful case. It sums up what Cincinnati is all about, if you ask me."

"How so?"

"It's all about forgiveness in the end. In Cincinnati, there are some things we can forgive and some we can't. If you're Pete Rose and you bet on baseball, you're forgiven. If you're Marge Schott and you say some ugly, racist things, you're forgiven. As mayor of this town, Jerry Springer visited a prostitute—*paid her with a check!*—and he was still reelected, still forgiven. But stealing? This city doesn't forgive that. Anything but that."

"Are you surprised that he could be responsible for the recent violence?" the Professor asked.

"It's funny, but I visited him in prison once. I had an idea for an article, a bit of satire, really. I was going to compare Cincinnati's upper-crust society with prison life—the idea being that they were not that different. So I visited Draker, thinking that could be the lead for my article. He'd been locked up for five years by then. I was surprised by our encounter. Physically, of course, he'd changed—the fat was gone—he was trim, even gaunt. His hair was turning grey. His forehead, wrinkled. But the biggest difference was in his eyes. They were hollow, lifeless. This was a man who threw giant galas, who used to laugh at his own jokes, who—for all of his faults—had been vibrant and full of life. But the man who sat across from me didn't answer my questions or even seem to acknowledge my existence. He wasn't rude. It just felt like he was a dead man. I don't know what happens in prisons, but I know that whatever happened killed Noel Draker." Knippinger paused. "So I never wrote the column, because, as it turns out, Cincinnati high society is not very much like prison at all."

"Did you like Noel Draker?" Dagny asked.

"I don't like or dislike anyone, really. It's an impediment to my job. But I suppose I had a certain fondness for him. I often wonder whether things would have worked out differently if he had listened to a bit of advice I gave him at our first meeting.

"It was at one of his early charity events, a black-tie affair right here, at this hotel, in the Hall of Mirrors—the nicest room in the city. Everyone who was anyone was here—the blue-chip suits from Fourth Street and a lot of the politicians—judges, councilmen, commissioners, congressmen. I was chatting with Draker at the bar. It was rather endearing really, he simply didn't have a clue how things worked. It was all well and good to throw charitable functions, but no one in that room really cared about the Children's Defense League or building a new wing at The Christ

Hospital. I pointed out the politicians and told him, 'That's where you need to start sending your money.' But Draker was a stubborn man. He found these people so odious, so distasteful, that for all the money he gave away, not a cent went to anyone that really mattered."

"Anyone ever love him?"

"There was often a beautiful woman on his arm. It was never the same woman twice. I don't think he was ever in love. Yet he always seemed like he was nursing a broken heart."

"Who really knew him? His software developers?"

"His programmers loved him, but they didn't know him. And that love faded once he pled guilty. Percy Reynolds liked him. Probably knew him as well as anyone. But when they found that memo, it must have broken Percy's heart. He had actually believed his client. I think that's why he gave up law and moved away."

"Draker's defense attorney?" Dagny had seen his name in the pleadings and newspaper articles about the case.

"He was the city's best trial attorney, one of the few in town with a national reputation. Bit of an iconoclast. Highest-paid attorney at Dresser and Edmunds, the top firm in the city. Quit the firm the day after Draker was sentenced. Disillusioned, I suppose. He'd put his credibility on the line for Draker. The whole thing made Reynolds nearly as hated as his client. Poor guy had to leave town."

"Where'd he go?"

"New Mexico, I heard. Truth or Consequences."

CHAPTER 41

April 26—Truth or Consequences, New Mexico

Under better circumstances, Dagny might have followed the sign to Trinity Crater, the hole in the ground created by the first nuclear bomb test in 1945. Instead, she kept driving south on I-25, past Polvadera and Socorro and a dozen other little towns full of busted barns and burned-out churches. New Mexico was beautiful and brown and broad and bare. A cool, dry desert breeze blew through the window, so clean and fresh and rich that one breath did the work of two.

The Professor had stayed in Cincinnati to follow other leads, so Dagny was traveling alone. Fumbling with the XM radio, Dagny settled on CNN and its nonstop coverage of Noel Draker, aka the Bubble Gum Thief, hoping she might learn something new, and relieved when she didn't. When a talking head mentioned her by name and referenced "her lover, Michael Brodsky," she changed the station.

Her lover. It sounded so illicit. But what then? "Boyfriend" sounded like an infatuation. "Partner" sounded like a business arrangement. There wasn't a word to accurately describe what Michael Brodsky had meant to her, just as there wasn't a word to describe the pain she felt hearing his name.

Percy Reynolds lived in the bulbous hills between downtown Truth or Consequences and Elephant Butte Lake, a forty-mile-long reservoir created by a concrete dam on the Rio Grande. It wasn't exactly lush, but it was green, and there weren't any tumbleweeds blowing around. It seemed like as good a place as any to run away to.

Dagny pulled into the driveway, walked up to the front door, and rang the bell. A barefoot man wearing red boxer shorts and a stained white undershirt answered. He was tall and thin and had long white scraggly hair, down to his shoulders. It had probably been a week since his last shower.

"Percy Reynolds?"

"Yes, ma'am." He had a deep, authoritative voice, the kind God must have.

She showed him her creds.

"Figured." He reached under his shirt and scratched his belly. "Well, c'mon in."

Reynolds led her across a tile floor into the living room, where Dagny took a seat on the couch. "Drink?"

"Water."

While Reynolds went off to the kitchen, Dagny surveyed the room. There were seven empty pizza boxes piled on the floor; eight wineglasses held remnants of red wine in the small cavities just above their stems. Crumpled paper towels and napkins had been tossed about. The house smelled a lot like a Blues Traveler concert Dagny had attended in 1995. "I guess you had a party?" Dagny asked when he returned.

"No," he said, handing Dagny a glass of water.

"Do you mind if we start?"

"I told you on the phone that this would be a waste of time, Agent Gray."

"Yeah, well, I thought I'd give it the old college try, since lives are in danger, you know."

"So I've heard."

"Two hundred and fifty-six people on May first. Sixty-some thousand on May fifteenth."

"I've seen the reports, yes."

"And you know that Noel Draker is believed to be responsible for the crimes in question."

"I am bound by the attorney-client privilege. Anything that I know about Mr. Draker is protected by that privilege."

"There are limits to the privilege, Mr. Reynolds."

"Please, call me Percy. A lawyer can and should reveal confidences when they reflect their client's intention to commit a future crime. Mr. Draker never said anything to me that would indicate an intention to commit a future crime."

"I'm a lawyer, too, Mr. Reynolds. And I believe that there are moral rules that supersede our profession's self-selected ethical canon."

Reynolds smiled. "If you wish to lambaste our profession, Agent Gray, then you've chosen the path to my heart. But this is the one time our profession got it right. If you take away the attorney-client privilege, no man will be free to speak with his lawyer, and if that happens, then no man can be fairly represented in court. And while I detest what my profession has become, I believe people should be fully and fairly represented in courts. A layman doesn't stand a chance alone. Hell, even with a lawyer, he's up a creek."

There had to be some way to break through. "Your client kidnapped me, Mr. Reynolds. He shot me with a tranquilizer and kept me in a basement."

"And he murdered your boyfriend, from what I hear. I understand your position, Agent Gray. You are a victim, quite possibly of my client. There are good reasons why we don't let victims determine the ethical rules of representation. I feel awful for your loss. I feel awful for what happened to you. But I don't feel responsible."

"He raped a girl."

"I doubt that."

"We've kept it out of the news for the girl's sake. She's nineteen—a college student. Frank Ryder's girl. You remember him. Your client shoved his calling card up Ryder's daughter's bloody vagina, Mr. Reynolds." She paused to let him think about this. "That's the man you're protecting with your ethical canons."

For a second or two, it looked as if Reynolds might break, but then he stiffened. "I'm sorry, but my principles are all I have."

If asking about Draker directly wasn't going to work, maybe she could take a different tack. "Why did you leave Dresser and Edmunds? You were the top trial attorney in the city. And you weren't so old that you had to retire."

"Why did you quit the law, Agent Gray?"

"It wasn't what I had hoped it would be," Dagny replied.

"It wasn't what I hoped it would be," he repeated. "Well, I guess I felt the same way."

"Will you tell me about it?"

He hesitated for a moment, and then said, "The more trouble the person is in, the more help they need. That's the nature of the profession. When you take a client, it's your duty to serve him to the best of your abilities. When I took Draker's case, the firm didn't care about anything except the money that came in the door. But then the Draker story got too big and the public got too angry. In the letters to the paper, people called me a 'hired gun,' a 'pariah,' a 'devil.' But around the office, it was worse. I'd over-hear it in the hallways, in the bathroom stalls. There wasn't a trial lawyer at Dresser and Edmunds who would have amounted to a hill of beans if I hadn't been there to teach them." His voice was rising, as if he were giving an anguished closing argument. "All the bankers and businessmen they represented were appalled and outraged that I represented Draker. Never mind that my partners never would have had those clients if it weren't for me!" Reynolds paused, then shook his head. "I'm sorry, I got a little carried away."

"No, Mr. Reynolds. Please continue."

His tone softened. "Dresser was a dying firm when I joined. I brought it back to life. My first big trial was a doctor who had been arrested for killing his wife. The doctor was a pillar of society, well respected in the community, so it was a big case. And I won it. And I won the next trial, and the one after that. The line of people wanting to hire the firm stretched out the door. In four years, we grew from forty lawyers to seventy-five. I didn't ask for credit. I didn't ask to be managing partner. I didn't even ask for a corner office. I asked only that I be allowed to try my cases."

"When Draker came around…"

"By then, the firm was on top. They didn't need the publicity. They didn't *want* the publicity. You know, Draker went bankrupt paying off the creditors, so the last few months, I worked his case for free. Everyone at the firm was outraged. 'Do you know how much you're costing the firm?' they'd ask. No one asked how much I'd made the firm over all those years. So I quit."

"Why did you move all the way out here?"

"I was married once, to a wonderful lady who moved out while I was asleep. She left a note behind that said 'I love you, but we both know that you're better off alone.' This is a good place to be alone. And I always liked the name of the town. You can have your truth, or you can have your consequences. That's kinda the way life is."

"Have you found the truth?"

"The more important question, Agent Gray, is whether you have."

"That's why I'm here."

"Well, then I guess you're going to have to keep looking."

"Even though the consequences are so huge, Mr. Reynolds?"

"The consequences are always huge, Agent Gray."

"I wish you didn't speak in riddles."

"What can I say? I'm still a lawyer." Reynolds scratched his head through the long white hair that didn't make him look like much of a lawyer at all. "When Noel Draker dies, I hope you keeping looking for the truth, Agent Gray."

"When and *if* Noel Draker dies, it will be too late for the truth."

"It's never too late for the truth, even if you've already suffered the consequences."

There was nothing more to be gained from the conversation. Dagny told him she was ready to leave, and he walked her to door.

As she headed to her car, Reynolds called out, "Good luck, Dagny Gray. I hope you save lots of lives. And find that baseball, too."

The baseball again. She turned around. "Find the baseball?"

"Waxton's ball."

She fixed her gaze on him. "I should find Waxton's ball?"

"If you can," Reynolds said.

"You've talked to Draker?"

"I can't answer that. Any conversations I've had with him are privileged."

"Draker told me to find that ball, too. You've talked with him! Recently!"

Reynolds shrugged. "Privileged. Sorry."

"If I had a board and some water—"

"Hypothetically, if I talked to him, we didn't talk about any future crimes, so again, it's privileged. And hypothetically, if I talked to him, it was so that I could urge him to stop. Beg him, really."

"And hypothetically, I assume, he said no."

"Hypothetically, he did. Hypothetically, it left me despondent. As maybe you can see, I've been on a bit more of a bender than usual. He's not a bad man, Dagny. He's just a broken one."

"Not broken enough for my tastes."

"Ten years, for a man like that, with murderers and gangbangers—"

"Not broken enough—"

"A learned man, scraping for survival—"

"It doesn't justify—"

"Trapped with a bunch of savages who called him Reed, because he was the only one who could read above a fifth-grade level. An educated man, locked in a place empty of knowledge. Indifferent guards—"

But she wasn't listening to him anymore. "You know what no one did to the man? No one killed him."

Reynolds nodded. "You're right."

"And you had the man here, at your house, and you didn't stop him. And you won't give me the slightest help."

"There's nothing about any of this that isn't tragic."

"And if I subpoena your phone records? Talk to your neighbors?"

"It wouldn't help. I wish it would. But you'd just be wasting your time."

Reynolds turned around and disappeared into the house. Dagny climbed behind the wheel of her car and put the key in the ignition. Every step of the investigation had led to another, but now she didn't know where to go. To Nashville, to find out more about the children? To Bethel again, now that she knew Draker was born there? Things seemed easier with Victor or the Professor at her side.

She looked into the rearview mirror and saw the saddest eyes she'd ever seen. Maybe it was time to go home. The whole endeavor was absurd—crisscross the country, track down Draker, avenge Mike's death. How did this ever seem remotely possible? It was lunacy, aided and abetted by the Professor's massive ego, Victor's naïveté, and the confluence of circumstance. If the Professor hadn't saved the life of the president's father thirty years ago, she would have attended Mike's funeral. She would have visited his grave. She would have gathered photographs and mementos and placed them in a box. She would have received flowers and condolences. She would have grieved the way normal people grieve after they lose a loved one. And maybe she would have even shed some of the sadness from her eyes.

She was lost in thought when a dark sedan pulled up next to her. Brent Davis climbed out of the car and headed toward Reynolds's door.

"Hey!" Dagny called, rolling down her window.

Brent turned around and smiled. "You stalking me?"

She stepped out of the car. "I was actually here first. Get the cheesecake, by the way."

His smile grew, and when she extended her hand, he embraced her instead. It was awkward, but not unpleasant, even comforting.

"I guess you came out here for the same reason I did," Dagny said. "Maybe you'll have better luck. He gave me nothing."

"Really?"

"Everything was privileged," Dagny said. "Doesn't matter that people have died, or that more will."

"Typical lawyer," he said, and then added, "Not that all lawyers are—"

"They are. Believe me. How's life with the Fabulous? Fabee got any leads?"

"There are so many people involved now, you wouldn't believe it. They're tracking down everything. Talking to Draker's grade-school teachers. Looking at his college transcripts. They think they have a make on his shoe from a print in Salt Lake, so they're trying to figure out where he might have bought it. Stuff like that, only thousands of things like that. Fabee's got two hundred people going through Draker's financial records, hoping to trace them to a base of operations. It's crazy. There's so much going on that no one can put it all together. Too much information and not enough processing. Maybe the Professor was right."

"I don't know," she said. "If a thousand people working a case are too many, I think it's pretty clear that three people aren't enough."

"Where are Victor and the Professor anyway?" Brent asked.

"Victor's back in Arlington, going through Draker's finances— trying to do the same thing Fabee has two hundred people doing."

"And the Professor?"

"Talking to people in Cincinnati."

"Like who?"

"He talked to Frank Ryder last night."

"Does Ryder know what happened to his daughter?"

"No. His daughter hasn't told him, and we're not going to."

"Did Ryder say anything interesting?"

"Not really. Said he discovered Draker's fraud while comparing an old printout of sales figures to the computer database. Noticed a discrepancy and realized that someone had changed the numbers to cheat Systematic out of its share of the profits. Ryder claims he was outraged, so he went to some of the company's biggest shareholders with what he found."

"Before he went to his bosses?"

"Before he went to his bosses, and without notifying Systematic." Dagny saw Brent raise his eyebrows at this. "Yeah, you'd think he'd go to Systematic first to tell them they were being cheated."

"What was up with that?"

"My guess is that he didn't go to the shareholders at all, but that he went to a lawyer, either to protect himself or to see how he could profit from the mess. And then the lawyer set him up with some shareholders, promising him a kickback from the proceeds of the lawsuit."

"Any evidence of this or just speculation?"

Dagny shrugged. "The Professor said he had a nice house."

"Are you guys going through Ryder's books?"

"Why bother? If anything illegal happened with the lawsuit, the statute of limitations has long run out; and anyway, there's a more important criminal to deal with."

"So where are you going now?" Brent asked.

"I haven't got a clue."

"I'm going to Nashville in a couple of days. Want to meet up there?" he suggested.

"Try to figure out why he went after the kids?"

"Yeah."

"Maybe. Let me check with the Professor."

"Just let me know," Brent said, starting toward Reynolds's house.

"It's a waste of time, Brent. He's not going to give you anything."

"I know. But I've got to put a check mark on a form."

She nodded. "It might be worth looking at his phone records, talking to his neighbors. Just in case Draker tried to talk to Reynolds."

"We've done that already. Nothing."

Reynolds was telling the truth—he just wouldn't tell all of it.

The sky was blue and almost clear, save for the thin wisp of a cloud that seemed to follow Dagny up I-25, dropping a light rain too soft for her to keep the wipers on, but enough to require an occasional swipe. Every few minutes, a car would pass the other way and the driver would wave hello. Nobody waved in DC. New Mexico felt like a different planet.

The cloud wasn't the only thing following Dagny. A black Navigator appeared behind her on the horizon, then gained on her. When it pulled within a car length, Dagny tapped her brake. The suggestion was not taken, and the driver drew even closer, tailing just a couple of feet from her rear bumper. Dagny grabbed her Glock and pulled to the side of the road. The Navigator parked behind her. Dagny marched toward the driver's side of the Navigator, leading with her gun. A young man with curly brown hair jumped out of the car, hands in the air. He was tall and gangly, wore a dark suit, and couldn't have been older than twenty-five.

"Jesus Mother of Mary, don't shoot!" he yelled, trembling so much that he fell back against the side of the SUV.

"Who are you?" Dagny demanded. The man started to reach his hand toward his back pocket. "Hands up!" she shouted, grabbing him by his arm and spinning him around so his chest was against the car. She cuffed his wrists and removed his wallet from his back pocket. He slumped to his knees. "Travis Bickelford?" she asked, reading his driver's license.

"I'm not here to hurt you!" He was crying, not just a few tears, but hysterical sobs. "I'm not. I'm not. I swear to you. Please, please."

"Then what are you doing?"

Bickelford spun around to face Dagny. He tried to wipe his tears away with his shoulders, but with his hands cuffed, they wouldn't reach his face. "I'm hoping to make you very, very rich," he stammered.

"Explain," she demanded with her gun still pointed at his chest.

"Can you lower the gun?"

"I could," she said. But she didn't.

"I work for Harvey Lettleman. Do you know who Harvey Lettleman is?"

"I haven't a clue."

"He produces movies. Big movies. Did you see *Catbird's Fall* with Angelina Jolie? That was his film. *A Moon to Rise*? *Three Strikes and Out*? Help me out here."

"I've heard of those movies."

"Well, he produced them. He's big. I can't believe you haven't heard of him. Lettleman Films? He's got four Oscars. Two for sound, but still…Look in my wallet. I've got business cards."

Dagny fumbled through Bickelford's wallet, past two condoms, several hundred dollars in bills, and a picture of Bickelford with Christina Aguilera. His business card seemed legitimate. Raised letters and no perforations.

"Why are you following me?"

"Harvey wants the rights to your story."

"You're kidding me."

"I swear I'm not. Your story is killer."

"You're wasting my time because of this?"

"Wasting your time? I don't think you understand how much money he's talking about. I'm supposed to start with two point five, and then negotiate points after that."

"I don't even know what that means, but I'm not interested."

"You don't understand. This thing is happening no matter what. Kate Beckinsale is already attached. They're looking at Matthew McConaughey for Mike. Look, there's going to be a movie, so you might as well make some money off of it."

If he hadn't mentioned Mike, she probably wouldn't have done it, but he did, so Dagny swung hard and hit him in the face. Bickelford fell to the ground.

"Two point five is just the starting point! I said we could negotiate!"

"I'm working a case, Mr. Bickelford, and you're wasting my time." She turned to walk to her car.

"Your boss is totally cool with you working with us. He doesn't need you anymore."

Dagny spun back around. "What are you talking about?"

"Fabee. He said he doesn't need you."

"You've talked to Fabee?"

"Not me. Harvey did. How do you think we knew where to find you?"

Fabee was a snake. "I'm sorry, Mr. Bickelford, but I'm working this case. You can make your movie and I can sue you later, but for now, I've got a plane to catch." Dagny tossed the young man his wallet and walked back to her car.

"What about the cuffs?" Bickelford yelled, his arms still bound behind him. "You can't leave me here in cuffs!"

"It'll be better for the movie," Dagny replied. "Makes my character more complex!"

Speeding away, Dagny felt good about roughing up Bickelford and leaving him cuffed. A few minutes later, she felt bad and turned the car around.

Bickelford was still sitting on the ground, leaning against his car. Dagny walked over to him and unlocked his cuffs.

"I knew you'd come back," he said, smiling. "I knew it. You're one of the good guys, and the good guys always come back. That's why we're going to make the movie, you know. Because people like to see good guys on the screen."

"Bickelford, you don't even know how this thing ends. How can you make a movie about it?"

"That's the great thing about Hollywood, Ms. Gray. We can end it any way we want. You sure you don't want in on this? We don't have to go with Beckinsale—we can go younger. Maybe Evangeline Lilly—you know, the girl from *Lost*?"

"Good-bye, Mr. Bickelford," she said, hopping into her car.

Two hours later, Dagny was standing in line at the ticket counter at Albuquerque International, studying the list of outgoing flights, trying to figure out where to go next. She was thinking about Kate Beckinsale and Matthew McConaughey when Officer Eduardo Perez called. After talking to him, she bought a ticket to San Diego.

CHAPTER 42

April 27—Chula Vista, California

On a normal day, she'd be running on pavement at a quarter past five, but the last month had worn her down and she needed that extra sleep. So she ignored the knock the first time, and the second, and the third. But the fourth knock was loud enough to get her out of bed.

Dagny grabbed her gun from the nightstand, tossed on a bathrobe, and walked slowly to the door. The peephole showed an empty hallway, but she could hear the soft murmur of hushed voices. *I know she's in there*, said one. *Oh, we're going to get her*, said another.

She flung open the door and pushed into the hallway. They were hugging the walls, a dozen of them, maybe more, and they pounced quickly, circling around her and firing a dozen shots from the front, and more from behind.

"Drop them!" she yelled, swinging her gun back and forth like a lawn sprinkler. No one obeyed. They knew she wouldn't fire inside the airport Hilton. It was too late anyway. They had gotten their photographs of the gun-wielding, bed headed abductee/special agent, and now they were headed for the elevator.

The only man without a camera stayed behind. He wore a grey herringbone suit and carried a brown leather briefcase that matched his shoes. The light from the wall sconces reflected off his hair. He smiled and shook his head. "Vultures, I know," he said.

"What's happening?" Dagny asked. Despite the adrenaline from the encounter, she was not yet fully removed from the haze of sleep.

"There's a price on your head. People are paying top dollar for pictures of you. It's only going to get worse. The video cameras will be next."

"Who wants this stuff?"

"These guys were from *People*, the *National Enquirer*, *OK!*, a bunch of freelancers, and the *Los Angeles Times*. Only one legitimate news outlet in the whole bunch. I'm talking about *People*, of course."

"Who are you?" she asked, rubbing the sleep from her eyes.

"Harold Booker," he said. "I'm not here for a hard sell. I book Anderson Cooper, and I'm just here to say we'd love to have you on."

"Your name is Booker and you're a booker?"

"Yeah. It happens. A guy named Bill Headline used to work at Headline News."

"Well, I'm sorry, Harold, but I'm not going to do Anderson Cooper, or anything else."

"I understand. You've got your investigation to worry about. That's cool. But being on our show could help the investigation. If you educate the public about what you're looking for, you get tips."

"I'm not interested."

"Fair enough." Booker reached into his suit jacket and pulled out his business card. "Just in case you change your mind," he said, handing it to Dagny.

"How did everyone know I was here?"

"I suspect that the hotel clerk noticed your name on the registry, made some calls, made some money."

"And that's how you found me?"

"No, no—not me. We're CNN, Ms. Gray. We're not like the vultures. Assistant Director Fabee said we'd find you here."

"How kind of him," she said.

Booker nodded and started to walk away, but turned back. "Look...use a fake name. Wear a hat. You're the pretty woman at the center of the biggest story in the country. You've got to be careful."

"Alright." It was good advice.

"And you look like a mess, by the way. Your hair is going every which way, and you've got pillow lines running across your face. Right now those vultures have some really atrocious pictures of you. Now, they don't *want* to run those pictures. They want pictures of you looking pretty—because that's what sells. You might not care right now, but these pictures are going to be on the Internet for fifty years, and you might care later. Clean yourself up, take a shower, put on some nice clothes, and then step out on your balcony for some fresh air. They'll be waiting in the parking lot below for the retakes. Then call the bellhop and promise him twenty bucks if he drives your car around to the service entrance, and sneak out of here." He started back down the hallway.

It sounded like a good plan. Dagny called out to him. "Thanks, Harold." He smiled, then went on his way.

Dagny showered and dressed, then spent twenty anxious minutes drying her hair, wondering if vanity would doom her, if she'd eventually find Draker twenty minutes too late to prevent his next act of violence, if people would die because she wanted to look pretty in some photographs. When she walked out onto the balcony, the cacophony of shutter-clicks was overwhelming. After three minutes of glamour shots, Dagny called the bellhop, picked up her car at the hotel's service entrance, and headed off for Chula Vista.

In the tumult of a chase, every decision is a nightmare. Little decisions, like sleeping in until six or spending twenty minutes drying hair. Big decisions, like spending—perhaps wasting—a day talking to a family about its murdered dog. It seemed unlikely that the Luberses held the key to the case. But then again, Draker chose them, didn't he? Chula Vista was a long haul to shoot a dog for no reason.

Officer Perez was waiting on the Luberses' lawn when Dagny pulled up. He was handsome and trim and younger than Dagny. She remembered a time when she was always the youngest person in the room, and then she remembered that it was a long time ago.

He smiled as she approached.

"It's nice to meet you, Eduardo."

"Dagny Gra-a-ay," he said, drawing out her last name. "I feel like we're old friends," he said, slightly embarrassed when it came out. "I mean, it's been a long month, hasn't it?"

"You have *no* idea."

"I've seen you on the news. There are a million questions I'd love to ask, but I know you're busy, so I won't."

"You can just wait for the movie."

"The what?"

"Long story."

The Luberses lived in a cul-de-sac kind of neighborhood, with thick, lustrous lawns and sidewalks large enough for a Big Wheel to comfortably pass a stroller. It was a quiet morning. There were no cars on the streets. No paparazzi snapping photographs. No federal agents trampling lawns. No Hollywood lackeys slowing her down.

"So they remember something about Draker?"

"Yep."

"Did you tell anyone about it?"

"Just you. I guess I probably should've called that guy running it all. What's his name? Fabee? But I thought I'd call you instead."

"Why's that?"

"I don't like that Fabee guy. A few weeks ago, he called and chewed me out for FedExing the bullet from Tucker to you. Said it violated protocol, chain of custody. What do I know about protocol for federal murder cases? I work in property crimes for the Chula Vista Police Department."

"Dog killing is a property crime?"

Perez shrugged.

"Michael Vick should have lived here," Dagny said, causing Perez to laugh a little.

"I've got a buddy who's a feeb on Fabee's team. Apparently, Fabee's not very happy that you and your partner were able to ID Draker before any of his guys could. And I kinda think that's great. So as far as I'm concerned, you're my official contact on the case."

It was nice to know they were annoying Fabee.

Martha Lubers led them inside, over and around piles of toys and children's books. She looked to be in her early thirties. Another younger person with an actual life. One more person to envy.

"I'm so sorry for the mess," Martha said. "We actually cleaned up. You wouldn't want to see it on a normal day."

"No problem," Dagny replied, taking a seat on the living-room couch.

Fred Lubers walked in and greeted them. He was a big, burly man, and his handshake was firm. "I saw you on the news," he said to Dagny.

"I've been getting that a lot lately."

"You're even prettier in person," Martha chimed in.

Any resentment Dagny felt toward the younger married woman evaporated. "Thank you very much. Officer Perez tells me that you two think that Tucker had a connection to Mr. Draker."

"Just Fred," Martha said. "I wasn't there."

"It's not really Tucker," Fred explained. "See, Tucker is really Tucker Two, but along the way, the Two got dropped. Tucker One was the dog I had when I was a kid."

"Where'd you grow up?" Dagny asked.

"In Washington, DC."

"What happened with Tucker One?"

Lubers lowered his head. "He died."

"No, I mean, with Noel Draker? What's the connection?"

"Oh, right," Lubers said, looking up. "I was walking Tucker—Tucker One that is—down the street in DC one day. This must have been twenty years ago. I was fifteen or sixteen. And Tucker was kind of a rambunctious dog, not at all like Tucker Two, who was a sweetheart—"

"He really was," Martha added.

"But Tucker One had never bit anyone before. He'd bark a lot, and sometimes jump up at a person. Excitable was all. But one day this fellow comes walking down the street with a lady friend—a cute woman with frizzy blonde hair—and they're holding hands and laughing, and something about him I guess Tucker didn't like. So as we're walking by, Tucker turns real fast and chomps on this guy's left hand. He's holding the lady's hand with his right, but his left hand was swinging free and easy. It wasn't a bad bite, but it pierced the skin and there was some bleeding. I yelled, 'Bad Tucker,' but it was too late—it had already happened. So the guy demanded my name and address, and the next day he came by with a medical bill and insisted that my father pay it."

"Did your father pay?" Dagny asked.

"No, he refused. He told the guy that Tucker'd been provoked." Lubers shook his head. "The guy hadn't provoked Tucker. I just told my dad that because I didn't want Tucker to get into trouble."

"The dog-bitten man…did he ever say his name?"

"Not that I remember. But they've been talking about this Bubble Gum Thief a lot, and they've been showing a lot of pictures of Noel Draker on the news, and especially the old ones, and I'm certain it's the same guy. Which is crazy, I know, because he didn't even seem that mad back then, even when my father refused to pay the bill. He just kinda nodded and went away. So for him to come out here, all these years later, and kill Tucker Two, who did nothing wrong, nothing at all…it just doesn't make sense."

"The woman Draker was with…could it have been Candice Whitman?" Dagny asked. It was just a hunch.

"The TV lady. No. It didn't look like her."

"I assume you never saw or heard from Draker after this incident?" Dagny asked.

"No, nothing." A dog barked from the backyard. "Tucker Three," Fred explained.

Dagny walked over to the back window and saw a German shepherd puppy frolicking in the grass. Maybe they were calling him Tucker Three for now, but in a couple of years, he'd be just Tucker. If only every loss were so easily replaced.

CHAPTER 43

April 28—Nashville, Tennessee

The numbers four, three, and zero cast a bright-red light upon the room. Dagny shoved a spare pillow in front of the alarm clock. It was too early to get out of bed, and she was too tired to try. She was about to drift back asleep when Brent Davis rolled over and gently caressed her cheek, then kissed her softly on the lips. Last night's wine was still on his breath, and probably hers, too.

"You should have picked me as your partner," he said. "We could've been doing this every night."

Brent cupped his right hand under the naked small of her back and pulled her toward him. "We could make this work, you know. I could move to Alexandria, get a job in the DC field office. Start a family. Settle down."

Dagny wrapped her hand around the back of his head and kissed his neck, then his lips.

"A little boy. A girl. Trick-or-treating on Halloween. Cupcakes for their school parties. Soccer games. We could do that," he said, his hand tracing her body from her thigh up to her face, then sliding around behind her head and gently tugging at her hair.

"But I barely know you," Dagny said.

The glowing green numbers on the alarm clock read 5:05. Dagny got out of bed, feeling guilty—feeling as though she'd cheated on Mike, even though it had only been a dream. She picked up the phone and dialed Brent's room. "Leave in ten?"

They were sitting at a booth in the Pancake Pantry, sharing a stack of Smoky Mountain Buckwheat Cakes drenched in butter and honey. It was Dagny's idea.

"So I have to ask, because it's been bugging me..."

Dagny couldn't look at his dark, smooth skin without thinking about her dream.

"What?"

"Why'd you pick Victor?"

She was glad it bothered him. "It was a close call, but I had to pick the best."

He laughed, but it was a nervous laugh. "No, really."

"You know why I picked him, Brent. I wanted to run the show."

"And you don't think I would have let you run the show?"

"You think you *are* the show."

This made him smile.

"Sometimes, anyway," she added, dabbing the corners of her lips with her napkin.

"Maybe you should get to know me before you jump to that kind of conclusion. Or maybe you should just get to know me." He smiled again. Two of the five cakes remained. He slid the plate toward her. "Rest are yours."

"Thanks." She speared another bite.

"I have to admit, Dagny, that I had an ulterior motive when I asked you to meet me in Nashville."

He was interested in her. She knew it. Didn't he understand that she was still grieving? Didn't he understand that she'd lost someone she loved? How could he possibly think that—

"I'd like to join your team. Work with you and Victor and the Professor."

"Oh," Dagny said. "Why? Life with the Fabulous isn't so fabulous?"

"There's nothing for me to do, really. After this, I'm supposed to report to a warehouse with a hundred other agents and flip through documents and spreadsheets that we've already reviewed five times. I'm not a flipping-through-documents kind of guy. And you've got to be able to use the help, right?"

May 1 was three days away. They needed all the help they could get. "Why would they waste you on document review?"

"Punishment."

"For what?"

Brent leaned forward and gave Dagny a look that meant *You know.*

"I didn't tell him that you told me about the Matisse," she protested.

"I know, Dagny, but he figured it out."

"How?"

He shrugged. "CPD denied it, maybe. I don't know."

"Why does he even care, Brent? Why does it matter?"

"I think you underestimate the threat you pose to him."

"I'm no threat, Brent."

"Of course you are. He's got a thousand people on the case, Dagny. If you find Draker first, Fabee's a laughingstock. His career is over."

"But if he gets to Draker first…"

"Then he's the next director and I'm stuck in the doghouse forever."

"So that's the real reason you're so eager to join our team. You need our side to win."

"You know, I had a nice little career going before a pretty girl made me tell her about a painting. You got me into this mess— you get me out of it."

"You realize that the odds of us finding Draker first are one in a million."

"Sometimes, when you're down and out, you buy a lottery ticket. And Dagny Gray, you are my lottery ticket."

All sixteen families welcomed Dagny and Brent into their homes with surprising graciousness. Despite their grief, they answered every question with elaborate detail and explanation, even though they'd endured the same inquisition several times already. Meals were offered and accepted. Tears fell, from the parents and siblings, of course, but also from Dagny, and even, more than once, from Brent. Altogether, Dagny and Brent spent thirteen hours with these families, probing into the painful and the uncomfortable, and yet they found no connection between any of the victims and Noel Draker.

And so they ordered dinner at a faux tavern in Nashville International, waiting for the last flight back to DC. Dagny ate a cheeseburger and all of the fries. Nine hundred calories. Forty-eight grams of fat. She'd get back to 125 soon. For dessert, Brent shared a peach cobbler that Dagny did not want, but felt obliged to eat. "You must have some fantastic metabolism, Dagny Gray. To eat like this and stay so thin."

She gave a fake chuckle in response.

The signboard flashed that the last flight to DC would be delayed another hour. "Wonderful." The way he said it didn't sound sarcastic. "The cobbler," Brent explained. "It's wonderful."

It was okay—it was not wonderful.

Dagny excused herself from the table and found an empty gate. Although she had accepted Brent into the team, she hadn't cleared it with the Professor first. It probably wouldn't be wise to show up with him unannounced. She dialed.

"Tell me what you found," he said.

"Nothing. No connection. We're coming home." She realized her mistake—that wasn't the way she wanted to reveal Brent's presence.

"Nothing at all?"

He hadn't noticed. "No, nothing."

"Who is we?" Of course he'd noticed. He noticed everything.

"I'm bringing Brent back with me." She added, "If it's okay."

"Davis?"

"I ran into him out West and then met up with him in Nashville. He wants off Fabee's team."

"We don't need him."

"So you've cracked this case?"

He laughed—probably because no one else spoke to him this way. "Never tell Victor this, but I thought you made the right choice from the start. My impression is that Brent can glad-hand, but I haven't seen much more than that from him. But if you think he can help, fine."

"I think he can help."

"He can help most by feeding us stuff from inside Fabee's investigation. We need an inside man."

"Maybe. Why don't we regroup tomorrow in person?"

"Okay." He paused, and then hummed the way he did when he was in deep thought. "Yes, yes, yes!"

"What is it?"

"How could we be so dumb? I know why you didn't get anything today. You talked with the wrong families."

"What do you mean?"

"If the actual victims bear no connection to Draker, could it really be that he was careless and missed his real target? This is a man who seems to have spent a great deal of time carefully constructing his spree. I think there was a specific child he wanted to kill, and I think this child had the great fortune of being ill on April fifteenth. Stay another day. Go to the school and find out which students were absent on the day of the crime and start with them. And hurry."

"We will," she promised.

"Divide and conquer, if you trust Brent."

Only eighteen kids had been absent from Haysworth Elementary School on April 15. Brent and Dagny divided the list of names. Dagny took the west side of the district; Brent took the east. They each spoke with five families before noon, then met for lunch, compared notes, and ventured out separately again. At two thirty, Dagny was sitting on Melanie Braxton's living-room sofa, surrounded by seven circling house cats, when Brent called and told her that he had found the link.

Forty minutes later they were sitting in Herman Deardrop's office on the thirty-first floor of the AT&T Building in downtown Nashville. Deardrop was in his late thirties. He wore suspenders and a bow tie. His hair seemed to be falling out in clumps, perhaps torn from his head in a fit of rage or anxiety. A short, spry man, Deardrop periodically jumped from his chair and paced in front of his floor-to-ceiling windows during the interview. Dagny might have viewed his behavior as suspicious if she hadn't worked with a dozen lawyers like him in New York.

"What are you trying to tell me? That he wanted to kill my son?" Deardrop pounded his fist against his office window with frightening force.

"Please, Mr. Deardrop, if you could just take a seat," Dagny said.

Deardrop walked behind his desk, but he did not take a seat. "I knew he was evil the whole time. He deserved even more than he got. I should have sent him away for twice as long."

Brent traded a puzzled look with Dagny, then said, "Well, Judge Nagel issued the sentence. You were just his clerk, right?"

Deardrop leaned forward, bracing himself with his palms facedown on the desktop. "Let me tell you something about the law, Mr. Davis."

"Special Agent Davis," Dagny corrected.

"Judges don't write shit. Clerks write their opinions. Every word of every order Nagel signed on the Draker case, I wrote. That's why the bastard wanted to kill my Daniel."

"If I might ask," Brent began, "why didn't you come forward when you realized that your son's school had been targeted?"

"Because no one knew that it was Draker then, shithead."

"Listen—" Dagny began.

"Right." Brent stepped in, calmly ignoring the insult in a way that Dagny couldn't. "But after it was known? Draker's been in the news for the past week."

"If I knew anything helpful, I'd have come forward. But all I know is that Draker is an evil guy, and you guys know that already. And I've got a deposition in twenty minutes, so you need to speed this up."

"Mr. Deardrop," Dagny said, "you're going to stay as long as we need you. This interview is not optional."

"Don't try your bullshit on a lawyer, lady. I know the law."

"So do I." Dagny looked up at the diploma hanging on the wall behind Deardrop's desk. "Then again, I went to Harvard Law, so I don't know what they taught you at the University of Dayton."

"I had a full scholarship. Bet you paid your way through Harvard, lady."

She had been on full scholarship, too, but she let it go. "Did you ever interact with Draker? Speak directly to him?"

"I was a clerk, Harvard. Judge does all the talking. We just do the work."

"Did Draker ever say anything to you?"

Deardrop hesitated before he answered. "No."

"Nothing?"

"Nothing."

"Are you sure?"

"Yes, dammit. He never said anything to me."

"What about his lawyer?"

"Nothing."

"Draker knew you were his clerk, I assume? That you were writing the decisions?"

"Yes, Harvard. Nagel had two clerks, but I was the one who sat in all the hearings on the Draker case, so I assume Draker knew it was me."

"Did Nagel tell you how long the sentence should be? Did he give you an idea?"

"You want me to break judge-clerk confidentiality?"

"There's no such thing," Dagny said.

"He told me to make it long."

"Did he tell you to make it ten years?"

"Not specifically. I came up with the justification that got him the full ten."

"Why were you aiming for ten years?"

"That's just what the guidelines said, Harvard. You should know you've got to follow the guidelines."

No one was bound to follow the guidelines anymore; the Supreme Court found them unconstitutional in 2004. They had been in effect, however, when Draker was sentenced. "The guidelines gave you some leeway," Dagny said. "You could have given him less."

"The guy's a monster. Are you seriously suggesting he should have been in jail for less time? Christ."

"I'm not trying to debate the merits of his sentence, Mr. Deardrop. I'm wondering if you went with ten years because that was the minimum to get him out of the federal camp system and into a medium-security prison."

"That was one of the reasons. And it was a nice round sentence. The double-digit years looked good in light of the public harm that Draker caused. And the bastard deserved every day of his sentence and probably more. What does it matter?"

Brent spoke softly. "Because we're trying to determine why Noel Draker would want to kill your son, Mr. Deardrop. Draker seems to have a long list of enemies—scores he's trying to settle. We're just trying to make sense of that list, and maybe figure out who he's going after next." Brent looked over to the wall, at a picture of young Daniel Deardrop holding a baseball bat; the oversize cap was falling down over his eyes. "In the meantime, you might want to keep an eye on your son."

"Isn't that your job, buddy?"

Brent and Dagny rose from their chairs. "No," Dagny said. "It's yours. You're the boy's father. Good luck with the deposition."

After they left, Brent placed a call to a friend on Fabee's team and arranged for someone to follow Deardrop and his son for the next few days.

The ticket agent told Dagny that she had been upgraded to Gold Medallion. In the past two months, she'd flown twenty-five thousand miles and lost the man she'd loved. The SkyMiles were hardly a fair trade.

The Gold Medallion status bumped her ahead of lowly Silver Medallion fliers on the waiting list for the free upgrade to first class. "You're not going to take it, are you?" Brent asked. "I'm in coach."

It was a silly question. Of course she was going to take it.

At the gate, Dagny floated something even more controversial. "You know that document warehouse you've been scheming to avoid?"

"Yes," he said with justified apprehension.

She smiled. He shook his head.

"Just one day?"

"You want me to go look through documents?"

"We want you to talk to people. Find out if Fabee has anything we should know about. Pick up on the gossip."

"You want a Liz Smith?"

"We want an inside man." She waited for him to relent. "Just one day."

"Grunt work and you won't even sit with me." He tilted his head up and bit his lower lip. "You're lucky you're beautiful."

The man in the seat next to her was reading *The New York Times*. He hadn't noticed Dagny's picture on the front page, next to the headline "For One Agent, It's Personal," but she had. A few minutes of a *30 Rock* episode on the monitor in front of her helped clear her mind, and she drifted off to sleep.

The plane finally landed at Reagan National at a quarter to midnight. Dagny didn't bother waiting for Brent—he was stuck in the back of the plane, and Dagny needed to crawl into bed. Although she expected the terminal to be empty, a couple hundred people were there, waiting for delayed flights. Many had their eyes fixed on the flat-screen televisions hanging overhead, tuned to CNN. A woman glanced at Dagny, then back up at the television, and then gasped and pointed at her. Soon, others were looking at her, too; then everyone seemed to be looking at her. Dagny raced past them. She caught a glimpse of the television hanging from the ceiling of the airport bar—her picture was on the left half of the screen, Mike's on the right.

What had Harold Booker said? *You're the pretty woman at the center of the biggest story in the country. Use a fake name*, he'd said. *Wear a hat.*

A souvenir shop was closed and the chain-link gate had been drawn nearly to the floor. A Hispanic man was stocking the shelves behind the gate. Dagny shook the gate gently. "Hey," she whispered, catching his attention. "Is there any way I could get a hat?"

"Sorry?" he said in a thick accent.

"A hat?" she said, miming the act of placing one atop her head.

The man smiled and nodded, then went around the corner and brought back a blue cap. He crouched down to the floor and held the hat under the gate.

"Twenty-five," he said.

A ball cap wasn't what she had in mind, but it would do. "Twenty?" she countered.

"Okay."

She folded the money and handed it to him under the gate. He pushed the cap into her hand. Dagny pulled her hair up into a ball and covered it with the cap, then ducked into the restroom to adjust her disguise. Only in DC, she thought, looking in the mirror and laughing at the three letters emblazoned on the cap—FBI. Dagny tossed it to a young boy at baggage claim, then took a shuttle to long-term parking and drove home. A handful of reporters were camped on her lawn. She drove past them to the Professor's house, wondering if she'd ever reclaim her life.

CHAPTER 44

....

April 30—Arlington, Virginia

Dagny woke at six, showered and dressed, then made her way down to the kitchen. Mrs. McDougal gave her scrambled eggs, bacon, and toast, and Dagny ate it all, as if it were medicine. It *was* medicine. What a revolutionary idea. Food—the cure for the common anorexia.

She wandered into the Professor's cluttered study. Whiteboards, graphs, charts perched on easels, diagrams, models, even a mobile, crowded every open space and surface. "So you've actually been doing something," Dagny said.

"I've got it narrowed down." The Professor walked behind his desk, picked up a stack of papers, and handed it to Dagny.

"What's this?"

"Draker's enemies," he explained. "It's funny. I've always compiled my own enemies list, but never someone else's."

Dagny thumbed through the pages. "You've got two hundred and twelve names here."

"And one of them will be next."

Dagny wasn't convinced. "I don't think you would have guessed about Tucker, and we still don't know his grievance against Waller's Food Mart."

"Oh, I know about Waller's Food Mart." The Professor smiled. She waited while he savored the moment. "Well?"

"Seven years old. Wanders into Waller's Food Mart with his father. The original Waller sees Draker remove a piece of gum from a pack and place it in his mouth. Waller demands that Draker's father pay. Draker insists that it was his pack and that he brought it into the store. Father doesn't believe him and berates him in front of Waller. Makes him promise to clean the floors of the store for a month. And beats him with a belt when they get home."

"Jeff Waller remembers this?"

"Jeff Waller has no idea, and the original Waller is dead. I heard the story from Draker's third-grade teacher."

"He complained to her?"

"He wrote a twenty-two-page essay on the injustice of it. One of those deals where you have to use up all the spelling words, but he kept going."

"Why did you end up talking to his third-grade teacher?"

"Because that's when monsters are made."

"And the teacher did nothing?"

"It was a different time, Dagny."

"Well, the man can sure hold a grudge." Maybe they really could unravel the logic to the crimes. The Luberses' first dog bit Draker. Melissa Ryder's father discovered the fraud. Chesley Waxton sued Draker. Silvers turned against Draker. Deardrop sent Draker to a medium-security prison. But there were still some loose ends. "We don't know anything about the second crime. And then there's Mike." She hadn't said his name often, and once it was uttered, she knew why.

"Again, I think Whitman was his intended target," the Professor said. "She was killed on the Ides of March."

"But what was Draker's motive?"

"Well, she advocated tougher sentences for white-collar criminals. Draker may have wanted to punish her for that."

"That's pretty weak. Draker's crimes are personal." Dagny sighed, then scanned through the Professor's list again. "So we have one day before his next crime and a list of two hundred and twelve potential victims. What do we do?"

"Since we think he's aiming to kill two hundred fifty-six people, there are some obvious targets. The courthouse, for example. The prison. The newspaper. I've urged Fabee to close them all for the day, and I hope he does."

"You can kill two hundred and fifty-six people almost anywhere."

"That's true. Which is why Victor's work is so important."

"Where is he?"

"He's in the basement, overseeing the team."

"The basement?" Wait, did he say 'team'? "The *team*?"

The Professor pushed a button under his desk, and one of the bookshelves behind Dagny swung open to reveal a hidden staircase.

"You've got to be kidding," Dagny said. "Who are you, Batman?"

"I have no idea who that is," the Professor said. Dagny wasn't sure she believed him this time.

She descended a wrought-iron spiral staircase into the basement, which looked like a small suburban office—Berber carpet, fluorescent lights, and a couple of desks. Victor sat at one of them, staring at his laptop. A dozen rows of metal shelves ran parallel across the rest of the room, holding neatly arranged boxes. Victor looked up at Dagny and smiled.

"You're looking good," he said.

She smiled back. "The Professor said something about a team, but you look like you're alone to me."

"Check this out," Victor said, pointing to his laptop screen. Dagny walked behind him and leaned over his shoulder. The web page listed the forty-eight contiguous states. "When I click on one of them, I get a list of cities," he said, demonstrating. "And if I click on the city, I get a list of properties that were once held by Draker, his company, and its subsidiaries, or by one of the shell corporations connected to Rowanhouse."

"Okay, I guess that's cool."

"That's not the cool part," he said. "Since Draker had a place in Nashville, I'm betting he has a place near all of the crimes. Somewhere he could have schemed without the hassle of credit cards or nosy motel clerks. I figure either Draker is squatting somewhere, or he's purchased properties under disguised names. If he's squatting, then I'm not going to find him—hopefully Fabee will. But if he purchased property, the money for it had to come from somewhere, and it has to be in someone's name. So I thought I'd trace Draker's assets to see if he could have hidden some land or some money before he went to jail."

"If he owned the Matisse and sold it through Rowanhouse, then there's four million right there."

"Enough for incidentals, maybe, after Rowanhouse takes his cut—but not enough to fund the whole thing. So I figured Draker must have laundered some other assets, not just the painting. I'm tracing all of Draker's old properties. It isn't as daunting as it sounds, because the bankruptcy dealt with most things. All of Drakersoft's assets were sold to Systematic at a discounted price in order to satisfy Systematic's claims against the company. And Draker's personal assets were sold at auction—we have detailed lists of that stuff. Fortunately, most of this was kept in electronic format, so it's easy to search."

"What about all the smaller companies—"

"That Draker set up to diversify his holdings? They were almost all indebted to Drakersoft—the parent company—which had lent them start-up money. So the Drakersoft bankruptcy trustee ended up suing most of these companies and foreclosing on their assets. By then, most of the subs had sold off their holdings, so there wasn't much to foreclose. These holdings included hundreds of pieces of property, scattered all over the country."

"Let me guess. Rowanhouse bought them."

"Yes."

"Then let's get warrants for these properties," Dagny said.

"Not so fast. All of these properties were immediately resold to legitimate buyers. Draker knew what he was doing. If any of the properties had been sold for *significantly* less than market value, the bankruptcy judge could have set the sale aside under—"

"A theory of fraudulent conveyance?" Dagny said, remembering her bankruptcy law class.

"Exactly. But each property was sold to Rowanhouse for *near*-market value. Maybe ninety-five percent of what it was really worth—consistent with property appraisals. Rowanhouse's companies then resold the property shortly after the sale, collecting a profit of about five percent."

"So Rowanhouse and Draker probably had these purchasers already lined up."

"And they probably agreed to split the profit from the resale, hiding it all from the bankruptcy court. Every sale looked legitimate if you looked at the selling price. On average, each resale netted just twenty-five thousand dollars. That's not much when you're talking about million-dollar properties, but if you consider that there were about five hundred pieces of property, it adds up to twelve and a half million dollars that Draker and Rowanhouse were able to hide from the bankruptcy court."

"So you're tracing the money?"

"There's no way to trace the money, so we're tracing properties. That means tracking down the deeds for all of Draker's old properties and driving out to see who actually lives there. If it's commercial, is there a business there now? If it's residential property, is there a family there now? Then we're looking at each of the companies Rowanhouse used to buy these properties. What other properties have they owned? Maybe they sold off all of Draker's properties, but bought new properties with his share of the proceeds of the sale. This means tracking down about two thousand more pieces of property—figuring out who really owns them. Unfortunately, there isn't a computer database with all of this property information. You can't even go to a state database for most of it. You have to go to the individual counties—some of which are online, but most of which aren't. It's a huge pain."

"So how are you doing this?"

"That's what's so cool. We're doing it with two thousand helpers. We set up a wiki."

"Like Wikipedia?"

"Exactly. I figured if you can recruit people to write an encyclopedia online, maybe you could recruit people to solve a crime. So I e-mailed Wikipedia editors, local police departments, and criminology professors, and asked for their help."

"Criminology professors?"

"College students have more free time than anyone, so I figured that criminology professors would be game for putting them to work on a case. Professors assign the work, and students go out and get the information. Stop by county auditor offices, photocopy deeds, and upload the information to the wiki." He clicked through a few links to a list of properties around Cincinnati. "If the homeowner checks out as legit, the property gets marked as safe. But if ownership seems questionable, it gets a red flag."

"And then what?"

"And then I get notified by e-mail that we have a red flag; I call the local police, and they go check it out."

"What if people make a mistake?"

"That's what the editors check. They review each entry and the information that supports it. If the deed is missing, for instance, they'll repost the property with a notation that the deed is missing. And someone will have to redo it."

"And this is working?"

"Yesterday, we found a safe house in Chula Vista, and Draker's prints are all over it. Right now we have cops visiting places in Bethel and Salt Lake City. It could be something; it could be nothing. We'll know within the hour."

"Does Fabee know about this?"

"We had to tell him about Chula Vista, of course, and we'll tell him about the others if they check out, too. But he doesn't know *how* I'm tracking it down. He thinks I did all the work. Probably driving him crazy, since he's got a huge team of his own sifting through much of the same data. They've probably gotten an earful about how one guy found the Chula Vista house by himself. When in fact, it's not one guy, but an army of Davids."

"An army of what?" Dagny asked.

"This law professor, Glenn Reynolds, wrote a book called *An Army of Davids*," Victor explained. "It's about how technology and the Internet let individuals work collaboratively to compete with big media or big government. Like the way bloggers got Dan Rather fired over the phony memos, or how they dug up stuff on Trent Lott. Reynolds says that Goliath is no match for an 'army of Davids,' at least not in the Internet age."

"And Draker is Goliath?"

"Actually, I think Fabee would be Goliath, in this particular metaphor," Victor said.

An army of Davids. Maybe it would change law enforcement, just as bloggers had changed the media. It was pretty darn smart—even smarter than her use of chain e-mails, which turned up the third crime.

"Hey, Dagny…something's been bothering me."

"Yes?"

"If Draker didn't try to run us over, shouldn't we be worried about who did?"

"Right now, we need to worry about the guy who's actually killing people. We can worry later about whoever tried but didn't."

"Two hundred and twelve names?" Brent was wearing a V-neck cardigan over a white T-shirt. He'd stopped home to change after spending a long day at Fabee's warehouse. They sat at the corner table at Oyamel, sharing ceviche and a view of the street.

"If you think that's a long list of enemies, you should see the Professor's."

He laughed. "You're joking."

"No. He showed it to me."

"How many names?"

"Thousands," Dagny said. "It looks like the phone book."

"Remind me not to cross that man." Brent called over the waitress and ordered two more beers. Dagny looked at her watch. It was almost midnight. "We have time," Brent said.

"Time is one of the things we don't have." Dagny spied a young couple kissing on the sidewalk. "It's amazing."

"What?"

"That life goes on." The waitress set the beers down on the table. "Tell me something comforting."

"Fabee's shutting down the courthouse, the prison. Draker's former schools. A golf club he used to belong to. Half of the Professor's list, Fabee will be watching. There's a good chance Draker won't be able to get near his intended target."

It wasn't comforting enough. "Danny Deardrop didn't show up for school, but Draker slaughtered those kids anyway."

"I'm just saying that we'll have people there to catch him, hopefully before he does anything."

Hopefully. "Tell me about the warehouse," she said, needing to change the subject.

"Imagine an aircraft hangar, shelves from front to back, floor to ceiling. Forty tables down the middle, with a hundred agents sifting through documents and evidence."

"What are they looking for?"

"No real rhyme or reason to it. Mostly trying to trace finances."

"Are they having any luck?"

"A lot less than Victor, it seems. Which apparently drives Fabee crazy. How is Victor doing it?"

She didn't have the energy to explain it in full, so she just said, "The boy's a genius."

"Yeah, but—"

Her phone rang. When she answered, the man's anguished words tumbled out. "However many you're planning to kill tomorrow, you can make it one less. They'll find my body hanging in my office in the morning." Click. The line went dead.

CHAPTER 45

May 1—Washington, DC

It was easy to trace the number. Convincing the taxi driver to run the red lights on Pennsylvania Avenue was hard. "They have the cameras."

"We'll reimburse you."

"No you won't," he muttered. But he obeyed nonetheless.

When the taxi skidded to a stop in front of the Hart Senate Office Building, two Capitol police officers rushed the vehicle. After Dagny and Brent showed their credentials and explained the situation, the officers quickly escorted them inside. The building was surprisingly modern and plush. A giant sculpture composed of large black aluminum triangles rose from the center of a nine-story atrium. Interior offices, reserved for congressional committees, looked down upon the sculpture through glass walls. The senators' suites circled the outer rim of the building. Each suite had two floors, connected by an internal staircase.

They raced past the triangle sculpture, bypassed the elevator bank, and darted up a plush, rounded stairwell to the third floor. Just past Senator Dianne Feinstein's office, they found Senator Brock Harrison's glass door. One of the Capitol officers knocked firmly and called to the senator. When no one answered, he pounded again on the door, rattling the glass. After a few seconds of silence, he grabbed a key from his pocket and unlocked the door.

The room was dark but for a faint horizontal line of light radiating from the bottom of a door on the left side of the room. Dagny flicked on the light switch. They were standing in a reception area; two desks were at the far end of the room. Chairs lined the walls. Copies of *The Washington Post* and *Washingtonian* were arranged neatly on the tables between the chairs. Pictures of Senator Harrison with other luminaries—presidents, prime ministers, Supreme Court justices, and Bono—adorned the walls. Brent opened the door on the left, and they ran past a conference room and several small offices. Harrison's office was in the back. His door was closed most of the way. Dagny pushed it open.

Harrison had removed one of the drop panels from the ceiling and looped his belt over a pipe. The senator was hanging from this belt in his dark-grey suit, swaying slightly from the air circulating through the vents. Brent felt for his pulse.

"Dead," he said.

One of the Capitol officers rushed to the body, but Brent blocked them. "We can't disturb the scene," he explained. It was obvious that they had never dealt with this kind of situation before. "What do you want to do?" Brent asked Dagny.

"I don't suppose you have a crime kit here?" she asked the officers. They shrugged. "Can you get us latex gloves and some ziplock bags then?"

After the officers had left to find the supplies she'd requested, Brent told Dagny, "We've got to call Fabee."

Dagny nodded, pacing around the senator's body. Brent grabbed her forearm and held her still. "If we start processing this scene ourselves, he'll have the Director pull us off this case. It won't matter how close the Professor is to the president."

"Fifteen minutes," Dagny said. She pulled out her cell phone and started to snap pictures. "Just to get a little head start."

Brent looked down at his watch. "Okay," he agreed and grabbed his cell phone from his suit pocket. "Just pictures."

Dagny circled to the front of the senator and photographed his face. His eyes were red. "Does hanging make your eyes bloodshot?"

"I found a man hanging once. I remember sweating and drooling, but I don't remember anything about his eyes."

"Then I think the senator was high," Dagny said. She took a dozen more pictures of the senator's body before noticing that something had been stuck to his tie. She used a pen to part his suit jacket. "Come look at this," Dagny said, snapping a picture. A card had been stapled to the tie.

THIS IS MY SECOND CRIME.
MY NEXT WILL BE BIGGER.

"Do you think he stapled this, or do you think Draker was here?"

"I'm guessing Harrison put it there," Dagny replied. "Figured it was something we needed to know."

The Capitol officers returned a few moments later with two pairs of gloves. "From the cleaning crew," one of them said, handing the gloves to Dagny. "We can't find any bags."

Dagny put on a pair and handed the other pair to Brent. "More agents should be coming. Don't let anyone through who doesn't have credentials," Dagny ordered. The officers understood, and made their way to the front door of the senator's suite.

"We've got to call Fabee," Brent said, anxiously. "He's going to ask the officers what time we got here and it better be pretty close to the time we called him."

"Okay," Dagny agreed.

While Brent placed his call to Fabee, Dagny phoned the Professor and explained the situation. "Check his calendar," the Professor said. "And his phone. See who was calling him."

"I will." Dagny hung up her phone, walked around to the senator's desk, and opened the center drawer. There was no calendar, but there was a bag of white powder. She snapped a picture.

"Second crime was a drug buy from Draker, I'm guessing," Dagny said.

"Maybe," Brent said, hanging up his phone. "Fabee's in town. He'll be here in less than twenty. With the whole cavalry, I imagine. He ordered us to stand down."

Dagny ignored the directive and continued her search. In the top right desk drawer she found a daily planner. There was no entry for the fifteenth of January; in fact most of the pages were empty. "I guess he didn't use this."

"Let me check the receptionist's desk. Maybe she kept his schedule," Brent said, jogging out of the room.

Dagny searched through the other drawers of the desk, then the credenza, but found no other calendars. Maybe he used Outlook, she thought. The computer wasn't on. She reached to press the power button, but Brent stopped her. "You do that and they'll know you turned it on."

"Nothing at the receptionist's?"

"No."

"We're FBI," Dagny argued. "I don't see why we can't turn his computer on."

"We had a stand-down order. The computer will register the time when we turned it on. Fabee will compare it to his phone log and see that we turned it on after his order."

"Why would he even look?"

"Because they're going to look at everything, Dagny. That's how they work."

Dagny sighed and turned away from the computer and back to the senator's body. Maybe he had a smartphone, she thought. She checked his pockets and found a BlackBerry. Fortunately, he hadn't turned on password protection. She scrolled through his calendar, but again there was no entry for January 15, and hardly any other entries either. Maybe he didn't keep his own calendar. Of course, even if he did, he probably wouldn't list his drug buys on it, she concluded.

Dagny switched to the senator's in-box and cycled through his most recent e-mails, photographing them with her cell phone. She scrolled down to e-mails from January and photographed them as well. None of them seemed suspicious, but she didn't have time to study them in any detail. Fabee would be here any minute. Dagny checked the senator's call register and saw that his last call had been to her phone. She scrolled through the long list of received and dialed calls, photographing them, wondering what other scandals lay buried in these numbers.

Fabee landed with his men like MacArthur in the Philippines. She heard them in the hallway and stuffed the BlackBerry back into the senator's pocket just before Fabee rounded the corner into the office.

"Out! Out!" he shouted at Dagny and Brent, pointing toward the door. As Brent passed by, Fabee muttered, "I see you've gone to the dark side, Davis." Brent just kept his head down and followed Dagny out of the room.

"That was awkward," Dagny whispered.

"I guess I'm not flying below the radar anymore," he replied.

Fabee's men took Dagny's and Brent's statements separately. There were logical reasons to do this—for instance, to make sure that they didn't accidentally convince each other of a temporal or factual mistake—but it still was insulting. Even more insulting was Fabee's insistence that Brent and Dagny stick around for another few hours in case further questions arose. As Dagny sat with Brent in a ten-by-ten conference room down the hall from Senator Harrison's office, she couldn't help but remember the last time she'd been locked away in a small room by a cruel, controlling man. Dagny looked at her watch. It was almost four in the morning.

She turned on her phone and flipped through the photographs she'd taken of Senator Harrison's call log. Maybe Draker had called the senator and had left Dagny's number for the return. The most recent call had a Virginia area code. Dagny dialed the number, and after a few rings, a woman answered groggily.

"This is Special Agent Dagny Gray. Can I ask who this is?

"This is Deborah Harrison."

It was a punch in the gut. Dagny hadn't planned to notify next of kin, and she wasn't sure what to say. She decided to tell her the truth. "Mrs. Harrison, I'm very sorry to tell you that your husband has been found dead."

The woman's voice trembled. "No. No." She started to cry. Dagny wanted to ask her questions about her husband—whether he had been acting strange, if he had received any unusual calls—but she knew Mrs. Harrison wasn't going to be much use for a while.

"I'm very sorry, Mrs. Harrison. Some agents will be at your house shortly to talk with you about this," Dagny said before hanging up the phone.

"That was brutal," Brent said.

"Your turn."

They spent the next half hour passing her cell phone back and forth, dividing the call duty. Most of the numbers belonged to lobbyists and lawyers; their offices were closed. One number belonged to a young-sounding woman. After Dagny explained the situation, the woman replied, "Jesus. I just talked to him yesterday. He seemed nervous and said he couldn't talk. It seemed like something was wrong."

When Brent dialed the next number on the log, Dagny's phone rang.

"What's the date on that call?" Dagny asked.

"April fifteenth."

"Then Draker used my phone to call Harrison. That's why he thought he was calling Draker." She imagined the call. Something like: *I just killed sixteen kids because you don't have the courage to come forward.* A call like that could drive a man to suicide.

"Why would he use your phone?"

"I think he wanted the senator to call me."

Two agents knocked on their door and split them again, subjecting them to more questioning. Like any good POW, Dagny divulged nothing, and after another hour, they let her go.

Fabee collared Dagny before she could escape, grabbing her arm and tugging her to an alcove at the end of the hallway. His face was red, and he was sweating through his shirt. The case had taken a considerable toll on the polished man she'd met in the Director's office just a few weeks earlier. "Why you, Gray? Can you tell me why?"

"I don't know."

"Is there something you aren't telling me, 'cause if there is, I will find it the fuck out."

"I don't know, Fabee."

"Is it just because you're pretty? Is he in love with you?"

"I don't know."

"You seem to know everything else, don't you? Laying the ID on Draker. Tracking his properties. If you know so much, why can't you answer the simplest question of all: Why you?"

Dagny just shrugged.

Fabee shook his head, then stormed off toward the senator's office. Brent passed Fabee on his way back to Dagny, but Fabee ignored him. "I don't think he likes us very much," Brent said to Dagny. "But we're free to go."

"Warwick. Warwick!" the Professor yelled at Dagny and Brent as they entered his study. "Does that mean anything?"

"Who is Warwick?" Dagny replied.

"That's where the senator was on January fifteenth. Warwick, Rhode Island."

"How do you know?"

"The event was listed on the website for the Warwick Museum of Art. The page is gone, but it shows up in the Google cache."

Dagny was impressed that the professor knew what a cache was.

"So what does that mean?" Brent asked, just as Victor entered the room carrying a six-inch-thick pile of documents.

"We found a whole new set of properties. It's never-ending," Victor said.

"It must mean something," the Professor muttered.

"The properties?" Victor asked.

"No, Warwick, Rhode Island," Dagny explained.

"Isn't that the place where the guitarist from Pantera was shot?" Victor said, setting down the papers.

"No, that was in Columbus," Dagny said. "You're thinking of the nightclub fire at the Great White concert. I think that was in Warwick." And then it hit her. Warwick and Columbus. The second and fourth crimes.

"There was the Who concert in Cincinnati where eleven people died," the Professor added, much to Dagny's surprise.

"Concerts with fatalities? Is that really it?" she said.

"Was Bethel where they held Woodstock?" Victor asked. "The kid's name was Crosby."

"Yeah," Brent replied. "But no one died at Woodstock."

Dagny wasn't so sure about that. She nudged the Professor away from his computer and ran a Google search. "Three people died at the original Woodstock," she announced. "One from a heroin overdose, another from a ruptured appendix, and a third was run over by a tractor."

"What about Chula Vista?" Brent asked.

Dagny searched the Internet for "Chula Vista," "concert," and "death," and found that someone had been stabbed at a Nelly concert in Chula Vista in 2002. It took her a few more searches, but she found that three people had been trampled at an AC/DC concert in Salt Lake City in 1991, and two people had been crushed to death at a Public Enemy concert in Nashville in 1987.

Dagny vaguely remembered a headline in the *Post* on the day she met Mike—something about a shooting on New Year's Eve at the 11:30 Club in Washington, DC. A quick google search confirmed it.

"Let's not get too excited," the Professor said. "Perhaps every major city has suffered a concert death."

"Maybe," Dagny said, but when she tried similar searches for Baltimore, St. Louis, Toledo, Houston, and Jacksonville, none of them turned up anything of note. "I think we've found his pattern."

Tragic concerts. It seemed absurd.

"So what's next for him?" Brent asked.

"Altamont?" Dagny suggested. "It's probably the most famous concert tragedy of all." In December 1969, eighteen-year-old Meredith Hunter was beaten and stabbed to death at the Rolling Stones concert at the Altamont Speedway. Cameras filming the concert captured the incident. Some people considered Altamont the bookend to the Woodstock era, so it made sense for Draker to start in Bethel and finish at Altamont. And then it hit Dagny. Draker had already given them the clue: Roberto Altamont.

She ran a search on Altamont. "Oh, my," Dagny exclaimed, pushing back from the keyboard. "Pearl Jam's scheduled to play a concert at Altamont on May fifteenth. That's his final crime." An article in the *San Francisco Chronicle* suggested that the racetrack expected to sell sixty to seventy thousand tickets.

"Then what about today? What's he going to hit today?" the Professor asked. Dagny searched various combinations on the web, pairing "concert" with words like "tragedy," "murder," "death," "stab," "kill," and "trample." There wasn't much left to find. In 2003, twenty-one people were killed in Chicago as they tried to flee a nightclub after someone used pepper spray in the audience. In 1991, eight people suffocated while trying to get into a gymnasium in New York City for a charity basketball game played by rappers. Three people died—one from a stabbing—at a Metallica and Ozzy Osbourne concert in Long Beach, California, in 1986. One man was beaten to death at a Korn concert in Atlanta in the summer of 2006.

"That company that Draker cheated..." Victor struggled for a second to remember the name. "Systematic! Systematic is in Atlanta."

Dagny searched Google for Systematic and confirmed that the company's four-story headquarters was located just south of downtown Atlanta, a few blocks west of Turner Field, along the Ralph David Abernathy Freeway. A recent company profile indicated that 307 employees worked at the building.

"They're on my list!" the Professor said.

"They aren't on Fabee's," Brent replied.

Dagny looked at her watch. "It's nearly eight. People are probably arriving at work."

Brent, Victor, and the Professor called the Atlanta police, Fabee, and Systematic's main switchboard, respectively. Dagny dialed Harold Booker's number at CNN.

CHAPTER 46

May 1—Atlanta, Georgia

When he was six years old, Seymour Dutton's favorite toy was a small rubber ball attached to five feet of elastic rope. He'd tie that rope around his little wrist, throw the ball as hard as he could, and try to catch it when it came rearing back at him. It was a nice toy for a boy who didn't have any friends. One day the rope snapped and the ball sailed into the china cabinet. Four plates shattered. When he heard his mother coming, Seymour ran to his father's study and hid under the desk.

Now, more than thirty years later, he was hiding under a desk again.

A second knock at the door—this one louder. He could see the door swing open through a small gap in the front of the desk. It was the security guard, holding on to the doorframe, leaning into the office. What was his name? Wallace. Or Willis, maybe. Friendly black man—said hello to Dutton every morning. Spoke with a funny accent. Maybe he was from Africa.

"Mr. Dutton, are you here? Hey-lo, Mr. Dutton? We must e-e-evacuate. Hey-lo!" The guard leaned back into the hallway, yelling, "He's not here! Maybe he's at the gym?"

He left, closing the door behind him.

Dutton crawled out from under the desk, scuttled to his office door, and turned the lock. He was not at the gym, and anyone who'd seen his belly should have known that was a lousy place to look for him. Dutton had gained five pounds each of the last ten years. It was amazing that such a small amount each year could leave him fifty pounds overweight.

Every morning, Dutton flipped through new e-mails, checked the mail pile, and went down the hall to get his first cup of coffee. This morning, he never made it to the coffee. He never made it past that first envelope on top of the stack. There was no stamp on it—it must have been delivered by hand, he thought. Maybe Draker had even placed it there himself.

During the awful hour between the opening of the envelope and the ordered evacuation, Dutton had sat alone at his desk, trembling in fear, compulsively checking the clock on the wall, sweat dripping from his forehead and down his back, praying that God would do something to stop what was about to happen. And then, finally, when his corporate security announced the evacuation over the building's speakers, Dutton assumed that God had answered his prayers—that God had intervened to save his employees since he lacked the courage to save them.

Dutton also lacked the courage to save himself. That's why he'd hidden under the desk. That's why he was looking out the window of his fourth-floor office, watching as workers left the building. Their faces were familiar, even if he didn't know all their names. He saw the janitor who waited for Dutton to leave each night—no matter how late—so that he could clean his office. They spoke every day, but what was his name? Rudy, maybe. Or Randy. He spotted Brenda—or was it Barbara?—the corporate chef. She'd left one of the best restaurants in New York to oversee dining operations for the Systematic campus. She was standing next to Phil, the new vice president of marketing, who was still in his first week on the job. He knew Phil's name, and Rhonda's, too. She was his secretary. She was leaning against the hood of a Honda Accord. Was that what she drove?

Dutton sat at his desk and folded his hands. Two weeks earlier, a journalist from *Businessweek* had sat across the desk. She was a small, pretty brunette, sharp as a tack, too. Jennifer Walters, was it? Something like that. Had an anchorwoman's haircut... shoulder-length hair, curling in just a little at the shoulders. She'd wanted to know whether business database systems could compete with open-source products, and he'd proudly described the upcoming release of Systematic Deluxe. It featured videoconferencing, real-time multiuser collaboration tools, desktop syncing, and remote access. He'd nailed the interview. But the woman had asked one question that had nothing to do with her article. It wasn't really even a question. More of a statement. "If Draker hadn't cheated you all those years ago, who knows how things would have played out. Maybe I'd be interviewing *him* about this." Was she just making conversation? Was she just joking around? Or had she pieced something together? Maybe she was working on a different kind of article, and the open-source angle was just a ruse.

Outside, police and fire sirens wailed. Helicopters hovered overhead. They were there to protect the workers and the building, so why did he feel like they were coming for him? Dutton felt his cell phone vibrate against his waist. He checked the number. It was his wife. He didn't answer it.

He picked the envelope up off his desk and pulled out the card. Dutton thought about the years that Draker had spent in prison, the way he'd been treated in the press, how he'd lost everything he had built. Why didn't Draker just kill himself? Was it courage, or something else, that had kept him alive? Dutton turned the card over in his hand and pulled away the piece of gum that was taped to the back, unwrapped the foil, and folded the gum into his mouth. Cinnamon.

Dutton tossed the empty envelope back onto the desk, and then realized the poetry of it all. He'd had the desk for so long he'd forgotten. It used to be Draker's—Dutton had bought it at auction during the Drakersoft bankruptcy. How could he have forgotten this? He'd been so proud of it at the time. It had been his trophy. His spoils. And yet, over the last ten years, he'd slowly forgotten that it ever belonged to Draker. He'd forgotten about Draker entirely, in fact.

His cell phone vibrated again, and Dutton tossed it onto his desk. He looked down at Draker's card, still in his hand, and then looked up at the clock on the wall. It was almost nine. Would it be a bomb? He assumed it would. But what if Draker wasn't coming after him at all? What if Draker was just playing a joke? How would Dutton explain the fact that he'd stayed in the building? Maybe he'd say that he'd fallen asleep. But then why didn't they see him when they opened his door? Because he liked to nap under his desk. Just like George Costanza. Still, could he have slept through the sirens, the loudspeaker? Sure, if he wore earplugs. What if they asked to see his earplugs? Christ, why would they ask to see those? It isn't a crime to stay in a building that's about to blow. They wouldn't care why he stayed. They'd just be happy he was alive.

Could a man wearing earplugs really sleep through the commotion of the morning? If he didn't go with the napping story, he could claim he'd had a stroke, couldn't he? No, of course not—there would be medical evidence of a stroke. They'd make him go to doctors, and they'd call him a liar. Okay, so if it wasn't a stroke, what was it? Maybe he just blacked out. Something generic. Doesn't even remember it happening. Amnesia. He could fake amnesia. All he would have to do is—

The floor tore open, and Dutton fell through broken pipes and wires, crashing into the office below. A flashing fireball raced through the room, burning Dutton's face and body. Though he'd closed his eyes, the light from the fire seared his eyelids. Every part of his body was in pain. Maybe he was dead and this was hell. Though debris burned around him, the worst seemed to be over. *I'm going to live*, he thought, just as a steel beam crashed from above and crushed his skull.

The card fluttered in the rubble, then settled in the growing flames.

THIS IS MY NINTH CRIME.
MY NEXT WILL BE BIGGER.

Seymour Dutton had thrown a ball on an elastic rope, and it had come rearing back at him.

CHAPTER 47

···

May 1—Arlington, Virginia

In an instant, the bright-orange fireball filled the screen and overflowed its edges, only to disappear just as quickly under a black cloud of soot and smoke. Victor was sifting through his pile of papers, but the rest of them stood in front of the television, transfixed by the spectacle. The Professor took a step closer to the monitor, then shook his head. "It takes a man years to build something and another man seconds to destroy it. If there were a benevolent God, wouldn't the opposite be true?"

"You don't believe in God?" Brent asked.

"Not a benevolent one," the Professor replied.

Over the next few minutes, CNN news anchors interviewed Systematic employees, local politicians, former special agents, psychologists, and profilers. The network moved so deftly and effortlessly from one interview to the next that it felt like a choreographed ballet. They'd even managed to create a three-dimensional computer animation of the explosion that had occurred only minutes before. "It's sad," Dagny noted. "We've become so used to crisis and disaster that they can do it in their sleep."

The only hitch in the broadcast was the network's unsuccessful attempt to track down Seymour Dutton, whose on-air denunciation of Noel Draker would have added a richer layer of personal drama to the day's events. But Dutton was nowhere to be found. "He was in his office," his secretary sobbed. "I assumed he was leaving with everyone else."

"I checked his office," Walter Davies, a security guard, explained. "He wasn't there. Unless he was hiding under his desk," he chuckled, until he realized that chuckling wasn't appropriate in the aftermath of an explosion.

"Dutton stayed behind," the Professor noted.

"But why?" Dagny asked.

"Another suicide," the Professor said. "First the senator and now Dutton."

Victor wasn't listening to any of them. He was sorting through his documents. "Got it!" he exclaimed, waving a piece of paper in his hand. "A property in Tracy, California. Probably only a couple of miles from the Altamont racetrack."

Dagny grabbed the page from Victor's hand. "I'm off to Dulles."

"I'm coming, too." Brent said.

The Professor grabbed Dagny's arm before she could reach the door. "Can I talk to you in private for a second?"

He led her down the hallway to the kitchen.

"I know what you're going to say, Professor."

"You do?"

"This is where you remind me that I shouldn't let my emotions get in the way. That I may want to shoot him, but that's not how we do things in the Bureau. That there is a system of justice in place and we should let it work. That Draker may have valuable information, and that we can't get it from him if he's dead.

"Well, I can't make any promises, Professor. Every second Draker breathes is another second evil lives. The man has killed children. He raped a woman. No matter what a bullet from my gun might do, any human being named Noel Draker is gone. The last thing the world needs is a trial where he sits in his suit and tie, dapper and suave, and women write to him in prison, visit him, fall in love with him, go on the talk shows and maintain that he is innocent or misunderstood, or that the world failed him before he failed the world.

"Yes, this case is personal for me. I know that killing Noel Draker won't bring Mike back, or undo anything else he did, but it will let me move forward. So I can't make you any promises."

The Professor cocked his head and smiled. "Actually, I wasn't going to say any of that. I was just going to give you some food." The Professor opened a drawer and pulled out a brown paper bag. "I'm happy you've been eating again, and I just want to make sure you keep it up. As for killing Draker, I couldn't care less. Go ahead and shoot the bastard."

CHAPTER 48

May 1—Tracy, California

"Ever read Kerouac?" Brent asked, sitting shotgun.

"Kerouac?"

"Yeah."

"No."

"Really? You're a smart, accomplished woman."

"Isn't he mostly for boys going through a hipster phase?"

"No," Brent huffed. "No."

"I didn't realize black men read Kerouac."

"That's right, Dagny. We just read Ralph Ellison and Ishmael Reed."

"Who is Ishmael Reed?"

"Typical." Brent drummed his fingers on the passenger door.

A moment of silence, and then Dagny asked, "So what about Kerouac?"

"Oh," Brent said. "He wrote, 'Tracy is a railroad town; brakemen eat surly meals in diners by the tracks. Trains howl away across the valley. The sun goes down long and red.'"

"Word for word? You're not paraphrasing?"

"Word for word."

"You have a photographic memory?"

"Close to it."

"Me, too. I don't think it's true anymore, though."

"About your memory?"

"About Tracy." The trains still stopped in Tracy, but it wasn't just a railroad town anymore. Some of the town's seventy-five thousand residents worked for Amtrak or the industrial parks and corporate farms that kept the rails bustling, but most commuted by highway to San Francisco or Sacramento and worked with their fingertips, not their backs.

They parked ten blocks away from the house. Dagny patted her gun, grabbed her bags, and hopped out of the car. Brent followed. They trespassed through dozens of backyards toward the Draker property. Like all the homes around it, Draker's house was a white stucco bungalow with an orange clay-tile roof. There was no car in the driveway. The lights were off and the shades were drawn. The house was at the end of a cul-de-sac, on a quarter-acre lot. Behind the property was a weathered picket fence, six feet tall. The fence hid a busy four-lane road.

Because children's toys littered the backyard of Draker's neighbor on the left, Dagny and Brent decided to camp in the yard of the neighbor on the right, crouching behind a row of shrubberies. "I'll circle the home with the scope. Wait here and watch," Dagny said.

"Why you?" Brent asked. "Why not me?"

"Draker doesn't want to kill me. You, I'm not so sure about." Dagny crouched close to the ground and scampered over to the side wall of Draker's house.

The Radar Scope was invented by the Defense Advanced Research Projects Agency and designed for urban warfare. Soldiers used it in Iraq. The Bureau hadn't gotten in on the action yet, but Dagny had a connection. In technical terms, the scope sent out stepped-frequency radar and read changes in the

Doppler signature of the returned signal. In layman's terms, it blinked if someone was inside the house.

Dagny pressed the scope against the wall and turned it on. Nothing blinked. She walked a few feet and tried it again. Still nothing. When she passed the back sliding glass door, she noticed that it had been painted black. She held the scope to the window. Nothing. After a few more tests around the perimeter of the house, Dagny was convinced that they had beaten Draker to Tracy. She wasn't surprised. With the whole country looking for him, Draker wasn't going to fly. He'd be coming from Atlanta by car.

Dagny ran back to Brent and told him the house was clear. "What if the scope doesn't work?" he asked.

Dagny held it to the side wall of the neighbors' house and pressed the button. The red light blinked. "Looks like someone's home. Let's ask them for their house."

Brent stood watch on the driveway while Dagny knocked on the front door. A short, elderly Mexican woman answered. She was wearing an apron, and her hands were covered in flour. Dagny flashed her creds. "Would you mind if I come in?"

The woman's elderly husband hurriedly hobbled in from the other room and fell to the floor, screaming, "We're legal!"

"No, no." Dagny grabbed his arm and pulled him to his feet. "You've done nothing wrong. I just need to borrow your house."

The woman started to cry. "But I'm baking a pie."

After twenty minutes of explanation, the promise of a suite at a luxury hotel in downtown San Francisco ("Room service, too?" "Of course"), and assurances that Dagny would remove the pie from the oven when the timer went off, Mr. and Mrs. Fernandez threw some clothes into a suitcase and drove away. Brent jogged back to their rental car while Dagny stood watch. When Brent returned, he parked the Impala inside the Fernandezes' garage, and they removed their bags.

There was only one window in the Fernandezes' house with a clear view of Draker's, and it faced the front door. If Draker were to enter through the back of his house, they wouldn't see him. "I can make some calls," Brent offered. "Get a camera in the back."

"Word would get back to Fabee," Dagny replied. "I've got another idea." It meant making a phone call that she didn't really want to make. Dagny pulled out her cell phone and scrolled through her history of received calls. The voice that answered was every bit as pompous and patronizing as she'd remembered.

"Calling to apologize? Or maybe you've been having naughty dreams about me, and you just needed to hear my voice."

"Hello, J. C."

"Saw your picture on the news. You're looking pretty fine."

"I don't believe for a second that you watch the news. You in LA?" Dagny asked.

"You bet."

"Want to drive up to Tracy and help me out?"

"Where the hell is Tracy?"

"A little east of San Francisco."

"Shit no. That's five hours, maybe six."

"I think it might be worth it to you."

"Why's that? You going to get down on your knees and—"

"Don't you dare say something sexual."

"—beg me for forgiveness?" Adams said.

"No."

"Okay, then, why would I want to drive up there?"

"To help me catch the guy who kept framing you?"

Eight hours later, J. C. Adams backed his Escalade into the garage. "I gave up a date with two chicks for this," Adams said.

"Well, I'm sorry that a mass murderer has interfered with your social life."

Smiling brightly, Brent sidled up to Adams and stuck out his hand. "Hey, J. C., I'm Brent Davis." All men swooned for J. C. Adams, it seemed. Men were idiots, Dagny thought.

"Nice to meet you, B. D."

The back of the Escalade was stuffed with boxes of electronics. "This is, like, ten thousand dollars' worth of stuff. It's more than it normally would be because of the remote battery. You said you need this stuff powered for days?"

"That's right."

"So do I just give you my receipts, or should I—"

"Why don't we get this stuff set up first, J. C., and then worry about reimbursement?" She wasn't sure how any of her expenses were going to be reimbursed, and she didn't really care.

"Cool."

Adams unpacked four television monitors, set them on the kitchen table, and plugged them in. Then he and Dagny took the cameras from their boxes and sneaked through the dark to plant them around Draker's house. Each of the cameras was no bigger than a stick of gum. Dagny fastened two up in the trees, along with external battery packs that would keep them filming for days. Adams attached one camera to the top of the neighbors' swing set, and taped another to the fence in Draker's backyard, burying the external battery in the ground and running a thin cable from the battery along a fence post to the camera. Brent stayed back in the Fernandezes' house, watching the monitors. He confirmed that the cameras were working by cell phone, requesting slight adjustments to improve the camera angles and picture quality.

"I don't get it," J. C. said to Dagny as they walked back to the Fernandezes'. "Why don't you just get a warrant and go in? Check it out. Maybe wait for him from the inside.

"He might have wired it for an intrusion," she explained. "An alarm or motion sensor. I don't want to risk scaring him away." That wasn't the real reason, but it was the only one she could give.

Dagny saw a car's headlights approaching. She grabbed Adams's arm and pulled him to the ground. They stayed low until the car pulled into a garage several houses away.

When they returned to the Fernandez home, Dagny studied each of the monitors and was impressed with the surveillance system. They had a clear view of each side of the house. Draker couldn't enter without them seeing. "Nice job, J. C."

"What else do you need?"

"That's it."

"For real?"

"For real."

"I don't get to stick around and watch you catch this bastard?"

"It could be days. And it could get ugly. Why don't you give me your receipts?"

Adams flashed his big white smile. "As long as you catch him, consider it a gift." The curly-haired quarterback hopped into his Escalade and drove away.

"Fuck," Brent muttered. "I forgot to get his autograph."

"I'll take night shift if you want to get some sleep."

"Forget it, Dagny. I'm taking night shift. You need to get some rest." Dagny didn't argue. She was tired. Brent sat at the kitchen table watching the monitors and Dagny crawled into the Fernandezes' guest bed. She slept soundly, until someone opened the garage door.

CHAPTER 49

May 2—Tracy, California

Dagny grabbed her gun from the nightstand, hopped out of bed, and peered out the bedroom door. The hallway was empty and quiet. She heard something—a car door, or a trunk—open. She edged along the wall until she came to the door to the garage. With a swift kick, she threw the door open and charged gun first.

"Just me!" Brent shouted, throwing his hands in the air and dropping the suitcase he'd been stuffing into the back of a blue Ford Explorer, newly parked next to the rented Impala.

"What are you doing?"

"I'm…I'm…" he stammered. Before he could finish his sentence, a cold hand grabbed Dagny's shoulder from behind.

"Your shift." It was a familiar Texas accent.

When Dagny turned, Justin Fabee was standing behind her. She turned back to Brent. "You called him?"

Brent shrugged. "We're all on the same team, Dagny."

"That's right, Dagny. We're on the same team. Now why don't you watch the screens while I rest up? That red-eye is a killer, even on a Bubird."

Brent closed the back of the Explorer and climbed into the driver's seat. He refused to meet Dagny's eyes as he pulled out of the garage. Dagny turned to Fabee. "Give me ten minutes to shower, and I'll take my post."

"Thatta girl," Fabee said, patting her on the back. "I know you want to get Draker just as much as I do, so this is going to work out just fine."

The hot water felt good. She closed her eyes and basked in the steam, thinking about the case, and mostly about Brent Davis. Why the betrayal? Maybe he'd become nervous now that they were close to catching Draker. By keeping information from Fabee, they were violating the ground rules established by the Director at the beginning of the investigation. If Fabee became director, their careers would be over. Even if Fabee never became director, they'd certainly be punished for this. Dagny didn't care about her career, and the Professor's career was essentially over. He'd have to use every last bit of goodwill with the president to protect Victor, leaving little for Brent. In calling Fabee, Brent was cowardly, but his actions were understandable.

As her fingertips began to prune, Dagny had a more troubling thought. Maybe Brent had been betraying her all along. Maybe Fabee asked Brent to befriend her, to share little bits of information to build trust, and then to infiltrate their investigation. Maybe it wasn't mere coincidence that Brent was at Percy Reynolds's house in New Mexico, or even that diner near Bethel.

Dagny dried off and dressed, and then headed to the kitchen and handed Fabee a Radar Scope. Fabee seemed puzzled. "It tells us if he's inside his house. For all we know, he slipped in while you were trying to scare me in the garage."

"I wasn't trying to scare you."

"Regardless. Take one of these and circle his house to make sure he isn't inside. To get it to work, you press—"

"I know how these things work," Fabee said, storming out the back door. She enjoyed giving orders to an assistant director. If she was going to throw away her career, she might as well do it in style.

Fabee returned a few minutes later, tossed the Radar Scope onto the kitchen counter, and pulled up a chair next to Dagny. "Davis is right, you know. We're on the same team. No reason for you to be upset."

"I'm not upset," Dagny lied.

"He was just following orders."

"An order to spy on us."

"Considering the Professor's background, I don't think you have any right to complain." Fabee paused for emphasis. "Besides, you were supposed to keep us informed of what you were doing. Director's orders."

"It seemed like you had your hands full."

"You know what I think, Dagny? You've got your own agenda, and you've been using the Professor and Victor, and you were using Brent, too. This case is personal for you. I'd feel the same way if I were you. But our job is to catch Draker, not kill him. That's why you want to keep a few steps ahead of me. Because you know that I'll catch him, but you'll kill him."

She hated Fabee for saying it, even though she knew it was true. "We all have our own agendas, Fabee. Even you." There was a reason he had come to Tracy, California, alone. Fabee wasn't looking to share credit with anyone. He wanted to be the one to catch Draker. So why was Dagny still there? Maybe he needed her.

Fabee smiled, rose from his chair, and walked to the refrigerator. "It's time for breakfast. You want eggs? Scrambled okay?"

Dagny sighed, keeping her eyes on the monitors. "Weren't you going to take a nap?"

"Hey, you and me—we may be here awhile," Fabee said. "So maybe we ought to be civil."

"Scrambled is fine."

They sat at the kitchen table, watching the camera feed. It wasn't easy to keep scanning from monitor to monitor, surveying static pictures, watching nothing happen for hours at a time. And it wasn't any easier sitting next to the man she'd viewed as a rival since the start of the case. She'd worked hard to try to get ahead of Fabee, and yet here they were, approaching the finish line together.

He made quesadillas for lunch and stuffed them with a blend of cheeses, chicken, peppers, and tomatoes. The tortillas were perfectly crisp. It was a good lunch, Dagny had to admit, but not out loud, since they weren't talking.

Finally, Fabee broke the silence. "I liked his paintings, you know. He was very, very good."

"Yes. He was."

"He really could capture the human spirit. Most painters try to capture the human condition, or the human pathos. I hate that stuff."

"Me, too."

Fabee pulled out his wallet and removed a picture of a little girl. He handed it to Dagny. "Her name is Veronica. She'll be three in July." She was standing next to a rocking chair full of stuffed animals, her hand grasping one of the spokes on the back of the chair, steadying her stance. She had big cheeks and an even bigger smile.

"She's adorable."

"I saw her yesterday for the first time since this whole thing started," Fabee said, tucking the picture back into his wallet. "The things we do…"

"It would only get worse if you're made director."

"Maybe. Long days, sure, but at least I'd stay in town more." He pulled the picture out of his wallet and studied it again. "Been divorced a year, almost. I could blame the job, I guess. But the problem isn't the job—it's me. I guess I'm just an asshole."

Dagny glanced over briefly at Fabee's hand and saw that he was still wearing his wedding ring. He noticed.

"Yeah, I'm an asshole, but I still love her. Just can't bear to take the ring off."

She wanted to look at Fabee—to read his face, his eyes, his expression—but she kept her gaze on the monitors instead. "Why do you want to be director so badly? You love the field, so why shoot for a desk job? You're supposed to work at a desk now, and you can't stay parked."

"I don't know." Fabee shrugged. "You went to Harvard Law, right? So you were one of those kids that always had to get the best grades, take the hardest courses. An AP geek?"

"Yep."

"I bet you didn't stop and ask yourself why you kept pushing yourself to do better. It's just ingrained in who you are. If you got an A minus, you wanted an A. And when you got an A, you wanted an A plus."

"That's right."

"When I was a special agent, I wanted to make ASAC, and once I got that, I wanted to be SAC, and so on. Maybe it's…I don't know. Low self-esteem? But I like what I do." Fabee got up from the table, walked over to the coffeepot, and poured himself a cup. "Want one?"

"No."

"The caffeine will help."

"I've been doing fine on adrenaline."

Fabee carried his mug back to the kitchen table and sat down, then leaned back in his chair. "When this is all over, what do you want to do, Dagny? Continue as an SA? Work with the Professor on his next academic paper?"

"I guess I sort of assumed that my career would be over. I've burned a lot of bridges."

"No," Fabee said. "You've done a stellar job."

"I'm sure I've made things difficult for others."

"Yeah, sure." Fabee laughed. "But you're tenacious and resourceful. And a hero, according to the papers. I think you're pretty safe at the Bureau, if that's what you want to do. I can understand if you want to keep working with the Professor. But then again, the Professor's an old man, you know."

"I know." She hadn't thought about the future in a long time, not since Mike was alive. "Right now, I have only one goal in mind."

"I hear you, Dagny. I do. But what if it doesn't do what you think it will for you?"

Fabee made a spicy chicken pasta with an olive-oil-and-garlic sauce for dinner. While they ate, they took turns staring at the surveillance feed while the other read the day's news aloud off the Internet. They agreed not to read anything about Draker. It was a relief to know that the Nationals were only three games back, that Congress was fighting over the minimum wage, and that two discount airlines were planning to merge, because this meant that the world continued to turn, and that maybe there would be something to head back to when the case was done.

Dagny read Fabee a restaurant review for the latest Asian-fusion restaurant in Dupont Circle—a combination Vietnamese noodle shop/English pub called Pho Britannica—then handed the laptop back to Fabee. He clicked around a bit and then started chuckling.

"What is it?"

"Nah, it's about the case. Can't read it."

"Read it."

"It's the gossip page."

"Go ahead."

"'Which skinny actress is so desperate to be cast in the planned Dagny Gray movie that she dressed as a secret agent and infiltrated Harvey Lettleman's office with fake FBI credentials, proceeding to handcuff the hefty mogul? Sources say that Lettleman liked the performance so much that he had her bring the handcuffs to his home later that night. We aren't saying who she is, but don't be surprised if Jana Bloom gets the part.'"

"Are you joking?"

"Swear to God, I'm not."

Dagny sighed. "I was hoping for Kate Beckinsale."

At ten o'clock, Dagny retreated to the guest bedroom for a short nap, leaving Fabee to watch the monitors. She set the alarm for two a.m. and crawled under the covers. Although she was never much for intuition, she fell asleep certain that tomorrow would be the day Draker would die.

CHAPTER 50

··

May 3—Tracy, California

In the black-and-white glow of the monitors, everything was still except the gentle shimmy of grass in the late-afternoon breeze. When the wind died, Dagny worried that the feed had frozen, but it hadn't. A photograph is just a movie of nothing happening, Dagny thought.

Fabee spent most of the day in the garage, yammering on his cell phone, coordinating the efforts of the Fabulous. The house walls muted all but the occasional expletive, so Dagny couldn't hear what they were planning. He was keeping his team at bay, he said, because more agents meant it was more likely they'd tip off Draker by accident. Dagny didn't buy this for a minute. Fabee was keeping the Fabulous away because Fabee and his ego wanted to be the one to capture Draker. She didn't care about Fabee's ego or the Fabulous; she just cared about the four monitors in front of her. Still, she wouldn't have minded if Fabee were sitting next to her, keeping her company, discussing the news or baseball scores or his daughter. In the past twenty-four hours, she'd grown to like the guy.

And then the picture from camera four shook.

It was the one attached to the fence. Dagny yelled for Fabee, who got there just in time to see the back of a man descending from the top of the frame.

Draker had just hopped the fence.

Fabee grabbed his gun and tossed Dagny hers. They stood at the monitor, watching Draker take a few steps toward the back patio, then drop to his knees in the grass. Was he looking for footprints? Draker ran his fingertips through the grass and then stood and walked to the far edge of the yard, shielding his eyes from the late-afternoon sun, studying his neighbor's house. After ten seconds, he turned and walked back to the middle of his yard, staring at the Fernandez house with a fixed and steady gaze. Dagny felt as though Draker was staring through the walls, looking at her. Although she couldn't see his face, she was sure that Draker was smiling.

Suddenly, Draker spun around and sprinted back toward the fence. He'd grown a thick, scraggly beard and looked haggard and worn. He was wearing an oversize T-shirt and loose blue jeans. His eyes fixed on the camera as he approached the fence. His sneakers hit the lens as he hopped the fence, knocking the camera to the ground.

Dagny and Fabee ran out the back door, darted through Draker's backyard, and jumped over the fence. They landed in an array of discarded soda cans and sandwich wrappers that littered an overgrown, grassy ditch alongside a busy four-lane highway. Draker was nowhere to be seen.

"Look," Fabee said, pointing at a footprint in a small spot of mud along the side of the road. The mud trailed onto the blacktop. "He crossed there."

A steady stream of semis blocked the view across the highway. She tried to catch the gaps between them with her eyes, looking for a bearded man in sneakers.

"He's in the woods," Dagny said, spotting a flash of movement visible between the passing trucks.

Traffic continued down the highway at a steady pace. "Ever play Frogger?" Fabee asked as he darted into the street, dodging oncoming cars and trucks. Dagny raced out behind him, beating a UPS truck to the first dashed white line, then waiting in the middle of traffic for another gap to take her to the double yellow line at the center of the highway. The wind from passing vehicles made it hard to stand still, and she almost teetered forward into an oncoming truck.

"I hate Frogger," Dagny yelled to Fabee, but he was already across the street. She waited for another truck to pass and then sprinted across the remaining two lanes. The driver of an oncoming Volvo slammed on her brakes and blasted her horn, but Dagny didn't notice—she was running at full speed.

Fabee was already deep into the woods. She followed him, trusting that he had his sights on Draker. Although Fabee was adept at weaving between the trees and hurdling fallen trucks, Dagny was, too, and she was faster. As the ground sloped down toward a rushing creek, Fabee slowed to keep his footing, and Dagny charged past. The ground near the creek was muddy, but she did not fall.

A thirty-foot-tall stone wall on the creek's far side kept the hillside from eroding. Dagny saw Draker pull his legs over the top of it. She leaped over the creek and ran to the wall, dug her left shoe into the crevice between the stone blocks, reached up to another stone with her right hand, and pulled herself up. Reaching higher with her left hand, she pulled up herself again until her right foot found another toehold, and then repeated the process.

Some of the stones along the way wobbled. She heard Fabee tumbling down the hill behind her, but she couldn't hear Draker ahead of her. When her left hand reached the top of the wall, the stone under her left foot fell to the ground, along with several stones below it. Dagny grabbed onto a twisted root above her right hand as the stone under her right foot gave way, too.

Grabbing onto the root with both hands, she hauled herself to the top of the cliff.

Thick trees were surrounded by deep brush. Dagny scanned from left to right and back again. No sign of Draker. She listened for him. Nothing, except the faint crack of a branch in the distance. She ran toward it, pounding her feet in the dirt, barreling through the brush-filled gaps between the trees, and then following a path of freshly trampled undergrowth out of the woods and onto an empty soccer field. Draker was running across a two-lane road on the other side of the field. Dagny pulled her gun out of its holster and charged ahead.

A large brick warehouse was set back about a hundred yards from the other side of the road. On the right side of the warehouse, rows of trailers were parked at garage bays. The front of the building was bare, save for a gated glass door at the top of three concrete steps. Draker ran up the steps and shook the door. It wouldn't give; the warehouse was locked. Dagny thought about taking a shot, but she was too far to get off a good one, and it would just slow her down. So she ran instead.

Draker darted to the right side of the warehouse, where two dozen trailers were lined up at garage bays on the right side of the building, twenty feet apart. A large white number painted in a black circle marked each bay. Draker ran behind the closest trailer at bay one.

Draker had cover now, and Dagny didn't. She ran toward the near end of the trailer and crouched behind the three clustered rear wheels. The sun was setting, casting long shadows on the ground, and Dagny's stretched well past the second trailer. Draker could see her shadow. She could hear his heavy breaths.

"Hello, Dagny," Draker wheezed. "You seem to be doing alright."

"I'll be feeling better in a few minutes," she called back.

The trailer was about eight feet wide, with a two-foot clearing underneath. Draker probably expected her to run around the back of the second trailer, but it was faster to roll under. When she got to the other side, Draker was gone. Looking under the next trailer, she saw Draker pushing himself up off the ground. He'd followed her lead and rolled under the second trailer just as she'd rolled under the first.

"You find Waxton's ball yet?" he called.

"I've had more important things on my plate," Dagny shouted. She ran to the second trailer and dove under it, banging her shoulder into the concrete, then rolling to the other side. Once again, Draker was gone. She heard the scuff of his shoes, yet another trailer over. "I can do this all day," Draker said from behind the third trailer.

"You'll run out of trailers," she yelled.

Draker laughed. "When we get to the end, we can go back the other way." Dagny heard him dive under the fourth trailer. She rolled under the third trailer and fired her gun toward him. "You missed," he said, safely on the other side.

Rolling under the trailers wasn't working, so Dagny tried running around the end of the fourth one, but Draker was too fast—he'd already rolled under the fifth. "You've got to go under. It takes too much time to go around." He coughed.

"Neither of us is having any fun, Draker." Her shoulder ached, and she was tired. Where was Fabee? "Why don't you turn yourself in?"

"That would be a pretty lousy ending to all this, don't you think?"

Dagny ran around the fifth trailer, but Draker rolled back the other way. "You can't win this game, Draker."

"Of course I can. You might not know this, but I do have a gun." Draker fired a shot under the fifth trailer, wide of Dagny, but close enough to make his point. Dagny hid behind the trailer wheels. She noticed that the fifth trailer had a couple of horizontal handles on the side, one three feet up, another three feet higher than that. The roof of the warehouse was only a couple of feet higher than the top of the trailer. Dagny holstered her gun, then grabbed the lower handle and stood on the top of the tire. From there, she jumped up and grabbed the second handle, then lifted herself until she could reach the top of the trailer. She pulled herself to the roof of the trailer, grabbed her gun, and peered over the other side. Draker had already rolled back under the fourth trailer and was standing a trailer away.

Dagny jumped from the top of the trailer to the roof of the garage, and ran along the edge toward Draker. She saw him roll under the second trailer and fired her gun into the space between the trailers. Draker stayed put.

"You ready to give up?" Dagny called.

"Unless you can shoot through this trailer, I don't think it's checkmate."

Dagny scanned the row of trailers for Fabee, and spotted him. She fired her gun to get his attention, then pointed down at the trailer in front of her. Fabee nodded and crept slowly around to the rear of the first trailer. Draker must have heard him coming. He fired a shot toward Fabee's feet, and Fabee jumped, then took shelter behind the wheels of the third trailer. "That's Assistant Director Fabee, I presume?" Draker asked.

"Yep."

"I can't believe you invited that guy to your big moment."

The sun had slipped past the horizon. It was starting to get dark. They had to end the game soon. Dagny took a couple of steps to her right and fired a half-dozen shots into the tires on the left side of the second trailer, then switched out the magazine and shot a half-dozen more, causing the left side of the trailer to dip down. Just as she'd hoped, Draker rolled out from the right side of the trailer, raising his gun toward Dagny. Without breaking his aim or using his arms, he arched his body, threw his legs into the air, and landed on his feet.

And then Draker spread his arms to his sides and dropped his gun to the ground.

Dagny stood at the edge of the warehouse roof, pointing her gun at Draker, gripping the trigger with her right index finger and steadying her aim with her left hand. Fabee came around the trailer and stood ten feet behind Draker, his gun fixed on him. Fabee looked up at Dagny. "Your shot," he said. "You've earned it."

One simple tug of her finger and Draker would be dead. Half an inch to justice. She'd been waiting for this moment since she learned of Mike's murder. And yet, she didn't feel close to relief or joy or closure. Instead, her mind swelled with a thousand questions. "Why the senator?"

Draker fell to his knees but kept his hands in the air.

"Why Candice?"

"Just shoot the SOB," Fabee yelled, but she had another question.

"Why Mike?" Draker lowered his gaze to the concrete. "Why Mike?" Dagny asked again, and Draker just shook his head slowly from side to side. "Why Mike?" Draker didn't answer. "Why Mike?" She rubbed her finger against the trigger, waiting for the will to pull it, waiting for it to feel right.

Draker lifted his head. "Because."

The bullet ripped through Draker's body, and he plunged forward, turned, and fell on his back. His dead face smiled up at her. Not just a smirk, but a big, happy smile. All she'd wanted was for him to show a little fear, a little pain—a fraction of the misery he had caused so many others. But he was smiling.

Fabee blew the muzzle of his Glock like a gunslinger before holstering it. He walked over to the body and picked up Draker's gun. "He had his gun pointed at you, and I came around and shot him in the back. It's that simple."

"Got it," Dagny said, releasing her finger from the trigger. Staring down at the body, she almost expected Draker to leap up and tackle Fabee, just like in the horror movies, where the first shot never kills the monster. Draker didn't leap up. He didn't move. He just lay there dead and happy.

PART IV

....

THE WHY

CHAPTER 51

May 6—Alexandria, Virginia

Dagny used a tape measure to find the center of the wall and marked the spot with a pencil. She drilled through the mark, then closed the wings of a toggle bolt and threaded them through the hole. After tightening the screw until it was firm against the wall, she lifted the painting and slid its wire onto the hook. Stepping back, she assessed its angle, then made adjustments until it looked even.

Mike's mother had given Dagny the paintings from his front wall. Dagny had burned the Monet and the Picasso. Mike's rendition of the portrait of Giovanni Arnolfini and his wife was now hanging in her entry hall.

Every time she looked at the painting, she saw things she'd never noticed before. This time, she saw the fruit hanging from a tree barely visible through the open window. The prayerful handclasp of the figure carved into the bed's headboard. The hint of a face in a small circle of stained glass.

Though each new detail thrilled her, Dagny longed to see a familiar one. She ran upstairs and picked through the boxes in her guest closet, found a magnifying glass she'd inherited from her grandfather, and carried it back downstairs. Lifting the magnifying glass to the painting, she peered into the mirror behind the Arnolfinis. It was a relief to find Michael Brodsky still there, holding his palette. Seeing his smile brought one to Dagny's face. She lowered the glass and looked at the blurred spot in the mirror, then raised the glass again and brought Mike back. Down and up; blurred, then clear. Amazing how a little magnification could transform a clouded dot into the man she'd loved. It was this thought that sent Dagny to her MacBook.

Although it took only a minute to power on, it felt like eternity. Dagny opened iPhoto and scrolled through the pictures she taken, past the photos of the crime scene and the fingerprints, finally settling on the picture she'd taken of the Williamsons' stolen Matisse. She enlarged the photograph so that it filled the screen. Behind the topless woman playing guitar were curved lines of blurry dots—the woman's audience. Dagny right-clicked and chose the zoom feature. She zoomed in close, scanning each row of dots, sliding the scroll bar at the bottom of the image to move it along. Every dot remained a blur, every single dot except for one. And that one dot was the unmistakable face of Michael Brodsky.

Noel Draker hadn't owned a Matisse. He had owned a Michael Brodsky forgery. The fact that Mike had placed himself in the painting meant that Draker and Mike must have been friends. And this meant that Dagny didn't understand anything that had happened at all.

CHAPTER 52

May 7—Washington, DC

Dagny walked up the steps of the Foggy Bottom row house and rang the bell. When Gloria Benton answered, Dagny noticed that her kinky blonde hair was now accented with red highlights, and she'd replaced her old glasses with a tortoiseshell pair. There was something sad about the publicist's desperate efforts to stay hip.

Benton greeted her with a smile and a hug. "Hello, Dagny. Come in, please."

Dagny followed Benton into her cluttered mess of an office, dropped her backpack to the floor, and took a seat. Benton settled behind her desk, cleared some stacks of papers, and then folded her hands on the desktop. "My, my, my. You've had quite the time of it, haven't you?"

"You have no idea," Dagny replied.

"How are you holding up?"

Dagny leaned back in her chair. "My phone won't stop ringing. The *Today* show. *Charlie Rose. 20/20.* They show up at my door, unannounced, sometimes at odd hours."

"It's awful, what goes on." Benton leaned closer and spoke softly. "But there are things we can do to make it easier. And considering how much you've suffered, you deserve to come out of this with something for your pain and troubles. The networks pay for interviews these days, you know. Everyone wants to be one of the first to tell your story, and once that chance is gone, everyone moves on." Benton paused. "Tell me, how do you feel about writing a book?"

"I'd love to, Gloria. I just don't think I'm ready."

"You need some time? To decompress and—"

"It's not that. It's just that there are some loose ends that I haven't wrapped up."

"What do you mean?"

"Well, there's this problem of coincidence." Dagny shook her head. "Coincidence—it's an awful thing."

"What do you mean?"

"A lot of agents—cops, too—don't believe in coincidence. Anything strange happens, and they assume it's fishy. But then there's Cortés."

Benton scrunched her eyebrows. "Cortés?"

"Yes."

"The explorer?"

"Yes. The Mayan calendar predicted that a pale-faced god named Quetzalcoatl would reclaim Tenochtitlán in 1519. And by coincidence, Cortés landed in Mexico in 1519, so the Aztecs assumed he was this god, and Cortés was able to capture Mexico. If Cortés had come in 1520 or 1521, who knows? Coming in 1519— that was pure coincidence. Do you believe in coincidence, Gloria?"

"Yes," she said. "I do."

"For instance, here's one right now: I'm in a position where I need a publicist, and I met you while working on this case. That's a coincidence, and it really happened, didn't it?"

"It did. I'm very happy that it—"

"Here's another coincidence I've been thinking about: I was chasing Draker, and Draker once bought a painting from my boyfriend." Dagny opened her bag and pulled out a copy of the photograph she'd taken of the Williamsons' stolen Matisse. She slid it across the desk. "Tell me about this, Gloria."

Gloria looked down the photograph, but did not touch it. "I don't know anything about this, Dagny."

"Please, Gloria."

"I don't."

"Michael used to forge paintings. Draker bought this one from him back when he lived in DC, so they must have known each other. What are the odds that Draker's old friend would be dating the FBI agent that was trying to catch him?" Although the question seemed rhetorical, Dagny waited for an answer.

"Small," Benton finally said.

"Freakishly small. Right? It's crazy. But I'll buy it, because crazy things happen. I can buy one coincidence. I just can't buy two." Dagny leaned back in her chair and looked directly into Benton's eyes. "The second coincidence is that you just happened to talk Michael into visiting Candice on the afternoon they were killed by Draker. I can't buy that coincidence."

Benton looked at Dagny. "What are you trying to say?"

"That didn't just happen by chance. Noel Draker asked you to send Michael to the bookstore with Candice." Dagny reached into her bag, then slid a photograph of a young woman across the table. "That's from your college yearbook, Gloria."

Gloria put on her glasses studied the picture. "So?"

"You were with Noel Draker when he was bitten by a dog."

"No—"

"I e-mailed a copy of this photo to the dog's owner, and he recognized you."

"You found the dog's owner?"

"Draker did. He killed the guy's dog."

Gloria handed the photograph back to Dagny. She sat in silence for a few seconds. "Is this all you have?"

"That's it."

"That's not enough to convict someone for a crime."

"You're right. It's not. But I'd like you to tell me what happened anyway."

"This is where I should call for a lawyer, I suppose." Gloria looked at her phone and then turned back to Dagny. A few seconds passed, and then she began. "Michael was still a student. Candice was a young professor. They were dating, but kept it under wraps to avoid a scandal. I knew Candice because she'd asked me to help her get a column in the paper. Being a professor wasn't enough for her, I guess."

"And Draker?"

"He was writing software for the Department of Defense, but also trying to raise capital to start his own company. Put every cent he had into an office on K Street. Tried to plush it up to impress the investors. And the word on the street was that you could get paintings of the masters on the cheap from a student at Georgetown."

"So that's how he met Mike?"

"They hit it off. Noel was the embodiment of everything Michael loved to paint—man conquering the world and all that jazz. And Noel wanted to be like Mike—handsome, suave, confident. Noel was none of those things—he was this nerd who had never fit in anywhere, this kid who'd been beaten by his father and made to feel worthless, even though he was a genius. Mike made him feel like he belonged in this world. I doubt Noel ever once felt good about himself before Mike."

Dagny knew something about the uplifting aura of Michael Brodsky. To share this with Draker felt strange. "How did you meet Noel?"

"Candice and Mike set us up on a double date. And then we became a regular foursome. Dinners and plays and benefits. We were in our twenties, but pretending to be adults. And we were always together. Laughing and crying. Supporting each other. Confiding in one another. Dreaming together. I've never had anything like it since. It was the happiest time of my life." A slight smile faded. "And then he left. Once he raised the capital he needed, he went back home to Cincinnati."

"Why?"

"He said he didn't want to build his empire in a government town. There was more to it than that. I think he wanted to show up the rich kids he went to high school with. Maybe prove something to his father. It's easier to become a big fish in a small pond. I don't know. He asked me to come with him. A publicist doesn't move from DC to Cincinnati, so I stayed. We flew back and forth to see each other, but that didn't last long. His company consumed him, and I wasn't eager for the life of a mistress."

"There was no falling out with Candice and Mike?"

"Not then. Later on, I think he felt abandoned by Candice. When his company was under investigation, it was rough for him. I called constantly, offering advice on the public relations aspect, but it didn't do much good. Michael called him a couple of times. I'm not sure Michael believed that Noel was innocent, but he remained cordial. But Candice stayed silent. She didn't return his calls. She was the one who could have really helped him, with her newspaper column and her political connections. But she chose not to. It would have looked bad, I suppose, for the tough-on-crime pundit to come to his aid. She certainly didn't want anyone to know they'd been friends." Gloria paused, and then added, "I didn't know he was going to kill them, Dagny."

It sounded sincere. "Tell me what happened."

"On the day before the murder, I was walking down the street and a man grabbed my arm. I turned, startled, and there was Noel Draker. He looked thin and sad and empty, but then he smiled and leaned forward and gave me a hug. We stopped at a coffee shop and caught up. He told me he'd been out of prison for a year, that he was working on a new business plan. He asked about Michael and Candice. Told me that he'd like to see them—said he had something he wanted to apologize for. He was vague about it, but I didn't think anything of it at the time. Said he was going to drop by Candice's book signing and try to catch her there. Asked if there was any way I could get Michael to show up. Told me not to tell him he'd be there, because he was worried that Michael would stay away. I never, not for a moment, thought Noel would harm them."

"And so you called Michael?"

She nodded. "I told him that Candice wasn't doing well and that I thought he might be able to help. Asked him to stop by the book signing, check in on her, give me his thoughts. He told me about you and that he didn't think he should see Candice. I told him that I wasn't asking him to date her again—just talk to her. He said he'd think about it."

"Did you talk to Draker again?"

"No. Never again."

"After Mike and Candice were killed, why didn't you tell anyone about this? Why did you protect Noel Draker?"

"You wouldn't understand."

"Try me."

She sighed. "Because I loved him."

It was something Dagny could understand. "You loved him?"

"Always. Even after we broke up. Even after I'd denied it a hundred times. I'm sure you can't imagine this, but he was kind and sweet and smart. I can't tell you how much it hurt to watch people tear him apart. Tear down everything he'd built. I can't tell you how much he suffered. I couldn't bear to watch him suffer again. I cried and cried when I heard Candice and Michael were killed. I loved them, too. But telling the police about Noel wouldn't have brought them back—it would have just added another tragedy to the pile. I couldn't do it."

"And what about the Silvers family, and the children in Nashville? You could have prevented their deaths."

A tear slid down Gloria Benton's cheek. "By then, I was afraid. I was implicated. I'd lied to investigators."

"Why did Draker kill Mike? You said that Candice let him down, but not Mike."

"Did Noel know you were working on the case?"

Yes, Dagny thought, if he'd been watching the police station or Waxton's bank after the robbery. He'd written Delta's reservation software years ago; maybe he'd tapped into it and found the name Dagny Gray, found her address, found her seating assignment, and then given himself the seat next to hers. Maybe he'd even hacked into the Cincinnati Police e-mail server and read the initial message she'd sent, back when the Professor was just curious and didn't want an investigation. "Yes," she said.

"Did he know you were seeing Michael?" Benton asked.

Yes, if he'd found the picture of them together at the National Gallery in *The Washington Post*. And he would have. Dagny nodded.

"Then I think *you* were the reason he killed Michael. From what I've read, Noel was trying to get back at everyone who was against him, right? If you were investigating the case, you were against him. He had no real gripe with Michael. But killing him was a way to get at you."

There it was: Michael Brodsky would have been alive if he'd never met Dagny Gray. She'd always known it, but had hoped it wasn't true.

Dagny grabbed her backpack and headed toward the door.

"Wait!"

Dagny turned back toward Gloria Benton. "Yes?"

"Aren't you going to arrest me?"

"I've got no evidence, Gloria."

"You've got my confession, here today," she shrieked, jumping from her chair. "You have my confession. You can't just leave. I've got blood on my hands, Dagny. I've got blood, and it won't wash away." She was sobbing.

Dagny just backed out of the doorway. Benton could have called a lawyer, but instead she'd answered Dagny's questions. That's all Dagny really wanted. Sending Gloria Benton to prison wouldn't have made the world any better. It would have just added one more tragedy to the pile. And besides, Dagny figured, for Benton to have to live with what she had done was punishment enough.

She left Benton's office feeling that the gaps had been filled, and though the answers weren't satisfying, at least they were answers. Dagny's worst fear—that her involvement in the case had led to Mike's death—had been confirmed, and though it did not bring comfort, it seemed to bring closure.

But on the drive home, her conviction began to waver, and the closure began to crumble. There were still holes in the story. If Draker had been lashing out at everyone who was against him, why hadn't he killed her behind Murgentroy's house? Why bother with the tranquilizer guns? And what did Senator Harrison have to do with the whole mess?

It was time to move forward, and it was time to leave Noel Draker behind. Still, Dagny couldn't help but think that if Mike and Draker had once been good friends, maybe Draker was someone worth knowing.

CHAPTER 53

....

May 9—Cincinnati, Ohio

Dagny parked under the Fountain Square she remembered from the opening credits of *WKRP in Cincinnati*, then walked three blocks to the public library. A dozen teenagers loitered by a fountain that cascaded over a sculpture of oversize and casually arranged leather-bound books. One teen looked at her with the kind of menace she'd never even felt from Draker. There was too much anger in the world.

Her morning visit to the Ryder house still had her shaking. Harrison, Dutton, and Ryder—there were still too many pieces missing. She walked through the library's glass doors, then took the elevator to the second floor. Newspapers hung from long sticks on a rack at the front of the periodicals department. Although five days had passed since his death, Draker was still featured on most of them. *The Cincinnati Enquirer* featured the biggest headline. The letters stretched from one side of the page to the other: "MONSTER." Dagny picked the paper off the rack and settled into a chair.

The story relayed much of what Dagny had already learned over the past few days. The discovery of Draker's handwritten enemies list, for instance. (There were 212 names on it; the Professor had guessed them all, and he was now insufferable). The dismantling of the dirty bomb that was sitting in Draker's California basement. (Dagny had believed that Draker never intended to commit his final crime. She was wrong.) A related article at the bottom of the page was titled *Why He Did It.* An abusive father. His parents' troubled marriage. Drugs. Alcohol. Pressure on their son. Supposed mental illness. Hearsay upon hearsay—everything was thirdhand or worse.

More articles about Draker were scattered throughout the rest of the newspaper. On the second page, Dagny learned that the Williamsons were going to auction their reclaimed Matisse and donate the proceeds to the victims of Draker's spree. Experts opined that it was one of Matisse's best works, so it was expected to fetch a hefty sum. Only Dagny and Benton knew it wasn't real. Although Mike had painted it, it was now a Matisse and forever would be.

A picture next to another article showed Fabee handing the stolen baseball back to a beaming Chesley Waxton. Fabee had found the ball inside of one of Draker's hideouts. The article noted that the ball had been badly scratched and damaged, but Waxton didn't care. "My baby has come home," Waxton reportedly said, weeping. The reporter noted that it was widely speculated that Fabee would succeed the current director.

Enough with the present, Dagny thought. She placed the newspaper back on the rack, walked to the counter, filled out a slip, and handed it to the librarian. "You know, you can read these online," he said.

"I know. I need the reels."

He placed her strip in a vacuum tube and handed her a number. Twenty minutes later, the number lit on an overhead screen. She collected the reels and carried them to a microfilm scanner, the likes of which she had not used since high school. After threading the first reel, she flicked on the power and began reading the story of Noel Draker once again.

Reading the paper in its published form was different from reading the text of the articles in an online database. The earliest Draker stories were small blurbs buried in the back of the business pages. As his company grew, these stories grew longer and inched toward the front of the business section. Pictures of him at various galas appeared on the second page of the Tempo section. When he established a scholarship for students at his old high school, it made the front page of the Metro section. Draker's IPO merited placement on page A4. Quarterly profits landed him on A2. Expansion plans pushed Draker to the front page, below the fold. But only scandal lifted Draker to the top of the front page.

The securities fraud dominated the headlines almost every day for a year. Tonally, they grew from a simmer to a boil. "Earnings Overstatement Alleged." "Improprieties at Drakersoft?" "Accounting Misdeeds Taint Success." "Books? Cooked." "Management Implicated." "Tales of the Unemployed." "Pensions Depleted." "Draker's House of Cards." "He Knew." "One Victim Asks, 'Why?'" "Childhood Classmates Not Surprised." "The Party Continues While The House Burns Down." "Victims Angry." "Lost Jobs, Lost Savings." "The Price of Arrogance." "Draker Admits Guilt, Takes Plea." "Monster." *Monster*—the same headline then as now. The first time, it wasn't fair. Even if he had been guilty, theft is not equivalent to murder, no matter how rich he'd been.

One man, Jeremy Hawkins, was quoted in seven different articles as saying, "The more we learn, the madder I get." An ex-employee, Loretta Stevens, appeared in five different articles, each time declaring, "I knew something was wrong when I worked for that man. The man had a case of the no-good." Spaced weeks apart, the recycling of quotes probably went unnoticed. Read cumulatively within a few hours, it was astonishing just how lazy the reporting had been.

The photographs—missing from the online databases—were the real revelation. The earliest photographs of Draker showed a man that was friendly and harmless. Over the months of the scandal, his smiled faded. Draker's eyes grew hollow. He seemed to shrink. One photograph captured the local US Attorney decrying Draker's behavior on the courthouse steps, encircled by a throng of reporters and photographers. Another showed Percy Reynolds, looking downright dapper and handsome in his navy pin-striped Armani suit; with short dark hair and a clean shave, he was a far cry from the man Dagny had met in New Mexico. Even Judge Nagel looked almost young in a series of pictures taken in his chambers. Photographs of the FBI's raid showed Dagny's brethren at their most Gestapo-like. The scope of the operation amazed Dagny. Dozens of agents were part of the raid. An endless stream of them carried boxes from Draker's headquarters. In one photograph, Murgentroy was smiling at the camera, mugging with fellow agents.

Dagny inserted a quarter into the machine and pressed "print," then packed up the reels and returned them to the counter. She had come to Cincinnati to look for answers, and she had found the biggest one of all.

CHAPTER 54

....

May 13—Truth or Consequences, New Mexico

A light flashed on, and Percy Reynolds opened the door, hair unkempt, eyes droopy, wearing slippers and an open bathrobe, red-checked boxers, and a torn white T-shirt. Reynolds rubbed his eyes, shook his head, and chuckled. "I figured you'd be back."

Dagny followed Reynolds to his living room. "I'll put on some coffee," he said. Dagny sat on the sofa and looked around. He'd cleaned up since the last time she'd been there. There were no pizza boxes or wineglasses, just magazines scattered on the coffee table—copies of attorney trade journals and newsletters, mostly.

"Black?" he called.

"Yes." She needed the coffee—adrenaline wasn't doing the trick anymore.

A few minutes later, he returned with two mugs and handed her the one that read "World's Worst Boss." "Parting gift from my secretary," he explained. He sat down in a recliner and extended the footrest.

"Mr. Reynolds, I need to ask you some questions."

"I doubt I'll be much help to you, Agent Gray. I'm afraid the attorney-client privilege survives the client's death."

"I'm not going to ask you to tell me anything that Draker told you in confidence. I'm just going to lay out what I think happened, step by step, and all I want you to do is tell me if you think I'm wrong. Can you do that?"

"I think so."

"Because I can't afford to be wrong."

"I understand."

"Let's start with the baseball."

She'd spent the last few days digging even deeper into the Draker case. She spent the next two hours laying out everything she believed about it. When she was finished, Reynolds did not say she was wrong.

There was a signboard at the front of the terminal. One side showed a map of the various gates, restaurants, and shops. The other featured the retouched photograph of a woman's face. The model looked familiar in the way that all models do. Her face was symmetrical, neither long nor round. Her chin was neither prominent nor recessed; her eyebrows thick, but not too thick, perfectly shaped, but not too shaped. Her features were average in every way, and therefore spectacular. She was, of course, thin. The photograph was black and white, except for the bright-pink shade of the woman's lips, and the bright-pink lipstick tip protruding from the tube she clenched in her mouth, the way a dog clenches a bone. Although dozens walked by this advertisement every second, no one seemed to notice it, except for a three-year-old boy who stopped in front of it and stared. It seemed like he was trying to make some sense of it.

Dagny watched the boy stare at the image, and tried to make sense of it. The Professor's voice jolted her out of her trance. "You want me to what?"

"I want you to call the president, because we're going to need more help on this," she whispered into the receiver. The man in front of her moved forward, and she followed, inching close to the counter.

"I can't do that."

"Professor, it's time to cash in your chips."

"Dagny, there aren't any chips."

"What?"

"I don't know the president."

"But you saved his father?"

"It never happened."

"You never saved his father?"

"No. It's just a rumor. Just a glorious rumor."

Dagny laughed. "But that's the only reason we got to work this case." The person in front of her was collecting his order.

"That's why it's a *glorious* rumor. But it only works when I *threaten* to call the president. I can't actually call the man."

"You really don't know the president?" And then to the woman behind the counter, "Minibon, light icing."

"What?"

"You really don't know the president?"

"No."

"It's just a rumor?"

"Yes."

"Did you start the rumor?"

"Yes."

"Well, then I guess it's time for plan B."

She hung up the phone, ate her cinnamon roll, and called plan B.

CHAPTER 55

May 14—Washington, DC

He was late.

Dagny sat at the corner table, taking turns with a Carta Blanca and the remnants of a basket of chips and guacamole. She looked at her watch again. Thirty minutes—maybe he wasn't going to come.

But he did. A dark man in a polo shirt and chinos entered the restaurant, blew past the hostess, and flashed a sheepish grin at Dagny. "Sorry," he said when he got to her table.

"For what? Showing up late, or selling me out to Fabee?"

He slid into the seat across from her. "Now this is exactly why I was afraid to come." And when Dagny said nothing, he added, "Sorry for both."

"You said I was your lottery ticket when I was your meal ticket."

"How long you been saving that one?"

"Since about ten minutes after you drove out of that garage."

"It would have been better then."

"I was too busy processing your betrayal to come up with the zinger."

"What was I supposed to do, Dagny? Ignore orders from my superior?"

"Yes. Yes. Exactly that."

"That's not realistic."

"When did you start selling me out? Was it when I ran into you in New Mexico? When you gave me the Matisse? Was it at the diner in Bethel?"

Brent laughed. "You don't know?"

"Know what?"

"It started in the Professor's classroom, Dagny."

That hadn't occurred to her. "Why?"

"HQ wanted someone to keep an eye on what the Professor was doing. And don't be all shocked about it. You yourself asked how a blue-flamer like me could make a mistake like taking that class. Well, the answer is I couldn't."

"I thought we were friends, Brent."

"We were. We *are*. I gave you the Matisse, by the way, on my own and at my peril. And anyway, some moral authority *you* have. You wanted me to be an 'inside man,' ratting out Fabee. Yet I don't sit in judgment of you."

"This case was personal."

"You got what you wanted. You got Draker." It wasn't going as she'd hoped. She needed some sign of remorse—some indication she could trust him. And then he gave it to her. "If it's any consolation, I've lost sleep over this. I didn't enjoy it one bit. I like you, Dagny Gray. I like you a lot, actually. Enough that this tore at me."

"Enough to want to heal the wound?"

He sighed. "You're not going to ask me to do something that could get me fired, are you?"

"Fired?" she laughed. "If I'm wrong and we're caught, we'll go to jail."

Brent flashed his badge in front of the sensor and the door unlocked. "You're lucky this stuff is still here. In another day or so, it's all being sent to deep storage."

Dagny wondered what "deep storage" was, because this warehouse, as big as a football field, seemed deep enough. Thousands of boxes filled dozens of rows of tall shelves. A tall, periscoping ladder was placed at the end of each row. "This is a bit overwhelming."

"It's not as bad as you think," Brent said. "Everything is indexed. Ninety-nine percent of this stuff is just financial documentation, deeds, canceled checks. The stuff you want will be up front." Brent paused for a second, looking puzzled. "Wait. What do you want?"

"I want the bullet that killed Tucker."

"The dog?"

"Yeah."

Brent walked over to a set of binders, flipped through the first one, and called out, "B-ninety-one-point-sixty-three." Dagny walked to the second aisle and worked her way down until she found the right box, then slid the ladder into place. She climbed up to the top shelf, opened the lid, and thumbed through the box. When she came to a folder marked "B-91.63," she found a bullet, wrapped in a clear plastic bag, marked with a sticker identifying the date and location of Tucker's death.

"Is it there?" Brent asked.

"It's here," she said, dejected.

"Sorry, Dag."

She stuffed the bag with the bullet into her backpack, closed the box lid, and climbed down the ladder. "How about the bullet that killed Murgentroy?" Brent walked back to the binders and called out "E-forty-one-point-thirty-two." Dagny tracked down the box, grabbed that bullet from the file, and stuffed it into her backpack, too. Then she collected the bullets from the Silverses' murders and from Waxton Savings and Loan. Every bullet was accounted for; she had been sure that one would be missing.

"Now what, Sherlock?"

If Dagny was right, there was only one more place to check for bullets. "DC Homicide."

CHAPTER 56

....

May 16—Leesburg, Virginia

Gravity seemed to pull a little harder than normal at Dagny. Her backpack felt like an anvil. Her knees wanted to buckle. Her body wanted to collapse, to lie down and doze. She'd spent two and a half days without sleep, chasing loose ends and filling in blanks with Brent. After the document warehouse, they'd visited DC Homicide, flown to Ohio and back, talked to Senator Harrison's wife, met with one of the Professor's friends at the FBI Laboratory, called TSA officials, and sworn affidavits before a judge. Among other things.

It would have been nice to lie down right there, on Fabee's front lawn, breathing in that fresh forest air, watching the glowing red sun sink to the horizon. Instead, Dagny pushed up the steps with a sense of dread. She had to tell Fabee that the case was not closed. After spending the last two weeks on a televised victory circuit, Fabee wasn't going to be happy. She rang the bell and waited.

He answered the door looking much as he had the last time she had come to his house—sleeves rolled up, a kitchen knife in his left hand. "Makin' chili?" she asked.

He smiled. "You must think that's all I eat." Dagny noticed that he wasn't wearing his wedding ring anymore. He followed her gaze, and his smile vanished. "I thought maybe it'd work out, but she says she's in love with someone else."

"I'm sorry to hear that."

Fabee shrugged. "Your call sounded urgent. What's up?"

"You're going to hate me, Justin, but I don't think we've closed the whole case yet."

He sighed. "Well, come in."

Dagny followed him into the kitchen. Fabee returned to his cutting board and a half-diced onion. Dagny walked to the other side of the counter, swung her backpack onto the kitchen table, and pulled out her MacBook.

"You going all PowerPoint on me?" Fabee asked, chopping through the rest of the onion.

"Something like that," Dagny said.

Fabee carried the cutting board to the stovetop, dumped the onion bits into a big pot, and brought the cutting board back to the counter. He ducked into the refrigerator, pulled out some green peppers, and carried them to the cutting board. "Well, let me see it."

Dagny opened her laptop. "I thought I only cared about getting Draker. But there were too many questions and loose ends. For example, I didn't understand why he targeted Senator Harrison until I found this." She clicked around a bit, then turned the computer so that it faced Fabee. "Back in the 1990s, when Harrison was still in the House, Seymour Dutton gave him a thousand dollars every year. His company, Systematic, had a PAC that gave Harrison five thousand each year. At least fifteen other Systematic employees gave a thousand each year to Harrison's campaign. None of them gave money to any other politicians. It seems strange—why would a bunch of Atlanta folks give money to a representative from Rhode Island? Between his own contributions and the ones he laundered through his employees, Dutton was buying something, right?"

A spreadsheet of campaign contributions that Dagny had downloaded from opensecrets.org was on the laptop screen. Fabee scanned the list.

"And yet, I couldn't find anything connecting Systematic and Harrison," Dagny continued. "No favors, no benefit—"

"No *quid* for the *quo*," Fabee said.

"Until I thought about Representative Brownman, from Colorado's Second District. You remember him? He held hearings on the Draker scandal. Pushed for prosecution. Called some of Draker's underlings before the panel. Got a lot of people to plead the Fifth."

"Sounds vaguely familiar." Fabee began slicing through the peppers.

"Brownman was doing Systematic a big favor with these hearings, and yet he didn't take any money from Dutton or Systematic or any of its employees. And although Harrison didn't hold any hearings about Draker, he had held a bunch of hearings about Microsoft. Hearings that helped out a lot of Microsoft's competitors. Companies, oddly, that didn't give any money to his campaign. Companies, oddly, that had given a lot of money to Representative Brownman." Dagny closed the spreadsheet window. "Obviously, Brownman and Harrison had a deal. 'You help my contributors and I'll help yours and—'"

"No one would spot the bribe."

"Exactly."

"Brownman's been dead for years, and Harrison's dead now, too," Fabee said. "Even if they weren't, the statute of limitations would have run out."

"I don't care about prosecuting them. I'm just trying to figure out why Draker did what he did."

"Because he went fucking nuts is why."

"Yeah. In part. But there's more. Like Frank Ryder."

"The accounting clerk?"

"Yeah. He discovers that Dutton's being defrauded, but doesn't run to Dutton, the victim. Doesn't run to the police. He runs to some lawyers, and they round up the investors so they could file suit. But you know what I really think?"

"No."

"I think Ryder orchestrated the whole fraud. And I think Dutton put him up to it."

Fabee had a skeptical look on his face. "You think Seymour Dutton paid Ryder to defraud him?"

"I'm guessing that no money changed hands. Dutton was too careful for that. Instead, he sent Ryder to some lawyers who would give him a kickback from the civil suit. Of course, they didn't call it a kickback. They just called Dutton a consultant and paid him for his time. Nothing illegal about that."

"Why would Systematic want a clerk at Drakersoft to cheat them out of profits?"

"To bring down Draker, of course, and then to buy off his assets. Which is what Dutton did. Seymour Dutton didn't want to *partner* with Noel Draker, he wanted to *own* him. But Drakersoft was bigger than Systematic, and Dutton didn't have anywhere near the kind of money that would take. Dutton struck the bundling deal because that's the best deal he could get, but he wasn't happy with the relationship. Draker controlled the bundled sales of *their* products."

"Even if Systematic wanted Ryder to set up an accounting scandal, couldn't he have set up some other kind of fraud? A fraud against someone else? Why defraud itself?"

"If anyone else were defrauded, they'd notice it, and they'd probably approach Draker and it would all work out. But if Ryder cheated Systematic, then Systematic could ignore the fraud for a couple of years, letting it bubble up into a bigger deal. Isn't it strange that Systematic didn't discover the fraud on its own? Wouldn't a company in its position conduct audits to make sure it was being paid correctly?"

"You have proof of this?"

"None. I went to talk to Ryder, ask him some questions. But it turns out he killed himself a couple weeks ago."

"I'm aware."

"I wasn't."

Fabee shrugged. "I'm not going to apologize for that. You weren't part of the official investigation."

"No offense taken. I don't know why Ryder killed himself, but I'm betting that he, like Harrison, was worried about someone poking around into this mess. And Dutton too, for that matter. Dutton stayed in the building to die when everyone else evacuated. Ryder, Harrison, Dutton—all dead by their own choice. Ryder was the inside man, and Harrison was the outside man, and that's all Dutton needed to frame an innocent man."

"All of Draker's employees turned on him, not just Ryder."

"C'mon, Justin. That's what we do; we threaten people with indictment until they flip and say what we want them to say. People will say anything to save their skin. Especially after Murgentroy planted a fake memorandum implicating Draker in the manufactured fraud. If the government's willing to do that to get a conviction, who is going to fight them?"

"So Dutton paid off Murgentroy, too?"

"He didn't have to. Harrison pressured the Bureau to get enough evidence for a conviction, and someone at the Bureau pressured Murgentroy to make it happen. When there wasn't a smoking gun, Murgentroy made one. Maybe he figured Draker was actually guilty anyway. It's been known to happen."

"I don't think I heard a shred of evidence in there."

"I found a little. But only after I found some evidence about something else."

"About what?" Fabee slammed his knife through the next pepper.

"Something always bothered me about Murgentroy's death." Dagny paused. "I was in front of the house when I heard Victor scream, and I started toward the backyard. I heard two shots before I turned the corner, and then I saw Victor on the ground, near the woods behind the house. Murgentroy was standing on his back patio, holding a rifle. I thought that Murgentroy had shot Victor. When I told Murgentroy to drop the gun, he ignored me. I told him again and he turned toward me. Another second and I would have shot Murgentroy, but he fell to the ground first. The thing is I didn't hear a gunshot. I ran over to Murgentroy and took his rifle, then started back toward Victor. And then I was hit by a tranquilizer dart. I didn't hear that shot either, so I assumed that Murgentroy had been hit by a tranquilizer just like me. And I was right." Dagny walked over to her backpack, pulled out a manila file folder, and handed it to Fabee. "His autopsy confirms it—a small needle penetration on his arm. So if Draker shot Murgentroy with a bullet, it was after he shot me with the tranquilizer."

Fabee set the file on the countertop. "We know that, Dagny," he said. "I don't think that's been in question." He did another heavy chop though the pepper. "He shot Murgentroy after he was already down."

"Why?"

"Probably because Murgentroy had seen him and could identify him."

"I don't think so. Draker must have been pretty far back in the woods. I couldn't see him when I ran into the backyard, and I doubt that Murgentroy could either. And besides, Draker wanted us to figure out who he was. He stole the Matisse and quoted Reginald Berry to lead us to Rowanhouse, and that's because he wanted us to find him. He gave me a Jeffery Deaver novel when he had me in that cell, and I think he did it to remind me of the

Deaver novel he was reading next to me on the plane. And he left his cell phone in my backyard, which..."

"Okay," Fabee argued, "so Draker wanted revenge against the guy who brought him down." Fabee carried the sliced peppers over to the pot, dumped them in, and returned with a handful of jalapeños he'd gotten from a basket on the counter next to the stove. He started to slice the jalapeños with the tip of the knife, peeling away the outer skin and flicking the seeds aside.

"If Draker had just waited a second, I would have shot Murgentroy. So why not let me do it?"

"He wanted the satisfaction of doing it himself."

"Perhaps. But something else bothered me. Take a look at this." Dagny opened the iPhoto program on her computer and scrolled to a scanned photograph of Murgentroy carrying a box out of Drakersoft. "This picture was taken by a photographer for *The Cincinnati Enquirer* during the raid at Draker's company. Murgentroy looks pretty gleeful here, as you can see. And he's not alone." Dagny enlarged the photograph on the screen and pointed at a hefty young agent. "That guy looked kinda familiar, but it took me a minute to recognize him because he lost all that weight. But that's Chunky. And the skinny man next to him, that's Bones."

Fabee looked up to the screen and squinted. "Okay."

Dagny enlarged the picture a bit more and pointed at a short, stocky man smoking a cigar. "And this guy. That's Jack. You see him?" She waited for Fabee to nod. "And next to Jack, this man here," she said, pointing at a blur of a man with a long, thin face and dusty-brown hair. "That's you, Justin. Isn't it? You were at the raid."

He shrugged his shoulders and tapped the broad edge of the knife against the countertop. "Yeah. Okay?"

"You didn't mention working on Draker's securities case before."

Fabee stepped back to the cutting board and continued slicing jalapeños. "They needed a big team to go through and collect evidence, so I came in and helped. It was a one-day assignment."

"When I was in the hospital and we identified Draker as the suspect, you said you'd never heard of him."

"One name from a thousand cases I've worked, Dagny. What are you trying to suggest?"

"When we were at Murgentroy's house, one of your goons mentioned that you had plane tickets in Murgentroy's name for flights from Nashville to Salt Lake City and from Cincinnati to DC. We know that Draker was booking flights in Murgentroy's name, or that maybe he booked them in his own name but later hacked into the reservation system to change the name on the record to Murgentroy. It wouldn't have been too hard for him to do this, since he wrote the reservation software for the airline. I didn't think about it at the time, but if you had his flight times, why didn't you check security footage to see who was coming on and off the planes? If you had, wouldn't you have seen Draker?"

"By then, the footage would have been erased."

"No. I checked today."

Fabee stopped slicing the jalapeños and spun toward Dagny, gripping the knife in his hand. His eyes narrowed. "Then it was an oversight, Dagny."

Dagny took a step back. "I was a little blind because of pride. I kept thinking that our team of three was beating your team of hundreds on the merits. But we weren't. Your team was dysfunctional chaos because that's what you wanted. You already knew that Draker was committing these crimes, and you didn't want your team to figure things out. So you made sure that no one was in communication with anyone else, that all of the information was filtered through you, and that no one started putting the pieces of the puzzle together.

"When the Professor and I went through the files from the Draker securities investigation in Cincinnati, they were in disarray, things were missing. At the time I figured it was just typical Bureau incompetence. But you'd been through the files the night before, and you'd removed everything that had your name on it. That's why things were missing."

Fabee crossed his arms, turning the knife handle over in his hand. "Keep going, Dagny. Your career is over, but I want to see where this goes."

"When Rowanhouse and Reynolds and Draker himself kept imploring me to keep going, I didn't know what they meant. But Draker wanted me to go after you. He believed that you had something to do with setting him up. Maybe he thought that Murgentroy was your pawn, that he planted that forged memo at your request. Maybe he thought that Senator—then Congressman—Harrison asked you to do this as a favor."

"Pure fantasy," Fabee scoffed.

"No, Justin," Dagny said. "Harrison's wife let me look through his calendars earlier today. He kept them in his home office, dating back to the nineties. You met with him during the investigation. Several times. You must have figured it would be good to have a congressman, a future senator, as an ally. You were aiming for director even then."

"If you're claiming I framed Draker, that's not much in the way of proof."

"You're right. I don't think I can prove that you framed Draker. But I do think I can prove you killed Murgentroy."

Fabee slammed the tip of the knife into the cutting board and marched into the living room. He pushed the curtains aside and looked out the windows to the backyard, then hurried to the front windows and checked them, too. Fabee moved through the dining room and his study, doing the same. When he finished, he returned to the kitchen and grabbed Dagny's arm, pulling her gun from her holster and tossing it into the dining room. Then he patted her down. "I'm not wearing a wire," she said, but he patted her down a second time anyway.

"You have no idea what you're talking about, Dagny."

"I saw Murgentroy fall. He fell facedown. But the autopsy said that the bullet wound was in the chest. I guess Draker could have rolled him over and shot him in the chest, but I checked the crime-scene photographs. There was blood splatter on the side of the house. Murgentroy was standing when he was shot. I don't think Draker would have waited around for Murgentroy to wake up. Draker was long gone when you shot him. I'd guess that Murgentroy woke up before Victor did, and that Murgentroy called you and told you what had happened. He was spooked by the whole thing, maybe he even said something about coming clean. Or maybe you'd already lost faith in him. That scene you guys put on for me and Victor—that whole interrogation bit—it was a great show, but Murgentroy wasn't faking the drunk part and that had to have you worried. So you shot Murgentroy, Justin."

Fabee stepped toward Dagny. His face was red—she could feel the heat radiating off his skin. But his voice was calm. "He was shot with Draker's gun."

"He was shot with yours."

"The ballistics matched Draker's gun, Dagny."

"But you were the one to retrieve the bullet from Murgentroy's body. You broke protocol. You should have left it for the examiner."

"Under our time constraints, I wanted a quick match. I wanted to check the lands."

"You retrieved the bullet from Murgentroy's body because it came from your gun. You needed to replace it with one of Draker's bullets so that it would look like Draker shot him."

"And where did I get that bullet, Dagny?"

She noticed that he was twirling the chopping knife in his fingers. It made her nervous, but she couldn't show it. She straightened up, standing even taller. "I figured it was the bullet from the dog. The one I brought you the last time I came out here. I figured that you still had that bullet—that you'd never sent it to the file—and that you substituted that bullet for the one that really killed Murgentroy when you sent it for analysis. But when I went through the file last night, Tucker's bullet was there. So then I thought that maybe you'd taken a bullet from the bank or the Silverses' house and substituted one of those for Tucker's bullet, but those bullets were all accounted for, too."

"So then you were wrong."

"No, Justin." Dagny took a step away from Fabee. "Because Draker committed another murder. All of his crimes took place in cities with tragic concerts. And since there wasn't one in Washington, DC, Draker made one. On New Year's Eve, Draker went to a rap concert at the 11:30 Club, fired his gun, and killed someone. I didn't realize this until a couple of days ago, but you figured this out a couple of weeks ago. You went to DC Homicide and got the bullet, and told them it was a match to Draker's gun so they could close the case. But you kept the bullet—I checked last night. DC Homicide never got it back. It's not listed in the Bureau's file contents either, but it's in the file. Since you'd substituted Tucker's bullet for the one that actually killed Murgentroy, you simply took the rap-concert bullet and placed it in the file where Tucker's bullet should have been. Tomorrow, that file was to have been sent off storage, never to be seen again. You would have been in the clear. That's the great thing about Draker being dead. No trial. No need to keep the file open. That's why you shot him when I wouldn't. And that's why you were desperate to be there to catch him, because you needed to make sure he died."

Fabee grabbed her wrist and held it tight. "And your proof for this insane theory is that we lost the bullet from DC Homicide? You'd throw away your livelihood on something so flimsy?"

She yanked her wrist from Fabee's hand and took another step back. "Well, then there's the baseball. And that's where you were just plain stupid, Justin. I thought it was strange that you were desperate to get control of this case after Michael and Candice were killed. No one knew at the time how big this case would become. Later, when everything snowballed, I figured that you were just particularly prescient. But that's not why you wanted in on the case. You knew from the start that Draker was committing these crimes. You knew it before Michael and Candice were murdered. You knew because Noel Draker told you."

"Yeah. He came right up to me and—"

"He threw a baseball through your window." She paused to try to read Fabee's face, but it wouldn't betray the thousand thoughts that must have been crowding his head. "Waxton's ball. You saw the signatures on the ball and realized it wasn't just some neighbor kid's. You did what anyone would do—you hopped on the Internet to find out about the ball and found an article about the bank robbery in Cincinnati. And maybe you thought about the only time you'd been to Cincinnati, back at the time of the Draker raid. You either figured out Waxton's connection to Draker yourself, or maybe Draker taped a note to the ball. The lab found traces of adhesive on the ball, along with tiny shards of glass. You can't get glass out of anything, Justin.

"You should have burned that ball and buried the ashes," Dagny continued. "But you kept it. Maybe you thought you could plant it as evidence, if you needed a warrant or wanted to frame someone. Or maybe you just figured it would get you one more picture in the paper when you gave it back to Waxton. But the article noted that the baseball was all scratched and damaged. The first time I came out here, to drop off Tucker's bullet, I noticed that one of your front windows looked a little different than the rest. I'm betting that there are little pieces of glass in your carpet that match the little pieces of glass in the ball. And I've got a warrant to get those pieces." Dagny pulled an envelope from her backpack and handed it to Fabee.

He tossed the warrant aside. "Glass is glass, Dagny."

"No, and you know that. We can match refraction. Break down the chemical composition of the glass, even analyze the sand. But it's not just the glass, Justin. It's Tucker's DNA, which we're lifting from the bullet you claimed killed Murgentroy, and the DNA on the bullet from the 11:30 Club."

Fabee raised his knife and lunged at Dagny. She ducked and pushed his arm aside, then barreled into his stomach, knocking him down. Her gun was on the dining-room floor, fifteen feet away. Dagny started toward it, but Fabee rammed his shoulder into her back and she fell forward. He drove his knee into her spine, holding her flat on the ground. "Where will you run, Justin?"

"Away," he said, raising the knife above Dagny. "Just away."

The shot hit Fabee in his right shoulder. He dropped the knife and fell to the floor. Victor walked over to him and cuffed his hands behind his back, then pulled him up to his knees and patted him down.

Dagny knelt next to Fabee and smiled. "My partner," she said, nodding toward Walton, "finally figured out how to fire a Glock."

Fabee looked over his shoulder at Victor, then turned back to Dagny. "Fuck the two of you if you think you'll bring me down. I've got the whole Bureau behind me. It'll play like the two of you trying to set me up. Breaking in here and trying to kill me. Fucking self-defense."

"It's not just the two of us," Dagny said.

Brent entered through the kitchen door and caught Fabee's glare. He smiled, then walked over to Dagny's laptop and pointed to the small camera lens in the bezel above the screen. "Little movie camera," he said. "Broadcasting live to the Director." Brent maximized the chat window that had been running in the background. The Professor and the Director appeared on the screen, staring back at them. The Director was scowling and shaking his head. The Professor was smiling broadly. "Even if we couldn't get you on Murgentroy, we'd get you for attempted murder on Dagny," Brent said, as he grabbed Fabee by his arm and lifted him to his feet.

While Brent read Fabee his rights, Victor fetched Dagny's gun from the dining room and returned it to her.

"Thanks," she said.

"No problem." He put his hands in his pockets and shuffled from foot to foot. "This was something else, wasn't it?"

"Yeah, it was."

"He hit you pretty hard. You okay?"

"I think so."

"You sure? That knee in the back was—"

"No, I'm good. I feel fine."

He took in a deep breath, then exhaled. "You know, that was the first time you've called me your partner."

"Yeah, well," Dagny said. And then she gave him an awkward hug.

CHAPTER 57

May 23—Alexandria, Virginia

The bell rang. They had come to her since she wouldn't answer her phone.

Bleary-eyed, she pushed herself out of bed, changed into sweatpants and a T-shirt, and answered the front door.

"Your hair is a mess," the Professor said. Victor and Brent stood to either side of him.

"I just woke up."

"It's eleven thirty," the Professor said. "You're not a teenager." Brent laughed at this.

"Noted."

"Are you eating?" Victor asked.

"Yes." She'd meant to tinge her reply with indignation, but it didn't quite come out that way.

"Come back to work," the Professor said. "It's been a week."

"You say it as though that's a long time."

"How long do you need?"

"I don't know. You said I could have as long as I needed."

"I didn't think it would take this long."

She laughed. "What work is there anyway? The case is finished."

"The Director likes what we did, so I've got approval to continue our little ad hoc group. We can pick and choose what we want to look at, and no one's going to get in our way."

"So Brent's included, even after selling us out to Fabee?"

"Hey, I sold him back to you, didn't I?"

"Probationary member," the Professor said. "So what do you say, Dagny?"

She hadn't given the future one thought since her confrontation with Fabee. She wasn't sure she was ready to now. "Four people can't solve cases like this, you know."

"But four people did," Victor said.

"No. Draker was helping us. We're not that good."

"So let's try," the Professor said. "And then we'll see just how good we are."

"I don't know that I want to come back."

"Of course you want to come back," the Professor said. "This is what we do. We don't push paper. We don't—"

"I haven't even paid my bills yet." She sighed. "They shut off the cable."

"You need help with your bills?" Victor asked.

"No, that's not what I'm saying. Let me call you when and if I'm ready."

"*If*?"

"*If*," she confirmed. "What's happening with Fabee?"

"Bones and Chunky have flipped. They're going to testify against Fabee in exchange for leniency," the Professor said.

"What can they get us that we didn't already have?"

"That Jack was the guy who tried to run us over in Cincinnati," Victor said.

"So it wasn't Draker."

"Nope."

"Also, Ryder wasn't a suicide," Brent said. "Fabee killed him."

Dagny wasn't too surprised by this. "I guess he was worried that Ryder would go public with Draker's innocence in the securities fraud case."

"Which could have prompted someone to take a closer look at that case, and eventually, Fabee's role in it," the Professor said. "So are you back in?"

"Look, I'll call when I'm ready."

Victor smiled.

"What?"

"You didn't say if."

CHAPTER 58

June 1—Alexandria, Virginia

Dagny pulled off her T-shirt and walked naked to the bathroom. She flipped the switch, shielding her eyes until they adjusted to the light. Squinting at the mirror, she looked at her stomach. Firm, flat. Not too skinny. She liked that her thighs didn't touch, and that her ribs could be seen but not counted. Turning away from the mirror, she stepped onto the bathroom scale. The number below flipped to 127 before settling back on 123. Dagny stepped off the scale, nudged it a couple inches along the floor with her foot, and stepped on it again. The number oscillated back and forth between 123 and 124. She leaned a little to the right and the scale finally settled on 125. Jackpot.

Dagny slipped on her running clothes and her sneakers, grabbed her phone and her gun, and bolted from her house. Morning clouds muted the light of the quarter moon and drizzled a light rain upon Del Ray. The streetlights shimmered off puddles and windshields. The neighbors mostly slept. A skinny, shirtless man worked on his car. He nudged the bill of his trucker cap upward and smiled at Dagny as she blew by. A few blocks later, a man tossed a suitcase into the trunk of a Buick while a woman berated him. A few neighbors turned on their lights and looked out their windows at the spectacle, but Dagny just turned up the volume on her iPod and continued past.

She followed the sidewalks of Alexandria to the Mount Vernon Trail, then sprinted past Reagan National Airport, past Theodore Roosevelt Island, all the way to the Key Bridge, which carried her into Georgetown. As the rising sun struggled to peek through the clouds, she ran over the hills of the campus and then paused in front of Mike Brodsky's home. The rain continued to fall as she splashed by the stalled traffic on M Street, Zegman's Gallery, and the bookstore where Mike was killed. She shot past Benton's office in Foggy Bottom, past the Kennedy Center, the Lincoln Memorial, and then the Washington Monument. She darted up to Pennsylvania Avenue and by the Old Post Office and FBI headquarters.

Drenched and drained, she followed a crowd of tourists and schoolchildren through the door of one of the buildings. She passed the information desk and walked through the open atrium to the stairs. At the top of the staircase, she turned right and then left into a large room. The walls were adorned with a blur of paintings; she ignored them. A collection of dancing triangles hung from the ceiling; she didn't see them. A bronze statue stood in the middle of the room. She walked up to it and smiled, then bit down on her lip to stifle her tears. Reaching out, she touched the statue's arm.

"Hey!" A security guard raced toward her. "No touching! No—" And then he looked at her, and at the statue. "You're..."

"Yes."

"Well...then I guess it's okay." He backed away, taking his post against the wall again.

She traced the statue's arms, her hips, her mouth, her eyes. At one time, this statue had been the first mirror to make her feel beautiful. Now, it wasn't a mirror—it was a snapshot reminding her that she could be happy, that her smile could be genuine, that her eyes could be bright.

She wasn't sure how long she stood there, or when the crowd started to gather around the beautiful bronze woman in the evening dress and her soaking-wet, flesh facsimile in running shorts. But it was a testament to Mike's talent that their eyes stayed with the statue as she slipped away. For the statue to be in the National Gallery, even if it was propelled there by tragedy, was a more fitting end than Dagny could deliver.

When she found her way to the museum's exit, she braced for the blinding rays of a fresh sun. But outside, it was still dark and rainy. She reached for her phone and dialed the Professor.

"Okay. I'm ready."

THE END

ACKNOWLEDGMENTS

One of the best things about getting a book published is that you get a forum to acknowledge the people who helped you along the way. My incredible wife, Kate, read through more versions of this book than anyone, and let me bombard her with questions about every chuckle or gasp. Joel and Linda Miller—the best parents in the world—offered their thoughts and encouragement throughout the revision process.

The following family and friends read through early drafts of the book: Stephanie Sellers, Marcia Miller, Carolyn Moore, Jim Bates, Mike Bronson, Rob Hegblom, Bradley Monton, Paige Petersen, Mike Rich, Michele Smith, Matt Tauber, Colette Wachtel, Victor Walton, Glenn Whitaker, and Mona Yousif.

Michael J. Sullivan, author of the the *Riyria Revelations* fantasy series, provided detailed and thoughtful advice that made the book better; Robin Sullivan, his wife, provided equally valuable advice concerning the path to publication.

I am a member of the Arlington Writers Group, and I cannot thank my fellow members enough for giving me feedback on some of the chapters of this book, and for letting me be part of their community. Special thanks to Michael Klein, the organizer of the group, for making it work so well, and for being a good friend.

My sons, Freeman and Calvin, are too young to read this book, but not too young to bring me joy on the most joyless of days.

When you write a book with a lot of characters, you scavenge for names anywhere you can. If I borrowed your first or last name, thank you, and I'm sorry; the character isn't you—I just needed a name, and you had a good one.

Before you write a story, you have to understand what you're writing about. I read stacks of memoirs and biographies before I began writing this book. Marya Hornbacher, Candice DeLong, Michael G. Santos, and Clifford Irving wrote the best of the bunch.

Thank you to the National Institute of Justice, for letting just anyone attend their great conferences. Thank you to Google for things like Street View. And thank you to Keith Blount for creating Scrivener, the best novel-writing software around.

Before she passed away, my first agent, Elaine Koster, and her amazing assistant, Ellen Twaddell, worked with me for many months to make this book better. I will always cherish my time working with them. It will forever be an honor to be associated with Elaine's incredible career. After Elaine's passing, my current agent, the lovely Victoria Skurnick, rescued me and found me a home, for which I shall always be grateful. Ingrid Emerick, my developmental editor, gave me invaluable assistance, and found things I missed a hundred times. Copy editor Elizabeth Johnson stopped Michael Brodsky from cooking with "red paper flakes," taught me the difference between "Bimmer" and "Beamer" (I still went with "Beamer"), and reminded me about rules of grammar that I'd long forgotten. If mistakes slipped through, it's probably because I'm lousy with Track Changes.

And, of course, many thanks to Andy Bartlett and the team at Thomas & Mercer, for believing in this book and bringing it to you.

ABOUT THE AUTHOR

Jeff Miller grew up in the suburbs of Cincinnati, Ohio, where Jerry Springer attended his temple and Pete Rose broke his heart. He's rafted down the Rio Grande with folksinger Butch Hancock, co-created an award-winning mockumentary about table tennis, and performed and written for a public-access sketch comedy series. Like many lawyers, the only thing he ever really wanted to do was write. *The Bubble Gum Thief* is his first book. He lives with his wonderful wife, Kate, and their two young sons.